LANDCASTER PRESS

The Great Landzman

Three Times the King

Thomas G. Jewusiak

The Great Landzman

(The incredible true story of the man they called Gatsby, as related by those who knew him personally, reported faithfully by his grandson)

or Three Times the King

Exploring Questions of Reality, Memory, Nostalgia, Identity, Race, Racism, Culture, Morality, the Self-made Man, the American Dream and Death

"Tell me your dreams and I will tell you who you are."
Francois Marichette

"Anyone turning biographer has committed himself to lies, concealment, to hypocrisy, to flattery, and even to hiding his own lack of understanding, for biographical truth is not to be had, and even if it were it couldn't be useful."   Sigmund Freud

"There is no such thing as real memory. There is only the fiction that we conjure to soothe our souls and turn down the heat of our brains. It is the duty of the state to mediate our memories for the preservation of ourselves and the state."   Wladislaw Gomulka

Jacket Design by Thomas G. Jewusiak

Back Cover Photo by Jewusiak   Cover Art by Jewusiak

Printed by Hand in Outer Mongolia

First Paperback Edition

Jewusiak, Thomas G.

The Great Landzman

ISBN-13: 978-0997096712

ISBN-10: 0997096713

Parts of this work were written in old growth ancient virgin forests. While the author was living in the woods, he hurt no old trees in any way. The paper in this book was made from the pulp of fallen trees. No live trees were cut-down. Only hand tools were used to cut and gather the fallen trees. Only horse and oxen drawn vehicles were used; mules were only sometimes used; donkeys never. The Humane Society monitored all animals, one human monitor per animal. The linen fiber in the paper was recycled from the white linen suits originally worn by Spanish grandees in pre-revolutionary Cuba.

LANDCASTER PRESS
West Palm Beach
LandcasterPress.com
LandcasterPress@aol.com

TheGreatLandzman.com
TheGreatLandzman@aol.com

Carramel at the Bucknells

Nicholas Carramel was invited to the Thomas Bucknell's at the desperate urging of an old mutual aunt back in Chicago, not yet demented. But it is Landzman that hung or hovered over the event, like a ghostly presence that would not go away.

Carramel was broken and abandoned in a summer cottage out in Great Neck that he could ill afford, hoodwinked into signing a lease by a coworker, a man called Outwater, who found that after only two days he couldn't stand to live under the same roof with Nick Carramel, or so he told anyone who would listen, and unceremoniously relocated to a cottage down the road.

In no shape to drive, they had Nick picked up and delivered to their door in neighboring Manhasset like a piece of cold meat covered with a thick brown coat of furry mold, like mutant peach fuzz. The outing would do him good; so they were told.

It didn't. It was a fiasco. He kept making uninvited passes at the two women, Delsey, his cousin and Jillian, her friend. Most of the time he seemed out of it, answering questions no one asked, referring to Delsey as the "bewitching Morgan La Fay":

> "You look like a rookie witch with her pointed hat knocked off and her hair all messed up."

And asking if she had just gotten in from her flight around the house:

> "How was the view up there?"

For reasons known only to himself he thought this was hilarious and giggled like an ass-backward little girl; everyone else smiled in apprehension. Tom was pressed into physically guiding him, maneuvering him like a comatose oversized checker through a complex of nonexistent squares. Bucknell, massive and seething, dwarfed the hollow, androgynous Carramel as he pushed him around without enthusiasm. Carramel, shaken, unnerved, neutered by the enormity of Bucknell's physical proximity which guttered whatever little residual confidence persisted in Nick.

He kept wanting to see the "barns" and fancied Tom a polo player, like out of the slicks, fully conceived in full polo regalia, at the dinner table no less, no doubt reeking from the stables: horse shit, piss and sweat; or was he sanitized and deodorized in Nick's busted brain, a photographer's pristine model peeled straight off the page of the rotogravure lying indecently spread-eagled face down and fingered on the side table, displacing the family bible which had been quietly interred in a mahogany box in the attic. This was an imitation of a life, a bad one that didn't work; skimmed hastily from a worn pile of popular magazines and pulp books.

Polo was a game for which the actual Thomas Bucknell, who invariably dressed for dinner, had utter and complete contempt. These incessant players of games were, in his mind, the inept, ineffectual destroyers of his own privileged class and he loathed them for it.

Nick kept repeating that he wasn't at all like a rose and none of them knew what he was talking about. They thought he might be trying to reference Shakespeare; but that wasn't it. It was he himself that he thought of as the rose.

It was an overwrought, high strung afternoon, tension ballooning exponentially, everyone jumpy, jittery. Delsey only half succumbed complaining of "a bad case of nerves"; a phrase that in her secure inbred circle was applied with equal imprecision to anything from compulsive nail-biting to funny farm psychosis. Jillian frantically wrestled to make her getaway, to disentangle from the cotton candy, Carramel's sickly sugar-sticky delusions which affixed by the feeblest touch; soggy enshrouding Muzak, taffy clogging arteries, congealing the blood, asphyxiating the brain. In his own muddled mind he was consummating a union with Jillian, twisting some innocuous remark of Delsey's about being set out in a boat together. Jillian cringed. There was nothing impersonal in her eyes and she was full of desire; she just had no desire of any kind for Mr. Carramel as she insisted on calling him; the name rolling off her tongue, shot out like an expectorated child's gumball.

It was as if they were all sitting around a keg of gun powder anticipating the inexorable ignition, never knowing what seemingly innocuous remark might set off the explosion. Little did they appreciate they would soon take turns tossing lighted matches at the ruptured drum, an out-of-time replay of a wicked children's game they once reveled in.

In a movie Paul Newman would be good for Nick Carramel. The perpetual boy excluded from proper society, a wounded, earnest, yearning outsider peering in, a screen persona Newman tried to perfect in some of his early movies. Also, Matt Damon as he played *The Talented Mr. Ripley* but not so murderous or quite so pathetic.

Nick:

"Have you come east for good?"

Tom:

"I'd be a fool not to stay."

Nick, as if a wicked switch had been flicked:

"New York has its thousands of Real Folks... I grant you that... but it is cursed with unnumbered foreigners. We came too late... too late. It's not fit for any decent white man... nobody who loves his wife and children and likes to shake the hand of his neighbor. New York is no longer white, native or Christian.

"There is, of course the Jew... the Jew, the incomprehensible alien, the corrupter. The Italians, the Poles, the Czechs, Scandinavians and Armenians all have the same remarkably ugly visages and that same smell. They all lack the symmetry of feature which is essential to the true Aryan... The Jew when he's not intruding... shouldering... muscling in... he has his enclaves... the slow upward creep... always growing... expanding... consolidating... moving...

8

always moving... watching over his goods with his sharp hawk's eye and his bee's attention... insect attention to detail."

Nick, hyper, talking a mile a minute:

"Your Jew arrived as part of the great inundation... that's what it was... they had a boost... a head start on your Micks, your Wops, your Greaseballs, even your Muffe or Heinie and your Pollacks... they fought with them all tooth and claw... and it wasn't an exceptional endowment of industry, sobriety, or ambition that pushed them ahead. No... No... Ya see... your Jew had for centuries been prohibited from owning land in Europe... the controlling powers erroneously believed that the land, the sanctified land was the source of all real wealth... that's how your Jew was liberated from being a mindless shit-kicker or clodhopper... they did him a big favor... they didn't mean to...Thomas Jefferson versus Alexander Hamilton and Hamilton triumphed hands down... no contest...

> Those who labor in the earth are the chosen people of God, if ever he had a chosen people.

So said Jefferson... a man so inept that he couldn't make money with a thousand slaves and thousands of acres of land and managed to pile up a crushing mountain of debt by shamelessly exploiting his position as ex-president. He built what he optimistically or delusionaly fancied a plantation on a

9

mountain... an act of peculiar idiocy... there was little level ground, and the soil was poor. He fashioned a mere architectural curiosity as enduring testimony to his childish dilettantism... driving... whipping his slaves into an incessant commotion... pulling it down and building it right back up again like some mad Winchester widow or the crazy man up on the hill. He was intoxicated by a mad acquisitiveness predictive of twentieth century consumerism... an oniomaniac ransacking Europe for silver, furniture, wine and fine comestibles, anything that struck his fevered materialistic fancy... this was no collector of art... mind you. He was petrified of speaking publically. He did write exceptionally well, though.

The Jew's persecution had been the means of his liberation... his elevation... his chains became his weapon and his tools... they herded him into cities with its trades and professions... his well-honed occupational skills served him well in America, with its urbanizing, industrializing... it's like they set the stage for him... ushering him in.

"And then they were money lenders, usurers... originally forbidden to Christians... They would take over the tables the Puritan Anglo-Saxon had so carefully set... beat them at their own game.

"This latest load of discharged Ellis Island cargo will worm their way like creeping bugs, make a cozy home among the neglected and abandoned residences of your own grandfathers and uncles. They'll step into the shoes of good solid Americans who won't be coming home, who died with their boots stuck in the mud, the perpetual quagmire which is Europe.

"These hordes we're letting in will poison our society... they are beaten men from beaten races, representing the worst failures in the ceaseless struggle for survival. We are interfering with a natural inevitable process in which they have singled themselves out by their incompetence for necessary destruction. We must cull the herd or the weak and inept will bring us down with them like a sick man on our back."

Tom, interrupting him, trying to get him to slow down, afraid his train was going to leave the tracks; that he would blow with the least provocation:

"This may be the very reason to stay... East, I mean.

"I thought the Johnson Quota Act solved that problem."

Jillian, grabbing the microphone, so to speak:

"Why are we all coming East? Isn't this a reverse migration? What happened to the great promise of the West, the Promised Land, the last frontier? The American Dream is turned on its ear. Now rich men trek East from the Middle West and West... to splurge... their pockets

11

bulging... bursting the seams with booty. The regular American law doesn't run here. It's a market place of commodities and everything but everything is reduced to bought-goods. Is there anything in New York that doesn't come out of money?

And poor boys from the farm instead of looking west look to the big city like a Mecca. There's a corruption here.

Maybe that accounts for the desperate debauchery we're drowning in. We are the first Americans sapped by our confrontation or lack of confrontation... with exhausted frontiers."

Delsey:

Oh, Jillian. You're beginning to sound like Tom. You're such a philosopher.

Jillian to Tom mostly, in a songful cadence, playfully:

"They came for baubles, bibelots and bows. The big spenders, the high rollers, the small town boosters chomping down on the big sloppy wet cigars, gathered like a great host from the provinces, the backwaters and boondocks to get plastered on the distilled spirits of exhilaration... and faster and faster did the hucksters unload of their trinkets and slippers, so the factories strained to labor into the night churning out more trinkets and slippers. Until a great roar arises from the mob swamping all peace and all quiet: 'More baubles. More bows. More trinkets. More slippers.'"

12

Delsey:

"What is that from?"

Jillian:

"I don't know. (pause) Where do you think it's from?"

Delsey:

"It sounds familiar."

Jillian:

"It does, doesn't it?"

Delsey:

"It sounds like the Bible."

Jillian:

"It's not the Bible, though. I think it's me but I'm not sure. I might have heard it somewhere. Ideas are in the air.... (whispering) The end is near.

"Every thought and act you have owes its complexion to the acts of your dead and living brothers. Somebody else said that too. I forgot who."

Delsey:

"No you didn't. You don't forget anything.

"What does it mean, though? The first part I mean, about the baubles and bows."

After a pause, Jillian:

"I'm not sure.

"New York... the East embodied... incarnate... Broadway... the façade of the American city... a false front... a cracking veneer beginning to peel... a set for a second-feature movie shot on the West Coast."

Picking up speed like a race car with its peddle stuck to the floor:

"The vaunted achievements of our material civilization... our hotels, our department stores, and our Woolworth towers are only symptoms of our spiritual impoverishment, papering over the vacancy of our manic acquisitiveness, the getting and the spending... as a consequence our existence is shallow, base and hollow, frittering our substance on worthless tchotchkes and flashy gewgaws... scatterbrained savages clawing each other over glass beads... We go gaga over wampum."

Delsey:

"We have to get you a church or at least a pulpit. We have to rent you a hall... that's it... or a big barn. You could speak on Balzac, Flaubert, Zola, Ibsen, Strindberg and Chekhov too. You just love Chekhov."

Nick kept trying to get off lame jokes that lay flat, crawled off, died and putrefied in the corner of the room; jokes that they felt compelled to anxiously laugh at; something about the women coming down from their balloons. He made some reference to a stop-over in Chicago and the town being in mourning with their rear wheels painted black as a wreath for Delsey. She gently reminded him she was not yet dead. There might have been something funny in there deep down but Carramel was so fractured, so inept and ill at ease that he couldn't pull it off. Re-rehearsed and re-spoken in the calm quiet loneliness of his overpriced rented bungalow these lines might actually come off as comical.

Tom expounded upon his favorite thesis: that ruling elites may maintain their power for a while through their exclusiveness but unless they have an avenue whereby they admit new competent, fresh, worthy blood their very exclusiveness will be the cause of their eventual doom. I think he purposely tried to calm things down, defuse the situation, by shifting the spotlight clear of Carramel.

> "This fellow Batsell predicts that this decade, the twenties, will mark the last decade in which members of the Anglo-Saxon establishment will hold sway. It is the beginning of their... our end. Up until now they have been safeguarded by countless caste barriers from the rest of the people and have had everything more or less their own way. This decade will be pervaded by a sense of impending loss of dominance, a sense of their own passing. Goldenhirst makes the point that the Jews are perceived by the writers of this generation as a kind of vanguard, as the representative, par excellence, of the postwar

15

assault on the upper social classes. And he does call it an assault. They are a stalking horse.

The American Anglo-Saxon privileged class is dumbfounding in its ill-conceived exclusionary clannishness. (Bucknell actually spoke like this.) They will wither and they will die for it and it will be their just desert... no one to blame but themselves. The English gave the Scots... regarded as an alien race... hated... land and titles and clutched them to their bosom. The Russians struck their deal and made the remnants of the Tartar chieftains into nobles. It has been estimated that ten percent of Russian noble blood is Tartar blood. You think this is because they loved the Tartars? They detested the Tartars. Expediency.

Who in the hell is this old-moneyed Anglo-Saxon elite... these people who dare to think of themselves as Patrician... of which I am a somewhat embarrassed member. They take themselves so deadly serious. They're nothing but the recent descendants of nouveau riche industrialists and merchants of the previous economic boom late in the last century... a pretentious... vicious mockery, a failed imitation of a defunct feudal regime... closed... violently egocentric and entirely un-chivalric. They assume all of the pretentions but take none of the responsibility.

"America is backward, not forward thinking. Hosts of previous societies would have welcomed this Landzman fellow... that nobody seems to be able to stop talking about ... They would have welcomed him with open arms... would have married him off to their fairest daughters.

"The military has traditionally been an avenue for social advancement from the very beginning of history. If the term 'officer and gentleman' means anything it means exactly that. If you are an officer... you are a gentleman... period. This Landzman was a Colonel for Christ's sake. What more do these bastards want? I'm told he was so covered over in medals you could hardly see the man. According to my sources the two major battles he fought in were the Battle of the Marne and the Battle of the Argonne Forest... both in 1918. Argonne probably the bloodiest of the war... involved more than a million Americans... resulting in over 25,000 dead and 100,000 wounded. These fools see him as the commoner in the king's chair while a legion of previous societies would have discerned in him the true and rightful king.

"I've done a little investigation of my own on this fellow... I've unearthed a rumor and it's only a rumor, mind you, that Landzman was up for the Congressional Medal of Honor... they sunk it, shot it down... political reasons... he wasn't American enough... too German looking.... the blond hair, those killer blue eyes... the erect military bearing... the clipped, correct speech... the quick step. You can practically hear the ghostly echo of boots clicking when he comes into a room; it shook them.

They say his mother was born in the Austrian... the Hapsburg Empire... Lemburg... On her citizenship papers she renounced allegiance to the Emperor of Austria... sounds like something out of a fairy tale... renouncing allegiance to the Emperor of Austria... but that wasn't good enough... spoke High German as everyone did in those conquered cities... who wanted to get anywhere.

"In any old society his military exploits alone would have conferred upon him vast estates and noble titles... Military prowess, after all, was the foundation of nobility... Thane of Cawdor... Forty acres in a former broken down fishing village, having to traverse the ash heaps of the Corona dump to get to the City, hardly does the trick... They forgot the damned mule.

"This Landzman was born in the wrong country in the wrong century... the wrong millennium. If one of the most decorated officers... who has fought heroically for this country... a Colonel no less... can be referred to as a Mr. Nobody from Nowhere by a member of the reigning caste of this country... whose immediate progenitor founded his prosperity upon dry goods or hardware or... wholesale pork bellies... then that fool is not fit to occupy that seat and should be displaced by any means... any means... necessary."

These remarks were met with deafening silence. Tom gave speeches... Delsey rolled her eyes... everyone's mouth dropped. He was famous for his turgid conversation stoppers.

Jillian:

> "And here I thought you were such a snob. I didn't know you cared about these people."

Tom:

> "Care? I don't care. I don't give the slightest damn about these people... I care about me and mine... my own... my race. I care about survival. And we are eating ourselves up as a class. In fifty years we may have the remnants of our money... some scattered enclaves... but our power, our control will be a fond memory, deliberated by historians and so-called 'social engineers', dissected and analyzed by the intellectuals... probably mostly Jews by then... who will supersede us. They will pick among our ruins like dispassionate archaeologists from a distant alien world.

> "We have the dimwitted audacity to turn up our noses at those who want nothing more than to join and strengthen our ranks, to be our allies... confederates... collaborators... our brothers... to fight alongside us."

Nick:

> "This kind of nativism is only natural... the fear that the alien will not fit in... cannot become

part of and therefore will disrupt the dominant social order and threaten it."

Tom, getting agitated:

"No... no... no... This isn't nativism... it is something far more complex and dangerous. Nativism is the fear that the new comer can't or won't adapt, that they are inferior and inimical to the existing structure... that identity is inherited, racially rooted and that this inheritance determines beliefs and customs.

"The fear of the ruling Anglo-Saxons is not that the newcomers will not be assimilated or that they are hostile or foreign but rather the very opposite... the fear is that they will become so identical to the privileged class as to be indistinguishable from it and so will pass... and I use that term very carefully... that these aliens can be excluded only by an exhaustive problematic tracing of roots. It's like the old aristocracy of Europe: 'Who is your father? What is your family?' or a crime family rooted in ethnicity... familia... to be accepted you need a rock solid provenance... and a trusted crime member to vouch for you with his life."

Delsey:

"I married an athlete and wound up with a thinker. Yale men aren't supposed to be cerebral. What about that tremendous stupid energy they're famous for... the obtuse tough stamina of the Yale Bull Dog?"

Jillian, who was not hesitant about giving her own speeches:

> "Have you ever noticed that even in the best American novels everyone sounds so brainless and speaks in these miniscule bites of sound while in foreign novels, especially the Russian ones, people give verbal expositions involving themselves in long protracted intellectual disputations... more accurately sequential monologues? You can't tell me those speeches are contrived or artificial. You take any stupid writing course and they tell you not to have your characters give speeches... but that's not reality. Give somebody just a little opportunity and you can't shut them up... you can't get a word in edgewise. I've heard Tom's brainier friends speak for an hour without coming up for air and what they say is sometimes actually worth listening to. Conversational speechmaking takes on the quality of an intellectual rant... trying ideas on for size. People say things they would hesitate to share with a larger audience or commit to paper. It's almost as if they're thinking to themselves out loud to hear themselves think."

Tom's mistake was attempting to undertake an intellectual colloquy, a Socratic dialectic which sadly but inevitably guttered into mudslinging matches, exchanges of juicy gossip or consumerist one-upmanship and posturing; mine is bigger than yours. The sedate social gatherings with intelligent conversation presided over by his powerful professorial grandfather had devolved with the years into wild jamborees, sexless orgies of drunkenness; leaderless, anarchic and utterly useless.

Jillian:

> "Are American writers slaves to their editors who insist on short clipped dialogue? Or are too many American writers plain stupid, incapable of sustained reasoned philosophical discourse... or do they want their characters to appear stupid... as one of 'the people'... as if the people were stupid... which is itself a kind of intellectual arrogance... or is it that they are afraid to appear too intelligent... the bottom line... afraid that they won't sell books.

> "This Fitzgerald character calls many of his so-called heroes brilliant... He compensates for his own intellectual regrets and shortcomings by claiming for several protagonists a profundity they can't carry... he can't pull it off... His characters while supposedly highly intelligent sound like ignorant fools."

Tom, not exactly on point, which to him was entirely irrelevant:

> "There's a culture clash here...the Englishman... the Anglo-Saxon was always tight lipped... distrusting words and philosophizing... considering it a fools game, unbecoming... unmanly even... shut your mouth and don't whine... as if words were inimical to action... a substitute for it and thus somehow cowardly... the American hero... like the cowboy... is a man

of few words... they're brave... trustworthy not eloquent.

"Those who found fault are considered malcontents as if their psyche is fundamentally flawed... It's like accusing the doctor of spreading the disease he uncovers.

"Have you read this Irishman, this Joyce? The words practically pour out of him like whiskey out of a cracked jug. Nick... you write..."

Nick, seizing his chance to jump in and hog the whole show:

"Yes I have. I certainly have as a matter of fact... and a muddy slovenly mess it is... no more than a monument of obscenity.... flashing phrase... calculating... even childish... limpid [sic] English... the pedantic scribbling of an eccentric... and this rubbish the intellectuals call literature. *Ulysses* suffers from an excess of design... he over-thinks it. Joyce has buried his story under the flair, flamboyance even, of his methodological technique. But there's a heavy suffocating weight to these sputtering pyrotechnics. He overruns the bounds of art into an arid ingenuity. He may be inimitable, but why would anyone want to imitate him in the first place. If writers try to imitate him literature as we know it will grind to a screeching halt... it will take decades to recover... He's also, possibly, quite mad".

"Personally... I didn't know enough Irish could read to sell a book like this... although it's not for sale in Ireland. How did you get a copy?"

Jillian:

"But not just the Irish are reading it. Actually, I think he's quite interesting. What about Eliot? Arthur Waugh compared Thomas Eliot to a drunken helot capable only of chastening the rising generation by his ignominious example ... or something to that effect."

Tom, ignoring the remark about Eliot:

"But the Irish I know... those that have what passes for intelligence, loath him... they see him for what he is... are overwhelmed by the pervasive body-stink the book exudes... They find the cloistered, insular atmosphere oppressive... the appallingly closed religiosity... Oh, he may claim to be irreligious but he's obsessed by it, entwined in and strangled by it... the small-mindedness... deathlike. One Irishman who writes tells me that this portrayal of middle-class Ireland depresses him, gives him a sort of hollow, cheerless pain... makes him feel appallingly naked... because his ancestors came from just such an Irish stratum. And this Joyce has not a clue as to how narrow-minded ... how claustrophobic and nauseating this prison house of the mind... this peculiar city of his is. What did he say...? "For myself I always write about Dublin, because if I can get to the heart of Dublin I can get to the heart of all the cities of the world. In the particular is contained the universal." But not when it comes to Dublin... no... not Dublin... definitely not Dublin, my friend. I, myself, have walked the streets of that foul grimy slum. Have you ever heard such arrogant solipsistic bullshit in your entire life? He's got his head so far up his dark ignorant ass he thinks he can pluck universal truths from a shithole."

Nick, back on his stage again:

"Yes... Yes... Joyce while claiming to reject this priest-ridden unholy Catholicism can't escape from it... he's mired in it... as much its prisoner as the most mindless true believer. I don't see why anyone else but the Irish would read this rubbish. Let us slay, as we would dragons, Wells, Joyce and Anatole France... so that the creation of literature may resume.

"And for chrissakes they're even imitating this bog Irishman. I'm in mortal fear of the latest spud in what's becoming a potato tradition."

This dropped like a lead balloon.

Trying to lighten things up Tom mentioned how much he and Delsey enjoyed Europe, that he was able to spend time in the museums, after hours. But the mere mention of Europe seemed to flick a switch in Nick's sick head, unleashing a withering, fanatical tirade... Nick, holding forth at the seized podium.

Nick:

"God damn the continent of Europe... God damn it to hell. It is of merely antiquarian interest. Rome is only a few years behind Tyre and Babylon.

"The Negroid streak creeps northward to defile the Nordic race. Already the Italians have the souls of blackamoors. Raise high the bars of immigration. Let only Scandinavians, Teutons, Anglo-Saxons and Celts enter."

It was Jillian who made the mistake of answering this hogwash.

Jillian:

"You remind me of Negroes who hate other Negroes or Jews who hate Jews. You want to ingratiate yourself into the company of those who can't tolerate you... who despise you. There is something sick about that... full of self-loathing. You cozy up to the Anglo-Saxons without being one of them. It's self-defeating. You're paving the road to your own ruin.

You're in love with the idea of your own failure. You plan for it. You wallow in it. It is grist for your mill. You will it, in spite of all your paeans to your dream of success. You prophesy your own doom. Yet while you have this conviction of the inevitability of your own failure you persist in this talk... this narcissistic determination to 'succeed'".

Nick, interrupting her abruptly:

"I don't understand how any of this applies to me. What are you implying? Not one of who? What are you saying?"

Jillian, interrupting Nick, stepping on, crushing his words as if he didn't exist or shouldn't:

"German was an often heard second language in this country until the War... then they started shrouding their ethnic background en mass... changing their names... to English sounding ones. Even in the past Germans were often lumped together with other non-Anglo-Saxon people. Benjamin Franklin considered them inferior... a swarthy people who shouldn't be allowed into the country... who were too stupid to learn English. Back then they were overrunning the good 'white' English stock in Pennsylvania.

"Just this year the Reader's Digest reprinted 'America for the Americans,' condensed from The Forum. They celebrated the passage of the Johnson Act. They want to shut the doors against everyone except the so-called Nordics. The article argues not only against the admission of black or yellow peoples but against Germans who they don't consider true Nordics... What did they say: Our institutions are Anglo-Saxon and can only be maintained by Anglo-Saxons and other Nordics... or something like that?

"During the War thousands of German-Americans were forced to buy war bonds to prove their loyalty. The Red Cross barred people with German last names from joining... they were afraid of sabotage. There was a Minnesota minister who was tarred and feathered because he was overheard praying in German with a woman... the woman was dying for the sake of God. Over 4,000 were imprisoned in 1917 through1918 for allegations of either spying or supporting the German war effort. In Iowa...the so-called 1918 Babel Proclamation... the governor prohibited all foreign languages in schools and public places. Nebraska banned instruction in any language but English... aimed specifically at the Germans. This is all a slippery slope.

"And the Germans in Germany hate other so-called Germans... this idea of a unified German Reich is a great lie... a myth incubating, impatient to be created by some dangerous crank. Arthur Moeller is in dread of the 'corrosive encrustation', as he calls it, of mixed blood... But the blood he fears is the tainted 'Latin blood' of the South Germans. Of course he hates the Jews even more. When intellectuals conspire to undermine what they call vulgar liberal democracy in favor of some rarified dream, it is entirely reasonable to condemn them for the subsequent and inevitable horror they fail to foresee.

"The Dutch traditionally despised the Germans, regarding them as racially inferior... In the late 16th century the Netherlands were the richest country in all Europe, and these people of what is now known as East Frisia and Emsland and also of Western Lower Saxony were extremely poor and a source for the prosperous Dutch of cheap slave-like labor. These Germans were regarded as unsophisticated. surly, stupid rubes... racially subordinate."

Ignoring this, as if in a daze, thinking back to what Nick had said previously, in a bit of a muddle, Delsey:

"I don't understand. How come all of a sudden the Scandinavians have become acceptable? Didn't you explain how you used to drool over the beautiful Swedish girls on their front porches in Saint Paul but that you couldn't even think of courting them because they were not socially acceptable? How did you put it? They weren't emerged enough economically to be part of what was then... 'society'... some society.

"Ha! Of course, maybe they wouldn't want you... would prefer big... big rugged Swedish boys who had actually graduated college... State College maybe but college nonetheless... who would appreciate them for who they were."

They invited him to comfort him, console him and here they wound up attacking, with the fury of piranha fish. He drew out the worst in them and made it fun... fun for them.

Nick:

"Oh no... no... no... that was because I was engaged to Ginevra."

Jillian:

> "Engaged? Maybe to Ginevra Benci... in the painting... on the wall... in your head"

Nick, entirely ignoring this:

> "But her parents broke it up, her father mostly... because I didn't have money."

Delsey:

> "Is that so? Money, you say? Was that the issue? Really? How convenient for your elevated self-regard.

> "Wasn't it because they thought you were weak... that she needed a strong, reliable husband... that you were unstable... that you hadn't graduated from college, had no career and drank too much.

> "When you asked her father for her hand in marriage he was dumbfounded more than outraged:

>> 'How can you ask for my daughter's hand in the condition you're in... your drunk? You're always drunk.'

> "Money had nothing to do with it. That's your excuse. You make believe you're a lady's man but you're a lady man. You affect a kind of dandyism but as you yourself admitted... after the war when dances and automobiles were prime fields of feminine conquest, you were a poor dancer and a worse driver... not to speak of

your other short comings. Yet women... your inept, pathetic pursuit of them are your obsession. You insist on playing a game with a losing hand... a game you can't possibly win."

Jillian, interrupting the interruption to Nick's relief:

"I notice you include the Celts in your superior group... those who should be allowed entry to this exclusive club of yours. If by Celts you include the Irish then you are performing intellectual acrobatics... more accurately contortions. The Irish were... are more loathed... by some... than these other groups. Some of my father's older friends wouldn't have Irish servants in the house.

"I would have thought that being Irish you would have more sympathy for these other groups instead of hating them the way you do."

Nick:

"That's a lie. That's an absolute bald-faced lie... a damnable lie. I don't have one iota, not one single, solitary drop of Irish blood in me.

"Who told you that? Where did you here that? What have you been saying... my god...oh my god... what have you been telling these people... Delsey?"

Delsey:

"Only what I thought everyone knew. On your other side, your mother's side.... didn't you

31

yourself describe your mother as straight 1850 potato famine Irish? I don't know if you were drunk or not... sometimes I can't tell... but then... you're almost always drunk. Molly, that's what they call her, isn't it? 'Black shoe, brown shoe Molly'... the one that says whatever comes into her head... no interlocutor between brain and mouth. One of our meaner relatives called her the most awkward and the homeliest woman she'd ever seen. That's why you're not invited to the family functions. I always thought that was so very stupid and bigoted. That's why I've always made a particular point of inviting you. You used to sob uncontrollably about how unjust it was, that the Irish were treated like subhumans... that the Irish were in fact 'whiter' than anybody else. But I think you misunderstand the criteria... colorlessness of complexion really has nothing to do with it and justice in this case is irrelevant. They may have been pasty-faced, unpigmented and ashen, like the untouchables of the hobo camp called Walden Woods who Thoreau reached out to; but they weren't "white" white; they were Irish."

Nick:

"Well, you are sadly mistaken, sadly misinformed. My mother's name is Gertrude, not that ridiculous name... you said. There was some Scotch-Irish... who aren't Irish at all... pure, solid, Protestant stock. They loathe the Irish Roman Catholics more than the old American English aristocracy does."

Jillian:

"I didn't know this country had an aristocracy, of which, you are, of course, a dues paying member. Did they issue you an identity card, or a secret badge, maybe? Do you flash it at opportune moments? Do you have one of those silly hand-shakes?

This is a theme that's haunted American writers... how a society without an old established class structure, where the whole notion of a privileged class comes from mimicking inane British models. How does an individual compete with the descendants of so-called 'old money' which isn't old at all and might derive from nothing more than the hardware business or wholesale pork bellies... who fabricate a royalish ancestry to fit into an artificial structure that money from the nineteenth century boom created which finally devolves down to race and religion.

"But I notice that the hillbillies, southern white trash and the old ruined Southern Planter class so purposely, ruthlessly impoverished by the mercantile Puritans... who are all as Protestant and Anglo-Saxon as the best of the elite... aren't included. There is an irony in that... this... this Southern class with its traditional flamboyance and elegance reminiscent of the English Cavaliers is... or at least was far more 'aristocratic' in its trappings... its manners and mores... then their tight-assed, tight-fisted, stiff-necked Anglo-Saxon cousins from the North who would plunder and murder in the name of good, clutching a bible with blood dripping hands, spouting scripture.

"This was the true noble, imagined south of your father which remains a symbol for you even if you don't recognize it, of an idea of life, destroyed not only by industrial urban civilization but by the Anglo-Saxon Puritan who had been its initial driving force, who gleefully ground that beloved South of yours into the dirt and slavery was only the excuse... the pretext. So what is this ineffable quality that makes them so exclusive and makes you want to become one of them? Not only are you a traitor to your race and class, you're a traitor to your father and your father's family. Your father, no matter what you say, remained an icon, a representation for you of a concept of life, a code of honor that disappeared, especially after the War with its fast forward acceleration of industrial urbanization.

"You have this harebrained dream that the ever eager parvenu will be allowed to join the debauched scions of this old money. You will never be allowed to join, never, no matter how useless and dissipated the moneyed Anglo-Saxons become... supplant...? Yes... replace...? maybe... conquer even... but join?... never... no... not ever. That's the tragedy of it all.

"You so often speak like a crazy man, being drunk is no excuse... as if no one is listening... and that no one will remember or care to remember what you say... that the poison you spew has no consequence... people die and will continue to die for the words you so carelessly give vent to. There is a kind of Karma... it's called memory. There are people writing down what you say and I guarantee... I guarantee... you will rue the day. These people you so despise will positively catapult into positions of power more quickly than you can conceive... positions of power in which to make or break you. While you're wasting your time ingratiating yourself to the fast declining Anglo-Saxons these people will make it on their own... create a universe of their own... apart from your beloved Anglo-Saxons and although they would invite you to join that world, your own words will come back armed... like an unjustly dismissed retainer... to haunt you. Your life would have been so much easier, so much better if you had made common cause against the Anglo-Saxon. You don't seem to understand that this is war. I assure you that whatever fame you reach... by some miracle... if posthumously, it would serve you right... no matter the beauty of your prose... what fame it finally attains... these words... most of all... these indelible words of your hate will be forever engraved as your epitaph... even if living men armed with chisels have to descend upon your grave stone in the middle of the night."

Jillian, in the heat of her peroration forgot who she was or rather who she was supposed to be; she was speaking words that might have lodged in her beloved father's rended heart, that he never would have dared to let out.

Nick, oblivious:

> "You don't know anything about my father.
>
> "Who are you calling a parvenu?"

Jillian:

> "I'm not calling anyone anything. I'm simply making an observation."

Delsey, finally getting to the subject in the back of everyone's mind:

> "Let's change the subject. This is all getting very confusing.
>
> "I understand you live right next to that absolutely gorgeous extravaganza of a house out on Great Neck, the one built by the mysterious and illustrious Mr. Landzman... the one who heads up the American Legion."

Nick, after a long pause, trying to collect his wits:

> "Yes... I live in his shadow... so to speak, almost... a cottage. He tried to buy it but they won't sell. They rent it to undesirables... to spite him... I was told... I don't mean me... not me. I didn't rent it... not personally... this fellow from

the office... but that's another... I guess they couldn't find an undesirable to rent it to."

Jillian:

"What about Landzman?"

She was teasing now.

Nick:

"I've only seen him from far away. He's waved to me, almost like a formal salute... even from the distance I could catch his smile... like he knew me, like he had met me before... like he knew who I was.

"I have to be careful, though.

"He has fierce looking men with ferocious dogs straining at the leash patrolling the perimeter of his estate.

"He's remarkably Nordic... in appearance... but I was told by my housekeeper whose friend says that he might be a secret Jew. That would explain a lot.

"Your Jew is a ferocious competitor. When a Jew is interested he has the strong sense of the track that we other races don't even know the sprinting time of.

"Your Jew is the vanguard, the stalking horse... he'll open the gates... in the night... while we sleep... let the other strangers in."

"But he's not like the others… Landzman… the other Jews I mean. With the Jew money and power are falling into the hands of certain of these people, who compared to the leader of a village Soviet would be a goldmine of judgment and culture."

Jillian:

"Landzman's not a Jew. He's the Great Silkie of Sule Skerry … who's seized command of the ship… while we were otherwise engaged below deck playing roulette."

Jillian, talk-singing very softly:

"'And thou shalt marry a proud gunner, And a very proud gunner I'm sure he'll be, And the very first shot that e're he shoots, he'll kill both my young son and me'."

which everyone, puzzled, ignored.

Nick:

"Did you notice how old Jews look like melted candles, like they're getting ready to waddle?"

Apropos of nothing.

Jillian to Nick:

"You've been to the Soviet Union?"

A question which was again ignored.

Jillian, again:

"Didn't Landzman's friend Belasco disguise his Jewish roots with the costume of a Catholic priest?"

Delsey:

"I thought Belasco was dead."

Tom:

"He didn't quite pretend to be a priest though... he just dressed up like one... a black suit with a stiff white Roman collar... the getup gave him the look of a Roman Catholic priest."

Delsey:

"Yeh... I remember, now... They nicknamed him: 'The Bishop of Broadway.' "

Tom:

"He's the fool who produced hokey melodrama and insisted it was a mirror of real life. He swore his preposterous stories were based on hard fact... that he himself knew they were true."

Jillian:

"But isn't it the truest stories that make bad fiction because they are so bizarre, so unbelievable. Though a good deal is too strange to be believed, nothing is too strange to have happened. Who said that?

"No, no, now that I remember, I think he purposely took on the affectations of a priest. He concocted some preposterous cover story about

39

being whisked off to a monastery for five years by a Father McGuire... who took him under his wing... his mentor... they became 'best friends'... but I'm not sure the benevolent priest McGuire existed except in his own head. His whole personality was his own invention like one of his overwrought scripts."

Delsey:

"His studio in the theater took on all the trappings of an old cathedral crypt. I think he was trying to relive old memories or trying to expunge them. I was in it... it was spooky... No, he's still living... I think. But I don't think they're friends."

Jillian, caught up in the enthusiasm of the subject, breathless:

"Yes, yes they are... or were at least. Belasco helped with his magic tricks... before the war... in the circus.

He helped with the floating houses, too... Him and the aviator... the one who broke the records. They met in the theater where Landzman directed and acted."

Delsey:

"Whose magic tricks?"

Tom:

"What circus?"

Jillian, composing herself:

> "Don't pay any attention to me. I just prattle on... and on. I have no idea what I'm talking about."

Tom, too full of himself, unable to shut-up; letting slip a potential goldmine of information:

> "In Elizabethan England actors were forbidden to wear their aristocratic costumes anywhere but on the stage... and if they did they were subject to flogging. I guess the fear was that they would pass themselves off as those they pretended to be, move into their great houses and take over and the whole structure of society would come crashing down around their ears. In many old societies, classes distinguished themselves by the dress they wore... which they were required to wear... they couldn't violate the prescribed dress of their own class."

Delsey:

> "Did you make that up?"

Tom:

> "Would I do that?"

Jillian and Delsey together:

> "Yes."

Tom:

> "And the King of England, James the First, used actors, his own King's Men to pretend to be

aristocratic courtiers to wait upon a visiting foreign dignitary... I think it was a king. They managed to pull it off..."

Delsey, interrupting Tom:

"Where do you get all this stuff from?"

Tom:

"Books. Books. They call them books."

But Jillian wasn't through with Nick:

"You are obsessed. You're afraid of him. It's mixed up with your fear... your race anxiety, if I can call it that... that identity itself might be a performance... an act... a magic trick loosely linked to some imitational reality and not to a rock hard definable reality based on something like family, blood... race. If Landzman can create an identity out of his own imagination, his own accomplishments, possibly a bag of tricks, then it makes the whole concept of identity as physically based unstable. If he is the perfect simulacrum of the American Patrician ... what is the basis for his exclusion? Are not the manners and effects of that group... after all... no more than a well-rehearsed, well-schooled show... isn't all such schooling just a matter of being taught how to act? And if they won't let him... invite him in... isn't he even more of a threat?

"Landzman... the unassimilable alien...? one of the foreign hordes who will overwhelm your closed tight privileged few... who closed you out... make it disappear before you have a chance to become one of them.

"You are aspiring for right of admission into a self-extinguishing clan... banging on the doors... trying to break into a quarantine hospital.

"You're being distracted and insulted by an uppity ticket clerk who won't let you book passage on the Titanic and puts you on a waiting list that waits forever.

"Are you really so incredibly dense or do you see it and are rendered impotent by your knowledge, like that man on the Titanic with haunting premonitions and icebergs in his head."

"Your dream transmogrifies into a lewd caricature of itself, struggling to hurdle into a decaying caste which is not only destroying itself but destroys all those who come into contact with it or seek to become a part of it."

Delsey:

"Enough... my head hurts."

Nick:

"What the hell are you talking about? They never closed me out. You are very confused... very confused.

Jillian:

"Doesn't your father run a hardware store?"

Nick:

"I beg your pardon. My father is in the wholesale hardware business as was my uncle before him."

Jillian:

"Oh, now I get it: retail hardware is déclassé... wholesale is crème de la crème."

Nick, shoots in:

"Do you personally know Landzman or are you like everyone else just shuffling hearsay around, making things up as you go along?"

He thought this would fix her, finally shoot her down, shut her up good.

Jillian:

"Do I know him? Why... I'm his... I... I work for him. We're as thick as thieves"

Jillian regretted this outburst almost immediately. The carefully kept secret was out.

Flabbergasted, Delsey interrupted, violently, jealously, never suspecting that Jillian worked at any thing:

"You work for Landzman? My god.... in what capacity... would you please tell me that... please?"

Jillian:

"Social secretary... mistress of etiquette... doyenne of doilies. I make sure the rules of social intercourse are minutely and scrupulously observed. We don't want any unrefined deadbeats, no riffraff sullying our hallowed halls.

"He's had you investigated if you live so close. I could guarantee it.

"It seems everybody is having everybody else investigated... they won't accept anything at face value... but whose investigating the investigators... that's what I'd like to know... maybe they exchange notes or make it all up...at the kitchen table at night... like some scribbler gone bonkers... formulating dossiers... they create our phony lives for us over ale and cold chicken... saves a lot of leg work.

"One art critic said that the biggest fraud of all is provenance... it's all nonsense... If the work is great and original it will reveal itself... it must stand on its own. Its history... its background... genealogy, if you will... by itself is meaningless... a diversion... the easiest thing in the world to fake.

"If a lost work of Shakespeare shows up we will know instantly that it is genuine simply by reading it... it will be its own proof. No one, but no one could have written Shakespeare except Shakespeare... no one who left a written record came close... they were all illiterate dunces in comparison. What galls all those that hoist up a pathetic pretender is that they cannot accept the miracle that is Shakespeare... who rose up out of nothing... thereby accusing them of their own inferiority... what excuse have they got... he was neither a Lord of the Realm nor University educated... the quintessential self-made man... and no one... no one has even come close in four hundred years. Why even bother?

"Probably only one in a thousand knows good writing from bad. The critics prove it, heaping exorbitant, orgasmic praise on unadulterated bunkum."

Jillian delivering the coup de grace:

"Landzman knows more about you than you do about yourself."

She had read the file. She had read all their files. She was enjoying herself now. She couldn't help herself. A stunned silence all around.

Jillian:

"Landzman... he's incredible... absolutely unbelievable."

Delsey:

"What... what on earth does that mean?"

Jillian with perfect aplomb, to Nick in particular:

"You must watch me play."

Nick:

"Uh...golf, right?"

Jillian:

"No, tennis, actually.

"Have you been to France, lately? We just got back."

The mere mention of France seemed to crack open the floodgates.

Nick:

"France? ... France? ... France makes me so sick. Its silly pose as the thing the world has to save. I think it's one goddamned shame that England and America didn t let Germany conquer Europe. It's the only thing that would have saved the fleet of tottering old wrecks."

Jillian:

"But you fought in the war, didn't you?"

Nick:

"Yes I did. I most certainly did. Yes... I was.... I was... wounded... sent home before I got a chance to really mix it up."

Jillian:

"Didn't you say something about having a sporting...? I did hear you correctly... a 'sporting interest' in the German dash for Paris but that it didn't thrill you... that you had hoped the whole thing would be bloody and long?

"But why would you want to 'mix it up', as you say, against your favorite heroes, the Germans? Couldn't you send a substitute, I mean to the war, or don't they do that anymore? You could have paid someone to impersonate you, which is the same thing. There's a lot of that going around... impersonation... I mean. Then you could impersonate your own wife and collect your own widow's pension. Give you a chance to dress-up, like at Yale.

"But you stayed in France... after the War I mean?"

Nick:

"No... I came home then went back... I lived in France for a year. I know the country intimately... I know its people as only a writer can."

Jillian:

"But that's just the point... you don't know the country at all... not at all.

"From listening to you, you resided in France without ever living there... without having any real connection with the country. The only French you came in contact with were servants... who hated you and grew rich cheating you. You met few French writers and had no interest in the intellectual avant-garde. Even your friend Dos Passos made the point that you never saw any of the architectural landmarks... never went to the museums or the great churches... cared nothing for art or music or great food or great wine even and never bothered to learn the language. You inhabited a Europe of displaced Americans with money...

ugly ignorant Americans... the habitués of hotels, nightclubs, bars and beaches. You remind me of why the English are so despised by their neighbors for their tourism... What a decadent concept... tourism... which looks down upon the natives as if they were an alien inferior species. These 'tourists' have all the manners of gawkers at a zoo.

"Your beloved Murphys, who you wasted so much time with, wallowed in hedonistic extravagance and squandered whatever money they inherited on the trivial perfection of frivolities."

Before he had a chance to counter this frontal attack Delsey chimed in:

"This is all getting much too complicated. Besides, Nick missed my wedding because of that silly war. Isn't that the reason? Isn't that why? Didn't you Nick?"

Delsey, revealing the ultimate solipsism of her ignorant, ridiculous self-absorption.

But Nick wouldn't give it up:

"I believe in the white man's burden. We are as far above the modern Frenchman as he is above the Negro. Even in art!

"We have to assert ascendancy being of the superior Nordic race. It is our duty, our destiny.

"Civilization is going to pieces."

But by some subtle intimation he didn't fully incorporate the women under the protection of his racialist umbrella.

Jillian was about to burst when Delsey gently touched her shoulder as if to say: be still, child, this too will pass.

Jillian:

> "When you say civilization is going to pieces what you really mean is white civilization... meaning that only white people are truly civilized. More particularly you mean the Anglo-Saxon or Nordic power structure... as if only the Nordics were the true keepers of the flame... that civilization's continued survival is dependent on the maintenance of that Nordic superiority. The very term 'civilization' is a politically and racially charged term used as a cudgel... much as the term 'culture' is used."

Before Jillian finished her last word Nick had passed out, almost as if the air had been let out of him; he buckled at the knees and collapsed at Tom's feet, a soused supplicant.

But this didn't slow them down; they continued to drink far into the night. The more Tom Bucknell drank the more sober he appeared at least to those who didn't know him. He grew more grave and correct and knowing he was drunk, stingier with his words, which he knew would make little sense; assuming a demeanor emulating his dead grandfather whom he had worshipped as a child. If he could, when half in the bag, he would resurrect that life style, the generous frugality, the friendly sobriety, discretion, and restraint; strict adherence to a moral code that raised a glass only on occasions of great moment; a vanishing world, in which the defining characteristics of good taste were, balance, proportion, appropriateness and understatement, a lack of ostentation. Nothing should be noticed. Intoxicated on illegal hard liquor furnished by bootleggers he became burdened by obsolete obligations, a reticent reserved style that used to be called 'breeding' but was reduced like so much else to a poor old shattered word by the nouveau riche. For Thomas Bucknell's father's father it was considered "vulgar", his grandfather's word, to give anything expensive in the way of "eatable or drinkable" at the evening or afternoons entertainment. He would have been appalled equally by Landzman and what his little grandson had swollen into.

It is a blessing in some ways that this grand paterfamilias did not live to see the day that his beloved privileged class, his particular tribe, dripping its invisible war paint, would be disparaged by their déclassé successors, the "ethnics", the despised interlopers, the loathed bouncers, heady in their exultantancy, triumphant over the remnants of his Anglo-Saxons, particularized and marginalized as: a Whartonian social ilk, the hereditarily rich American, as if they were some over-the-hill decayed untouchable, retreated to their fetid mountain lair, retrogressed to donning animal skins and telling stories, lies around the fire about the imagined days of empire; Solomon and his 700 wives, princesses of royal birth and 300 concubines.

The Bucknells had hired a car for Carramel just for the occasion; Tom being stingy in the use of his own car and driver for such circumstances, feeling that it was an imposition on his own man and not included in the unspoken terms of the man's employment:

> "I don't run a taxi service for every Tom, Dick and Harry who visits."

The hired driver waited patiently in the area designated for such help, it being considered inappropriate to allow him to mingle freely with Bucknell's own personal servants who were more privileged in Tom's eyes. But by 3:30 AM the driver, groggy and exhausted had the temerity to enquire gently at the servant's door whether Mr. Carramel would be leaving any time soon or staying the night, in which case he could return in the morning. Nick, informed of the driver's query, lashed out with a withering drunken barrage of billingsgate and had to be physically restrained by Tom from attacking the man with a large wooden object which came to hand nearby, an irreplaceable museum piece, which looked like an antique ornamental truncheon but would better be described as a fasces. Nick often acted on the misperception that his professed superiority in social status would protect him from any backlash from what he looked upon as the cheeky lower orders crying out for the discipline of a stern hand. The driver, composing his wits was not falling for it, ran around his car twice, like in some children's game or cheap movie comedy, something with Chaplin or The Keystone Cops, chased by a tripping Nick getting tangled up in his own feet and when he had the chance the driver jumped into his own seat and simply drove off with Nick clinging to the running board precariously, screaming obscenities and stumbling after him half way down the drive. Nick was not so lucky in other similar instances and was beaten bloody and insensate by a taxicab driver over a fare dispute in Italy and dragged in by the police and beaten further and more methodically at the station house.

Bucknell, not wanting a loose cannon rolling around his house, guest wing or not, in the middle of the night, refused to invite Nick to spend the night; to hell with his condition. At 4:00 AM, a taxicab for some reason being unavailable, he finally had his own driver rousted assuring the driver personally that it was exigent circumstances. With the typical faux egalitarianism of an asinine classist Nick insisted on sitting in the front seat although the car was obviously not designed for such an accommodation.

> "Sir, I believe we both would be more comfortable if you sat in the proper seat."

Nick:

> "Wouldn't dream of it. What da ya think I am?"

They all knew what he was. The driver knew enough to hold his tongue.

Nick, however, had forgotten his own street and number while at the same time swearing he knew exactly where he lived. The one driver who knew the address for sure was long gone. Tom's driver knew Great Neck and yet could make no sense of Nick's directions and so they drove around in circles for two hours with Nick shouting out incomprehendable commands and non-existent landmarks. It is only with the sun risen and Nick approaching closer to what passed for sobriety that he regained the presence of mind to shout out in a moment of epiphany, an act of self-discovery:

"Landzman... right next to Landzman...

"The little house next to the big one."

Thomas Bucknell, unable to go to sleep, stumbling up his own steps, leaning on Delsey, who almost tripped him up, remarked mockingly, as if the gathering had been an imperfect success:

"At least he didn't expose himself... But then again the night was young and spring was in the air."

I Loved My Grandfather

I loved my grandfather. My grandfather was a great man. Some said he was a gangster, a bootlegger, a gambler, a womanizer: that's a quaint, old fashioned piece of cant, but then, he was an old-school kind of fellow. If he was something of a conman he was one short of pretentions; none-the-less always in the process of relentless, ruthless self-invention. But there are those who say that my grandfather didn't exist at all, at least not as I portray him. Of course, how can you prove someone's existence? Could I prove my own? Would you like me to take the testimony of proven liars? What footprints in the sand are ever recast in concrete?

They said he'd killed a man, maybe a great many men. But then they had it coming. He was in the war you know; still called the Great War when he came marching home, in one hard piece; a war hero they said, with medals to prove it, which he carried with him (around his neck) to his death. The rest of his life was an extension of hostilities, with less apparent blood. It was a war in which he exhibited such a superfluity of bravery and for which he was exulted with such intemperate praise that the remainder of his life appeared a postscript in soft lead pencil, an indistinct afterthought.

Courage, he objected is overrated as virtue, if virtue at all:

> "Our highest crimes are begotten by our audacity; courage: the mother's milk of notorious corruption. Hell is bursting with heroes, prison slopping over with monsters devoid of fear."

The war may have been his; notwithstanding, he did not relish the excursion. If he had blood on his hands, he gave as good as he got and more and nursed no regrets.

I loved my grandfather. A day does not go by that I do not miss the dominion of his smile. I will never lay eyes upon his like again. I would hang on to his every word for hours on end and time stood still while I listened transfixed as he weaved his story. I write, long after it can make any difference, because of my father.

Not being a bookish man he did not want his own father identified with a man in a book, no matter the fame of the book; neither anecdotal nor Dostoevsky; however, he found it not a trivial book, but thought it trivialized the man, his father; put down in words by Nick "Castaway", which is what he called him, a fool not equipped to try to depict the very different man, that was my father's father.

My grandfather was more generous in his judgment... he watched over Nick to the bitter end; sent out agents to the drunk tank to bail him out, to run him home in the middle of the night; counted him his friend and never called him Castaway, because he never was, not while James Landzman lived.

Carramel titled one of Landzman's hired toughs his angel, guardian perhaps, his oblivious acolyte... for simply being there... always, showing up... whisking maggots off his still sentient flesh with a footman's brush... posting vigil at the lockup door as John Law bundled him in, beaten, humiliated, bloodied and bruised; tanked-up, stumbling in, in tight bloody cuffs digging into wounded flesh.

If it strikes you as childlike that I refer to this man repeatedly as grandfather, it is from a wealth of affection. From now on like everybody else I'll call him Landzman, J. Landzman, that's who he was; the initial not the name and not ever, no never, Jay. He signed himself that way, with a grand magisterial flourish. Only Carramel called him Jay... never to his face...

dense to the arrogance of calling anyone by other than the name they gave themselves; the supreme usurpation, the arrogated intimacy, the rechristening granted without a blessing, of best friends and even then. Nick was Landzman's best friend though Landzman hardly knew it at the time.

I always found it odd that Nick projected his own weaknesses on to my grandfather, imperfect as he was.

We want our heroes vulnerable, even those, especially those, we worship. We want them to be godlike but damaged, injured, unfinished, incomplete, alienated; plagued and crippled by kryptonite hidden in strange, undiscoverable places; lesser gods trapped on an even lesser planet; they deserve better; they're in a purgatory which they haven't earned; a superior entity serving hard time for a crime they've not been charged with and are ignorant of.

Carramel Mostly Loved Himself

Carramel mostly loved himself or his ideal or not so ideal self that he thought he saw in Landzman or injected into him. He was an unembarrassed and embarrassing hero worshipper:

> "When I like men I want to be just like them. I want to lose the external traits that give me my individuality and be like them. I don't want the man. I want to absorb into myself all the

qualities that make him attractive and leave him out. I hang on to my own guts."

This is the kind of statement no heterosexual male makes today for fear of being accused of homoerotic inclinations. It got worse; at a basketball game he said of himself, how:

> "...he fell madly into admiration for a dark haired boy who played with melancholy defiance."

We can't understand Landzman or rather Nick's Gatsby without understanding Nick's purposeful and not so purposeful misrepresentation of him and why he should bring forth such an erroneous story. These characters are all tied together. Thomas Bucknell analyzed Carramel's work, extensively and voluminously years later for reasons unknown; well they're not entirely unknown.

Thomas Bucknell, uncatalogued archives, undated, untitled, unnumbered:

> "The writer can do nothing that the hero does; he can only admire, love, and take pleasure in him.... He is memory's genius. He can do nothing but recollect what has been done, can do nothing but venerate what has been done ... so that all may admire the hero as he does.... This is his calling, his self-effacing task; this is his faithful service in the abode of the hero...

> "Therefore, no one who was great will be forgotten, and even though it takes time, even though a cloud of misunderstanding takes away

58

the hero, his lover, the writer, will nevertheless come, the more time passes, the more devotedly he clings to him.

"A young lad falls in love with a princess, and this love is the total essence of his life, and yet the relation is such that it cannot possibly be realized, cannot possibly be translated from the ideal to the real. Of course, the slaves of the finite, the frogs in the swamps of life, scream: That kind of love is foolishness... Let them go on croaking in the swamp. The knight of infinite resignation does not do any such thing; he does not give up the love, not for all the glories of the world. He is no fool."

This sounds like a bad translation of Kierkegaard.

For Carramel the history of the universe no less was the history of god creating himself. The ultimate self-made man is a god-man, spilling genuine blood; the American dream made flesh in Landzman, finally shattering himself like blown glass against the hard malice of a ruthless world oblivious to his glorious incarnation.

This is the profound drivel that gives poignancy to Carramel and prevails upon us to take notice of this particular man. The fact is that Landzman never cracked while Carramel withered and crumbled.

Landzman was astounded by the book:

"I never said ten words to the man and this. Maybe if I spoke more to him, acknowledged

59

him, thought whether he existed or not, he would never have written it."

Ten words is not true; this was Broadway sounding off, holding forth in a mock unassuming manner, shifting speech patterns that belied his meaning, utilizing words like unobtrusive time bombs that self-detonate, mines consigned to a dying sea from a long forgotten war.

A self-serving plagiarist once insisted: good writers borrow furtively from other writers while great writers steal outright, which is total bullshit as most quotable quotes are. Whoever said this was an inveterate, unembarrassed word thief.

However, I do believe in 'omage, that ridiculous word with the dropped H, of the soi-disant cognoscenti: to echo back previous authors or auteurs, to praise or mock them; or have a little fun with them or just to signify that you too know the terrain, have lost and wasted scouts in the badlands, exhausted your horses to early, unnecessary deaths and dismemberments, leaving only your sturdy pack mules standing but half dead; have trekked the barren ground until your poor feet bleed, leaving footprints from the rain dance in inhospitable towns.

Carramel lifted some of his best lines from Landzman, laid claim to them as his own, a mortal larceny in the minds of both men who knew the magic dwelt in the word itself; the spirit was not called forth by the word but existed in the word, reincarnated with the invocation.

We have in the book the borrowed splendor, the precision of a great lyric poem; the ritual incantation creating the godhead. It is no fluke that Nick never touched these heights either before or after. The fundamental proof is the man's body of work. There is only one piece. He rose once and only once, as if by enchanted proximity, to the wellspring.

Fitzgerald left more trash in his wake than a garbage scow on its watery way to the Staten Island dump, more than any other author of equal gifts. He was lethally smitten with the inauthentic cello throb of *Colliers* and *The Saturday Evening Post,* purveying with slick effrontery the fancies Horatio Alger never woke up from in his wet homoerotic reveries; poor boys latching on to older men. He crooned pedestrian music to the hoi polloi with pretentions; pandering to a tin ear; a muzzled, beaten, blood and feces caked circus bear droning agonizingly, painfully to a plastic ukulele, strummed by a stumbling clown crying make-up tears.

Landzman loved neglected clichés, which by anachronistic use he infused with immaculate significance. One oblivious wag supposed that Shakespeare just exploited the platitudes, the worn old saws of his own day, which achieve a sharp awakening only by the very fact of having their soiled context overlooked.

Landzman never met an old cliché he didn't make love to; he danced with all the old dowagers in the ancient ballroom and they adored him for it and crooned neglected ditties from another world in his good ear which he committed to a perfect memory.

Carramel Takes the House

It is by an inexplicable confluence of calamities that Carramel laid hands on Landzman's papers, an imperfect storm of missteps, of stepping away when they should have stepped in or up. On the day of the killings, the police (there was no one left with a wallet thick enough) emptied the house of witnesses, protective custody for the butler, the footman and the cooks. The chief of police was there with his hand out, left waving in the wind which incensed him. The chauffeur left with the silver and the upstairs maid (surprised weeks later in his girlfriend's lair by Wolf's men who took back the silver and exacted interest); the phalanx of hired dicks hopped the first train in a limp panic.

But Landzman had been in no position to stake his claim; boxed into a corner, a tight coffin. His proud castle was for a transitory moment an abandoned ship, adrift, ripe for salvage, land pirates crawling all over it.

Even Wolf kept his distance; the great fixer couldn't fix this. The place was crawling with newspapermen, like roaches scurrying wildly in the light, when he showed up, forcing his driver to back up down the endless drive of Landzman's citadel at a reckless speed, losing a back wheel.

And it was a citadel, a castle, an exact replica of a late medieval fortress perfected in the concrete dreams of a master architect. Just like Mad King Ludwig who was not so mad that he couldn't fabricate his wildest imaginings in the forests of Bavaria. To this day it is Ludwig's masterpieces that grace the tourist posters beckoning foreigners into the visions of a dead daft king with perfect pitch.

But it was Wolf who finally did step in, storming the battlements, with the slick connivance of an actor acquaintance, a degenerate gambler deep into debt who couldn't stomach the vig; with forged credentials, a denizen, habitué, he liked to say, of Broadway, a cornpone genuine character, who could slip into Shakespeare like a well-worn kid glove. He adlibbed Landzman's concocted father to riotous effect reduced the audience in on it to rolling in stitches on the floor. He assumed the permanent persona of the "shiftless and unsuccessful farm person"; part of his repertoire, the myth, the back story; the back story is just that and seldom true.

We All Tell Stories

We all tell stories and listen to each other's; the deal we conceive and call a compact; we hush and nod enthusiastic approval to each other's lies, shoring up the ruins which we are. We reinforce, bolster the mutual hallucination we persist in calling reality against every shred of hard evidence. We could not survive a clear glimpse at things as they are.

Those who claim stories are a worthless mind sop are clueless, ensnared in an involuted whorl. What clear eyed business type doesn't ambition to be a raconteur, the lifeblood of the party, the orator spellbinding at the fire; the high priest in holy robes intoning the magic words? It is the word that is magic, summoning forth the demons and the angels to frolic with; or war to the death with.

The word held sway long before universal literacy or literacy at all; the word is not dead; if it dies we die. Whether we read is largely irrelevant, especially, the mindless pap served up to us, which mostly is not worth the vegetative death or the momentary flicker of dancing electrons on a fading Kindle screen. Print is not the word it is merely the medium. How many third rate films are momentarily redeemed by a well-crafted speech mouthed by an inferior actor entirely out of his depth, oblivious to its meaning.

We love stories; we live for them; they soothe; they comfort; they lull us into a running catatonia from which we never wish to wake or a fever pitch of unconsciousness or stark, blatant consciousness; they keep the wolf at bay and mock the bull into a tango of death, taunted by the preposterous executioner in tight pants and dancing slippers. They fashion order out of the chaos and impose order and meaning where there is neither. And some, the best, rouse us from our stupor.

Myth is the story that vibrates in and strums our soul and plumbs our depths.

Myth is a culturally authorized and endorsed propaganda using images with universal reverberations and ordinarily recognized meanings to communicate to individuals what and how to feel about being human. This is what Barthe said or something close to it.

Jacques Barzun wrote that figures, whether of fact or fiction, insofar as they express destinies, aspirations, attitudes typical of man or particular groups, are invested with a mythical character. Gatsby and Landzman both fit the bill.

The lower social classes, even those with money, have no interest in and indeed are threatened to the quick, frightened by any knowledge of experience beyond their own everyday preoccupations. Literature, art, is despised by them, regarded as a dangerous threat because it will blow apart their hovels, no matter how grand, where they eat and sleep and make a mockery of how they comfortably conceive of themselves.

It is a consummate irony that the Anglo-Saxon has internalized and made a core value of what is essentially an impoverished class's value system. For the Anglo-Saxon "soul searching" is undignified and unmanly; the examined life is a fool's life; not worth living and it is that very examination that makes it so. No whining, no complaining, stiff upper lip, no inerasable stigma of the malcontent:

> Theirs not to make reply,
> Theirs not to reason why,
> Theirs but to do and die

While proclaiming their own love of freedom this is a self-imposed slavery more appropriate to a totalitarian slave state requiring its citizens to march lock-step to their own unquestioning slaughter. How supremely ironic that Shakespeare with his quintessential Hamlet, with his archetypal Russian soul should perfect and write in the language of these constricted English.

There is myth that is art and myth that is anti-art, kitsch.

Myth, in contemporary culture, often kitsch, is simultaneously a simplified explanation of human experience and a mask protecting everyday humanity from the despairing, existential depths of that experience. Myth is indispensable and destructive at the same time; necessary because it keeps humanity from full consciousness of the dangers associated with the blacker side by offering palatable explanations and dangerous because it keeps humanity from full consciousness of the hazards associated with the more "realistic" view.

Popular escape novels, even if gussied up in faux intellectual trappings, are destructive of the human condition. They are the translation of the stupidity of received ideas into the language of beauty and feeling thus moving us to tears of self-pity for the utter banality of what we think and feel. Milan Kundera said this or something very like it. True literature sharpens the focus on reality even if it means evisceration.

Pauline Kael insisted that trash gives us an appetite for art. She was dead wrong; it stifles any possibility of recognizing art when we see it, much less the possibility of appreciating it or being ennobled by it. Human appreciation of artistic beauty is cruelly, irreparably distorted and ruined by the requirements of mass culture and the mud gods it constrains us to kneel before and offer obeisance to.

But Kael did finally acknowledge the fundamental error of her ways, acknowledging that although the previous generation was persuaded to disdain trash, the newer generation, with the media and schools in hot pursuit, had begun to talk about trash as if it were serious art. But worse still these new cheerleaders for trash on a raucous joyride in the stolen car of self-inflating egos, having killed off the Master in the big house and his lovely wife and all his beautiful children, the babies, too, became the new Vandals with empty degrees attacking not just the Anglo-Saxons but all European White Men, Jews especially included, bursting open the treasure house to toss the riches to the clawing, trampling multitude, grinning cannibals in top hats from the explorers that they ate, picking human flesh from their teeth with pilfered gold toothpicks. The great museums and the great books are not just vaults to preserve the past, or monuments to edited histories; they are a storehouse of collected human genius; they preserve the possibility of our future, if we are to have any future worth living.

Pauline Kael called movies a tawdry corrupt art for a tawdry corrupt world and if we don't learn to indulge in great trash and there is great trash, what movies shall we see or books read? Movies are so rarely great art, that if we cannot appreciate their great trashiness, we have very little reason to be interested in them; or so she dangerously pontificated.

Indulging in trash is going to an Irish wake for the death of souls; having such a grand old time that you forget entirely about the corpse stinking up the room or the flies blotting out the light and clogging your nose, much less the quintessential tragedy of death.

I remember guiltily reading the works of a particular author deeply ashamed of my self-indulgence. I read all of him. He takes his Daddy, who, no doubt, reading between the lines, was a mean vicious lazy drunken bum in real life, unalloyed white trash, who abandoned his son, responsibility and everything else that mattered, and this poor dumb writer returns the favor, as so many crippled children are compelled to do, by magically turning his dad into a fantasy hero worthy of Disney, salt of the earth, an aching wish fulfillment made into fictional flesh. And he does it again and again and again. The effect is mesmerizing; his pipedreams talk and walk and seem to have a human face and smile at you and sit with you late into the night, hold on tight and won't let you go. They gave him the Pulitzer for this intoxicating kind of shit; which shit is subversive. He has his cartoonish bogeymen who he foists upon us the reader, who distracts him and us from the greater evil under his very nose. Eugene O'Neil understood that it was not enough that these glamorized drunks accepted that they themselves were drunks and barflies, they had to turn drunkenness, gambling and whoring into a positive value, a thing to be applauded and glorified even, a sign of manhood. Russo's is a dream that will put you to sleep at the wheel. And when your head cracks open like an egg crashing through the windshield, who do you blame? Oh, you won't blame anybody because you'll be dead; you stupid fuck.

Popular pulp fiction, trash, even when bleak evades and denies reality partly to avoid the stain and stigma of infuriation and skepticism. Instead of telling a story of desperate survival and perhaps even triumph of a kind, it wallows in a fantasy of benign rescue. It makes us eager collaborators in our own emasculation and devitalization. We're waiting for superman to fly in or our ships to come in or the Fairytale Prince or the king's golden haired daughter to come down from her tower; to be plucked from obscurity or poverty or disgrace by a magic mentor or an astonishing savior or a quirk of fate.

Vargas Llosa said that one of the most important functions of literature is to remind us that however firm the ground we walk on appears and however brightly the city we live in shines, there are demons lurking everywhere; and I would add, the most dangerous demons are in the garb of saints wanting to lead us by the hand enthusiastically to our own damnation by means of sugar sweet persuasion.

But the demons also lurk within us needing only an urging, or some primordial hint to leap suddenly to life or sneak out at night. Hegel was wrong: Macbeth didn't step out of nature to cling to alien beings; the alien beings sprung out whole from Macbeth's own soul and weren't alien at all. It's like meeting your double in the street and failing to recognize it for what it is and flailing at it uselessly with an old buggy whip or asking it to afternoon tea, which is worse.

By educating and sharpening critical perception, the accepted and revered works of high culture seek to subject any conventionally accepted canon to a withering barrage of truth, to pull down the idols, demythologize the established pieties, a sharp stiletto point to burst the pompous, bloated and pretentious. It is the great equalizer.

In a world of universal deceit unveiling the truth is an act of revolution or revulsion or pure mindless anarchy.

I disliked popular fiction as a child and regarded it as a kind of cataleptic undeath, an escape to a La La land, a total and absolute waste. There is nothing wrong with escape in its place and some children especially those of adult age need this protective cocoon, a deep, supposedly healing sleep until the deadly fever of their childhood has past; but the time comes to wake up, to leave sleep behind, not to worship the bronzed baby shoes which bound and crippled our little feet or to gild our old wooden crutches like holy trophies but which made our legs withered and weak or to keep our antiquated iron lung like a consecrated precious object in the middle of the living room to ooh and aah over but which still secretly sucks the air out of us and the entire room. I listen to these poor fools today in astonishment as they wax nostalgically ecstatic about the novels they loved which they pretended to be literature. "You must read... read... read." What, to have ill-conceived words tumble through your brain like an adulterated street drug that leaves only a throbbing hangover in your dulled down damaged psyche? Most so-called educated people read too much. I am especially blessed in having regarded shit as shit; and "then discovered Shakespeare. Why is any other book needed?"

We are addicted to trash: the smothering, suffocating big tit that squashes against our face and blocks our nose and kills the air; that we can't wean ourselves from, that we're stuck to with a mawkish glue. Pauline Kael though wildly opinionated, contrarian and downright wacky was: incendiary, provocative and at times enlightening, if often wrong; but she had some idea what she was doing. What reviewer today would acknowledge even to themselves that 99% of what they review is pure garbage? They haven't got a clue.

Kael, speaking of trash movies might just as well have been speaking about trash books:

> Movies are our cheap and easy expression, the sullen art of displaced persons. Because we feel low we sink in the boredom, relax in the irresponsibility.

"The sullen art of displaced persons", a line worth repeating and posting on every theater marquee and on every video recording right before the FBI warning and on the cover of every pulp book which books are now printed on fine paper the better to deceive and entrap us.

Trash opens up the soul to raw sewage; it can taint whatever purity that soul might have possessed, cheapening existence, disconnecting us from any struggle to come to terms with reality or in any way ameliorating it. Most popularly acclaimed writers, best sellers, hawk a kind of mawkish barely sentient death and a special place in hell will be reserved for these money whores who sell themselves to the public taste and have the gall to call their academically embellished garbage literature. They diminish our righteous rage and lull us into a self-induced narcolepsy. They are minutely skilled gilders of shit. They hollow out our cores with a skillfully wielded razor knife and reduce us to servile cowards submitting to a puerile fantasy of external intervention.

We are reduced to facing down the homicidal apathy of a fat girl serving up candy bars to the morbidly obese on silver platters at state dinners.

If anything, it is literature that will save us; literature, which is a matter of life and death. But even true literature is habitually ruined by being entrusted into the wrong hands, desiccated school-marms, shrunken and shriveled, male and female, who suck the life-blood out of it. The schools and Universities are a death trap.

If someone came from another world and wanted to know the truth about what it was to be human, what and who we are, quintessentially, he should not waste his time reading our history or science books; looking at our great construction projects or our scientific achievements will only reduce him to laughter or tears. Rather, he should learn our languages and read our great books of literature which if he has a soul himself will reveal to him the soul of man, both the good and the bad of it; that we are brothers under the skin. And if the visitor does have a soul what he sees of us will not save us; quite the contrary it will sign our death decree; only these few great books will grant us a reprieve from that doom of certain annihilation.

Protean Man

"The vaudevillian" assumed the mantle, possessed the house.

The son was not amused by the pulp factory that was Wolf's mind. Landzman bristled at Wolf's self-serving wisecracks:

> ... an exotic man directing a protean man.

Was Landzman the protean man? Did Wolf think of himself as exotic or did he read this shit somewhere? Wolf was always quoting someone, pretending he had forgotten who, assuming a mock ignorance but really quoting ironically, attempting to blow up both the quote and quoted with it.

Modern psychiatry thinks it has discovered something new, proclaiming:

> The protean style is distinguished by continuous shifts in identification and belief which results from such dynamics as the accelerating rapidity

of historical transformation (fancy talk for things are changing more quickly than ever) and the revolution in mass media.

In this cocoon of self-serving involuted bullshit the "self" is no longer regarded as fixed and the jargon "self-process" is substituted. The emphasis is now upon change and flux usurping the old nomenclature "character" and "personality." This is intellectual gobbledygook. These terms never suggested fixity or stagnation.

The personality of any intelligent aggressive human has always been a process, a composition in development, an act of creation. Ever since the rise of the cities has facilitated a man's opportunity to liberate himself from the strict psychic confines of the village or small town the self has been a work in progress; no longer cast by entrenched opinions, bad and good, by people who have always 'known' us and our family, from the time we crawled in the dirt and soiled our diapers. Every time we encounter a new person or group we can debut a new play; we are given the opportunity to recreate ourselves, to grow and evolve. In stories old and new the characters that grab us are multifaceted, complex, tortuous, evolving and often contradictory and confused. Who was it that said?

> There never was a good biography of a good novelist. There couldn't be. He is too many people if he's any good.

There are good writers who make convolution and disorder the core, a molten, magnetic hot swirling core, of their best characters?

I will make my hero laugh when sensible people think he ought to cry.

Gentleman from another World

Landzman:

"Wolf's an older gentleman from another world... strangely naïve in some respects."

But Landzman often found it difficult to overlook Wolf's condescending utterances.

It was Landzman that said of Wolf:

"I made him...I raised him up out of nothing."

Out of the grave is harder. Did the son create the father or the father the son? Are they coequal or were each the others doppelganger? Are they the arrivistes commanding entrance like the barbarian at the gate who hollers up undisguised in the stolen uniform of Rome? Is it capital they have sliced out of their confined peripheral worlds by the bluff, bravado and sheer swagger of their self-transformation, fashioned into the compelling devices that will thrust them into the upper crust which they pierce like a dagger, ousting the old moneyed Anglo-Saxons?

But was it Wolf who crowed of Landzman:

"I could use him good.

"So thick like that in everything... thick as thieves... all the time allied together".

Was this a false rumor spread to sow discord? It was always a subtle question of exactly who was using who.

Landzman loathed Carramel's bit where he was forever turning him into a girly bootlicker. Wolf was decidedly Landzman's man. As for Dan Kodi, Landzman reserved a particular distaste from the old dead debauchee.

Kodiac

Landzman was minding his own business trekking the white, fine sand beaches of the Long Island Sound, his family had a beach house there, when Kodi, that's what he called himself, Kodiac to be exact, half sloshed, enquired whether he knew the hour of the receding tide; Landzman did. Kodi whined that he was in a "terrible bind"; that "one of my crew jumped ship"; that he needed a replacement "pronto". Landzman was only surprised that he wasn't looking for his little lost dog. The old fart offered him "triple the usual rate"... "would train him on the job as First Mate"... "was desperate to weigh anchor without delay." Kodi called the spot "Little Girl Bay" which was no doubt his own private sick joke; little girls, little boys, it didn't seem to matter much which to Don Kodi on the prowl.

Landzman would soon enough find out. A few days later Kodi, docked at a Hudson River pier, took him to New York City and bought him two navy blue blazers, six pairs of white duck trousers, unplaited, and a yachting cap with an inappropriate scrambled egg brim; looking like he stepped off the pages of some imaginary "Yachting Life". In his own mind he looked like a ding-dong, a fancy-pants dipshit on a fashion runway traipsing through Kodi's warped mind. He didn't like the way Kodi looked at him, didn't like the way he asked him to turn around so he could admire the fit; didn't like the way the other crew members, mostly good looking young men, eyed him like fresh meat or competition. After only two weeks he confided in one of the boys, a handsome boy about his own age that he intended to jump ship the first chance he got.

> "But you can't quit. Don't you understand? If you ask to leave he'll throw you overboard in the open sea with buckets of chum for the trailing sharks; if you jump ship he'll report you as a thief.

> "In one-half hour we'll be rounding Sandy Hook. It's a short swim but the currents are vicious. This may be the last chance you'll get. It's worth a shot. Kodi's got his eye on you. If you jump now just before the open sea, he'll think you fell over-board and drowned. He'll never report it. He'd be scared to."

This sounded wild, like he was being suckered by a tall tale; but for some reason he believed him, just a little. Maybe he was just trying to get rid of the competition.

This boy seemed quite content, in his own way, in his privileged position; he showed great personal deference toward Kodi in his presence. Landzman swore that Kodi never made a pass at him. But then he would never admit something like that, not in those days; it would be a blot on his personal honor; somehow he would be responsible. That's how boy-rapists stayed in business. Even those victims who manage to fend off their advances are often afflicted with disgust, guilt and self-hatred, an unholy transference, of which feelings the guilty perpetrator is immaculately free. So there is a double crime; not only the crime itself but the guilt that should accrue to the offender which is thrust instead upon the victim.

He cut the picture of Kodi out of a photogravure years later and kept it on his dresser as a warning or was it a sign, a talisman of his enduring luck. Kodi had given him one hundred dollars as a signing bonus, although they didn't call it that in those days: "walking around money", a very pretty penny in 1906. He jumped ship with the money carefully wrapped in oil cloth but would definitely have drowned if not for an old tug pulling an over-laden barge seeming to sink from its load that just happened to be passing by.

Kodi named his big yacht the Tuolomne, which he pronounced "To All o' Me", with a silent N and which he translated Straight Up Steep or as he would sing to himself when narcissistically drunk: to all of me straight up steep. It was lost crossing the Atlantic with all hands; no trace ever found. Landzman would sometimes mention the possibility of a mutiny but then the crew seemed so inexpert, so jarringly handsome, decked out in their fine pretty clothes. Advertisements can be treacherous in their propaganda, in their self-defeating lies. There were not enough experienced old weathered tars below deck. The Atlantic was wracked by ferocious storms that year. An extra hand that actually knew the ropes might have made all the difference.

But being a drunk Kodi did leave at least one enduring, positive legacy by way of example; for himself Landzman formed the habit of letting liquor alone. As for the millions, as far as Landzman knew they might as well have gone down with the ship.

Landzman Was Not Dead

Most believed that Landzman was not dead, that he could not die. The others were more afraid he was still alive.

He was waked in a closed mahogany casket in the early Fall of '22.

A second player intoned the 23rd psalm with a deep vibrato baritone as he- slipped into the warm, sandy Long Island earth. Carramel couldn't stand to see the dead man's face or his hands for that matter, overcome as he was, which spared his life; the monkey wrench in the works.

Landzman became a story, a myth, the legend before the book. But it was a very different story. Like any good story, in it, Landzman lives:

"He couldn't be killed so easy by a crazy man... he was always rung round by body guards... troopers ... three... at least, who never left his side."

These loyal Tontos, all a crack shot:

"...would'a took a bullet for the Colonel."

"They would'a shot that bum down like the dog that he was, in the street, before he got to fifty feet of the boss."

They were his soldiers, men who had trudged behind him, in the mud and blood, of war, into the proverbial canon's mouth and lived to tell the tale; the tale was horror and death; the imperceptible salute, the stand-to of staunch ex-troops overstepping the threshold, invariably addressed him as Colonel, always Colonel.

And Landzman himself was no paper pusher, no mere map gazer, no General on the hill:

"...a gunman, a pistollero, armed to the teeth with three hidden revolvers and a knife in each boot."

However, for the life of me, I don't remember the boots. They ached to have him live, like Kennedy or Elvis.

The Sightings

Then there were the sightings, the avowals and denials: Palm Beach, Switzerland and always Paris.

Some claimed that he secretly owned the casinos in Monte Carlo with Grimaldi as his front man:

> "They couldn't tie their shoe laces without Landzman".

that he was:

> "...three times the king that Grimaldi ever was".

> "Grimaldi... that plump little frog... was just window dressing, an empty suit with a rotten ancient name".

Some claimed that Landzman lived openly as himself in Geneva, that he travelled freely through the Soviet Union, procuring the late lamented Tsar's secreted treasures; that he carried letters of transit signed by Lenin, irrevocable; a ridiculous fiction; that he spoke Russian and German like a native and could pass; that he assumed preposterous poses like an actor playing parts:

> "...Fooled all the rich swells."

No, that was neither Landzman's voice nor his style.

Landzman had no prejudices against the old moneyed rich; in fact he liked their air, their style, the way the old ones carried themselves; the younger ones he pitied. In small irrelevant things he imitated the old ones. He, also, found something woeful about what they had become; even then they showed signs of passing like a sad old inbred race refusing to transfuse new blood. (The Romans confronted with the Ostrogoths.) They had what so many wasted their lives trying to get; those that were self-deceived, distracted, sidetracked; chasing a prize that inevitably proved empty to them.

Landzman knew money as freedom, power, the power to create. He grasped that one could not be even a lesser god without money, a boat load of money. The luxuries were beside the point, a distraction, irrelevant tchotchkes, toys for the brainless. He kept an original painting of Benjamin Franklin prominently on his wall and a bust on his desk. For Franklin money was not an end in itself but a means to independence, liberation, time for the pursuit of creative knowledge and good works. For Landzman it was the toys that helped devour the Anglo-Saxon rich like some Darwinian imperative making way, felling a wide, clear swath for the bold New Man.

The Irish Bootlegger

I know that Landzman was comrade in arms with "old man Joe", the Irish bootlegger. They ran a pipeline out of Canada together. Why do people find it hard to believe in that storied pipeline, a mere 8 inches in diameter; that it was somehow beyond the ingenuity of a man who could float mansions up and down Long Island Sound and pitch them up like a circus tent in the middle of the night, a charmed caravansary, appearing like a vision made manifest in the morning vapors rising off the Long Island Sound?

Landzman, like his predecessor was mysteriously seen along the shores in places which amazed the people.

The fine scotch whiskey gushed like spring water through the astonishing pipes and made them both more moneyed than story book potentates.

They say Landzman in later years was a secret caller at the White House; that he never logged in, that he swept through security without a pass like a privileged apparition, that he was a maker of presidents because he could never be one. Thrice the kingmaker never the king.

These were stories, stories of a distinguished, commanding gentleman at state dinners, a mesmerizing raconteur with a studied clipped manner of speech, and an accent that modulated with the company he chose to keep. If he called you old sport it would be best to dive quickly for the exit. It was an epithet employed with biting irony.

"Oxford"?

they would ask.

"Yes"

He would hesitate, wavering.

"I took my degree in literature and stayed on to teach. I studied architecture privately, designed a home for Lord Heathrow... school connection."

"Too much personal information" he would later think. "Less is more. Less is more. Keep it mysterious."

He kept the photographs at home in a drawer; never on the wall.

He was married to a movie star, two movie stars, they say; not at the same time. He made movies, bought a studio, to meet beautiful woman they say; as good a reason as any.

Married My Grandmother

I know for a fact that Landzman married my grandmother or rather the woman who would become my grandmother; a young tennis player, recently graduated, (Radcliffe, Smith? I forgot which), with family money and impeccable manners, irreproachable credentials.

She spoke four languages perfectly, by a strange coincidence, the same ones Landzman spoke; enough to get her a plum job as a concierge's assistant in a second string European hotel or the chairmanship of the linguistics department of an American university. She would slip into the embassies on her "shopping" trips to the city to earn her own money, translating. She was thrown together with Landzman at the French embassy; there for a presentation ceremony, for Landzman.

> "I understand that you are their ace translator. It would be a pleasure for me to practice my French on you"

opened Landzman in nearly perfect French.

Her grandfather had made his mint in haberdashery, feigned a new adherence, changed his name; disappeared during the high holy days, rose to become a bastion of Charlestown society. But her pedigree was secretly suspect and subject to purposeful slights. She cringed at the word Kike, clutched these slights tightly to her bosom, gestating to bear a wombful of toxic fruit.

Landzman took her on in the summer of '22 to enlist with his squad of "social secretaries". She became his head fishermen, an authentic whaler with a hungry eye for the kill, hounding down the big fish, methodically, culling, combing, sifting the social register, the society columns, the financial journals, the Broadway rags and the tax rolls to fashion a "guest list", which is what they euphemistically called it, an inspired amalgamation of old and new money with the common denominator being money, money, lots of money; also a certain talent on the new money side.

For these nouveau riche admission required more scrutiny than a poor boy's scholarship to the Ivy League, all with an eye to the prize. Accommodations could be made for the Cophetua complex. The field was sown with the more than willing amateur lovelies for the likes of Tom Bucknell to pluck from.

Landzman had a force of his own confidential erstwhile Pinkertons who sifted the truth from authorial fancy, composing thickening dossiers; a job more for minor deities than gumshoes. What man is not the sorry author of his own dumb biography, re-scribbled in a spilled pool of warm, stale beer, or chilled champagne poured in his hair?

Son of the Last Tsar

There is a family account that Landzman is the out of wedlock son of the last Tsar of Russia, the murdered one, who, in fact, was mostly German by blood. This tenacious rumor is outlandish, without a scrap of genuine hard evidence. He called himself pure Rus when the light spirit moved him, (unremembered in more sober moments though he did not drink), the scion of a vanished empire.

He looked like a lost Viking, barreling down Main Street in a Brooks Brothers suit and a wide grin, claiming all he could survey in the name of the forgotten king; tall, blond, with the cheekbones of a Finn, the guts of a burglar and the manner of a king.

The Tsar connection is grounded on cracked, glass plate photographs, uncanny resemblances and lost letters suspiciously rediscovered. But we all know that photographs lie and so do letters.

Calls in the night can easily be bogus, asylum internees with surreptitious access to an open line for a trifling bribe to an inexperienced orderly.

The real Anastasia reached out and settled for a time in the new wing.

There was an ancient woman with elegant manners and a suggestion of a Russian accent in her English, when she wasn't speaking perfect French, sequestered in her own cottage, incommunicado on the Long Island grounds with direct access to the Sound. She handed him down her rubies and the Rembrandts; reputed to be bogus, which charge incensed her. She insisted that it was the phonies, that's what she called them, that hung in the museums and the great houses of Europe and that hers were the "real" thing; that is painted by Rembrandt himself. She personally knew the forger, commissioned him, married him; who she swore stood heads over Rembrandt, just unrecognized. She insisted that the so-called fakes in the museum were actually a cut above the originals.

Landzman hung them openly, the Rembrandts, attempted to have them authenticated. But no art expert would stand up to make fools of the museums and their procurers and their carefully nurtured provenance. They risked being ruined, hooted out of the field, never to labor in the sphere again.

Her priceless Persian rugs were looted during the interregnum when Carramel held sway. He meant no harm but couldn't keep the keys straight.

Landzman longed to return to a homeland that was no longer there, if it had ever been; locked out in a diasporic expulsion.

I Know He Worked the Circus

I know Landzman worked the circus before the outbreak of the War, a high wire walker, aerial illusionist, billing himself: "The Great Gatsby", hence the moniker which stuck; ironic that he should attain undying fame in the name of a forgotten circus act which folded in a year or two. His specialty was vanishing while striding the tight rope, dancing the wire in the lingo of the carn. He executed the high flip backward summersault, the salto mortale and never touched down; "plucked by an angel, a bird taking flight", intoned the hokey script; a quick trick minus trap doors; diversion and distraction, distance and height, pulled by a catapulting wire through a painted cloud on the canvas ceiling sky in the merest puff of white, smoke, and a sound effects whoosh which blew hats off on the ground followed by a ground shaking thump which shook the patrons off their seats. The thumper, as it was christened, consisted of a contraption which lifted, by means of pulleys, hauled by three men, a two thousand pound weight, up a track, like a guillotine, timed to hit the ground the split second of the explosions, the blast of air and the white puff of smoke; all coming from different directions and never perfectly timed; the effect disorienting and profound.

A historian of magic informed me in no uncertain terms that no such trick had ever been performed in the whole history of magic; that the logistics were impossible. Yet Landzman had the posters pronouncing himself the Vanishing Magus, "The Great Gatsby", carefully conserved. I had them hanging on my office wall. The historian insisted that the posters in themselves were insufficient evidence, not proof; publishing substantiates nothing. Like any good shaman Landzman never divulged the tricks behind his miracles, as he was adamant in calling them. After all, he billed himself a wizard.

He turned water into wine, fine wine, the best that money could buy, Bordeaux, the best vintage year; that was the real trick. Cheap "winers" were a dime a dozen. He was picketed by angry Anabaptists, with their shiny impeccably crafted horse carriages boldly blocking the motor car congested street. Anabaptist, an epithet which they themselves rejected and refused to recognize, who carried signs calling it a blasphemous trick, upstaging "the Lord", making fun of miracles. Nothing could be further from the truth, Landzman insisted. The wine trick was a hands down cinch.

High on strong wings to perceive all kingdoms, eyes to outstare the sun, he disappeared up, the audience searched down, mumbling in awe that it was "no trick". "He vanished". They felt cheated; they wanted him back. They paid for a trick, prestidigitation, entertaining artifice, convivial conjuring, not cold hard reality. For some reason they dreaded his death. They yearned for resurrection. Masses thronged the gates. He did the magic only once every stop, to further the illusion; departed under cover of night. His knack was knowing when to stay dead.

He would be hailed on the street by travelling strangers as if he had come back from the empire of the departed with tales to tell. They yearned for the story. He pleaded ignorance. He had to stop. It was a matter of time. His number was up.

He took to the trapeze but had to give that up; lost faith in his catcher who eyed him cagily and his young pretty wife. He was saved by the Great War.

Carramel's War

I speak of Carramel's part in the war only because of his bizarre drivel about Teutonic migrations. Carramel ran so fast to the rear in such a state of blind screaming hysteria that he had to be tackled by two soldiers who feared he might sow further panic. He was restrained in a strait jacket mumbling incoherently, court martial unthinkable in his raving state. It is easy for cowards to make light of carnage. He sank into soothing amnesia, erasing inconvenient memories of the "war interlude", as he called it.

Strings were pulled from above and he managed a less than honorable discharge. His record was expunged, including in his own head; so he never existed, not to the War Department at least and he slumped whimpering home, broken, hollowed and abused.

Landzman recognized him instantly as the lunatic who had run him over, imaginary Huns screaming at his heels. He had tried to console him. It is the secretly terrified who especially despise the weak at heart. In the coward they spy themselves.

Though not an accomplished killer or any killer at all, Nick was not untouched by the slaughter. He never shot his gun. It remained secure in its tightly buckled holster; less than standard Government Issue for his lighter more delicate hand; none-the-less the stench of death would lodge ceaselessly in his broken head as he succumbed nightly to fitful, terrifying torpor. As he was known to remark: You never really get the smell of burning flesh out of your nose entirely, no matter how long you live.

Landzman's Lover, Tom's Wife

It is Carramel who was obsessed with Landzman's lover, Tom's wife, and his own true love, such as she was; he fantasizes that he has a chance with her. She flirts with him, mercilessly, toys with him. There was in Carramel the insuperable, uninitiated boy, habitually spurned or ignored by women and who, yet, keeps coming back for more, plodding annoyingly on, in love with the punishment.

He plays the go-between, intermediary for his stand-in, to quench his own thwarted desire. It is his vision of Landzman and not Landzman who drowns in the blue lakes of Delsey's eyes and is strangled in a tangle of her golden hair, slogging through the morasses sparing not his horse or sword; the fustian porter robbed him of his treasure and broke his little sword. The fact he refuses to face: she was never a princess and had no wish to be freed, was in fact enraptured by her slavery; her eyes stagnant, dark, drowning pools, her tower not of ivory but broken rubble stone and not so high; she loved to play the strumpet, her siren voice devoid of all but the chinks.

The irony is that Carramel, in the piece, is the obliging panderer, warming to the calling, happily divulging her impostership, unceremoniously unrobing, uncrowning the king's flaxen daughter, standing picket outside his thatched peasant's cottage while Landzman, the imagined king, fucked Delsey inside, partaking as he only could, listening, deriving vicarious satisfaction from the sounds of ecstatic orgasm emanating from within.

Some idea of himself had gone into loving Delsey and when she rebukes him; to save himself he projects it onto Landzman. He becomes more confused and disordered; he shatters, breaks down, runs away so fast that even the hounds couldn't catch him, just like in the War. Writing the book, telling his story, pinning his trauma on Landzman, externalizing his devouring demons allowed him to persist as best he could. The poor son of a bitch.

Intricate Web of Make-believe

Carramel's life as he recounts it is an intricate web of make-believe; the yarn he whispers in his own ear to lull himself to sleep. He needs to set it down in the book to keep the lies straight; the playbook to document, legitimize his dream of himself, the paper pages to prop against his ruin.

If his family were prominent, well-to-do people once, they are no longer; his father once formidable, crutched by impeccable courtly manners, a ruin of a man, alcoholic, launching his son to oblivion with pathetic, high flown platitudes, all that his poor, alcohol sodden brain could summon. He made it to Yale with handouts from a maiden aunt in her dotage who mistook him for the favored cousin.

Thomas Bucknell Was a Scholar

Thomas Bucknell was a scholar, plodding away doggedly at his doctoral thesis at Yale, interrupted permanently by his shotgun wedding to Delsey, although I doubt shotguns were anywhere to be found; more likely a civilized deliberation among the families, or what remained of them, in the library; the conversation suddenly hushed when the coffee is carried in, care of the servants, no finger sandwiches to be found, not appropriate, under the circumstances. Money was no doubt discussed.

Tom prided himself on his mastery of language, his learning, always meaning to come back to his thesis at Yale, whittled away as the years wore down; mocked by Delsey for reading deep books with "big words", he finally succumbed completely.

Thomas Bucknell had been a big man with a big practiced voice, a deep base echoing from the bottom of an oak barrel bursting the staves. In a movie Charlton Heston would have been a good choice to play him; Gregory Peck with blond hair; Bruce Dern was all wrong; Barry Sullivan was just okay. The looks but not the mannerisms or voice of Richard Denning or Peter Graves; the voice and accent of Kelsey Gammer or the voice of Paul Frees of god writing checks or the voice of Alexander Scourbey with only a touch of the demonic presence of the over-the-top character Mike Lagana in Fritz Lang's *The Big Heat* but with the sound and speech patterns of his famous King James Bible recorded for the blind.

Delsey:

"You bully me with your big words... you big brute. I have no idea what you're talking about half the time. It's rude to use words that nobody understands".

She consumed him, busted him, plundered his season. She was a wastrel, a destroyer. She pulled him under with the seductiveness of the irrational, the common, the plebian. He was born into the wrong class. It was he that said that his fellow idle rich thought every day had to be a fiesta and that he was ruined by it. The celebrated writer whom he had grandly feted quoted him without attribution. That was his story; he would die without attribution. It is the same Bucknell who abandoned his own notes to storage praising the other writer.

Hemingway

Hemingway's wet fecund prose is succinct, laconic; its legacy was done in by the cut-rate copycats latching on, unfatted leeches flaking off unrequited, bloodless, like dead dry skin, desiccated, mold infected.

Hemingway's prose was distilled poetry, especially immune to obvious mimics; epigones with razor teeth devoured by acclaiming him, drowning him, choiring an avalanche of Halleluiahs; unacknowledged idiot progeny with unnerving caricaturistic similitude, stomping up to the bottom of his castle keep, squinting up, slobbering to claim their patrimony, which will teach you to fuck with the native girls who only look pretty, notwithstanding their tight young pussies pulsating; but squeak and speak gibberish.

The Hemingway sentence perished from too many inept descendants. It will be resurrected by a nameless savior, god sent, who never heard of him. His worst imitators sound like deponents seated, handcuffed, before a court stenographer. Or are his characters dictating a telegram? To whom? Certainly not to each other.

Fine writers don't deliver a message they cast a spell. Most of them haven't a clue as to how they do it. What Hemingway does is more difficult than it seems. Pare down your prose and you run the risk of self-evisceration, seppuku, a painful procedure, especially when done properly. Remove what you think is excess baggage and it turns out to be a vital unheard of organ the purpose of which will be discovered by some obscure unlicensed physician twenty years from now who flunked out of a Caribbean medical school. If you want to convey simple information or write an operating manual or a how-to book read Strunk and White or whoever; none of these ever wrote poetry nor do they have any idea what poetry is; great prose is poetry. Hemingway wrote poetry, so did Fitzgerald in a different way. Take out all the excess words and you run the risk of taking out the mortar that holds the bricks together. Expand your vocabulary; expand the language, rival Shakespeare. Shakespeare used 31,534 different words; 14,376 words appeared only once. It is estimated that he knew 35,000 more words that he didn't use; would that he had. As far as big words, the bigger the better; searching for the right word is like searching for an exotic beast thought to be extinct in a tropical rainforest; there are not enough words in the English language to express the mind of man, pathetically small as it is.

And if you're so arrogant as to think the proletariat is stupid, write to them in crayon on big poster boards carried by homeless men decked out in dirty clown suits, jumping around and pointing to it, like the updated sandwich board men, by the side of the highway doing an erratic d t's dance to get you to get your taxes done.

But never forget that Hemingway's style is a perfected act; it is a stylized naturalism if I can call it that. It is craft but with all the screws showing for effect and the pieces hewn smooth with a razor sharp ax.

It is like the method actors that try so hard to be real that they bust a gut. Who in the world acts like this? Who manages to exist teetering on this edge of hysteria? Brando is just as mannered as any stage ham, as mannered as Olivier. With the early Brando we may forget that he is acting for a moment; he pulls us into his whirlpool so we can drown with him but we always pull back, come to our wits, in time to see the stage he's on. With Olivier we never forget the stage; we hear the machinery creak which drowns out the speech. Olivier was persona non grata in old Hollywood; the moguls hated him; knew he couldn't act at least not movie act which is all they cared about. Olivier himself tells the story of one of the Jewish moguls coming down to the set on a regular basis to berate and belittle him publically and loudly in front of the other actors; for his lack of acting talent. He tells the story to prove what idiots and vulgarians the moguls were. But these men had superb instincts, far better than his. He only proves how right they were.

The Academy gave Olivier the Oscar for the most hilarious over the top caricature to hit the big screen. Was this an inside joke? The whole movie was a hoot. Even Gregory Peck, not famous for his comedic touch, was hilarious.

Never quote your critics even to prove what fools they are.

Steve McQueen quotes one of his early reviewers who compared his looks to that of a Botticellian angel crossed with a chimpanzee. He thought it was funny or so he said.

The American public craves self-deprecation; they want their elected gods to wallow in it: "shucks, twere't nuthin". Reagan had it down to a science, concocting his persona from a mishmash of old B-movies. Sometimes he forgot what was real, if he ever knew. He practically toed the ground, shyly looking down when he spoke. He took a page from the book of Charles de Gaulle who never would have made it in America. But the McQueen image sticks, indelibly.

This Hemingway of which we speak was the same Hemingway, the magician, who scoffed at Fitzgerald: like a tough little boy sneering at a delicate but talented sissy little boy, and Hemingway never once came close to forgetting that where he came from the

Irish were scum. Hemingway wrote as if he was part of the club. We like to forget how much of a bigot he was and how he and his first wife, Elizabeth Hadley Richardson, could joke hilariously about going to "Wopland".

Closeted, Schooled Pet

Bucknell craved work, yearned, ached for it. Delsey reduced him to entertaining a closed circle; a closeted, schooled pet, probing for an exit, propelling him in desperation to wagering, prostitutes and beggar maids. It was Delsey that got him started gambling; she "just loved the casinos." It was his manic concentration, his defiant perseverance, his best traits that militated against him; pitted him against an army of his own clones. He couldn't stand to lose which made him lose more. He couldn't do anything half-way. He bet and lost a king's ransom in the gambling halls of Monaco, which set him up as a permanent mark. He was being dressed to kill or better, dressed for the kill, the Eternal Tailor, the Universe's Pervert, taking intimate measurements at the inseam with impunity and he didn't have a clue. By the time Delsey left there was nothing left to leave; he was a spent shell; an egg sucked dry with only the shell left perfectly intact; the night's work of an egg-sucking possum; he shot his load at a moving target that wasn't there.

Landzman Was In Business

Carramel never understood Landzman, that Landzman was in business, a businessman. It was an elemental misunderstanding, profound, even.

Landzman didn't throw parties; he conceived events; a producer of his own life's theater, not host but impresario, a master of ceremonies staging extravaganzas to lure in life's plungers, risk-takers, high rollers; at least that's how they flattered themselves; Las Vegas before its time. His house gained fame as the only honest game in five states. When Rot-Gut Ferret was cleaned out it was the result of Ferret being both drunk and stupid, a money guttering combination. But there was much more to it than that. What might seem a huge gambling haul for a night was small potatoes for James Landzman; something else was afoot, something bigger.

He was tired of constantly pulling up stakes; of floating the big boat down the never ending lake.

The Saint Paul Girl

Carramel was induced to leave Saint Paul because of a series of ugly incidents involving the harassment of some poor young girl. He had gotten it into his head that they were engaged. The family intervened and agreed not to pursue it with the police if Carramel would get out of town, go east, far from their daughter. He had relatives in New York; Delsey it would turn out. But he continued to write the poor girl every week.

Things got worse. There were rumors that he used to roam the New York City streets at night and had been detained by the police for following young women home to their apartments. As far as anyone could tell nothing ever came of it. But then he loved the City, like a young girl does, with a crush that made her heart beat fast with excitement. He would moon about the vast, breathless bustle that was the City.

Friends had seen him peering into restaurant windows searching, searching for god knows what; lurking, as if he were a poor boy without the price of a meal or as if there were a party inside that he had not been invited to. I think he lived his life as if there were some fabulous party going on somewhere from which he had been purposely excluded and if only he searched hard enough he would find it and if he jumped through the right hoops, made enough money, he would come up with the entry fee; that they would reconsider and let him in.

Landzman's Merry Men

Years later Carramel was brutally beaten with a billy club, a policemen's truncheon, back in the day when cops gloried and got away scot free with such savagery. Ham-fisted meat-faced ape with badge and gun:

> "Ya like followin young girls around the street, do ya? Ya like lookin, do ya? Ya like scarin 'em, do ya?"

In a brogue which thickened to the cracking beat: "Do ya? Do ya?" like an obscene ditty to a tune by Stephen Foster from a vicious drunk more drunk than he.

He had been following the cop's sister for weeks in some drunken romantic reverie and kept screaming to the club as it came down relentlessly, mercilessly upon his bloodied head. The cop broke his nose, his left cheek bone, his jaw, four fingers in his right hand, his writing hand, and broke the drum in his left ear:

> "She smiled at me. You don't understand; she smiled at me."

She may very well have smiled at him. She was no beauty. She could have done a lot worse and did, often. No, Nick had long since stopped courting beauty. He had forsaken her entirely; it was fickle beauty that had cleaved his heart in two.

It was Landzman's merry men who paid the cop a quiet late night visit he would not soon forget; to be sure he would not likely use his billy club again in such wise fashion or any fashion at all.

Innate Longing for a World Fairer

Nick's Carramel, that is Nick's portrayal of himself, is at odds with the real Carramel. The real Nick always carried the guilt for the murder of Landzman although he never acknowledged it. He was an accessory before and after the fact. If he had revealed Delsey's guilt in the slaughter of Tom's lover to the police he would have saved the lives of both Winslow and the putative Landzman.

The fact that he proclaimed himself an innocent, an honest man, does not convince us that he himself believed it. Run when anyone insists how honest they are. Could he be so deluded? His life is nothing but a series of facile compromises. Despite his protestations, even as he describes himself, he is a man without a moral compass much less a moral anchor. He is irresponsible, careless, a moral bankrupt. Carramel, self-obsessed, self-consciously writing auto-biographically:

> "His boyhood passed more given to contemplation than to action. Less prosperous in fortune than at an earlier age he had every reason to expect; he retreated into the realm of the imagination and became a kind of idealist fabricating the world for himself from within through his formidable meditative power. He had an innate longing for a world fairer than the one outside of himself. "

What thinking man does not?

This would as well describe Landzman, with the exception of the arduously acquired worldly riches which exacted its own inestimable price. They were not the polar opposites they might appear. They were brothers under the skin. Landzman made manifest the fictions of his mind. But Carramel's dreams came to being in the word, the book. Carramel mercifully died in a real way on that day of death. It is Landzman who lived on, his protector, his guardian, his doppelganger.

Landzman's Resurrection

Landzman held Nick accountable for the carnage that inauspicious day, for his own needless sacrifice and suffering. He longed, if not to punish him, to reprove him; to make him see.

But, even so, Landzman revealed himself, made his presence known to Carramel years later; that he was still alive or back from the dead; he refused to explain which.

But Carramel denied him, refused to believe in him, thought he was an impostor or a ghost.

Landzman:

> "Don't you recognize me, Nick?"

Nick:

> "Recognize you? Why should I recognize you? I've never laid eyes on you before in my life. What is this? What are you trying to pull? Who are you, anyway?

> "Get away from me. I don't know you. What do you want from me? Do you take me for a fool?"

Years before, at one of his own extravaganzas Landzman came up, unassumingly. Everybody knew him... everybody it seems, except poor Nick, the bungling gatecrasher who stuck out so conspicuously.

Landzman:

"Don't you recognize me, Nick?

Nick:

"No, I'm afraid..."

Landzman:

"You almost knocked me over, once. Do you remember?"

Nick, visibly shaken as if he is talking to a ghost:

"No... of course...

Long pause, Nick:

The war... the war. How could I forget? You helped me... the one who...

"Yes, Yes. Yes, of course, the Colonel... Colonel Landzman! My god... the hero. The man himself... The conquering hero... They told me you died... in battle... in the war.

"You're that Landzman? I mean... you... you own this place? You... built it? You're that man? The man... My god... you're alive... back from the dead."

Landzman ignored the clumsiness, the inappropriateness of Nick's remark.

Nick, unnerved:

"What on earth are you doing here?"

Landzman:

"I might ask you the same thing."

Nick:

"Well, you see... you see... I live just next door... in that bungalow way over there... you can't see it... not now... its hidden...obscured by the house, this house... It seems to disappear next to it... but it's there... and since there are no fences... well, not very big ones anyway and so many people... I just thought... I thought... well... why not?"

Landzman:

"Well you have to be careful... old sport. In this neck of the woods trespassing could get you shot or permanently lost."

Nick:

"But it's so crowded. Why does it... How could they...?

Landzman:

"They've been watching you for quite some time... shadowing you ever since you slipped in. It seems you've eaten enough for a party of guests. How did you like the caviar?

"Listen, if I can be of any service... any help at all..?"

Nick:

"No! Oh no. No. I'm fine, just fine."

Landzman:

"They didn't want to create a scene. I thought you looked familiar so I thought... I'd...

"The next time I'll send you an engraved invitation, hand delivered by a uniformed messenger in robin's egg blue. In the meantime, you're welcomed to stay as long as you like. Enjoy the show. We'll wrap some of the food up for you so you can take some home. If you eat any more now you'll get sick.

"Do you know anyone here? Do you recognize anyone? Someone to talk to?"

Nick:

"I thought I saw my cousin Delsey's friend but she disappeared when I got close... into thin air."

Landzman spoke to Nick the way a parent would to a clumsy child not because he thought he was stupid but because he perceived in him the child that he was and in some ways always would be.

And with that Landzman dematerialized as was his custom only to suddenly resurrect in the far distance among another group of guests. The butcher in town said that his delivery boy insisted he was a shape-shifter but I'm not sure the delivery boy was smart enough to know what a shape-shifter was, exactly, or understand its implication.

All the Private Dicks

All the private dicks, all the lawyers, bail bondsman and literary agents, all the legions of hired intermediaries couldn't save Carramel from himself.

After the deaths and an interlude in Europe Landzman came back to America; he would always return; hid in plain sight, found it unnecessary to change his name, a name common enough. He was tired of creating names for himself. He always expected history to catch up with him, the infernal revenue to come knocking at his door, or the demoniac off-spring of some long dead desperado with an imagined score to settle.

Through mutual friends he formally made the reacquaintance of Nicholas Carramel, who bought whole heartedly into the pretense that he was someone else entirely. Carramel, after the denial, approached him warily, with trepidation, as if he were a real spirit this time, a genuine holy ghost. Carramel exploited this perceived friendship, would telephone him, late at night. But Landzman got the distinct impression that Carramel was unhinged, thought he was talking to himself or part of himself and would carry on the most intimate soul searching conversations. Nick sometimes imagined that it was Landzman himself, the dead one, that he had somehow managed to reach, calling out to him into the nether regions beyond the grave. For some reason that I don't understand Landzman recorded these conversations; it may be that it was just because the equipment was already in place. The early voice recorders were hooked up by his Serbian friend, his distant cousin. They weren't really conversations, more like confessions or ravings; he had them transcribed and bound, but with time the binding disintegrated, the heading pages with dates dislocated and scattered.

Landzman Not Westinghouse

Contrary to popular belief it was Landzman not Westinghouse who paid Tesla's hotel and restaurant bill to the bitter end. He managed to keep Edison at bay as best he could, who he regarded as an ignorant gangster and racketeer with disgustingly dirty personal habits. He had his own private bitter experiences with Edison and his so-called Trust which sent in its hired goons to break up his very expensive custom-made, custom perfected camera equipment, which Edison alleged or imagined he had a patent on, having stolen the idea fair and square from the French. It was Edison's thugs that drove Landzman into his first acquaintance and then alliance with Wolf. But Landzman could retaliate just so far. Edison possessed a certain unique immunity because of his undeserved status as a revered public icon; sacred societal idols were safeguarded, untouchable, whether criminal or not.

Edison (his father, Samuel Edison, was thought to be of Dutch extraction) and his cohorts, Anglo-Saxons or what passed for them, didn't grasp that this was war, that the battle was generational, cultural, philosophical, and religious. For them it was protecting business, movies a novelty. For Landzman and the Independents who were ethnics, mostly Catholics, Jews and non-patrician Protestants, it was a struggle for the soul of a nation, for possession of the country itself. Although Edison was a truculent agnostic who thought all religion bunk and all bibles man-made fairytales, he listened in silent if unvoiced acquiescence to his illiterate friend, Henry Ford, who harbored particular loathing for the Jews as the source of all evil in the world.

Recorded Everyone Who Mattered

In fact, Landzman recorded everyone who mattered; he had an in with the phone company; he owned controlling interest, voting stock. There wasn't a phone in the country he couldn't listen in on. It's been alleged that the telephone was invented and funded at the behest of a secret, secret police force to more effectively spy on people; but it wasn't the FBI.

Landzman had a file drawer on J. Edgar including pictures, which granted him immunity of sorts. He knew where the bodies were buried, literally; he had detailed maps with pins.

Hoover stayed up nights with his good buddy Tolson, listening to phone calls rerouted, amended, custom tailored for his predilections; some of them out and out fabrications voiced by actors. Landzman employed a solid corps of voice imitators, to skillfully elicit information and sow confusion among his adversaries.

Landzman told me that although it was great for business it tended to be destructive of personal relationships. He knew too much, everyone's secret, what they thought of him; no, I take that back, what they said about him which is very different, full of empty posturing and not at all close to the truth. This almost omniscient knowledge in some ways crippled him, isolated him. He had a small army of transcribers, readers, recapitulaters, condensers and abridgers. He had virtual mystics combing for diamonds in the sewage, like listening for alien intelligence from the static emanating from deep space which you answered at your peril. He wasted too much time reading digests to learn that people mostly lied.

Under the Freedom of Information Act

Under the Freedom of Information Act certain files were released which purport to be transcripts of the telephone conversations of Carramel with a personage identified only as J. No further information or conjecture is offered about the identity or possible location of this "J" individual. There is a note that his location could not be traced but no reason is given for this failure. The files are also heavily redacted without explanation for what is being redacted or why. There is no reason given for the wiretaps except the broad umbrella title of "Subversive" which is stamped across the covers where the covers are intact. Since all good writers should be subversive it is not explained if all writers of note are being bugged. There is also the possibility that this J person is the target of the tapping or at least the reason why Carramel is being tapped.

There is also the troubling anomaly: the recordings of Carramel continue until 1944, four years after his death. There is the possibility that since these bugs were for technical reasons always manned that the continued recording represents a boondoggle, a deception on the part of individual agents looking for a cushy assignment, a gold brick with little danger of being shot dead in the street by bank robbers. Since from their own scribbled notes, accidentally left in the file, it is evident they regarded the Director as a pompous ass or worse, this would have been a great joke on him. The agents were always looking for ways to mislead or deceive the Director, "do a dance on his head", which lead to some interesting case files. They also kept a poster hanging in their recording room which looked like it was professionally and expensively printed in quantity, entitled: "The Little Negro"; and included photographs of the director which could possibly have been retouched and also representing in detail what purported to be director's "family tree". This was stashed in the archives probably by the accident of a clerk not knowing it was a joke and meant to be destroyed; it included a note as to its source.

The agents seemed to have been well schooled in Carramel, since he was at times under continual surveillance. They may have known him better than he knew himself, a circumstance which seems to repeat itself. They could thus concoct the record of the so-called "postmortem" tapes at their leisure at night seated at the kitchen table, over ale and cold chicken.

There is also some obscure reference in the file that a previous agent had been suborned by the mysterious J character, became a friend and accomplice; opening the possibility that they all sat down together and fabricated the entire file; it could therefore be regarded as a literary construct, a production, fiction; something the Director could read late at night for his titillation. Some of the events described are wildly improbable and must be a joke. Many of the Bureau files may have been in fact fabricated entirely for the Director's "entertainment" or befuddlement, unbeknownst to him, made up especially, to appeal to his prurient taste for intrigue and dark conspiracy. One agent reading the transcript said: "It's not like bullshit; it's more like poetry, bad poetry or lady pornography." The Director was called the little lady by his men.

There is an unsubstantiated story in the Bureau that one of these gumshoes created a brand new identity for himself and became an early biographer of Carramel mining the wiretap transcripts as a primary source. He became a professor at Princeton, counterfeiting a doctorate for himself, teaching freshman English while formulating his book; through this infiltration getting a better feel for the exact bullshit required.

However the most plausible and simple explanation is that these are clerical errors on the part of some low level typists. However, there are what seem to be oblique references to happenings after 1940 which would make the dates correct or implausibly, in the alternative, that those speaking could foresee the future or more implausibly still, could create it.

Carramel Didn't Die in 1940

The other explanation is that Carramel didn't die in 1940; which I grant you is farfetched. His death was plastered all over the newspapers; the publicity was widespread and there was an open casket. My grandfather went to the funeral and said that he was dead or at least it seemed that he was. But Landzman had a friend who made a good living creating corpses for those wishing for reasons of their own to fake their deaths or attend their own funerals incognito; he did special effects in the movies and life-like masks and waxwork figures. It got to the point where a glass dome wasn't required on the open casket; the "remains" felt real dead to the touch.

This movie special effects artist was also in partnership with the New York City medical examiner who grew exceedingly rich signing death certificates and rigging autopsies. He spread the money around which was prudent. The Examiner had a summer mansion on the gold coast, just down from Landzman; he claimed an inheritance from his wife's fabulously rich family in Argentina which clan seems to have been extinguished in one fell swoop leaving every cent to poor dumb Mildred; which puzzled those who actually knew Mildred McGuire's people, penniless, shiftless boozehounds from the Lower East Side. The

Examiner also lectured at City College about Retributive Justice. Being a medical examiner, a scholar in forensics and crime scene reconstruction, he had a lucrative sideline faking suicides and "accidental" deaths for an early Murder Incorporated with the consummate skill of an impresario constructing a stage set.

There are also transcripts of the Landzman voice recordings of Carramel that seem to indicate that at times there was no one on the other end of the line even though the line was open, live, connected, whatever you call it when the electricity runs through the wire. But even these "exchanges" partake of what seems to be an active dialogue, a give and take. One cannot necessarily assume that Carramel was entirely crazy or hallucinating. Good writers, after all, conceive very real characters out of their own minds. Carramel might have used these "conversations", the telephone, as an imaginating device, to help bring forth, midwife, the life he was creating.

But at other times the person on the other end seems quite real; they step on each other's lines and finish each other's sentences, falling all over themselves, stealing the punch lines. There is also the real possibility that Carramel was "imitating" the voice of this J character and talking to himself like a deranged ventriloquist.

The calls start in 1923; continue on an intermittent basis spanning twenty-one years. Many of the files are undated, out of order, and some are so badly water and mold damaged they are currently unreadable.

Someone with deep pockets and the aid of a battalion of forensic document experts will no doubt be able to extract further precious gems, someday.

I've compared some of the Bureau's files with Landzman's files where the dates still exist and match-up. Some of the subjects are the same but the words are entirely different which could be the fault of the transcribers. If you have ever given testimony before a court reporter and later read a transcript, you know that these are often the work of the reporter's imagination only suggested by the sworn testimony or enlivened by a bribe.

Carramel Who Will Live

But in a hundred years it is Carramel who will live, immortally, while Landzman, with all his limitless wealth and inexhaustible power, will live on in the written down make-believe of others, as recreations, recollected mistakenly, if innocently, sifted through necessarily alien psyches, funhouse mirror images in unquiet pools; unless of course by some miracle I manage to set the record straight. Although as yet unheard I am to a very real extent the very last man standing. But then there are the other accounts: Thomas Bucknell's voluminous unsifted record of which I have only begun to touch the surface and then of course Jillian, my grandmother, the wildest of wildcards.

Can we not quite possibly invent the future by means of our dreams, our delusions made substantial?

My father insisted that I romanticized my grandfather, that after all he sometimes operated outside the law; but what law would that be? He took the law into his own capable hands where there was no possibility of justice. Weren't they all criminals in their own way, a rotten crowd, the whole damned bunch of them?

To Be a Great Criminal

From the James Jacob Landzman archives, dated 1949, numbered document 5,652, untitled, catalogued by the executor's staff:

> A couple of kids sitting in the front row of a Saturday movie matinee were overheard saying that the greatest line in "literature" occurred in Arsene Lupin, a series of pulp novels about a gentleman thief and master of disguise, usually a force for good, while technically working independent of the law to overcome with Gallic panache those truly criminal who work inside the law:
>
> "If one can't be a great artist or a great soldier, the next best thing is to be a great criminal."
>
> Someone described the Jazz Age hero as both murderer and saint.
>
> Sometimes it's hard to tell one from the other.

Committed Liars

From the Thomas Reginald Bucknell papers, uncatalogued, undated, untitled:

> But aren't most writers committed liars even those who swear to unearth the truth? Don't they put a brighter color on the world? Aren't they all part of the vast underground conspiracy, constructors of the mutual hallucination we call reality, without a nod or a wink, to make life palatable, to make it livable, so we don't all take the long swim, or a slow boat to China or turn into really nasty criminals. (In the Loesser lyrics "a slow boat to China" completely changed the meaning of the expression; however the phrase originally meant and was still often used to mean resigning from existence after having had enough, exiting the world.)

Letter from the Catholic Harvard

November 2, 1913

Dear Father,

You have to save me. I just can't stand it any longer. I've made such a terrible mistake.

I'm sorry I didn't tell you sooner but I just couldn't. I know how you feel about the "stinking Papists". I just didn't see that I had any other options.

Aunt Sally called it the Catholic Harvard and was willing to foot the entire bill including a ridiculously generous weekly stipend and I just didn't think I could turn her down. I've saved almost all of the allowance money. I've saved it for you, Dad. How is the new job? I'm so proud of you.

I sometimes feel I've died and gone to hell. This place is a looney-bin with the inmates as trustys.

You wouldn't believe the stuff they talk about: the shroud of Turin, the sighting of the Lady by some uneducated peasant girls in a dump and when they're going to reveal the predictions she made to them. They go on about whether Mary Magdalene was really a prostitute. They talk about the Trinity, the Immaculate Conception, the virgin birth, that the Eucharist becomes the actual, the actual body and blood of Christ and that even a mass murderer who tortures and rapes little children could go to heaven if he was really, truly sorry, and made a good confession thereby proving God's infinite mercy; but an innocent child that wasn't baptized couldn't get in, neither could anyone who died before the atoning death of Jesus, neither could John the Baptist, because he wasn't baptized, not by Jesus anyway and that's the only way that counts. They take this stuff deadly serious. I thought at first that it was an elaborate put on, some sort of a lame initiation. They consider this intense intellectual conversation. Those who can make you believe absurdities can make you commit atrocities. Anybody who believes crap like this is capable of anything, any crime.

And it's not like they are all stupid. That's the frightening part; they're not. It's like some essential part of their brain has been removed, all critical capacity burned out with sulfuric acid poured into precise holes drilled into their skulls. Either that or they're born slaves or they have somehow been reengineered into thralldom. These are all geeks who have formed a tight clique; a union of girly boys salivating, panting like beaten bitches in heat, shamelessly sucking up to the wolfish sissy priests. I was told that the admission standards are somewhat exclusive. But they are looking for a particular type; then there's the self-selection. Who else would want to come here but the kind that are here? The term Catholic University is an oxymoron. To call a Papist a Catholic is an absurdity, buying into their big lie; there is absolutely nothing "catholic" about the so-called Roman Catholic Church; it's like surrendering the field before the battle has even begun. It just proves that by corrupting the language we corrupt our souls and surrender even the possibility of conveying reality.

And they all have bad skin. And they're all fat, not necessarily overweight but fat, soft, even the athletes; like they lack muscle tone, hardness; they all look sick, like they do filthy things, gorge on putrid, maggot infested meat. They dress badly and eat like pigs and speak in these heavy low-class accents, not English, really.

And they're the most self-important group of people. The fact that they don't know how to eat, don't know how to dress, don't know how to speak, are ill-educated doesn't bother them in the very least. They're too pig-headed to hang their bloated pig heads in shame. They're Catholic: God's chosen ones, with their own exclusive back door into heaven.

There's a careful selection process at work here. It's like wheat gone rotten that's been sifted and resifted again and again until all the iron is out, all the grit, all the germ with nothing left but a fine worthless white dust devoid of nutritional value puffed into an insubstantial breeze to eventually vanish into nothingness.

The worst thing about it is their priests. I learned very early on never to be alone with one of these. But it's like all the students and their parents are in on it. It's like this is the way the game is played and if you don't know the rules you'll be locked out. I haven't seen an overt nod and wink but it's there, just beneath the surface or a quick nod when you're not looking. This is their club. They are all collaborators, just as guilty, guiltier than the prime perpetrators. Let them have it. Let them have each other. They deserve it. Let them send their sons off to be buggered, send them off like lambs to ritual slaughter for an empty pocket full of change.

Evil in high places is an incubator of evil; it infects and spreads the pestilence like a medieval plague house. The predator priests run rampant unembarrassed by their boy-rape. And if the minds they infect are locked shut, it does not inoculate them against the infection; these voluntary internees are incapable of any sense of smell, they carry the infection with them like shit on their shoes spreading it as they go about the world.

And what do they become: fifth rank attorneys thieving and padding their rates, prosecutors mercilessly entrapping the merely avaricious, college professors as dumb as a post thoroughly demoralizing their charges by the impenetrable depth of their stupidity?

Also, I found out that cousin Jimmie, Doctor Jimmie is a big imposter. His really nice guy routine is a racket to suck you in. By never making any waves, by bending over backwards, never disagreeing, he's avoided scrutiny. His whole life is a fraud, volunteer doctor for all the sport's teams, the CYO, Boy Scouts; team doctor isn't that what he called himself; ready supply of boys is what it is; to play doctor with. He's part of it; one of them. They must have some sort of spy network, scouts looking out for prime meat. I've had two of those come up to me grinning like idiots, wanting to know if I went in for the same things as Jimmie, wanting to give me their number, wanting mine. When I told one of them Jimmie was married he almost busted a gut and said: "You're not serious" and then "I thought he was going to become a priest. His priest friends must be broken hearted. I guess he made a deal. Maybe she likes to watch." I guess his wife is in on it too. I made the mistake of telling this to Jimmie when he came up to see me. He wanted to make sure the shackles were good and tight. Maybe he thought it was time to make his move. I ruined it for him, rained on his parade. I don't know what possessed me to tell him, to stick it in his face like that; it was a wicked, reckless thing to do. Maybe I was trying to get back at him. He is a thoroughly disgusting human being, if you can even call him that. I got sick when this all happened, sick in the pit of my

121

stomach. I had to vomit. You have to remember that with mother and Aunt Sally Jimmie was on a pedestal, a paragon of virtue and hard work, to be admired and imitated; no, someone to emulate. The earth had shifted off its axis, which is ridiculous; I'm embarrassed to say that, embarrassed that I made myself vulnerable, that I'm not made of tougher stuff. These people are worse than murderers; they are devourers of souls; they eat you up. I know I haven't been in war, that I haven't been hunted down in the streets like an animal or tortured on a rack. But this is in some ways worse, more nightmarish. This is the demons in disguise as saints. Where do you turn? Who do you tell? Satan had more dignity, was a Prince of the realm compared to these lowlife pigs.

I don't know if Uncle Frank knows, whether he's in on it. But how could he not know? From what I was able to learn, when Jimmie was president of the student body at Regents, which made him General, or whatever they called it, he preyed upon the younger boys with the collusion of the priests, offering his choice picks to them, softening them up for the kill; schooling, grooming, priming them; he was one of the elect, singled out for special privileges, their private pimp; the priests were crazy for him... because of his huge physical attributes, that's what they say. I'm sorry to talk like this; it's very embarrassing. But I'm desperate. I can't take it anymore. Now it all comes together, makes peculiar crazy sense.

Everything is topsy-turvy, upside down, helter-skelter; I'm stuck down the rabbit hole. The Irish who are the lowest of the low everywhere else reign like tin pot despots here; the sons of pipe-laying contractors, ambulance chasing lawyers and crooked politicians, lording it over the Italians and Poles who they treat like their inferiors, calling them Wops, Guineas and Polacks; the Germans stand on the side laughing. But they all hate each other; the Poles, Italians and Germans think the Irish are scum. I have to get out of here. This is a crazy house.

Please come and get me. I'm afraid they'll try to stop me, call the police if I try to leave by myself. They know the police; they're all "devout" Catholics; they keep the priests well stocked, pick up boys in off the street for them, for "counseling and mentorship". In the future I will run like hell if I even hear the word mentor or protégé.

Please, I've learned my lesson. I've had enough. This is it. I am so sorry that I didn't listen to you. I was so wrong.

I love you and think about you often.

Your Devoted Son,

Nicolas

Who Knew Hell Could Be Bucolic

A day after sending the letter Nick stopped going to classes and tried his best to guardedly untangle any knots, extricate himself, and waited for his father. He packed his suitcases and waited. He left the school books piled on his desk and would not touch them, as if they were contaminated.

During the day he waited by the iron gate at the entrance to campus; who knew hell could be bucolic. As the sun set he watched from his dormitory window like a young boy, though he was already sixteen, his face pressed and distorted against the window glass.

And on the third day, as if by some miracle, a massive black car pulled up just under his window. It was as big as a tank and might as well have been.

Nick could not have been happier if his father had galloped up on a pure white charger in full armor and flicked off all the predator priests like bowling pins in a dark alley or picked gorging flies off his wounded body struggling to stay alive; thrown open the doors to the cathedral and marched his high-stepping stallion, with a crunch of leather and the sparkle of silver spurs, straight into the sanctuary of evil and plucked his son up as if an enchanted eagle, from the high altar an instant before the obsidian dagger plunge and away from the priest with the filthy hands who would thrust in and rip out his still beating heart and bite out a bleeding piece of it with his teeth to eat.

An enormous man exited from the driver's side, walked around and with much fanfare opened the door for Nick's father. Maybe he, too, understood the portent of this moment: the father coming to rescue the son or was it the other way around, the son redeeming the father.

Nick's father looked rejuvenated, just like the old days, full of his old confidence, his essential drive, his immaculateness of purpose, as if the South would rise again out of the ashes.

Nick met his father half way.

Nick:

> "I've been waiting for you... at the window... by the gate. I've been in hell."

Father:

> "I left as soon as I got word."

Nick:

> "You look wonderful, dad.
>
> "But how could you know... so quick?"

Father:

> "The miracle of the United States Post Office."

Nick knew this was one of his father's little jokes but thought there was more to it, as if his father knew, had another way of knowing, another source. But there would be time enough for that, he thought.

Father:

> "We're leaving, now, right now, this very minute."

Nick:

> "But don't we have to sign out."

Father:

"We don't have to sign a god-damned thing. They won't give us a refund... they're thieves."

Nick:

"But don't we have to fill out some forms? Won't they stop us?"

Father:

"I don't see any chains. Where're the armed guards? Where's their fucking army?"

Nick, shocked, his father never spoke like this:

"Dad?

"We have to get my clothes".

I think deep down that his father had the same irrational, visceral fear as the son, that once the Papists got their hooks into you, sunk their teeth deep, that there would be no escaping them.

Father:

"Buster, will get your personal stuff. Stay out here. Don't go near that place."

A nod and a smile from Buster as if he were a co-conspirator with the father and the son, in on the happy enterprise from the beginning.

Nick:

"My clothes? I have to get my clothes."

Father:

"Are they the same clothes you left home with?"

Nick:

"Yes."

Father:

"Leave the clothes. Leave the books. Leave the old luggage.

"This hell hole just happens to be in New York City, son.

"We're going to buy you new clothes and new books. We'll get the stink of candle wax and incense out of you. Have you exorcized by a genuine bible thumper from Missouri.

"You can spend Sally's blood money on yourself. Celebrate. What kind of motor car would you like?"

Not waiting for an answer he continued:

"You can start Yale next fall... if that's what you want... that's what you wanted all along, your dream. They have your application from a year ago. You're accepted. You've been accepted. You can spend the rest of this school year reading and writing your stories."

Not appreciating it at all at the time, Nick would come to cherish this brief period as an almost enchanted interlude; he practiced his writing unhindered and would look back upon the spell with deep nostalgia. He would never be so happy and yet at the time he seemed not happy at all, not happy in the least when it was all happening.

Father:

> "I talked to Dean Michaels. They're not going to recognize any credits from this shithole, so you'll have to start all over, fresh, a new beginning, a true commencement. My sister is going to help and I'll manage the rest... somehow, I'll do it. I promise you that, if it's the last thing I do."

The Old Priest Tried to Bugger You

Seven years after the cataclysmic event, the hit and run, Nick and Delsey met for lunch at the Plaza seemingly reconciled to a past that bound them conjointly like prisoners chained together who might make their escape but never from each other.

Nick had confessed something to Delsey and made her swear to never tell another living soul; Delsey, his lady love, who he infused with a depth her shallowness could not begin to encompass. But Nick understood at some level that at its most degenerate and decadent the corrupted American Dream is personified by, becomes one with the American Debutante's Dream, young undeserving girls with the chinks, pluming themselves like bright birds with their brains extracted, embodied by Delsey's vapidity, an object of deadly, deathly, materialistic meaninglessness. To this woman, who he referred to as a ninny at times, he bared his soul in moments of supreme, if drunken, truth.

He confessed that no woman had ever loved him the way Sigourney Fey had. I think she was personally affronted, sincerely nauseated by the tawdriness of it all, which is a hoot.

Nick:

> "No woman ever loved me or will love me the way Monsignor Sigourney Fey did. He was my best friend in the whole world."

Delsey:

> "Isn't he the old priest who tried to bugger you?"

Nick:

> "Who told you that? I never said any such thing."

Delsey:

> "Yes you did. You most certainly did.... Just like now in one of your moments of inebriated truth... your moment of well-oiled crystalline clarity.
>
> "You have these epiphanies... these awakenings, as you call them.
>
> "You were sloshed... just like you are now... a little more so.
>
> "You said you would never have become a successful writer if it hadn't been for Fey".

Nick:

> "I never said any such thing. You made that up... to get back at me. You blame me for Landzman when it was all your fault. I protected you. I... I lied for you. You might have gone to jail and Tom would have left you.
>
> "I lost my soul for you."

Delsey:

> "Uh, you're what? That's a joke. I'm not sure you ever had a soul to lose ....or worth losing. You'd already sold it. You made your pact.
>
> "Your father didn't come quick enough to save you."

Nick:

> "What do you know about my father...? You don't know my father."

Delsey:

> "You read me the letter you wrote to him... the one you found with his things when he died... that he saved with his most valuable personal belongings. If only you had listened to him, confided in him... if he had come sooner. You loved your father, in your own crippled way. Going there was the ultimate betrayal... it wounded him to the quick... he hated the stinking Papists. Sometimes "hate is a saving grace". Are they your words or were you quoting

your father's...? You soiled the letter when you found it... weeping into it... the ink running.

He took you out of hell but you remained in communion with one of its principal demons. The tentacles struck deep. You left your luggage but packed up hell in a suitcase.... Or is it a hand basket...? and took it with you. The fiend found its way to your belly, worming its way, making itself a cozy home. You already made your pact.

"You said that Monsignor Sigourney Fey, the perfume reeking dandy, loved you and mentored you and told you you would become a great writer... that he believed in you when no one else did... that he would read your work over and over... editing it, help you polish it... that's when you were writing junk... he helped you gild the turd... he brought you to the mountain top and showed you the world waiting for you.

"Sigourney Fey... a 'fin-de-siècle aesthete and dandy'... Isn't that what you called him...? who just 'adored' and turned you on to Decadent authors like Swinburne and Oscar Wilde.

"It's hysterical if it weren't so obscene... the self-proclaiming Right Reverend Monsignor bragging that his vestments are too gorgeous for words:

> 'I look like a Turner sunset when I am in full regalia.'

"He was a profligate nightmare. Didn't he squander most of his inherited family fortune on antique, mostly Renaissance, priestly dress. He would show it off with the least provocation and perform one man fashion shows, pirouetting foppishly like a peacock in a tutu.

"He celebrated high mass for a private select audience in the resplendent apparel of an ancient Borgia cardinal, hands shuddering as he elevated the jewel encrusted communion chalice skyward. Didn't he switch to Catholicism because they'd put up with his wardrobe predilections, which earned him the violent hatred of his previous Episcopalian bishop... who practically chased him out... calling him lewd.

Nick:

"My god! You are positively evil, the garbage you cook up."

Delsey:

"How could I know enough to make this up? My imagination isn't squalid enough. You're the writer.... Not me. Besides, all your so-called revelations are marred by an obvious suppression. You always lie to yourself and call it honor.

"Let me explain the pattern... you get drunk, in vino veritas, confess your mortal and venial sins, experience an epiphany, forget the epiphany come back drunk again, sense a breakthrough, deny the confession but know in your heart of hearts it is true "

132

Nick:

"You've taken all the bits ...the pieces, all my soul searching scraps and regurgitated this crap. You've extrapolated?"

Delsey:

"I don't even know what that means. I'm the dummy. Remember calling me that?

"'How could I love such a dummy'? Your very words... Well this dummy doesn't forget.

"You told me how he loved young boys... unembarrassedly... that he would plant these young dainty sweet little things in front of the classroom facing it... he was so proud... as if they were trophies and stare and swoon over them and positively melt... during class... like he couldn't stand to be away from them."

Nick:

"Yes, he may have been a pederast but it wasn't like that with me. He was capable of pure, unreserved love. He loved me"

Delsey:

"He was a full-blown narcissist, a mean bastard when he didn't get what he wanted. Isn't that what you told me? He made a gross physical pass, misunderstood the signals, tried to kiss some boy or felt his crotch or something like that and the boy lashed out viscerally without thinking and the little priest fell to the floor, mostly with wounded pride. And that your little saint got his revenge, hounded and humiliated this boy who had the audacity, the cheek, to reject him... drove the boy to drop out of school.

"Don't give me this saint crap. The picture you paint is of a monster among monsters who inveigled, cajoled and intimidated to have his way with them. He paid you off with attention and gross flattery and bought you like a cheap whore.

"I may have filled in some of the blanks but you painted the big picture for me. I may be dumb.... But I'm nowhere near as dumb as you think I am.

"You told me you wheedled an invitation for him to some of Landzman's shindigs so that he might develop an interest in older young men. But he was spoiled by easy prey. He didn't know how to make his move, didn't know the signals, didn't know who was who and incensed by his high pitched girlish giggles they got together, lured him and took turns beating the crap out of him.

"And that one time he showed up in a byzantine cardinal's get-up. He looked like a pontiff in drag... they wouldn't let him in ... said it wasn't a Halloween party or a masquerade ball.

"Then there was the time he started performing the Catholic mass in Gaelic. Isn't that anathema, forbidden?"

Nick:

"That's another often repeated lie... a vicious... vicious, dirty lie. It was not Gaelic. It was Church Slavonic... a sanctioned Greek Catholic Uniate rite... recognized... under the Church of Rome. He got a special dispensation... from the bishop."

Delsey:

"Oh, was that the bishop, his bosom buddy, who used to go hunting young boys with him? I'm not religious but that <u>was</u> a sacrilege; he <u>is</u> a sacrilege. Did he get a dispensation from the bishop or did he have to go directly to the pope...? Then, when out of it drunk, he was hearing confessions and granting mass absolutions at ten dollars a pop... a small donation for the poor and the lepers. Boy, he loved those lepers. What is it with you Papists and the fucking lepers?

"The last time he was booted... no carried out by Landzman's heavies... they dropped him like a hot potato... at the postern of his favorite seminary in the wilds of Westchester... and then skedaddled.

"You're a panderer, coming and going... your own special little niche in life.

"You lived through Landzman. You were hopeless.

"'Her voice compelled me forward breathlessly as I listened.' You love-sick putz. 'Give me a break' as they say in Brooklyn.

135

"You have a mind made for the Saturday Evening Post and Colliers. How did you ever manage to rise above the incredible shit you wrote? By what miracle did you not drown in it? When you told your writer friend, the bullfighter wanabee... how you tailored, cheapened your stories for the slicks, the unfreeest of all forms of writing... writing by the numbers... to rake in the money, he called you a whore, swearing such whoring would ruin your talent.

"And on the priest who you whored yourself to... you got your revenge... on your mentor, your best friend... the man who loved you... who you loved... revenge but good.

"When the priest showed up at your door, like an abandoned, beaten, old hound, drunk, demoralized and delirious that night, you turned him away and said he disgusted you... made you sick. That was the night he was beaten to death.

"Didn't you say that his death was like an awakening and made you nearly sure that you would become a priest just like him, just like him... how very touching... that his mantle had fallen upon you from on high... to recreate the atmosphere of him? What mantle would that be? And when he died it was as if the evil spell was broken... the wicked witch was dead and his power usurped by Mencken's violent hostility to Papism."

Nick:

"He was not beaten to death... that is totally untrue... totally untrue, a false rumor... Who told you that? He went to a place he shouldn't have gone to... He was roughed up a little... that's all, just roughed up. He was in the hospital... just for a while... He's fine now. I visit him in the home."

Delsey:

"What? What home would that be? The home for old pederast priests... they must have a grand old time all together... sending out for little boys to share?... or is it... the lost home locked in your own warped little brain?

"Besides, in your pilfered tome you describe, in what is no doubt your personal contribution, being alone in the bedroom of the pale, feminine McKee sitting up between his sheets clad in his underwear... you and McKee, a match made in whatever passes for hell these days.

"It's very expedient to use a narrator as a cover, a shield and when the readers, the critics, discover how banal, how stupid, how immoral that narrator really is, another fool critic sallies forth to reveal the true author's brilliance ingeniously hidden beneath this unreliable, fatuous narrator. There is no confusion like the confusion of a simple mind.

"And you associate your two main female characters... by name, for the sake of almighty god... with that depraved debauchee... that disgusting, degenerate old semi-albino.

"Are you... serious? How sick is that?"

Nick:

"Oh, you like to appear so innocent, so innocent... but you're the malevolent manipulator, the prime perpetrator of that old first slaughter... on the dump road, at the marble pool. I'm a piker next to you.

"Landzman may have stage-managed you but you worked Landzman back when you realized he might be using you. You instigated the confrontation between Tom and Landzman. Landzman called me at your request 'would I come to lunch at your house.' Tomorrow? Jillian would be there. You yourself called and seemed relieved to find I was coming. Something was up. You planned the whole bloody debacle and wanted an audience for the spectacle, your own production.

"You flaunt your relationship with Landzman right under Tom's eyes. 'You look so cool. You always look so cool.'

"It is you who choreographed the macabre dance of death.

"It is you who suggested that we all go to New York.

"'But it's so hot,' you whined like a peevish little girl ... 'Let's all go to town. ... Who wants to go to town?' you practically demanded.

"It is you who determined who went with whom and in what car,

"'Tom, You take Nick and Jillian. We'll follow in the coup' remember.

"In New York, you tell Tom to break out the whiskey which brings things to a drunken boil. That's what you wanted, a tournament between dark knights for the love of the dark queen... You orchestrated the whole black catastrophe like a maniac impresario.

"The joust, with you as prize, ends with you choosing Tom when Tom vows to treat you better which is what you had been maneuvering for. But the whole thing is a sham because Landzman doesn't want you, well, at least not the way you want him to want you, which Tom doesn't have a clue to.

"Landzman played his part... to ease you out.

"'I want to speak to Delsey alone,' He wanted to know what the hell was going on.

"Do you remember your words? 'Even alone I can't say I never loved Tom... It wouldn't be true.' 'Of course it wouldn't,' Tom stupidly agreed. Shades of those cello chords. 'As if it mattered to you,'

"This is where you act out your so called 'choice' although there is no choice to be made. This is all kabuki, a puppet show, charade, cheap melodrama with Tom forever the dupe. 'Of course it matters to me. I'm going to treat you better, take care of you from now on.'

"You made it... just what you wanted. You couldn't have Landzman but you got Tom or at least extracted a new treaty... new rules of engagement.

"You choreographed the entire death scene. You wanted Miranda to see Tom with Jillian so she'd go crazy with jealousy, over his new 'girlfriend'. Miranda knew what you looked like; you were in the papers, all the time, that wouldn't drive her nuts. I think you might even have murdered her in that instantaneous moment of decision, which way to swerve... run her down like a dog, purposely... to lock up the whole package nice and neat. Wasn't it you who in mocking me said we have to beat down the lower orders? Or was that Tom? Wasn't Miranda one of the lower orders, out of control, literally at the gates, intruding aggressively with her phone calls at the most intimate 'family' moments?

"Go and run off with your darkie grease-ball, your Flamenco adoring greaser spick. Did you know that high class Spaniards hate the Flamenco and how it reflects upon their nation... call it a whorehouse Gypsy dance? It's the flacks for the great unwashed who call it a masterpiece of the oral and intangible heritage of humanity. There is an anarchist society that demands that clog dancing be declared the cultural equal of the classic ballet? They want an official proclamation... equal time with the Bolshoi or they'll blow it up. Next it will be that asinine Irish jigging where they are paralyzed from the waist up... dreamt up by some jokester who wanted to perfectly imitate wooden marionettes strung-up, spastic below the waist.

"You think we don't know. Everybody knows. Tom knows. He doesn't understand. Tom's the one who said: 'Africa begins at the Pyrenees'. Or was that me."

No Respect

From the papers of Thomas Bucknell, written in pencil in a strange hand; without explanation:

> Fitzgerald was never accorded the respect he deserved. In his mind's eye he was a great writer and as such a great man. We are social beings even the most self-reliant and self-sufficient of us. It is inevitable that we see ourselves as reflected in the eyes of others. In his photographs there is not the slightest air of greatness. He appears wimp-like, weak and beaten.
>
> There is a story of him going to a Hollywood party thrown by Norma Shearer and Irving

Thalberg and performing some skit as the other guests were doing and being drowned out with boos by some pompous silent film star, John Gilbert or some such clown; one of the finest writers of the twentieth century booed by an arrogant fool. That's a potent image for Fitzgerald's entire life.

Suitable Behavior in Hollywood

From the papers of Thomas Bucknell, uncatalogued, unnumbered, undated:

> The Fitzgeralds didn't comprehend correctly what was suitable behavior in Hollywood. These were not the decadent lazy rich Fitzgerald and Zelda were accustomed to back home, but rather a kind of self-made aristocracy, industrious and self-disciplined professionals steeling themselves for the long hours on the movie set.
>
> > "Hollywood is not gay like the magazines say but very quiet. The stars never go out in public and everyplace closes at midnight." Zelda
>
> Yeh. They have to get up in the morning to work.

An Old Dodge from Winslow

After his first visit to the Bucknells Nick was eventually able to pull himself together enough to buy himself an old Dodge from Winslow, of all people, at an inflated price. Nick kept making outrageous passes at the woman at the garage and was absolutely thrilled, if somewhat taken aback, that they reciprocated. They misinterpreted his signals and he theirs. He didn't seem to understand that a trip upstairs was part of the deal, part of what he bargained for.

Actually driving the Dodge was another matter; it was back in the "shop" for body work on a weekly basis. Winslow proffered a poor man's transport service; he would drive whatever repaired or purchased car to the customer and then walk back to his own pintsized Main Street; he knew all the shortcuts and where he could trespass with impunity. He actually looked forward to the walks, an excuse to take hours off from the wasteland of soot and cinders and walk in the providential shadow of millionaires. He could have had one of the women follow him and drive him back; Miranda knew how to drive, haltingly. He claimed he didn't want to leave the place alone; that he couldn't afford to sacrifice the business; but that wasn't the reason. At first he had been stopped by police cars who would invariably enquire:

"May we help you? Have you broken down?"

which really meant:

"What the hell are you doing here, you dumb fuck? Don't you know you don't belong out here? We got our eye on you."

The first few times they would deliver him back to his down scale Main Street to confirm his story. But after a while they knew him by sight, made an exception and would shrug: "It's only Winslow." Only Winslow. It became an ironic mantra before and after the bloody murders with a different twist:

"It's only Winslow."

On the fateful day he had been seen by a motorcycle cop and calls of complaint had tumbled in about a crazed man trekking the roads and trespassing the wide lawns and entangling hedges. "It's only Winslow." It was repeated so often it was no longer vaguely funny, if it ever was.

Winslow was a practiced, wary walker attuning himself to the particular sounds of approaching cars which he learned to recognize, even as they were gaining ground on him from his rear. On that future inauspicious day he would blaze his own path chopping with his body through the meticulously pruned ornamental bushes like a shark gone berserk on fresh surfer chum served up bloody and raw.

One cop who recognized him from his solitary treks called him, lying there "deader an a mackerel", blood simple, "poor blood simple fool", which was misinterpreted and misquoted by the press which blared the headline: Cop Calls Assassin BLOOD THIRSTY. But blood simple is not blood thirsty. He went blood simple in Poisonville, not from The War but from the aftermath; the befuddled, frightened mentality after a long-drawn-out entanglement in ferocious conditions; so steeped in violence or the violence of intolerable circumstances of one kind or another that sensitivity to it has evaporated. His neighbor in purgatory, Mike Elias said of him:

> "He used to tell me that God forsook America, skipped out... ditched... left it to its own devices... sat back and laughed, dropping matches to watch us... scurry like ants. He was so close... so... so close. He just about made it atta here alive... against all the odds. But the empty ghost of god, Doctor T. J. Mecklenburger... him with the dead vacant eyes... wouldn't let him go... took him close, held him tight and whispered in his ear the way to hell."

This was back in the day when a host thought nothing of letting his drunken guests drive off with a friendly wave-off at the door, the kiss-off as an accessory to negligent homicide, to play a life and death variation of bumper cars, a blood sport, while divining their way home aimlessly, targeting the ambulatory locals for their delectation, to see how quick they can jump, like scared rabbits, into the roadside bushes.

Engine of Death

Thomas Bucknell, from his archives, uncatalogued, undated:

> "The motor car evolved into an engine of death; its shiny skin the exoskeleton of a giant, stinking, if often beautiful pest, sheet metal its steel armor; the combatant's shell, rolling womb,

quick, anonymous instrument, secreted, cocooned, alien inside his ship of slaughter.

"Automobiles: the faster they go the more they drag us down and back, yanking us away from civilization; pulling our chain behind it. They bring no beauty to the world, no enlightenment to men's souls? They are going to change everything whether we like it or not; the way we make war; the way we accept peace; the way we think about who we are and what it is we want. There is blood on our streets and the blood will flow; the more roads we build and streets we pave the higher the body count will rise. There will be more carnage on our roads than in all the wars this country ever fought. President Harding proclaimed this the age of the motor car which 'reflects our standard of living and gauges the speed of our present-day life.' Speed without forward movement, distance without genuine progress. We tax the poor man to build highways to oblivion; the downtrodden funding the means to be run down like dogs. Did this consummate conman ever get it right; the first Hollywood president before Hollywood really existed, blurring politics into entertainment; with his self-promoting 'press conferences' and his perceived matinee idol looks he mesmerized a nation on the road to ruin which road they surfaced with their own blood."

Dodge Under the Shed Roof

By celestial navigation a thoroughly well-oiled Nick managed to inch back to his Great Neck Manse after another night of drunken revelry, or what passed for revelry, at the Bucknells; Jillian failed to show; again.

He pulled the old Dodge under the shed roof, shrouding it from the rain and dark and took off his shoe gingerly, almost indecently, lewdly peeling off the moist, sticky sock with a peculiar delicacy, nauseated by the festering stink, as if undressing a wound that declined to heal; he rubbed and stroked the small, repulsive, bone tired foot, a foot which he dared never expose to anyone, staring sneakily, with embarrassed covetousness, at Landzman's colossal mansion, glowing like Coney Island in the night, looming over him like a hulking giant, massively erect, a portent, a tethered balloon, outlandish in captivity, meant only to travel in, a balloon which when you weren't looking would float high into the sky and disappear; only the never-ending rope remained visible, an astonishing rope which only the trickster could cut without losing it irretrievably; levitating, a big yellow Chinese lantern with the pole knocked out from under it.

It was the devil that stalked him in his dreams clomping around with monstrous feet; in answer to his demonical prayers his own ugly little feet ballooning to gargantuan size, lifted him off the ground, just high enough to make him lose his balance and hit the hard ground.

A Matter of Size

I think Fitzgerald never appreciated what an act of kindness it was for Hemingway to suggest that they go to museums to check out the size of male genitalia, to assure Fitzgerald that he was perfectly alright in that department. It is well known that the penises on surviving classical statues are unnaturally small. There are various theories for this; one, that the artist wished to flatter his patron who, not well endowed himself, would by comparison think himself a superman. There is nothing strange in this form of hyped duplicity. There was an advertising campaign years ago showing a very average man shaving with the caption emblazoned: "Are you one of the one in four men who must shave every single day, then you need...?" One can almost envision the self-satisfied nebbish puffed out with pride, positively dripping imaginary testosterone.

The larger phalluses of course had been broken off, either to be used as dildos or through some mass orgy of broken marble, some celebratory protest, the "rape" of whatever. Rather than discard the whole statue or append a clumsy add-on, the sculptor or his successor decided to work with what was left and fashion a new, much smaller penis on the stone remnants. The sculptors, in time, getting wise to the caper decided to preempt the inevitable vandal sacrilege and sculpt a penis and testicles so small that nothing could be broken off. The sculptors found to their surprise that these new statues were exceedingly popular. Certain men loved them, parading their wives in front of them, strutting like brazen peacocks, presuming their wives to be blind virginal idiots, and the wives, knowing better, with wan smiles, kept their mouths shut tight.

Write Out of their Experiences

It has been said that authors do not write about their experiences they write out of their experiences. Perhaps the word out should be taken literally; they extricate themselves from their own lives, recreate those lives, themselves, in their better image; or even more, writing is a means of quelling demons, of assuming power over a life in which one is seemingly powerless. A great writer may be the one that gives meaning to experiences that have no intrinsic meaning and that god-like attempts to bring order out of the senseless chaos.

Good writing was essential to Fitzgerald's sense of himself, perhaps to his very sanity; and rooted himself and his world in a genuine more authentic world, a world of his own creation; it was his anchor not his drain and if he plumbed the depths he came up purer, cleaner, sanctified. It was a catharsis, a holy ordeal, a wrestling with demons. And if the world he portrayed was absurd, grotesque even, in the true sense of that word, then he was at least able to confront the absurdity head on.

He and Hemingway are brothers under the skin and perhaps this is why Hemingway despised Fitzgerald so much; he recognized his own shattered self in his adversary. Hemingway is the most misunderstood of writers. The Hemingway hero is not a "Hemingway hero"; he is a man on the brink, at his wit's end, teetering on the edge of the abyss, desperately clutching for his sanity for dear life. If he grasps for a code to steady himself and if that code seems to become an end in itself, what man has not sought solace in the repetition of comforting rituals, of rites which try and reaffirm the soul?

Fitzgerald:

> "Ernest is quite as nervously broken down as I am. But it manifests itself in different ways. His inclination is toward megalomania and mine toward melancholy."

Both men are good writers, each in his own way. Both are magicians dependent for their very existences on their magic. When Hemingway loses the magic, his power, the potent wizard's wand, he can no longer summon the courage to live.

But if the Salt Hath Lost its Savor

Found with Fitzgerald's personal papers by Sheila Graham, undated, not part of his official papers:

> "Ye are the salt of the earth. But if the salt hath lost its savor, wherewith shall it be salted?"

> You are the salt of the earth which salt preserves from decay. It is the writer who is the salt, who commands the Word and through his ministry of that Word preserves the world from rot. The salt that has lost its savor is valueless, it preserves

no longer. So, too, if those who are the salt of the earth cease to communicate saving power, if the writer loses his potency he too is corrupted, fit only to be cast out, and trodden under foot by wild swine.

Whip Out Like a Magician

Only a Fitzgerald, the wizard, the creator, could whip out like a magician from his old bag of tricks the intoxicating metaphor from the spilt blood of his ink; could find the dizzying image on the point of his pen, a way of expelling the Roman Catholic demons howling inside of him. His images are hallucinogenic and press up against, cozy-up to the boundaries of terrifying irrationality.

He paid an extravagant price for everything. He courted, no he made love to failure; personal humiliation was his private catastrophe; reality could climb the ladder but never touch the dream; illusion itself was the climbing rope from which he hanged himself in an Irish style suicide by whiskey dragged out pitilessly over a sinking lifetime. How many decent writers drove themselves to distraction and exhaustion to cover their debts of one kind or another: Walter Scott, Dumas, Dostoevsky, Balzac, Lamartine and countless others?

Let us blame no writer that drowns himself in a whiskey death; in a one hundred proof goblet of fake dreams; or are dreams fake by their very definition or are they the only "reality" that matters?

Bernard Shaw, (an Anglo-Irishman who went native and pretended otherwise) has said of the Irish:

> "An Irishman's imagination never lets him alone, never convinces him, never satisfies him; but it makes him that he can't face reality nor deal with it nor handle it nor conquer it: he can only sneer at them that do ... and imagination's such a torture that you can't bear it without whisky... And all the while there goes on a horrible, senseless, mischievous laughter."

An accurate perception of reality may spur the imagination which should ideally serve as wings to escape from that unacceptable reality. But an escape to whiskey is not the exclusive refuge of the Irish. Of America's Nobel Prize winners for Literature five were drunks including Sinclair Lewis, Eugene O'Neill, William Faulkner, Ernest Hemingway, F. Scott Fitzgerald, John Steinbeck and then there was: Dashiell Hammett, Thomas Wolfe, James Thurber, John O'Hara, Jack London, Tennessee Williams, Raymond Chandler; and from across the sea: Dylan Thomas, Kingsley Amis, Malcolm Lowry and Philip Larkin.

There are those who have proposed an existential explanation for Fitzgerald's drunken debauchery, which even Edmund Wilson alludes to with the typical pompous airs of the prissy disapproving schoolmarm that he remained steadfastly to the very end of his fat, bloated life.

If society's most revered institutions are in fact ridiculous, the deserving object of the merciless scorn which Fitzgerald subjected them to, then the sanest and even most honorable course may be to escape the absurdity through the exhilaration and thrill of a descent into the immediate. If these inescapable structures of society are absurd and irremediable, why not... why not drown in whiskey?

But if institutions, the structures of society, at least in theory, <u>can</u> be redeemed, reformed, this leads to anarchism, bloody revolution and endless class war not necessarily to death by alcohol.

But even if beyond its corrupt institutions the world itself is utterly absurd, inevitably and necessarily corrupting those institutions, it does not mean we have to succumb to its absurdity. There is the power of the mind to create meaning where there is none; call this delusion if you will, but an empowering delusion it can be. To wallow hopelessly in the absurdity of the world is useless if often wildly entertaining, preciously trendy, puerile and prurient, pornographic even, an ignoble, obscene capitulation, abject prostration. This kind of pessimism or rather realism leads to weakness, is weakness; optimism, no matter how insubstantially founded more likely leads to power even if that optimism is a mind trick, the power is real, an exercise of will, an assertion of identity, an end in itself.

It is better to be an optimist and a fool than a pessimist and right.

Life has to be given a meaning because of the obvious fact that it has absolutely no meaning. Henry Miller said something like this.

Tell the truth, and they'll accuse you of writing black humor.

> "We are fabulists, all of us; we reconstruct with handicapped brains what we half-knowingly fantasize as the factual truth and vehemently deny that we lie through rotten teeth."

Abject failure was the proximate cause of Fitzgerald's personal calamity; also the breakdown of that vulnerable, susceptible manner of self-confidence which is founded on illusion, on this dream, this imagination of self. Like Nick's Gatsby he grudgingly came to realize that experience could never measure up to the dream; increasingly he learned how pathetic his efforts were, to be the man he struggled in his own way to be. He knew, too, that only the imagination can bridge the gap; but only with a suspension bridge of hanging rope weathering ominously in the sun.

To be possessed of ideals is to be self-deceived, because of the very nature of ideals, but to attempt to endure bereft of them is to live vacantly and vainly, thwarting an innate, ingrained, human craving. A commitment to a grand ideal by those rare men, while by the evidence of the world is dubious at best, it is none-the-less worthy of our conscientious scrutiny; more properly it should be observed with a reverential, if dumbfounding wonder.

New World, New Eden

The Puritans believed that the community they established in America, not a new country but a New World, a new Eden, was sustained by a fresh covenant with God which delivered and spared them from the vicissitudes of the Christian history and perhaps even the heavy burden of original sin; they were the new Adam. But with this came a new, more demanding responsibility to keep this new world pure, simple and free of that sin. Much of the isolationism that fought to keep us out of the War was rooted in this idea of a pure New World that needed to protect itself from the contamination of the Old World. In 1796, the French minister to the United States, Pierre August Adet, reported to his government: "Jefferson, I say, is American, and by that name, he cannot be sincerely our friend. An American is the born enemy of all European peoples."

The Old Testament concept of a new commonwealth was supplanted or rather joined by the revolutionary republicans who adopted the Enlightenment and with it the idea that the society of the American colonies is founded upon natural principles that emerged with the Revolution, principles that established a new covenant but this one with Nature which also freed it from its chains to the Old World, its corruption, its kings, its aristocrats and the decadence of its ill-gotten, illegitimate concentration of wealth. The American dream morphed into something un-Calvinistic, Deistic, believing in its place in the goodness of Nature's God, Nature and Natural Man.

There was a fundamental "democratic" basis to the Declaration of Independence, and its particular American Dream, which was based on the "rights of man". Whereas the American upper classes were staking out their independence from the British Empire, the lower classes were seeking to redefine the entire structure of society not only of the governing bodies but of the governing class. This was not only about overthrowing the tyranny of Britain it was about overthrowing the tyranny of elites who lorded over them; it was a declaration of freedom from the very idea of the inherent inequality of class privilege.

It has been remarked by many early visitors that their most arresting impression of America was the way that every one of every rank looks you straight in the eye, without so much as a flinch, or a stray thought of inferiority or inequality.

By assuming privileges associated with a rejected and loathed European class system the Bucknells and their ilk were doubly violating the American Dream and the Revolution which was both its instrument and culmination.

The American Dream is intimately allied to the Frontier and the magic West. When everybody is coming East it is a sign that the idea of the charmed West has collapsed, closed down and is emptying out and with it an essential part of the dream of America has been abandoned.

A year after the Oklahoma Land Rush, the director of the U.S. Census Bureau announced that the frontier was closed; based on the 1890 census. It has almost been taken as gospel that the experience of the frontier was what made America unique, distinguishing it from Europe; that it shaped the practicality, energy, and individualism of the American character; that any man could re-create himself in a new land and there had always been a new land within the new land just beyond the horizon. As the cities became corrupted by the encroachment of the European diseases, commercialization, industrialization and the old monster of rigid class distinctions rearing its lurid head, a man had only to go West to rediscover the purity of the original dream. Even the equalization of the six-gun had a democratic almost chivalric integrity to its seeming barbarity.

This perhaps over-hyped proclamation by the census bureau signaled the final winding-up of the youthful, individualistic, Natural West subcategory of the American Dream, the one that had roused or rousted homesteaders, prospectors, wildcatters, and railroad men. From the very beginning of America our sequential ever migrating "West", the moving Last Frontier, had a mesmerizing effect on the yearnings of the poor, the restless, the discontented, the ambitious, the trailblazers and the pioneers as it had equally on the speculators, the entrepreneurs, the wheeler-dealers, the confidence men and the politicians; in their own way fortune hunters all, looking to strike it rich.

Kodi represents a corruption of that Western ideal; there's nothing pure about his Nature. He is not a self-made man but a pioneer debauchee, hard and empty, who stepped in shit, won the lottery; finds and creates nothing but debasement in the West bringing back to the East the savage violence of the frontier brothel and saloon like a contaminating virus; the uncivilized and uncivilizable coming back from the wilderness with enough gold in his pockets to wreak havoc on the City; white trash with money, the perennial American Nightmare.

Cast Their 'Characters' in Concrete

Thomas Bucknell in the middle of one of his perorations:

> "Writers too often cast their 'characters' in concrete; they craft a type, a caricature, consistent, cohesive and predictable while people in the world are unpredictable, complex, contradictory, ambiguous. Such a writer's characters may develop but they develop in highly predictable ways.

> "This Joyce fellow does a decent job creating or recreating a world but it is a nauseating world of small, mean, stupid, insular people that makes you want to slam down the book so that you catch it before it invades, poisons your consciousness, sickens your soul.

> "And he's not the first to create this 'stream of consciousness' crap which is too often a cover for muddle and a deficiency of discipline.

"This Norwegian fellow does it better, making instability of character his core. What does he say? I will make my hero laugh when sensible people think he ought to cry. The disconnected... the outcast.... They are his heroes... alienation, existentialism, surrealism... his subject."

Delsey:

Tom. Would you please, please be quiet? You're making my brain hurt.

Tom:

I'm so very sorry Delsey. I had no idea you had a brain.

Jillian:

Come now children, play nice.

Delsey:

I just can't stand it anymore. Nobody knows what he's talking about or cares.

Jillian:

That's not fair. I care. Where did you get a translation from the Norwegian?

Delsey:

Stop it. Stop it... both of you. You're ganging up on me. I can't stand it. You both planned this little farce between you... this charade. There is nobody with that ridiculous name. Tom does that, he makes things up. He doesn't like the

159

way the world is so he makes things up, invents his own world. He tells me stories, false facts that I'm not well-informed enough to know are phony, then he laughs up his sleeve at me. He tried to reinvent himself but it didn't stick. Nobody believed him. So he's stuck, stuck with the same old self which he doesn't like very much.

Tom, paying absolutely no attention to Delsey:

"Actually, I had a tutor who happened to be Norwegian... University graduate who used to sing to me in Nor...

At this point Delsey screamed as if mortally wounded. Everyone ran to Delsey's aid. But Tom accustomed to Delsey's violent theatrics, as if oblivious, held forth in a tongue only he, of those in the room, understood. If it were French or Spanish I think Delsey's reaction would have been less hysterical. But the fact that it was to her mind such an exotic tongue, whether it was Norwegian or old Anglo-Saxon, or Old High German or the opening stanza of Beowulf, really didn't matter; it burned through Delsey like some magic incantation accusing her of what she was. Tom later told Jillian it was the opening passage of a book he had read. But Tom was known to lie, was famous for his ironic lies, like an old timey newspaperman concocting hoaxes and watching to see who gets the joke. The incantation might have been no more than skillfully harmonious Germanic sounding gibberish.

Tom:

Den lange, lange Sti over Myrene og ind I Skogene, hvem har trakket op den? Manden, Mennesket, den forste som var her. Det var ingen Sti for ham. Siden fulgte et og andet Dyr de svake Spor over Moer og Myrer og gjorde dem tydeligere og siden igjen begyndte rawi anden Lap at snuse Stien op og gaa den naar han skulde fra Fjaeld til Fjaeld og se til sin Ren.

The chant was melodic in a Gregorian way, each word searing, a red hot rivet and still they poured forth unstoppable, scalding water from a broken volcanic spigot.

The Mysterious Stranger

It was only years later that I heard the story that helped explain Tom's seeming mastery of what turned out to be the Norwegian tongue. The story of the Norwegian tutor who sang Norwegian songs to him was patently absurd. And yet not so absurd.

When his mother was a young woman there was an assistant to Mister Thomas Bucknell Senior who originally showed up for a gardener's job but so impressed the Senior Bucknell that he made him his personal driver and in short order promoted him to secretary and personal assistant. The Senior Bucknell was usually a stickler for flawless references carefully verified, but in this case, inexplicably, he threw all caution to the wind for a man who may well have descended from the clouds or risen out of the primordial swamps of Louisiana. The mysterious stranger was possessed of no formal education or at least no evidence of any in the form of credentials or degrees; he was self-made, such as he was, and self-educated with a voluminous knowledge much of it in error, a learning with vast gaping holes in it typical of the supremely arrogant autodidact and he was gripped by a passion, a compulsion, to get it all down, to write. Although he stepped or washed upon these very foreign shores penniless, an itinerant wanderer with an uncanny knack to insinuate himself; devoid of outside connections; he had the natural air of a born aristocrat or rather of a stage actor one imagines would play an aristocrat; tall with striking good looks he made most of the reigning grandees resident to the place look genetically degenerate.

Mrs. Bucknell resented her husband's new man, begrudging him the obvious dispensations which to her mind he was unworthy of. There are rumors that she too fell sway to the power of his charms but she in no way ever openly acknowledged this fact.

She had been barren her seven years with Thomas Bucknell and yearned desperately for a child. Bucknell longed equally for an heir. Bucknell never suspected a thing and Mrs. Bucknell projected the image of the ever proper lady. Mr. and Mrs. Bucknell linked together, joyously, proclaimed it a miracle. He would fulfill his responsibility and continue his line; his house would stand.

And if the Senior didn't believe in the basic decency of mankind then at least he himself would be decent, regardless. Bucknell was staunch in his conservative principles, believing in noblesse oblige with an emphasis on the oblige. And if he believed in the born superiority of the ruling class he also believed that any one demonstrating superior talent should be welcomed to become part of that ruling class, with an appropriate initiation, of course. The aspirer had a responsibility to take pains to prove himself. Willing! Intelligent! Quiet! Honest! Grateful! Modest! These were the essential characteristics required from the new man. The fact that Knut possessed only one of these traits seems to have escaped Master Tom entirely. The fact that the "Norwegian fellow", as the staff called him, although he spoke far better English than they did, might have no inclination whatever to prove anything to anybody was simply beyond his frame of reference.

Bucknell had been astounded to learn that his charge, (as he condescendingly thought of him), in his few free hours, had become a valued assistant to a local Lutheran minister, wrote incendiary editorials for a local temperance magazine and preached sparsely attended lectures on Balzac, Flaubert, Zola, Ibsen, Strindberg and other Scandinavian writers. The problem was his tendency to give impromptu orations to whoever would listen and often to those who wouldn't and resisted.

The new man was not let go for cause, quite the contrary; he bolted as soon as he had the chance. Bucknell obligingly provided the excuse.

Bucknell came from a long line of self-righteous abolitionists; the kind that burned and pillaged the

South with a kind of priggish bravado and sanctimonious manic glee, exacting god's revenge as they saw fit. His kind had always adopted the Negro with a paternalistic, condescending, untouching embrace.

When Bucknell took on the new Black driver with impeccable credentials it was too much for Knut; it chased him straight off the continent in a rage. Before departing he held forth with an Old Testament fury venting his hatred not for the Black Man, not in the least, but for stupid America:

> "The Negros are and will remain Negros, an emergent human form forcibly extracted from the jungle, rudimentary appendages on the corpus of white society. Instead of founding an intellectual elite, America has established a mulatto stud farm."

If it was any consolation he also hated the British, viscerally, who he regarded as a pest to all their neighboring countries where they spread their tourism, gawking at the native folk like an inferior species, props for their amusement; and more despicable still, their vile sports enthusiasm.

He loathed the American baseball more than Wolf ever did. He found it juvenile, silly, unmanly, "sisterish", beyond ridiculous. He lacked the meticulous elegance, contacts and clout to rig the World Series, which he would have done if he could, simply for the fun of it. He yearned instead to blow it sky high along with all its harebrained fans: "overgrown idiot kinder folk", he called them, with the help of well-placed high explosives and the cooperation of the anarchists whose intimate company he liked to keep. Sports represented to him an area of American customs where democratic inclination, which he loathed in any event, inevitably surrendered to:

> "...atavistic impulses, reversion to the mad howling of a backward savage tribe: the worship of authority, the celebration of discipline and conformity, the absorption of the individual's voice drowned in the mindless roar of the crowd:

> "They unembarrassedly cavort like big sissies in funny clothes and make believe it is an easy substitute for the manliness they obviously lack."

He did not consider fisticuffs a sport in any way related to these infantile ball games: rather it was the manly art of self-defense. He had been a formidable bare-knuckle boxer in his youth and a lethal streetfighter.

I Rigged the Stupid World Series

Wolf knew Comiskey, dealt with him personally, knew him to be a crook, although a "secret crook" and carefully connived his scrupulous revenge:

> "Comiskey comes from the world of the established, deep-rooted wealth, which, though straitlaced and sneering at barefaced kinds of illegality... goes in for bribery, blackmail, and

scheming to keep and amalgamate its dirty criminal power."

Everybody hated Comiskey, especially his own players, who he repeatedly cheated out of promised bonuses. They were called the Black Sox long before the fix. Comiskey made them pay to launder their own uniforms and they protested by coming out on the field covered in filth. But Wolf seemed to hate everybody connected to this "amusement" as he called it.

Wolf:

> "This was a game played by ignorant thugs and bigots, who hated Jews and Negroes... with disgusting habits, barflies incapable of an honest day's work... even my guys, not exactly the crème de la crème, didn't like delivering bags of payola to this lowlife scum. Ty Cobb beat up his teammate, Ed Siever, continuing to pummel him as he lay unconscious on the ground, kicking him mercilessly in the head. He stormed into the stands viciously attacking a heckler who was missing most of one hand, and part of the other having been wounded in a workplace accident, with spectators screaming for Cobb to stop:

> 'He has no hands. He has no hands!'

> "I knew this one guy, and he was not a totally stupid guy... talked about this inane game as if it were really important... this professor, this putz... some professor. How did he put it:

'I am not one of those who can live without illusion or without the hope of illusion; I am not that grown-up or up-to-date. I am a simpler creature, tied to more primitive patterns and cycles. I need to think something lasts forever, and it might as well be that state of being that is a game.'

"Or some such shit... Would you believe this is baseball he's talking about? This is from a professor... in a genuine university, which has students that pay good money, which gives out degrees... What kind of a university would have such a professor? This is a child... stuck in his crib with shit in his diaper and probably shit smeared all over his face because he doesn't know any better. This is a professor? This is a putz.

"This is the kind of clown who inspired me. For him and his ilk, but especially with him in mind, I rigged the stupid World Series. And I'd do it again, every year... and I did, I did. But after the first they never found out it was rigged... that's the incredible beauty of it. The bets were placed more carefully. Fixing is easy... the bums practically fall all over themselves scuffling for the payoff. It's them that came to me. Like cheap whores come begging at my door for their fix:

'Please fuck me Wolfie. Please fuck me more.'

It's putting down the bets without showing your hand... that's the trick. The real art is screwing

167

the chumps good but them never finding out they got fucked. Kind of like rape after being slipped a mickey. They wake up with this strange feeling but no precise recollection.

"This Lardner character had it all wrong. The crooks didn't corrupt baseball... baseball was always corrupt to its rotten core from the start. We only cashed in on the corruption and made them eat their own shit with gusto while they sent compliments to the chef and left a big tip."

"Kenesaw Mountain Landis, who tried to clean out the city sewers with a box of wet Kleenex:

'Baseball is something more than a game to an American boy; it is his training field for life work. Destroy his faith in its squareness and honesty and you have destroyed something more; you have planted suspicion of all things in his heart.'

"America has been brought low... down into the gutter, from the Puritans... tight assed bastards though they were... they had their real dream and their New Eden... to the New Republic of the men who started this county like Jefferson, Washington, Madison, Franklyn and Hamilton and my personal hero Thomas Paine... and like that racketeer Carnegie... who though he crushed his competitors like bugs talked a good... a very good line. His God-chosen rich men would lead us out of the wilderness and make all America rich... from this to a dopey children's game played by hooligans who you wouldn't let your sisters go anywhere near, never mind your mother."

Wolf thought it was a fraud and maybe he got some perverse joy in methodically bursting balloons, a hopping mad trickster armed with pins. It wasn't enough to expose the feet of their (by "their" he meant the idiot goyim, who make an athletic performance the repository of all their pathetic hopes; though he never says as much) gods as unfired clay; he had to pulverize the feet to fine dust with a ballpeen hammer wielded with an intoxicated glee, watching the feetless gods lose their balance, teeter, totter, shake violently then tip over; rotten trees in an empty wood, fall and shatter; all the while laughing hilariously.

Wolf had been a superb athlete, a "real athlete", which he was careful to distinguish from the little boys playing with their balls or the beer gut couch potatoes, semi-comatose, reminiscing vicariously of a glory that was never theirs. He was a warrior, a boxer in his youth; set a state record for the 100 yard dash while in high school and could swim like a fish. But most of all he loved boxing, "the purity, the cleanness of it", pitting one man directly against another, "mano a mano". He also loved the ponies, which he rigged; taking some of the enthusiasm out of it.

He would if he could, bring back gladiatorial combat, fighting to the death for the honor of the good fight which brought into serious question the soundness of his judgment on the entire issue.

Wolf:

"This is what we've degenerated into... that some queer coach can stand up and pontificate in front of these poor boys... that sports represented the most direct and secure passage into the world of men.

"This is no initiation into real manhood... it's a way to sidestep manhood... to substitute a phony rite of passage because you could never reach the standards to pass any real test. And you don't even have to play sports... all you have to do is watch, pick up the patter like you're interested... pure voyeurism. This whole thing is for very sick fucks who can't get it up. I'd like to shove a spear into the little hand of one of these armchair jocks and launch them with a boot in the ass into the jungle... to kill a lion... a fucking lion with a spear and their bare hands... then and only then would they have earned their manhood... then and only then would they be allowed to fuck women."

Old Communist

Knut's views were akin to that of the ancient Communist woman who had fought fiercely alongside now dead comrades and had always been willing to sacrifice herself selflessly for the Cause. But this Communist was cursed to witness the demise of her formerly beloved Soviet Union; the so-called death of Communism. However, in her view, the creature did not cease to exist but morphed itself into a self-devouring fiend. To her, Communism's penultimate demonic fruition was not Russia but the United States of America with its graduated income tax, forty hour week, minimum wage, unemployment insurance, Medicaid, food stamps, junk culture and junk food, food turned into poison. In the Soviet Union if you didn't work you didn't eat. To her America was the exact opposite. America hadn't defeated the enemy, it became the enemy with a bizarre unholy twist; like a second feature horror flick in which the hero battles the fiend hand to claw, fluid to fluid, sweat to sweat, and by intimate contact becomes irretrievably infected, mutating into a whacky doppelganger making animated mouths at itself in the hazy morning mirror tumbling into fractured consciousness. Her Frankenstein monsters were gobbling their soul's away from the inside out, curdling everything into an ugly sour stew.

It had been her fervent desire that her beloved proletariat finally liberated from the slavery of their incessant labor and from their captors, the capitalist blood suckers, would embrace literature, the arts and great music; that they would stand in awe of beauty and labor tirelessly at its creation in whatever new form they might devise from their native genius. She looked around in utter, profound disgust at the poisoned fruits of her life's work; at the unexpected, unintended consequence, "popular culture" run amok: mindless sports enthusiasm, junk movies, fan magazines, gambling, idiot idols, and pulp novels. It was her steadfast belief that they could not possibly get any genuine pleasure from these abysmally stupid pursuits, that their very pleasure was a delusion. They were corrupted, suborned by some insidious collective compulsion; that this is what they were supposed to like, so they liked it or pretended they did in order to bond with the group.

She firmly believed that the ex-proletariat were their own worst enemy. She didn't swallow the Marxist cant that art in capitalist countries is an instrument of the bourgeoisie in maintaining its social privilege and power. She did not buy into the enduring party line that the poor were subdued by the rich by means of these mind-numbing, soul-killing entertainments and gadgetry and ever evolving pharmaceuticals. Walmart may be full of garbage that nobody needs but the finer shops of the rich are chock full of more finely wrought rubbish and ingeniously crafted contraptions that are equally worthless. The rich swill analogous poison in more gargantuan portions.

The old Anglo-Saxon elite had fallen back in precipitous disarray, the unguarded rear falling away like flies swatted at, retrenched into their walled enclaves, anxiously shielding the remnants of their booty and the ragged loose ends of their assiduously acquired good taste. The old Communist especially despised the new power elite who either pretended to share the public's insatiable taste for guzzling garbage, or were afraid to oppose it, afraid they would be regarded as supercilious elitists looking down their snobby noses at the untouchables; or were they themselves mindless vulgarians to the very core, indistinguishable by manner, look or taste from the plebeians they lorded it over; these plebeians who would come to enjoy and even need the generous application of the whip and would be gladly subjugated but only by those no better than themselves.

Old Communist Woman:

"They were better off working eighty hours a week... hell, they were better off as serfs, instead of slaves to their own abysmal bad taste. You give these idiots money and time and they infect society like a flesh eating black plague with their big stupid boats dragged behind their monstrous, shiny pickup trucks and slinking back into their appalling macmansions without a trace of shame.

"In Russia we used to call it poshlost. America is awash in poshlost... sinking... drowning in poshlost... base self-satisfied vulgarity... highfalutin banal superficiality... taste so bad that it becomes more than an esthetic offence and becomes a moral obscenity... complacent hackneyed mediocrity curdling into moral degeneracy... Dostoyevsky applied the word to the Devil... smug narcissistic inferiority... not only the obviously trashy but the falsely important, the falsely beautiful, the falsely clever... corny, treacly trash, cutsypie clichés... the sentimental... the saccharine... the mawkish and maudlin. Philistinism in all its phases, bogus profundities, crude, moronic dishonest pseudo-literature parading as the real thing stealing away the souls of the gullible, parading up and down decked out, garbed in garbage."

Norwegian Cook

Young Tom Bucknell was taken under the wing of the Norwegian cook who was a second nanny to him. It was rumored that the cook was Knut's mother and that it was she who was the stalking horse who insinuated her son into the household with the subversive idea of cuckolding the master and initiating a new race of supermen; but this was ludicrous since she had never laid eyes on Knut before that first day he materialized like a strayed dog coming home. The cook suspected what the others couldn't see. She adopted Knut in her own mind long after he deserted them; in her heart she considered his abrupt departure an abandonment; he didn't even so much as say goodbye.

By the time Tom grew into the image of his father there were conveniently few left who remembered that father, the staff rotated, new blood brought in. The cook having formed a bond with the young Tom was one of the few who could in no way be induced to leave even by way of bribery. Although she was never given formal notice it would have taken a forcible eviction by burly men to drag her howling from her stove with the young Tom clinging to her apron. The Senior Bucknell, who saw only Tom's Nordic good looks and amazingly quick intelligence, was either blind or chose not to see.

But there were those like the holdout cook who suspected that taking-on the black driver so long ago was no coincidence. The Senior Bucknell was well aware of Knut's tenacious judgments. The driver stayed less than a year and exploited his position to step up in the world. Though a professed ardent believer in Negro rights this was the first Black person Senior had ever hired and strangely or not so strangely, it would be his last.

Exactly what Knut knew is the unanswered question. There was never a question of whether Mrs. Bucknell would run off with him or whether he wanted her to. The fact that he was impoverished was entirely beside the point, at least as far as Knut was concerned; it was irrelevant. Knut thought too highly of himself to let a mere lack of money stand in the way of his exalted self-regard. He was no egalitarian, nor even a democrat. "Egalitarianism was the enemy of excellence" he pontificated. He believed that social harmony existed only where each person knew his place which place would be based on talent, intelligence and hard work; his own place was naturally at the very top and he resolutely believed that he would rise inevitably to that pinnacle.

The Senior Bucknell was the better man, by his own dim lights, an ethical man, although one could say the same of Knut, by his own lights; kinder, more understanding, a better husband than Knut could even conceive of being.

Mrs. Bucknell was mesmerized or dumb-founded by Knut's speeches and they were speeches:

> "I take life as it comes, as it is. Who am I to change it? If I don't like it I will enumerate that which is unacceptable (not I will tell you what I don't like). It is absurd and to the best of my ability I will tell you why it is absurd or will tell

you in my own way I don't care that it is absurd. I may laugh at it, but as far as changing it; the fight would be futile. I would be crashing my head into a brick wall."

This was his idea of intimate, compelling conversation, wooing the womenfolk, and it worked. Knut spoke English with a studied precise excellence which just missed being ridiculous. He was very much missed by all, except, of course, the Black driver who marveled at his own unaccustomed position and the new power at his fingertips; there was an added triumphalism in his step which the Master found disconcerting, if not positively ludicrous. He wrote him sterling references and aided him in his move up in the world and out of his house.

Purposeful Resolute Action

A single-minded commitment to a life-long course of purposeful resolute action is thinkable only if one is deluded, mired in a deficient perception of the nature of things as they are. As contradictory as it sounds such a commitment to ideals gains particular traction in times of corrosive skepticism and mordant relativism; such commitment can be regarded as a mindless surrender, a purposeful shutting down of the critical mind.

Such was the time in the early 1920s when Americans had recently come back from the tired Old World having fought its War, long after we had thought our break with that corrupt world had been clean, permanent and complete. They came back more in vanquishment than in victory, infected as if with the old disease they thought they had been cured of, with a sense of philosophical defeat, having succumbed as many Europeans had to a morbid absorption with death, downfall and repudiation; haunted by a sense of the decline of Western Civilization to which America was once again inextricably bound like an anchor sinking in a bottomless sea. The War's aftermath presented a barrier that abruptly cut off Western Civilization's expanding confidence in its own ability. We, in America, came face to face with a long lost father, a degenerate, who re-insinuated himself into our lives, stole our savings, re-entrapped us and the discovery had unsettled our confidence. Is this what we came from? Are we no better than this?

Faulkner's *The Bear*.

> For a... "thousand years... men fought over the fragments of that collapse until at last even the fragments were exhausted and men snarled over the gnawed bones of the old world's worthless evening until an accidental egg discovered to them a new hemisphere."

Pound:

> "For an old bitch gone in the teeth,
>
> For a botched civilization..."

We gave our blood and treasure to prop up the teetering old wrecks, the crooked masts splintered and cracked; that will never be sea worthy, no, not ever again.

Modern Man

Found in the archives of Thomas Bucknell, untitled, undated, uncatalogued:

> Does not the artist, especially the writer create his own world while existing exclusively in his imagination; does he not achieve a reality through his creations more beautiful and transcendent than the humdrum, stale, grubby "real" world in which we are doomed to drag our leaden feet?
>
> Nick's Gatsby's quest is not for an external treasure or the object of his desire but rather for himself; not by looking within to discover it but by creation and recreation, to give birth to it. This is a greater burden, a higher task than seeking a grail or rescuing a damsel in deadly distress.
>
> He is modern man, which is man as artist; existence precedes essence; he defines his own; he does not search outside of himself for the meaning of existence, for some holy grail, for some secret that if discovered will explain everything; nor does he look within himself, as if contemplation will reveal that same secret.
>
> He is the man of action; for the conception cannot live alone in his head but must be fulfilled, proved and proofed in the world outside of him. This essence exists not in the mind of some God but in the mind of modern man the self-creator.

The artist like the self-made man, who is the artist-creator of himself, is god-like; he creates an existence limited only by that which he can envisage, alive in his own world only, in which his dreams materialize, ghosts incarnated in vulnerable flesh and red blood.

And if he comes crashing down, blown out of the sky by the iron cannon balls of actuality shot high, to the hard unyielding concrete earth beneath, he can be sustained by the memory of that flight, for his moment of transcendent glory, broken, bleeding, beating wings singed but glorified by the flames of an imaginary sun that dwarfs our own with a blinding light.

The Ghost

The following is a verbatim transcript from the files of James Landzman based presumably on a voice recording. It is also possible that Bucknell is one of the speakers and transcribed the conversation from memory; which, however, doesn't explain how it came into the possession of Landzman. It is not based on one of Landzman's recordings because it would have been designated as such and the speakers would have been identified. It is dated 1929 and specifies that three or perhaps four people are speaking but does not name the speakers nor does it distinguish between them in the transcript. I originally separated the words among four speakers titled speakers one, two, three and four; but since this is conjecture on my part I thought it would be better to let the reader make up

Did you notice that Nick's ghost seems to understand Landzman better than Nick?

What ghost? What are you talking about?

Oh, I'm sorry. The writer... the writer.

What writer? Do you mean Fitzgerald?

He means the one who helped Nick polish the work: the ghost writer.

Well, call him that instead of being cute and calling him the ghost.

But it seems so appropriate, like a magic muse taking corporeal form. Who else but a supernatural spirit called forth by a magician, a wizard could produce such a work.

Some people think Nick doesn't even exist... that he's a construct of the ghost or of Fitzgerald.

That's ridiculous.

Did you read Nick's original?

I didn't but a friend of mine at Scribner's did. He says the ghost is the real writer. He didn't believe in Nick... in Fitzgerald either.

But the ghost was a drunk, a fool... he exposed himself at dinner parties.

No... that was Fitzgerald... because he didn't think he was big enough.

You're making excuses. I didn't know you knew him.

Not well.

Does the fact that you're a drunk and ineffectual buffoon who exposes himself mean you can't be a fine writer?

I grant you, he was a boob, a real lame.

The question stands: can you write wisely without being wise?

How did the ghost know Landzman?

I didn't know he knew him.

Did he know him?

I saw him at one of the parties.

Saw who? Which party?

Landzman's.

No, I mean which one.

I don't know which one.

But the ghost wrote nothing but mostly trash before and after.

You're confusing him with Fitzgerald... but the same can be said of Nick.

Who said Nick doesn't exist... in reality?

Lots.

That's absurd. You might as well say Landzman doesn't exist.

Whose Landzman?

Do you mean who is Landzman or whose Landzman?

Both, I guess.

You can't mean both; it's either one or the other.

No I mean whose Landzman. If you answer the one it answers the other, well, to some extent.

No it doesn't.

Didn't you say, they say Landzman didn't exist? You might as well say you don't exist or I don't exist... that we are all creations of some hack.

The question stands. You can't question whether he exists unless you know which one you are questioning. The question stands. Whose Landzman?

Nick's Landzman, Gatsby, is pure fantasy... the wishful conjurings of an overwrought adolescent mind... exaggerated, unstable. He himself admits his incredulity was submerged in fascination. Because of his impressionability, Nick clutches an image; he's an old lady with a holy picture, a persona and clothes it with his wishes... fascination generates credulity. The

Landzman or Gatsby, if you prefer, that he foists upon us is a cliché and on insubstantial bona fides he becomes a supernatural wonder.

Who said fascination generates credulity, wonder makes us need to believe?

You just did.

The ghost comes closer but he's necessarily lashed to Nick... can only manage to get the word out through Nick.

That's not true. There are other devises. Fitzgerald undermines Nick repeatedly and by calling him into question we manage to get the picture.

What? We have Nick, who even the ghost regards as a fool but who is a fool himself and maybe even a greater fool than Nick. And from this mishmash we expect to get at the truth

Who says?

What do you mean who says?

I mean who says we have to unearth the truth?

What's the point of reading it if we can't find the truth?

The truth. The truth, you say. Whose truth? You can't stand the truth. The truth is impossible. You, excuse me, we can't stand the truth. We will wither at its touch; shrivel up at its sight. It will make us miserable. It will destroy us.... How about just the glory of the experience... confused, misled, delusional as we are, the imaginative experience itself... transcendental... the mind experience, an end in itself, the only meaningful end.

If you're going to live in or for this magical imaginational experience you might as well trip out on drugs; if the reality of it is irrelevant.... if truth doesn't matter.

And what megalomaniac has the unmitigated gall to shove the truth, his version of the truth in our face, with the idea of rousing us from our supposed stupor, like a dog's face smeared with his own shit to house break him, not to make him free? Truth? The truth will set you free only after it's eaten you alive and spit you out. I get back to the question: whose truth?

Fuck the truth.

I am not talking about some big truth; I'm just talking about the truth of the story, the facts.

But that's the point; maybe the truth of the story is tied up with some big truth. You can't discover one without the other.

That's bullshit. And for Christ's sake stop calling him the ghost... it's a little bit too clever by half for me. Call him what he is... a ghostwriter or collaborator or alter ego or living muse or whatever.

A dim-witted person can make only certain, limited kinds of blunders, limited as they are by the size of his mind; but the mistakes open to a really intelligent fellow are far greater. But to the one who knows how terribly smart he is compared to the rest of the stupid world, the possibilities for true idiocy are breathtaking.

Who are you talking about? Are you trying to start a fight?

If the shoe...? (long pause) No not at all.

Besides I don't think it makes any sense. It's too clever by...

I think it does make sense.

You would... you said it.

Besides... I don't think the idea is original.

So few ideas are. But why would somebody repeat such a lame idea.

People are always repeating lame ideas. If they really thought about it themselves they probably wouldn't repeat it. They'd realize how stupid it was.

Nick or the ghost, or whoever, seriously misleads us. He tells us Landzman turned out all right. Is he serious? He's murdered, at least so far as the story is concerned. Everybody thinks he's murdered. Nick is a full-blown narcissist. He is directly complicit in three murders and he thinks Landzman, or the creative fantasy which replaces him, turned out all right. He's fucking dead.

But the point is he's not dead.

Nick doesn't know that. Nick thinks he's dead. Besides, three people are dead, one of them very close to Landzman.

Besides one was a prostitute the other her pimp.

You make it sound so black and white... a little money on the side... trying to make ends meet... to put together a nest egg... get away from it all. It was so much more complex. Winslow loved her and she was run down like a dog. He went crazy... he couldn't make her happy himself. She didn't walk the streets. She picked her lovers, clients, or whatever... from Manhasset and Great Neck... those who didn't want to make the trip in... all the way to the City.

It's as clear as day that Tom's affair with Miranda is a financial transaction. She was carefully attuned to price and market place values... she prudently chooses Tom, picks him up impressed by his shoes and suit. He's a commodity as much as she is. It was like a family business. Her sister came in on it... to share the overflow... to watch her back.

You keep confusing Nick's book with reality.

Winslow was so proud of the place. He was like a little kid who just built a palace with an erector set... giving his friends the grand tour. The interior apartments rivalled any penthouse on Park Avenue or so he bragged... though he had never been anywhere near a penthouse on Park Avenue. I think he honestly forgot that it was a whorehouse. If you called it that he would have been dumbstruck for a moment... his feelings wounded. He was a skilled carpenter and furniture maker... he missed his calling... he was a miserable motor car mechanic... good but miserable... he hated cars. The men he served with came by on Sundays to do the plumbing, electrical and marble work. They all asked him why he didn't fix up the outside... he said he liked it that way. He liked the surprise, the shock when they walked inside and up the magic steps ascending into another kingdom.

I thought it was business... he lost his money maker... that why he killed himself.

He didn't kill himself... that was the story they concocted for press consumption... less questions asked. He had six bullets in him. How do you shoot yourself six times? He took six bullets before he fired the one final fatal shot that went straight through the heart. He was a pistol marksman in the Marines, also a sniper in The War... 4th Marine Brigade... he picked off twenty-one Germans from on top of a church bell tower. They blew the tower out from under him with a howitzer, but he managed to survive... spread-eagle on top of a pile of rubble like he was claiming it or embracing it... it collapsed from under him... making him loose his footing. They say it was a sight to behold as the blasted rock tower descended ahead of him as if in a slow motion movie... as if he was somehow the cause of the collapse and orchestrating it from above as a spectacular deception: the disappearing tower.

I remember him saying almost as if he had memorized it, repeating it like a holy incantation:

> '...a Marine who is proficient in pistol marksmanship handles any challenge without escalating the level of violence or causing unnecessary collateral damage.'

And he was a Marine, a committed warrior conjured out of the mists of the past... like a Samurai on the streets of New York City... just like Landzman. With six clumsily aimed bullets in him, he just had time to take out the three soldiers who were methodically, if inaccurately, filling him full of lead... he chose not to... he had hit his only chosen target dead on. In that sense he did kill himself. I don't think he ever signed the Armistice... he never declared peace... he didn't want to live... not without Miranda... she was his love and she loved him too in her own way... she did it all for him, for the both of them. Nick got the wrong love story... he missed the real one... he was too stupid to see it. He was too stupid to see anything. And she was not plump... she was voluptuous, curvaceous and quite beautiful... stunningly athletic. She had been a dancer in her youth and stayed fit until the death car reduced her firm dancer's body to butcher cuts. Nick liked them anorexic with boy-like builds, wraiths, unsexed gamines minus the mesmerizing effervescence often erroneously associated with the term... devoid of flesh, unthreatening disembodied voices jingling only with the chinks.

But weren't they rolling in dough with Tom's deep pockets.

You don't understand. Tom didn't pay in so much hard cash money.

But he must have known that she was a prostitute.

He did.... but he didn't. I don't think he ever quite admitted it, to himself. He was such a pompous fool in so many ways that he thought she loved him for his undeniable charms.

But everyone knew. It was a kind of landmark... the whorehouse in the dump by the gas pumps... Mrs. Winslow and her sister displaying themselves incongruously, shoving in the nozzle suggestively with a wink, intoxicated by the rich organic smell emanating from the gas nozzle... making them breathless: Fuck under the ever watchful eyes of Doctor Mecklenburger... he knows what you've done or more accurately couldn't care less... even if you do it again and again. The deus absconditus or more precisely deus otiosus, the idle god, the irresponsible creator retiring from the tired world... set the whole shebang in motion, didn't like what he started... then slipped out through a trap door like a third rate conjuror to let in all run down like a racing automobile with a full tank of gas and no one at the wheel. His sightless, empty gaze, though without judgement, is without sense or reason. This creation was a Frankenstein horror; maybe he just ran from it; or stepped on it, a broken fiasco abandoned on the floor.

There were always motor cars out front.

But that was his legitimate business... he actually repaired and bought and sold motor cars. Tom paid without exactly admitting to himself that he paid... he supplied Winslow with a steady stream of customers, for the motor cars... he sold him his own cars at less than market value. That's why Winslow became so agitated... the accustomed car from Tom wasn't coming, not on schedule. He was in a panic. He didn't know how to go about collecting what was owed them without spoiling the show. Tom was descending into some kind of fantasy... some imaginative recreation of reality... breaking down... in a way. Winslow was saving to make their getaway. He had unearthed a buyer for his little Main Street, his diminutive version of the American Dream... living smack dab in the middle of New York City's garbage... and he almost had enough. He was going to start a medicinal herb farm in Hunterdon County New

Jersey just west of Clinton... he loved it out there... he said it was like something out of a picture postcard that you tack on to the kitchen door, like those towns in Vermont that seem lost in time... some pre-industrial pastoral paradise... like America used to be or what we think it used to be. He wanted to go back. He wanted to find something he had lost... to get back to something he started with but hadn't been able to find again. He had lived there as a child. His father had owned a large and prosperous farm but had somehow been cheated out of it by means Winslow could never understand. The magic memory of that farm, that time, that place, was the only happiness Winslow had ever known; but it was a happiness after the fact in memory only.

But Tom was hogging too much of Miranda's time... expecting exclusive rights. The apartment in the city created a bigger problem... it took her away from her steady cash paying clientele and it was dangerous without Winslow's ever watchful eyes protecting the women and there is no doubt that he would protect them... that was his purpose... with his life if the occasion came up.

Metaphor

Discovered in Landzman's archives, unpublished, undated, numbered 12,467 by the executor's staff:

> Metaphor bridges the borderline which divides the everyday from the fantastic, the whimsically grotesque. Metaphor contrives another mode of being; the speaker expands the hearer, extends the scope and imposes a novel, even surrealistic means of seeing, feeling and evaluating through his depiction. The reader when challenged with this kind of image, that seems to misrepresent their own preconceived notions of actuality, will redefine the meaning they give to words in light of this experience which alters the mind.

No Outside Commanding Authority

From the papers of Thomas Bucknell, uncatalogued, unnumbered, undated:

> In Nick's book we are given no outside commanding authority against which to judge Nick's unreliable testimony.
>
> Everything is filtered, distorted through the inept ignorant narrator, Nick. Even if he stumbled on the truth he wouldn't recognize it. The pursuit of some accurate authority, the truth, is undercut repeatedly by the process of his searching. The more he searches the more he mucks things up; the muddier the water gets.

Like some film noir gumshoe, he never sees the whole picture clearly; he isn't part of the solution he's part of the problem. He makes things worse. He is an ignorant bit player but equally complicit with the leading actors.

He's like the reporter in *Citizen Kane*; the more he investigates the less he really knows. He never figures it out; he's as lost in the end as in the beginning; more so.

The Horatio Obligation

From Thomas Bucknell's papers:

Isn't the very process of the narrator who is seeking to discover the truth inevitably distorting, the process itself frustrating and misleading. Even if Nick were whole and healthy, which he is not, his conclusions would be self-serving, glimpsed as they are through the prism of his own warped psyche. He is the bungling private investigator unearthing clues, in some cheap detective novel, who is manipulated and deceived and who never grasps the whole picture, completely misunderstands; accumulating evidence or at least what he thinks of as evidence or imagines is evidence. He is a drunkard riveted to a jigsaw puzzle; but the pieces don't fit; he keeps jamming the fragments together anyway, distorting and disfiguring them even further in the attempt to coerce them into a cohesive rational whole but thereby making the discovery of the truth, the facts even more problematical.

Didn't someone call it apostolic reporting or maybe it was survivor's testimony; the last man standing left with the load of bearing witness to the way it really happened, the Horatio obligation. Landzman, or rather Gatsby, is the dead hero whose existence must be justified.

Two Unidentified Speakers

Transcript from the F.B.I. records, two unidentified speakers, date and circumstances unreadable, cover water and mold damaged:

"See, the problem is these guys all write. They may not consider themselves writers... may not publish what passes for the slicks these days... but they are all intoxicated with words... they love them... they all leave their testimony... their record... you just have to dig for it. The best record is Jillian's but it's locked in a vault and her executor has the key... or the combination and nobody can even look at it until 2018.

Why that date?

I have no idea.

Maybe she wants to have the last word. I always had the feeling she was smarter than all of them... the real power behind the thrown.

But Landzman was very rich before he met her.

Only in money.

But she's dead. Why would it matter?

With this crowd you never know. She was so strong willed I wouldn't be surprised if she lived forever. She might be writing the definitive book right now under an assumed name, taking on the guise of a stumbling narrator to set the record straight once and for all."

Valley of Ashes, Flushing Meadow

I remember walking the Valley of Ashes, rechristened Flushing Meadow, which brings to mind a toilet, filled full of Manhattan's shit; floating on this buried dump was what they proclaimed a World's Fair with infinite hubris, an amalgamation of Hollywood showmanship and Madison Avenue hype, dirty money married to a paucity of imagination. They shipped in Michelangelo's Pieta all the way from Italy to swamp it in a garish, frigid blue light more appropriate to the night shift at the downtown city morgue. But I quibble. We have come full circle. Seen through the imagination of wonder which suspends disbelief; it is the vision of Father Schwartzenegger; but sullied; how perfect the name, dark, black, of the whacko priest slipping loose the bounds of the tangible:

"Well, you just have to do it. Go and see it... they call it an amusement park... that's what they call it. It's like a fair... actually... only it sparkles more. But you must go at night and you must stand off... way off... in a dark place... under the trees and it will seem to hang there in the air... like a balloon glowing in the night... but made of paper... like one of those big yellow Chinese lanterns... on a pole... sky wishing lanterns. But what do you do when it rains... with the lanterns I mean? I worry about the lanterns."

By the Rivers of Babylon

Found in Nick Carramel's papers, handwritten on a legal yellow pad in pencil, undated and without heading:

> By the rivers of Babylon, there we sat down and we wept, when we remembered the Zion we had lost.
>
> We regret that we have allowed ourselves to come into such a state, and we wish we could go back to having things the way they were; that we ourselves are guilty of our captivity; that we can never retrieve what we have forfeited.
>
> We lost the Dream called America; we lost our Eden, the New World; we can never go back again; we can only sit and weep in the pathetic knowledge of what we have thrown away.

Love of High Art

The Soviet communists wished to instill in their proletariat a love of high art. They warred against what they decried as the decadent culture seeping in from the dissolute west; the harder they tightened, the more it oozed through like poison from an old toothpaste tube. The American anti-capitalists leftists ironically were the opposite and embraced the lowest of what they called popular culture and pretended it was as good as high art because it emanated from the people. It would be of no use to remind these connoisseurs that the highest of high art often came from the humblest of origins. They didn't want to appear to be snobs, looking down their noses. It is with the collaboration of the new self-ordained elites that the masses elevated their mud gods onto golden pedestals misappropriated from their "betters".

Even presidents embraced this charade and as with so many charades and so many con men, may have bought into their own silliest duplicities. Ever the politician, Franklin Roosevelt proclaimed with a straight tear stained face:

> "The world of art is poorer with the passing of Irving Thalberg. His high ideals, insight and imagination went into the production of his masterpieces."

"World of art"? Thalberg was a shlockmeister heaving slops to the credulous for a pretty penny, which paraded shamelessly as culture, for the gullible too ignorant to distinguish. Franklin Roosevelt was expert at this kind of common man posturing, famously, flamboyantly serving hotdogs to the King of England at Hyde Park.

The movies had been tainted by their origin as inexpensive recreation for workers and immigrants. With their cheap admission prices, movies took their initial stimulus not from the dried out imitation of European high culture, but from the peep show, low-brow nickelodeons, pornography, the music hall, Vaudeville, from what was lowdown, dirty and vulgar.

But the savvy movie tycoons subsequently went in search of redemption by way of Broadway stage actors, classic novels and literary writers. And so was born this strange fever for operetta, not quite opera but kind of like opera only watchable by the masses and given the cultural imprimatur by certain critics always anxious to ingratiate themselves with the rabble. These newer movie moguls craved the feel and prestige of old time class without the snobbery associated with it. So we have Lawrence Tibbett who had a crack at bridging the gap between high and low, a superb baritone, he sang leading roles with the New York Metropolitan Opera before singing in the movies; also Grace Moore and Jeanette MacDonald. People took their families to it supposing it was culturally enriching, high-class stuff, just like the rich folks watch.

Some Lewd Ditty

Some lewd ditty warbled by an old whore in the streets inspired politicians to glory. We have the very word of martyrs and patriots that it was the forbidden music insinuating itself from the magic west misconstrued as celestial harmony which helped bring down the Communist monolith.

Esteemed jurists and competent lawyers claimed to have been inspired by a fanciful fabrication in what is no more than a wildly popular children's book, made more saleable by another author of genuine gifts who rewrote it as a goof repaying his childhood friend who did yeoman's service as his amanuensis and gofer. He may have proved the academic point in his head about making kitsch marketable but didn't want his name associated with it and he didn't laugh last; he stopped laughing completely. His little joke became a gargantuan beast he had unwittingly unleashed and lost control of, which haunted him. Even the putative author, no fool herself, was ashamed of her currying favor with the gullible, ignorant multitude yearning for its pap: "I wonder what their reaction would have been if [the book] had been complex, sour, unsentimental, racially unpaternalistic because Atticus was a bastard." There is no end to the self-indulgent melodrama that we ourselves love to wallow in. We cry real tears for fake concoctions which mock us mercilessly by their gross stupidity.

Nick may have been a dupe, blew a silly little fool into a goddess, but his creation, the creation of his own imagination at least; the goddess was worthy of at least some worship.

Thoroughgoing Vulgarian

It has been observed that jazz in Fitzgerald's *The Great Gatsby* exemplifies the debasement of the era. Jazz is seen as the consequence of the Anglo-Saxon upper crust surrendering its belief in itself, of losing its sustaining cultural myths, of voluntarily relinquishing the high culture for the low and pretending the low is just as good and tweaking it to make it more palatable to save face. According to this view they have lost the war and declared victory by adopting as their own the uniform and weapons of their enemies.

But Fitzgerald was not that perceptive, not consciously. He was himself a thoroughgoing vulgarian. He had no love of great art or music or even great literature; his reading list of chosen author's appalled his more culturally sophisticated friends.

One of the surest signs of the Philistine is his reverence for the superior tastes of those who put him down, who humiliate him. Somebody else said this first, particularly in regard to Fitzgerald; while cute it's worth repeating. It may not be true but it certainly applies to Fitzgerald who invited humiliation.

Edmund Wilson contrasts their reading at Princeton:

> "I had been reading Plato and Dante. Scott had been reading Booth Tarkington, Compton Mackenzie, H. G. Wells and Swinburne".

What a reading list. By what miracle did he escape the permanent taint of his early influences?

Like O'Hara, the "taint of his personality seeped into the way his books were received." We dislike Fitzgerald and his harebrained attitudes so much, consider him such an ignorant, self-indulgent, self-destructive fool that it does irreparable harm to our judgment of his work. As a second rate poet who loathed the man is famous for observing:

> Fitzgerald was a stupid old woman with whom someone has left a diamond; she is extremely proud of the diamond and shows it to everyone who comes by, and everyone is surprised that such an ignorant old woman should possess so valuable a jewel; for in nothing does she appear so inept as in the remarks she makes about the diamond.

The image itself is dead on, right down to the "old woman".

Fitzgerald had no desire to emulate the high culture of the previous generation of the select rich; he wished to mimic, instead, their most degenerate issue, with their compulsive and indeed perverse socializing, their unquenchable need to satiate their own vacuity with a daily carnival.

Zelda was perfectly literal and not entirely crazy and quite consistent when she expressed the wisdom to Hemingway that Al Jolson was greater than Jesus Christ. Fitzgerald practically wets himself in venting his ridiculous, misplaced enthusiasm for Charlie Chaplin. He was heard to gush girlishly that Chaplin was:

"...one of the greatest men in the world... and that his pictures are sophisticated and hilarious and will make him immortal".

Chaplin, a man who took himself very seriously and when off the screen carried himself like an aristocrat, significantly, was never heard to return the compliment. And though Chaplin may have been more than simply a slapstick clown we are astounded when we steel ourselves to suffer through his admittedly skillful, if dated, shtick today as an exercise in cultural anthropology and sit slack-jawed in utter amazement at the level of mass hypnosis, the enormity of the infectious big lie that elevated him to the rank of a semi-deity. Chaplin's two-reelers are often coarse and vulgar, with the equivalent of adolescent fart jokes and a declared class warfare aversion to work and simple decent manners.

Both Fitzgerald and Zelda were thrilled by popular entertainment, Fitzgerald emasculated by it, always eager to play the fool, humiliating himself with his idiot opinions, ever the schoolboy juvenile panting breathlessly, the stage door Johnnie coming too soon. We are mortally embarrassed to disinter his facile gibberish:

> "We trembled in the presence of the familiar face of *The Birth of a Nation...*"

He wallowed in low culture and was besotted with junk writers. Fitzgerald wrote more tripe than any author of equal talent. And for those inept, incoherent fools who wish to redeem his whoredom by positing some supposed symbiotic relationship between his garbage and his masterpiece we have Fitzgerald's own words.

He wrote to Mencken in May 1925: "My trash for the Post grows worse". In a letter to Hemingway of September 9, 1929: "The Post now pays the old whore $4,000 a screw." But he'd been tramping those mean streets so long they were rote. He'd been a whore for so long that only the price fluctuated. In 1921, T. A. Boyd wrote in the St. Paul Daily News:

> "His short stories, almost without exception, show that there was one thing uppermost in his mind when he was writing them and that was no more nor less than $350."

In a letter to Maxwell Perkins concerning *The Great Gatsby* Fitzgerald acknowledges the "trashy imaginings as in my stories."

As for *This Side of Paradise* the consensus of informed critical judgment found it sophomoric, a novelty, pretentious, utterly puerile, coming along at the perfect time when the public had an insatiable appetite for this kind of twaddle. His good friend hit the target:

> "*This Side of Paradise* ... is really not about anything: its intellectual and moral content amounts to little more than a gesture... a gesture of indefinite revolt. The story itself, furthermore, is very immaturely imagined: it is always just verging on the ludicrous. And, finally, [it] is one of the most illiterate books of any merit ever published (a fault which the

publisher's proofreader seems to have made no effort to remedy). Not only is it ornamented with bogus ideas and faked literary references, but it is full of literary words tossed about with the most reckless inaccuracy ... full of malapropisms of the most disconcerting kind."

Although he lamented himself a prostitute and flagellated himself accordingly, he, nonetheless, gloried in the big bucks he reaped, rolled hilariously drunk in its muck and the interminable, incessant festival it bankrolled. And if his Gatsby's money was perceived as ill-gotten how much more so was Fitzgerald's own, who degraded and shilled a magnificent talent for a cheap, tawdry thrill. He was a fine bred race horse who harnessed himself to the plow, to bury potatoes in rocky dirt which spit out money. Whores only sell their bodies. Fitzgerald mutilated the best of his own soul, its pieces thrown to unworthy swine for filthy lucre. Gatsby, Nick's alter ego, his ideal self, was the most honest man of the bunch. I would rather be a gangster than a whore, any day; streetwalkers had a jump on him; better to sell your body than to sell your soul.

Baudelaire lamented to himself: "What is art? Prostitution." Perhaps he was having a bad day or having trouble figuring out what art was. Whether we write for the dollar or for the public taste or for the perceived taste of some imagined elevated intelligentsia who will pat us on the back like good dogs but pay us nothing, like the deadbeats that they are, or some future nebulous posterity which we naively presume will be wiser. Who is to say we who write are not all in danger of falling into prostitution.

Since the late nineteenth century artists have been obsessed with prostitutes. The conman, the shapeshifter, the self-made man, the man on the make, the man without a rock-solid inviolable core, if there is such a thing, became the new man. The new world, the city, was oily and slick, shifty, racing without a printed roadmap, ambiguous, an empty spectacle. Who the hell was who? With the passing of arranged marriages, without the careful knitting of family connections and the compulsive examination of roots, of provenance, how could we be certain? Was anyone what they pretended to be?

Sheila Graham whose proclaimed background was nothing but a carefully constructed sham, a fabricated past as a British society lady, was branded by Fitzgerald, who had been taken in, as a prostitute. He wrote it in his own hand in big letters on her picture, on its back, while displaying its front.

Graham's parents were in fact Ukrainian Jews. Her father, a tailor, fled the pogroms, died of tuberculosis in Berlin. Her mother took the eight children to England and lived in a basement in a Stepney Green slum. She provided for her children as best she could by cleaning public toilets. In 1914, her mother in desperation was forced to give her up to the Jews' Hospital and Orphanage at Norwood. Graham's daughter Wendy Fairey tells us:

> "Entering this institution at age six, my mother had her golden hair shaved to the scalp as a precaution against lice. To the end of her life, she was haunted by the degradation of this

experience. Eight years later when she 'graduated,' she had established herself as Norwood's 'head girl': captain of the cricket team and recipient of many prizes, including both the Hebrew prize and a prize for reciting a poem by Elizabeth Barrett Browning."

At eighteen, she married John Graham Gillam, whom her daughter Wendy Fairey describes as:

"...a kindly older man who proved impotent, went bankrupt, and looked the other way when she went out with other men."

This husband became her Professor Henry Higgins, educating her in speech and manners and bankrolling her further social climb. She enrolled herself in the Royal Academy of Dramatic Arts and became a music hall dancer, one of the 'Cochran Girls.'

Graham had the uncanny ability to advance herself by latching on to a succession of older, powerful, wealthy men. How is this different than Fitzgerald's imagined Horatio Alger sycophant attaching himself to a Kodi or a Wolf? She shamelessly, if justifiably, advanced her career by concocting a self-serving fiction, *Beloved Infidel*, exploiting her relationship with Fitzgerald after he was dead. There is ample evidence that Fitzgerald not only despised her but despised himself for having been so totally taken in. He took his vicious revenge by broadcasting the secrets of her origins to her enemies; revealed by her in their most intimate revelatory moments together. The irony is that she is a product of self-creation every bit as astounding as that of the fictive Gatsby and is infinitely more admirable than

Fitzgerald's undying, institutionalized love, Zelda. There is no snobbery quite so extreme as the snobbery of the "failed snob", the exposed bounder, the single-minded snobbery of the viciously snubbed. Fitzgerald remained a prisoner of his corrosive bigotry and racism right to the bitter end, poisoning even his final years.

Letters to his Daughter

Following are the words of Jillian Landzman as found in the archives of James Landzman. Jillian preserved the bulk of her writing in her own papers, which are still "under seal", as my father mockingly referred to their safe-keeping. I think he was offended that their guardian, more properly their trustee is a literary agent acting on behalf of all of her children and grandchildren. This doesn't sound like a transcript of a voice recording; more like a short essay. It has no heading and is undated:

> "There are those who love his work, who love to imagine a wisdom gained by Fitzgerald as he aged; there is none. Some cite the letters to his daughter as evidence of a ripening. Unfortunately they are nothing more than the pathetic, vapid, weary reveries of an unregenerate sophomore romantic in a beaten and bloodied man of forty, a callow, fatuous, misguided, gifted little boy who got old, crumbled and fell apart without ever growing up; he rotted without ever ripening. He was not

'young to the bitter end' but merely juvenile and puerile to his very bitterest end.

"And if he regretted his vicious bigotry as he neared his demise it was voiced more out of defeat than enlightenment; the pathetic pleadings of a pounded man bleeding on the ground in utter rout. It is always too convenient when people get religion and sing Halleluiah as they are about to fall into the grave they've been digging assiduously for themselves their entire lives. Finally his abhorrence was properly directed:

> 'I hated Italians once. Jews too. Most foreigners. Mostly my fault like everything else. Now I only hate myself.'

"This from the most despised of 'foreigners'. These words should be carved on his gravestone along with 'No Irish Need Apply'.

"There is no arrogance like the arrogated arrogance of the inferior, the excluded, who lay down a barrage of blinding smoke to hide what they are or what people think they are and are inadvertently poisoned by it.

"Fitzgerald loathed himself, loathed what he came from. He was morbidly, self-eviseratingly conscious of being Irish. As John O'Hara's alter ego in BUtterfield 8, Jimmy Malloy explains to the old money debutante Isabel Stannard: 'I am a Mick. I wear Brooks Brothers clothes and I don't eat salad with a spoon and I could

208

probably play five-goal polo in two years, but I am a Mick. Still a Mick ... The people who think I am a Yale man aren't very observing about people.' O'Hara himself had the further disadvantage of looking the part he so despised; fat, big ears and dopey face, a caricature of a drunken bartender. Who was it that said: 'To me, O'Hara is the real Fitzgerald.' Well, maybe not, but both were hounded by identical demons and both succumbed. O'Hara could be an embarrassingly bad writer, wallowing in it, while Fitzgerald could rise through his art, above the tacky, self-indulgent melodrama that was his own life.

"O'Hara, at least, had the moral superiority to empathize and identify with the others who were also excluded by the old money Anglo Saxons, while Fitzgerald, pathetically deluded as he was, fancied himself in league with this old moneyed elite who wanted no part of him, to look down upon the Jews, the Italians, the French, the Armenians, the Poles or anyone else he could find to kick around.

"But a man who learned absolutely nothing, took away nothing."

The Mutilations, the Beheadings

All good writing is moral writing; how to be a good person in an evil world or how to survive on your feet, remain standing, in an environment of corruption. And if you don't think the world is evil you're part of the problem; your ignorance fosters a conspiracy of deadening suppression.

Novelists who indulge in a portrayal of pure evil, standing apart as witness but unvictimized, run the risk of cheapening it, winding up with a harrowing melodrama drained of substance. There are also good writers who have a naïve, a miniscule notion of evil. The mutilations, the beheadings, the snuff films, the predations of the Mexican, Columbia cartel, the Chinese, Russian, Georgian Mafia or whatever permutation; they're all small potatoes.

It's the evil in high places, the corruption of power that wears everyman's soul to a nub. A man who shakes hands with the Mafias or the Cartels, who does business, can expect to have that hand severed and shoved down his beloved's throat; there's a kind of rough jungle justice in it. What the hell do you expect? They're accessories before during and after the fact. A plague on all their fucking houses; may they all rot.

Today the powerful have simply become more adept and efficient at absolute theft and death. Terror with them is passé. It's left to the gangsters and warlords; the clumsy, inefficient murderers.

Power, whether military or governmental has traditionally used terror as its effective instrument.

Peter the Great, holy head of the Orthodox Faith, slaughtered by Devine Right, tortured his rebellious Streltsy for weeks, until, in his infinite mercy, he intervened putting them out of their misery by personally slitting their throats and cutting their heads off. In the golden Elizabethan age men were drawn and quartered, their heads displayed on pikes over a difference of opinion. Henry the Eighth's unfaithful wife had the gaudy avenue to her execution festooned with the tarred, parboiled heads of her purported lovers.

It is Shakespeare's beloved, merry Prince Harry, Falstaff's Hal, who becomes Henry 5th raging without bluff of what is to come, before the walls of Harfleur, threatening like any simulacrum of Genghis Khan:

> "........The blind and bloody soldier with foul hand
> Defile the locks of your shrill-shrieking daughters;
> Your fathers taken by the silver beards,
> And their most reverend heads dash'd to the walls,
> Your naked infants spitted upon pikes..."

No, the real evil is evil parading as good: the judge bribed by a private prison to fill it with the innocent, the demon pretending to be God's chosen one, the priest raping boys and convincing himself and them it is God's work, the bishop in league with them, shifting the evil one methodically from place to place, into virgin territory, the better to entrap the innocent, the unwary. The politician paid off after the fact by obscene "speaking fees", consulting fees and phony foundations. That poor dumb mayor of Chicago was bush league, not part of the club and simply didn't understand the legal pitfall of quid pro quo.

History Is Wrong, Happiness Is Right

One writer said:

> History is wrong, tragedy is right. The action is momentary, fading as the memory of man, but the suffering partakes of the nature of infinity.

It has also been said:

> "History is wrong; happiness is right. What actually happened is secondary. It is the magical perception, the illusion, the carefully constructed 'remembered' moment of ecstatic happiness that really matters, the profound feeling rather that the circumstances that produced those feelings; it is that feeling, the happiness, that is beyond the bounds of time and partakes of the infinite."

Emperor's New Clothes

"The Emperor's new clothes": the saying has evolved into a universal metaphor for pretentiousness, pomposity, social hypocrisy, collective denial, or hollow ostentatiousness.

The Emperor's New Clothes (Danish: Kejserens nye Klæder) is a short tale by Hans Christian Andersen about two weavers who promise an Emperor a new suit of clothes that is invisible to those unfit for their positions, stupid, or incompetent. When the Emperor parades before his subjects in his new clothes, a child cries out, "But he isn't wearing anything at all!" The tale has been translated into over a hundred languages.

But the parable is censored, sanitized and disinfected. In the true story, the one that I read as a child at night, the king's thugs are ever vigilant, watching, not the king, but the subject's faces for any inadvertently divulged doubt of the king's glory and the splendor of his wardrobe. They pounce quickly with their clubs and pummel to death any disbeliever. But in most cases the king's men need not even nod or raise a finger, for the crowds ever heedful themselves descend upon the doubter, the disrupter, en masse like a single amebic organism devouring his body and his blood.

It is the story of the ability, or the self-protecting curse of deceiving oneself because of societal requirements, of hypnotic mass hallucination keeping the wheels of a (corrupt) social structure grinding on.

Who was it that said: all communities are imagined? Communities are to be distinguished, not by their falsity or truth, but only by the "style" in which they are imagined.

And if we, by force of perceived will, break free of the socially imposed delusion, it is often to find refuge in a delusion more of our own making, but delusion none the less.

The truth will not make you free. It may make you insane; insanity, the feeling of detachment or disconnect, the disintegration of a carefully constructed structure of the conscious mind we call reality.

If reality is a carefully constructed illusion, that very illusion may be essential to our functioning in the "real" world, this together with the illusion that we are in control. It is these illusions that keep us in what we think is control, what the world calls sanity.

Evolution has endowed us with an unconscious mind which allows us to endure and persist in a world which necessitates an enormous consumption and processing of information of which the conscious mind is incapable.

It is not repression alone that accounts for the gaps and inaccuracies in our memory but also an energetic, forceful act of re-formation that is also beyond the conscious. We structure our memories to keep our illusions intact. If those memories threaten those carefully crafted illusions, necessary illusions by which we survive, then we reconstruct, misremember or purposelessly forget; if the experience is illusion shattering, thus threatening our ability to function and thus our sanity we will pound it down with a sledge hammer deep into our psyches, to keep from consciously remembering. The mind is kind to itself; it lies to itself; it allows itself to go on.

We fall into the world as if tumbling into a dark but warm sea. If we climb out of it toward the light we drown on the air burning our lungs on its fire.

It is an oversimplification to call Freud's unconscious, as one silly neuroscientist, a simplistic critic did as: "hot and wet" seething with lust and anger, hallucinatory, primitive, and irrational.

Lévi-Strauss said that the mind is a structuring mechanism that imposes form upon whatever it finds. Freud's subconscious in its way attempts to impose a structure where there is no structure, order where there is no order; it refuses to consciously acknowledge the cruelty and evil inflicted upon us; it allows us to function in a fragile fabricated world which we mutually create and constantly reinforce with our fellow illusionists, mutual hypnotists, practitioner and practiced upon, to symbiotically maintain viable social structures cocooning us, in which we are able to carry on.

Kant's theory was that we actively construct a picture of the world rather than merely documenting objective events as we accurately observe them; that our perceptions are not based on what exists but, rather, are created and constricted by the characteristics of the mind and also the entirety of our experiences both conscious and unconscious.

Homo-sapiens had the most malleable brain of any earth species for the very purpose of forming complex social bonds, to subsume critical capacity, to suspend disbelief, to partake of a mutual fantasy, all absolutely essential especially to his early survival on the planet.

Our big brain is mostly a dream machine. This ability to integrate into the group at all costs makes it indispensable that as individuals we switch off high functioning critical ability. The social consequences of holding societal structures to any rational critical account would simply be too disruptive to social order and cooperative activity. This is why the social critic is an outcast, a pariah, a capital threat. More than one ancient tribe, among them the Bulgars, singled out their brightest and best, their most incisive and intelligent for elimination:

> "They are too good for us, too good to walk among us always finding fault, always pointing out all our flaws, always with new disruptive ways of doing things; showing us what idiots we are; making us miserable; let us send them to the gods where they belong."

Just as the unhinged mind sees conspiracies everywhere, intricate patterns, codes and signals extracted from chaos, so the "functioning" conscious mind creates order where there is none, meaning in the meaningless and so plods on in lockstep to oblivion.

Incorruptible Man in a Thoroughly Unscrupulous World

Discovered in the archives of Thomas Bucknell, untitled, undated and uncatalogued; author uncertain:

And if Fitzgerald's personal life was tawdry, chaotic, pathetic and absurd, tumbling clownishly down a drunken path of dissolution, sickness, failure and rejection, it is Fitzgerald the great writer standing over the ruin who never lost his majesty, the great man, wise and knowing, deep in his subconscious, manifesting himself through the sweat of endless rewrites, like the godly spirit that was himself, exacting hard labor to be set free, to come to life on the flimsy paper page and live forever.

This may all seem bleak, even nihilistic, but it's not, not necessarily. It suggests that we are all delusional, in it all together cooperatively, reinforcing each other's delusions. It is not the "reality" of what happened that so much matters but the way we remember it, creatively through a godlike imagining. It is that blissful memory which exists timelessly, which supersedes time, time, which is, after all but a construct of our conscious workaday mind. Landzman gives testimony to this truth.

And if you tell me he was a gangster, a racketeer, I say what of it. He helped me when I was in desperate need of it. He was better than all the lot of us; better than the perpetually campaigning politician always with his hand out, the judges on the take and the predator priest who rape the young sons of the criminally credulous, unembarrassedly, as if by divine right.

No Landzman was all right; it was the small corrupt, mean world, unfit to encompass his godly dreams that finally broke his heart.

Landzman, Gatsby, Nick and the ghost who is holy; they are all in this together. And they are each other in many ways. Landzman may not have died that night and may have been as tough as Damascus steel, but Fitzgerald in his almost infinite ineptitude got just a part of him fundamentally right. He lived on, an incorruptible man in a thoroughly unscrupulous world.

Zerobbabel

The following is a purported conversation between Thomas Bucknell and an unknown person as found in the archives of Landzman. The cover of the transcript is missing; the date and circumstances unknown:

In the 1920s Halbwachs and Durkheim argued that societal groups determine what is memorable and also how it will be remembered. Zerobbabel argues that we need to recognize society's ubiquitous cognitive role as mediator between individuals and their own experiences. Some fool preferred to refer to it as a remembrance environment, as the harmless sounding defanged mechanism through which ideas and concepts of a culture, culture mind you, culture without culture, gain access to individual brains.

Excuse me, I forgot who Zerobbabel was.

Fuck you.

What kind of way is that to talk? I'm just trying to learn. Talking to you is like going to school. Did I say talking? I meant listening. Do I get course credit for this? Is there going to be a test?

Fuck you, again.... No wait... I'm sorry... I like to bounce ideas off of you... they coalesce this way.

Bounce... did you say bounce? How about hitting me in the head with them and having them fall with a dead thud.

No... No... you're a good audience.

That's because I don't say anything.

That's not true... You're an incisive critic.

Would you just let me finish this thought? And then let me know what you think.

Societal groups determine not only how reality is remembered but how reality is perceived in the first place. We are suborned by our social environment, society's pervasive cognitive role as intermediary, intercessor between persons and what they only perceive as their own experiences. Reality is a mass hallucination into which we are coerced with all the magic guile of an underground secret police state. We are bombarded incessantly with the drumbeat of its relentless, insidious propaganda. How else to explain societal structures which are corrupt to their core; these structures would disintegrate, fly apart into social chaos without the illusion of justice, fairness and order.

We elevate mountebanks and buffoons to lead us, applauding these nincompoops as deities because they reinforce our convenient and meticulously crafted lies. There is in fact no such thing as normal human memory; we have only culturally contrived memory molded to serve distinct objectives corresponding to diverse structural stratagems of society. Our minds are structured to manipulate and deceive us so that we can function efficiently in a corrupt society.

Wow. Do you expect me to comment on that?

Megalomaniacally Holding Forth

Leslie A. Fiedler megalomaniacally holding forth on Rip Van Winkle and Huckleberry Finn:

> "The typical male protagonist of our fiction has been a man on the run, harried into the forest and out to sea, down the river or into combat — anywhere to avoid 'civilization,' .... One of the factors that determine theme and form in our great books is this strategy of evasion, this retreat to nature and childhood which makes our literature (and life!) so charmingly and infuriatingly 'boyish.' "

I think Fiedler got it absolutely, totally wrong like he did most things. It is the old stodgy prigs entrenched in their routine mind numbing status quo, their appallingly normal surrender which they doggedly proclaim a life, the staunch defenders of the soul rot they are mired in; these are the walking, putrefying dead men who fail to sniff out their own stink, who complement themselves as "adults", as mature.

It was Aleksandr Solzhenitsyn, no boyish dilettante running away to the woods, who said, that at all costs, he structured his life to avoid a tedious everyday existence, life as the vast majority of people lived it. One gets the feeling that even the gulag was preferable, was in some sense a choice, an alternative; he wasn't talking about Communism but about life itself, or what we call life, civilization, what life has degenerated into.

The dropping into unconsciousness, into rote, doing what everyone expects you to do, what they do, the default settings, the cop out, the rat's race, the endless, self-defeating, mindless pursuit of nothing worth anything, the gnawing, corrosive sense of having held it in your hand, having been distracted for just a moment and lost, some infinitely fine and infinitely wonderful thing.

It is Holden Caulfield who refuses to enter the world, call it the "adult" world if you like, a world that Caulfield considers unethical, a fraud, a pack of lies, a world of self-deceptions and pretentious bad taste. He is Huck Finn whose innocence and down to earth decency contrasts with the corruption and hypocrisy of the (adult) world. Everyone wants Holden to learn to play the game, to adapt to the world as it is, to find his place. In one of the most misunderstood quotes in what passes as literature Holden quotes one of his teachers who quotes Wilhelm Stekel:

> "The mark of the immature man is that he wants to die nobly for a cause, while the mark of the mature man is that he wants to live humbly for one."

This kind of a "mature" man, the kind Stekel is talking about lives an existence of quiet, cowardly desperation. There are things we must be prepared to die for or life is not worth living. There are times that demand that we call Stalin the "plowman", in correspondence we know will be opened by his ever vigilant sensors.

Wisdom with Age

Thomas Bucknell, from his own archives, undated:

> "Fools say that you gain wisdom with age. That's crap. You become beaten and bloodied and so weakened, so defeated that you compromise readily where you never would have dreamed of compromising in your youth. It is with the acceptance of the unacceptable that the cowards who rule aggrandize themselves, calling it wisdom and thus themselves wise. It is only the once brave who still have a vestige, a memory of courage, that grasp their own rout. Wisdom, magnanimity are the hollow words designed to disguise the shame of those who have sold out."

Saints Out of Charlatans

Thomas Bucknell from his archives, untitled, unnumbered:

> The Roman Catholic Church is habituated to making saints out of charlatans. There is something blasphemous in presuming to write God's book of stars. There was one particular mountebank who had all the presence of a demonic carnival barker, with his mad monk's eyes, but without the sexual prowess of the authentically charismatic Russian, at least not with the ladies. He nauseated a solid minority of the faithful reigning as he did on the early days of TV, neck and neck with Uncle Miltie.
>
> Later on, past his prime, he exuded what passed for oily charm on the television talk shows, appearing on Johnny Carson to tell the uplifting Hallmark tale of one of the staunchest of the Roman Catholic faithful, a desiccated leper, eaten out limbs, crawling on his belly to catch up with the holy man as he traversed the jungle quick of foot; to partake from the fakir's very hands, into his diseased stubs, hungrily, the genuine body and blood of Christ. Carson, in disbelieving horror as much as shock with a journeyman's professional, practiced poker face wondered almost out loud what mad house this creep, steeped in his own brand of dementia, slithered out of.

The priest with the mad monk eyes fell upon hard times; ostracized; a falling out with the all-powerful archbishop of New York, who he had best not fuck with, ostensibly about powdered milk money but really a jealous rivalry over matters of the heart.

Acknowledgment

This book would not have been possible without the generous and encouraging help of countless people many of whom labored with me over the manuscript, working tirelessly correcting many erroneous facts. There were the Millhouses and the Barnabies, the Cronkeits, the Weisenhauers, the Millers and the Peers, the Phillips, the Executors who everyone called the Executioners, the Miners and the Moores, the Bronsons, Bragnarts, the Fishers and the Floods, the Fleishbaums , the Haggerties, whose fathers, grandfathers, mothers, grandmothers or great uncles, butchers or tailors or haberdashers, livery men and fishmongers, barbers or bricklayers, all claimed to have known him, some on a first name basis, or claimed to have drunk ale and eaten cold chicken with him at odd hours in his private Rathskeller, all of whom had many tales to tell some of them quite possibly true. Word spread as if by an underground telegraph tapping code deep in the earth emanating as an annoying low frequency vibration which could be picked up by merely prostrating oneself naked on the bare earth; (one poor fool, misunderstanding, listening for an oncoming train put his ear to the third rail, but

224

that has nothing to do with anything) most sought me out; some called in the middle of the night, whispering, conspiratorially.

Make Up Stupid Names

Quite obviously many of the names in this acknowledgement were changed or fabricated, ridiculously, at the specific request of the acknowledgee, (some suggested their own fictitious funny names) wishing to remain nameless; they say for their own safety; but I don't know who's left to settle the score or whose score they wish to settle and if that score settling wouldn't set up another score to settle. I always thought the ridiculous names reeled off in Nick's book hurt the reality of that book; they were two cute by half. They had the effect of shaking the reader out of any suspended dis-belief that had been so carefully crafted. The fact that Eliot liked to make up stupid names didn't give it any more legitimacy or verisimilitude.

Delsey's Granddaughter

I got a phone call from someone claiming to be Delsey's granddaughter. She revealed that her mother, Delsey's daughter, her only child, never died in that car wreck; that it was a hoax engineered by her loving father, Tom Bucknell with the help of Landzman. She just wanted out; she couldn't stand the burden of the history, the interminable cars cruising by the house on a summer night like an endless funeral caravan. Everybody knew the story or thought they did thanks to the book. She was sick to death of gawkers. She hated the book.

Delsey's daughter, escaped to California, became a movie actress though not a big star; she worked for Landzman for a while; retired at her height, modest though it was, to write the genuine true story which she claimed "no one dared to publish". She promised to send me the manuscript convinced it was a potential blockbuster. She refused to give me her real name, or address and I never did receive the book. Maybe she had second thoughts.

I started watching all of Landzman's movies into the middle of the night seeing if I could get a glimpse of a familial look; I had seen many photographs of Delsey and of her daughter. I looked for Thomas Bucknell and James Landzman. I unearthed a promising lead and hired a private investigator who filed encouraging reports weekly for six months and then stopped returning my phone calls. I guess he milked it for all it was worth or maybe there were secrets powerful people didn't want uncovered. Finally his phone was disconnected; he seemed to have closed up shop. I discovered that his license wasn't renewed. A neighbor told me he had gone to Tahiti but for some reason I didn't believe him. Tahiti? That's preposterous. I don't think he was murdered; that would have been plain stupid. He struck me as the type of man who could be bought off at a very reasonable price.

Then there was the priceless nitrate film footage turning up, ready to explode at the softest touch, purporting to show everyone, including Landzman playing the impresario with the exaggerated hokey panache of a silent film star. For a time I believed it was my grandfather but one old timer watching the film said it wasn't Landzman at all but a look-a-like, an actor playing Landzman in a film at a later date than that depicted. It was produced by Landzman himself, when he owned the studio, but for some reason never released, or more likely released and subsequently lost. He might have had second thoughts, not wishing to dredge up painful memories or throwing it in their face; besides by this time he was already quite dead, technically.

And then there was the film from a lost Edison archive showing an acrobat magician on the high wire doing a double summersault backward flip and then disappearing in a puff of smoke; it could have been The Great Gatsby; it might have been him; but the film was of such questionable quality and from such a distance that it was impossible to tell for sure; it could also have been an early example of trick photography; however the audience would have had to have been professional actors because they looked genuinely awe struck.

Then there was what seemed like an early documentary or "how to" film, explicating in detail what was represented as an engineering feat; hauling this huge floating house out of the Sound like a gigantic whale fighting them the whole way, with hundreds of roustabouts choreographed in a precision caper; demonic June Taylor dancers hoofing to the rapid fire beat; or Volga boatmen trudging with a lightning step tripping the light fantastic. How many must have marveled at the ghostly apparitions floating from the fog of some inland waterway, lagoon, inlet, fjord, firth or sound, ultimately rejecting it as some transitory hallucination, trick of the mind or eye. The nameless man with the "how to" film wanted a sizable sum for it, seeming to think it answered some essential riddle. But you have to know the question and how to pose that question in precise language before the answer does you any good. I half suspected that he believed that I would use its trade secrets as the basis of a lucrative future business, hauling the homes of the rich like monstrous waterborne Winnebagos. What he didn't seem to realize is that they would sink like a stone if launched in the open stormy sea; but these tranquil waterways, cast upon, lead nowhere or to the uttermost ends of the earth, flowing ever into a hollow immense darkness dismal under a graying sky.

Old Man Joe's Issue

Old man Joe's issue seem to have entrenched themselves into the warped psyche of the nation... its septic fantasy life and its corrupt structures of influence. I have been told that the Ambassador was naively benign compared to his more ruthless offspring. They all refused to speak to me concerning this book and would not open their archives. In unison the progeny all proclaimed, in unholy chorus, like a packed nest of demoniac birds screaming for the worms ripped flesh; that their progenitor was an entirely legitimate businessman who had absolutely no dealings with any man called Landzman, Gatsby or whatever. In fact they questioned the very existence of Gatsby or Landzman in almost identical words as if they had been given a script or coached. They swore that it was all a fairytale; some called it a myth; one called it the never-ending saga and laughed up his fashionable sleeve and insisted that I leave.

The Irish Ambassador

The Irish Ambassador was a master of bribery if you could use so humble an expression. He suborned people, corrupted, despoiled them, remolded them into his implements. If a simple suitcase of cash would do it, so be it, bought and paid for, open and shut, simple. But he knew what people craved, needed, secretly desired, even before they did. He wasn't a simple pimp, a whore master, a provider. He had hundreds of woman in his stable all carefully groomed and finished; interviewed and hired; on the payroll in legitimate businesses, at least outwardly legitimate. He didn't only deal in simple currency, but in advantage and advancement; he could clear the way to power and prestige. On his intimate staff he was called the matchmaker. Most of the girls were new to the business, college graduates, models, actresses, agents, no track record to track down.

It is said that hundreds of powerful men had actually married woman the ambassador had siged on them.

Most of these marriages ended in divorce with the added irony that payment for services was rendered by the mark, the victim, saving the Ambassador a bundle. But some of the "girls" liked the easy, steady stipends and remained on the payroll for decades; the higher their husbands rose the fatter the wad of cash and the more intricate and insidious the perks. He was remembered for all his more than generous wedding gifts.

He kept the Roman Catholic priests, who knew what he was and he knew what they were, in his pocket with his gifts. He kept meticulous dossiers on the entire hierarchy. They may not have voted for him but knew enough to keep their mouths locked shut; a Mexican standoff. He never sent his sons to Catholic schools; he knew better. With the girls it was different; with the priests, he knew they would be untouched.

But then there was his collaboration with the Cardinal, his partner in crime, 29 years his senior, who took young Joe under his wing, married him in 1914, threatened Gloria Swanson to break it off, in-league in his war against the Anglo-Saxons, helped him appease the Nazis, helped Joe's father trash the bank so young Joe could ride in to the rescue; brokered Joe's deal for RKO (the K is for Keith).

Satanic Joke of the Roman Church

William H. O'Connell, the unchristian priest, elevated to Cardinal as a satanic joke of the Roman Church, was a steadfast champion of cheap child labor who denounced movies from the pulpit as the "scandal of the nation" infested by Jew promoters. He was always eager to stick it in the eye of the despised Boston Brahmins who looked down their noses, seeing only Irish riffraff decked out like demonic clowns in outlandish get-ups. He crowed ecstatically from his faux Renaissance villa fabricated with Benjamin Franklin Keith's Vaudevillian loot whose louche empire the Church funded:

"The Puritan has passed; the Catholic remains,"

Leading to the celebrated Yankee rejoinder:

"The Puritan endures while the Roman Catholic will eventually drown in its own stinking manure, its face contorted into a snarling rictus from self-inflicted death."

Words uttered by a sadly diminished Yankee whose intellect had been savagely compromised by devouring too many pulp war novels. It is poetically appropriate that O'Connell's faux Beaux-Art mausoleum was utterly demolished and his stinking remains excavated as a stipulation of the crookedly contrived sale by one culpable corrupt entity to another culpable corrupt entity of his gutted mansion to settle the claims for pennies on the dollar of the victims of endemic priest-rape of young boys.

For the reporters in his pocket, the Ambassador would get their books published, edited and rewritten if necessary; have them favorably reviewed. He had ghost writers write their columns when they got lost on benders. He sent them "secretaries" who worked long hours for peanuts, who wrote better prose than they did and had impeccable sources. He had reviewers in the bag. He knew how to manipulate the best seller's lists by sending out his agents to buy up books. The book prizes were a cinch; it didn't take suitcases; mere handbags of money clinched it.

One Very Old Woman

One very old woman, at the periphery of the clan, was a gold mine and sat for a total of 36 hours of taped conversations. She was extremely lucid and convincing and seemed to be possessed of total recall, describing Landzman in the minutest detail as an absolutely charming man who the women were crazy for. She hinted but only hinted that she had been "intimate" with him. She was in many ways pre Jazz Age and quite conservative in an almost coquettish way which sounds absurd for a woman of her age. While chattering she seemed to go back in time and re-inhabit the experience, to bring it all back. She despised the Ambassador who she said attempted to "violate" her. She suspected from what she knew that his sons and daughters acted as his pimps, procurers, whether knowingly she didn't know. They would bring their friends home who the big man would proposition and if that failed he would rape them. But what she loathed the Ambassador for most of all was:

> "...foisting his incompetent crippled son, his debauched, debased, degenerate progeny... the emanation of his poisoned loins to foul an unsuspecting, gullible nation... spraying his

toxic ejaculate on the ecstatic populi squealing like giggly girls for more, more. This was his greatest criminal act, the consummation of his evil, the ultimate megalomania. The rest was peanuts, a lark, boyish pranks.... this was far worse than his murders, his extortions and all the noxious remainder.

"Don't get me wrong... I liked this second son... he managed to pull it off in spite of himself... miracle of marketing... and mass hypnosis. I just couldn't stand his high pitched whiney nasally voice... pretentions of Harvard."

Which she imitated to great effect, amusing herself exceedingly, laughing immoderately. Her late first husband had been to Harvard and:

"I can assure you sonny-boy did not have a Harvard accent... it's phony, an affectation... a fraud... a failure to realize the desired affect... a peculiar amalgam, like mercury and silver but mistaken for silver through corrupt dental industry propaganda."

She always loved "Dick Nixon" as she called him and his:

"...beautiful deep base baritone with a perfect stage actor accent".

"Sonny-boy was a lousy speaker with his anachronistic, bombastic, 'stump-grinder' style.

I think she used the wrong expression here but she seemed perfectly happy with it and I dared not correct her.

> "Sonny-boy. I think it was Lyndon who called him that."

She liked Lyndon, a "seducer", that's what she called him, not a rapist like that "pig" Joe.

> "A honey-dewed hillbilly who knew how to lay it on thick."

That he came from Texas and not the hills was irrelevant.

> "Everyone and I mean everyone... all the men of power, thought sonny-boy was a putz."

She was showing-off, using a jarring word for effect, not part of her everyday vocabulary.

> "The General [Eisenhower], I think it was, who called him little boy blue or something like that.

> "The General, everyone loved the General. He was so energetic and powerful when he started. They infiltrated his inner staff... You know that... The ones that should have protected him betrayed him... after his heart attacks... his strokes. He spoke beautifully during his first campaign... during the war. Watch those films... they're out there.

> There was absolutely no need to give those incessant interminable press conferences... that convoluted, fractured prose... like a dog chasing

234

his tale but unable to find it, but trying, oh so hard, non-the-less. They sent him out there to make a fool of himself, to seem old, worn-out and confused. This was no accident, no, no... this was all part of the plan... the strategy... the bastards... they sent him out there to humiliate him... to die publically. He could have given one very carefully rehearsed, carefully scripted speech, once a month and no one would have been the wiser. He would have preserved his former glory. And that god-damned golf with its old man stink and rich man's decadence. Whose idea was that? He would have been better off cavorting with high class prostitutes in the Whitehouse basement bowling alley... I don't think Truman's bowling alley was in the basement though... was it...? Couldn't they find a more private pastime? Even then people didn't hate him... they just felt sorry for him. They were exhausted and befuddled just staring at him falling apart on that infernal TV screen. That medium eviscerated him. Sonny-boy was the lazy son-of-a-bitch... What did some writer not on the take call his work ethic... "Seigneurial"... that was it... decadent nouveau riche... that's more like it.

"They all thought the country was going to hell in a hand basket with baby blue and his rickety hands at the helm. That's what Lyndon called him... a "rickety cripple". They all had names for him... none of them good... You know, I have to confess... I didn't vote for Roosevelt... my first husband loathed him... but whatever you say about him... he was no cripple. That monument or statue, the memorial where they have him bound in a wheelchair is an absolute disgrace to the man. I knew people who swore... swore that they saw him walk... walk right up the capitol steps... the entire flight... double time... quick on his feet. They believed he could walk and by god he did walk. If the connivance of the press could make Roosevelt walk how much easier to change lead into gold, water into wine and the rickety cripple into a great orator.

"He should have excused himself from powwows with big men. They despised him, bullied and overpowered him. They sensed his weakness like dogs smelling fear ... he reeked his incompetence. It leaked out of his pores like putrid sebum, which stuck to everyone's shoes and soiled the floor. He shrunk and shriveled in their presence. He should never have met with Khrushchev in Vienna or wherever. Khrushchev famously dismissed sonny-boy... brushed him off as a lightweight, someone to push around just for fun. I'm surprised Khrushchev didn't induce... that's the word, induce him to dance for him... pull down his pants and make him do the hula-hula. He was no great shakes."

She explained in detail that Khrushchev's men, writing years later, lamented that they were actually embarrassed for the United States, saddened that it had fallen to such depths. She had her secretary search for the passages in her library but could come up with only two. The part where they pitied us and

236

lamented our sad inglorious fate, the humiliation of a once great nation, demeaned and degraded, lorded over by a weak-kneed Lilliputian, a self-infatuated weakling, I found self-serving.

"Sonny-boy should have sent in the real men to speak to the real men... they knew the language. The Russians never would have made their move if General Eisenhower had been in charge... The clumsy, inadvertent... arsonist... bumbling... fumbling matches ... sonny-boy set the fire... then... only, just, managed to put it out, grabbing extravagant credit... no doubt willing to murder every last one of us to show the Russkis that he was no pussy... that they got him wrong, that he knew how to play chicken with the big boys.

We must remember... he had a Rendezvous with Death... also a wicked need to drag us along to keep him company on his way down to midnight in some flaming town. That he was willing to risk, even court the death of his withered, sick, decrepit own corpus could not be classed as courage... more like self-slaughter masquerading as valor... taking out his own rotting garbage.

He was the terminal, bullied nerd on his own death watch... fingering his Uzi in his underwear... in his daddy's basement bunker with fantasies of mowing down the school cafeteria during second period lunch... he'd show them a thing or two... blow the whole town to the moon... the moon."

She spit out these words with a sharp, visceral fluency dripping with purified contempt. She sounded like Norman Mailer... who hungered for an Ezra Pound as his editor. She laughed. There was a joke here somewhere, more than one but I'm not sure which ones she thought were the funniest.

She insisted:

> "Sonny-boy should have been a nightclub comic... a stand-up... Vaudeville or the Borscht Belt... No, No... more like the seedy Holiday Inn at the edge of town bypassed by the Interstate... one of those top bananas with the trick pants... delivering one-liners. He was hugely entertaining... he missed his calling... I just loved his 'routine'... so well-rehearsed... the press, his lapdogs, panting orgasmically for their bone, barking like trained seals, bought and paid for by the big man... delivering the setups on cue for sonny-boy to knock down. It was all an hilarious show, a circus for his credulous 'constichency'."

She loved this mispronunciation and repeated it and laughed again.

She had heard one rumor that they had rehearsals with the reporters who sonny-boy was scripted to recognize, which would devolve into orgies catered by old man Joe; but the orgy part she did not believe; her imagination could not take her there. I assured her he had in fact gone to Harvard but she discarded this as hype.

"The Ambassador bought the degree, rigged his transcript? He hung out there for a few years... yes... he was seen... Yes, I grant you that... You'd be amazed at what enough money will buy. He had ghosts write the book. But I can't understand... why he talked so funny, that whiney, high pitched, ridiculous voice with the preposterous cadence: thumpety thumpety, thump, thump, thump. Imitation must not be as easy as it seems. It must take a magician or a great actor.

"I know for a fact that voice coaches had trooped in and out, battalions of them... but all to absolutely no avail... he was hopeless... this man was no quick study. I read that he practiced his one pathetic Berliner phrase for days on end. It was all so contrived... it didn't gel... very careful ... too careful. Who is this man? Some said he had a tin ear for languages... more like a tin head. 'Lay-oss'. Who in hell talks like this? He couldn't even learn to pronounce the name of the country he was destroying. This accent, a poison stew of low class Boston Irish Catholiceeze tacked on to a reluctant, resistant Harvard Brahman fighting back tooth and nail and winning hands down. Old Man Joe promoted his ne'er-do-well son the way he would a nubile young female into a Hollywood star. But the incipient star had potential at least... Jack, entirely lacking, had none.

"In some cases it is easier to manipulate the perceiver than the one being perceived? It was easier to change the perception of his speaking ability than the ability itself, which was immutable. He was hopeless, beyond improvement?"

But when I tried to follow-up, after speaking with the people she sent me to, in confidence, the sons and daughters of those who could and did verify her "testimony", but only second hand. When I came back, I was told by a servant, but more a secretary-jailer, who intercepted her phone calls, that the lady was suffering from dementia and had probably gotten her information from publications she had studied (she was a "voracious" reader) and had "internalized these sources, creating false memories" or that these facts were "planted" in her by her first husband who was a "powerful mesmerizing presence," who "loathed the Ambassador" and was a "staunch Republican". But after a dogged search I could find no publications with such exact, particular accounts as she gave. She named names, places and dates. Her keepers assured me that she had not been "cogent" for at least a decade; they explained that she had "moments of clarity" which was "deceptive" and could "lasso you in" and "disappeared without warning". But a friend who she referred me to for corroboration assured me she was as sharp as a tack; she had been caught writing a book; the manuscript was confiscated; she was a virtual prisoner in her own house. Suitcases full of money changed hands; the same forces were still at work with different names. The Ambassador had, after everything, succeeded in raping her, belatedly, in old age; reaching through his myriad progeny, his desiccated hand from out of his stinking grave to strangle her.

Photographed Together

From various family and private collections, libraries and foundations a total of seven photographs showed up of the two of them, Landzman and the Ambassador, together and they appeared to be on friendly terms or enemies in a stand-off eyeing each other warily; it's hard to tell which.

John Dean's Elaborate Figment

However, one must always remember John Dean whose colossal, pitch perfect memory before a live audience, under oath, in front of Congress, was all an elaborate figment of his overwrought boy's imagination, as the Nixon tapes, later, definitively reveal. Was he lying, did he misremember, was he self-deceived, half way into early onset dementia; did he crave the attention like poison sweets, or did he like to be seen as a man with a steel trap memory, super mensch or all of these? Was he manipulated without his knowledge? Was his Halloween Kewpie doll, Kansas homecoming queen from hell, ever in attendance consort, really a high end hooker picked and groomed by higher ups, the grownups, to playact his real life wife? But didn't he win that case? Was her creepy vigil meant to help or hurt? Was she his handler, his dominatrix, his watcher? Was her proximity essential? Did she transfuse him with hidden bloody tubes underneath her skirt? Would he instantly fold if the puppet master's puppet master failed to materialize or never came back from lunch? Would he crumple to the floor; wind up in the janitor's rag pile? Could Dean even hope to get a real girl on his own?

Graciousness of Bucknell's Grandson

Through the generosity and graciousness of Tom Bucknell's grandson I was allowed to spend extensive time studying the wide-ranging records that he left; none have been catalogued but they have been carefully preserved, waiting anxiously on the shelf for some driven and determined descendant looking for the secret of how such a vast immeasurable treasure could possibly have been so depleted in one single generation. He seems to have written manically and continually without stop as if keeping the wolf at bay; as if as long as he could write he could substantiate his existence and continue to live.

There are three finished novels; all having been submitted anonymously and summarily rejected by publishers; the rejection slips are markers in the books as if to prove to posterity what fools these publishers had been. He was too proud to purchase the publishing house, although a few well-placed phone calls would have done the trick; too proud to even underwrite the cost of publication which was a big mistake, considering what a crap shoot getting published is. As far as I could tell they would be eminently publishable today and would probably sell given the unique provenance. The press would have a field day loving the corny chronicle of resurrected ruined "aristocracy": The Suspected Murderer of Landzman Resurgent. What an irony if Landzman's descendant should be the instrument of Thomas Bucknell's posthumous fame and reconstructed riches.

However, there was enough money left so that none of his issue were absolutely obliged to grunt and toil by their own sweat. His descendants have reentered the workforce with a vengeance. Most have graduated from his alma mater no doubt helped by the formidable buildings which bear the family name squat down in the middle of campus ready to stand against Armageddon; but his descendants were too collectively embarrassed to apply for the scholarships which his endowment underwrote. It was a kind of code that they kept, though not without rancor. They would remain in ferocious competition with poor men's sons and daughters, the descendants of the huddled masses, the wretched refuse seeking solace on these shores and need to claw their way back up and trot hat in hand, mere supplicants, to lay out their heart and soul, their germinal schemes for scrutiny before venture capitalists who they regarded as vultures. Even the Silicon Valley little boys club, was doomed, at least initially, to perfect the subtleties of the kowtow, the dance of abject submission, to lure the magic seminal seed from angel investors, although enriching demons they may be. The days of raising working capital by going on a strict diet of hasty pudding (gruel) and potatoes is long gone.

Deep-rooted Spanish Family

Tom's daughter with Delsey died in a car crash when she was seventeen. There was no funeral service, at her dying request; cremated and relegated to her beloved Sound, scattered at the end of the dock, the famous one, her favorite spot. Fact follows fiction, fiction fact. It was said that Delsey had abandoned her when she was young and broke her heart; ran off with a bullfighter. Although appropriately histrionic this was too melodramatic to be true. In fact she married into a deep-rooted Spanish family in a fungus encrusted, crumbling Madrid cathedral, very old world, which mirrored perfectly the family's straitened condition.

Jillian attempted to attend the wedding but was given the bum's rush out the door of the cathedral by a group of ominous black draped nuns who moved in upon her in a dense wave like a single organism, a devouring giant amoebic macrophage flapping their vulturous bat habits like bloodsucking brides of Dracula. Jillian it seems was "disrespectfully dressed" to enter "God's holy house", although decked in the height of fashion, straight out of a magazine cover, for an early summer wedding in Newport.

Delsey's marriage to Thomas Bucknell of the renowned Chicago Bucknells did not exist according to the Spanish family's church which was especially adept at ignoring cold hard facts. The family treated her no better than a whore, a "non-Catholic fornicatress", in spite of her coerced conversion to the one true faith; a pagan, nouveau riche trash, "low-born gutter slut", who their none-too-intelligent son, "blinded by the glitz", had picked up on one of his boozy sojourns, strike that, "mining" trips to America.

She did not bear children to the Spaniard, thanks to one too many clandestine abortions of Thomas Bucknell's posterity. Tom had given her a solid platinum watch, trying to persuade her to have another child; she grabbed the watch and had the abortion anyway, behind his back.

But it was the Spaniard's merest touch that had come to give her the heebee-jeebees, to use her infantile locution as she shivered in pantomime. In a movie the Spaniard might be played by Marc Anthony as he projected himself from the screen in *Man on Fire*. Coincidently the Spaniard also kept an elaborate shrine to the Blessed Virgin Mary Immaculate Mother of God (with the name tacked on to one of her numerous special appearances.)

It wasn't the Lady of Guadalupe, I don't think. There she appeared to an Indian peasant, Juan Diego, in the appropriated body of a Mestizo and magically spoke to him in his native Nahuatl language, the language of the Aztec empire, thus establishing Mexican legitimacy against Spain at least in the eyes of God. The lady came out firmly against human sacrifice which was a very good thing and much appreciated by the potential sacrificees.

Trying to establish that not all Catholics were complete idiots, a level headed abbot of her basilica for thirty years, Monsignor Guillermo Schulenburg, openly doubted even the existence of this Juan Diego, a symbol, not a reality, of course opposing this nonentity's canonization, which would entail the recognition of a stupid cult. Politically insensitive to the danger of killing off a tourist attraction that drew a million people a month he was forced to resign his position.

To the Lady of Whatever the Spaniard worshipped on his knees continually and lit up enough candles to make it look like the room was on fire. It's a miracle he didn't burn the house down.

They whispered behind Delsey's back of her barrenness and snickered. She fell out of a church tower while making plans for its restoration. The police chief, surrounded by his epauleted underlings, insisted she was inebriated and laughed hilariously up his dirty sleeve, immune to the earnest pleas of the foreign inquisitors newly arrived; but Delsey did not drink.

Tom, for old times' sake, for the mother of his beloved daughter, sent over a contingent of Pinkertons and family retainers and spoke to the American Ambassador, a family friend. Stonewalled by the corrupt officials in the pocket of the husband's family, Tom's people were all rounded up, arrested and beaten savagely, one to death, for good measure, as a warning; carrying firearms without permission; and deported.

The paterfamilias screamed uproariously in broken but unaccented English:

"I don't give shit for Ambassador American."

He was having such a grand old time it was almost a shame to disillusion him. He had no clue as to what a mountain of shit was about to descend upon him.

It was Tom who sought out Landzman, implored him, although he only had a vague idea of who Landzman was, exactly, or what price would be exacted of him. He pleaded for his help, "for justice". How perfect, Landzman the instrument of justice, commander-in-chief of the celestial dominions, Saint Michael the Archangel, Prince of the Heavenly Host who would cast into the perpetual fires of hell all the evil spirits who prowl through the Earth seeking the ruination of souls.

> "Where there is no law, where the law is corrupt, a man is required to take the law into his own hands."

Landzman:

> "If you're going to assume the role of avenging angel you damn well better get your facts straight."

Who's to doom when the judge himself is dragged to the bar.

The Gangster Who Fucked his Wife

I'm not certain that Bucknell ever connected Landzman with the gangster who fucked his wife, got shot to death in his own marble swimming pool and had lived across the bay in the great big house; or that he himself may have had the pivotal role in engineering this Landzman's murder. Tom's memory grew increasingly forgiving both of himself and others; age does that or is it early onset dementia?

But it was Delsey's young daughter whose appeal persuaded. She liked to imagine herself as Landzman's secret daughter, his "love child", an antiquated idiom seldom used even at the time; gifted as she was at quirky self-dramatization.

Landzman, more formidable than Bucknell, procured indigenous help, greased with sacks full of greenbacks and newly minted coin; and himself disembarked with a small army all speaking colloquial Spanish, including a leathery Mexican with well-honed Indian gifts who did not speak at all. They smoked out the murderers, the lowly henchman, quickly, who gratefully confessed, naming all the names for the mercy of a swifter death.

They came clean to a gratuitous bevy of gruesome bloodbaths. This family was a Machiavellian version, Old World, of Murder Incorporated, about to be subjected to unanticipated Yankee know-how from a very un-Yankee. This, after being exposed to medieval implements which through unfamiliarity had to be improvised clumsily with much superfluous blood; looted from the local church, a proud Inquisition collection celebrated for miles which the faithful trooped in droves to marvel at in nostalgia, the just old tools to deal with Infidels and secret Jews.

They were hunted down systematically, with alacrity. It seems there had been a family conclave with a unanimous vote taken, presided over by the family priest, a "saintly man", a distant cousin, revered locally, who granted his own ecclesiastical sanction; who got it first, twice in the head and once in the heart another in the private parts for the unrevealed privileged reasons of the particular hired assassin locally recruited who reveled ecstatically in his mission, settling his own special family score; (it is he who personally delivered the rotting precious piece of the priest now housed in a venerated reliquary which pious old ladies and stupid young girls light candles and pretend there is no stench while gagging unperceptively as they mumble their mindless singsong prayers by rote). The police chief was slaughtered next, with all his minions, every damned one of them.

They died unanimously, the utter extinction of an ancient rotted name; obliteration; their Renaissance family mausoleum fashioned by an unrecognized apprentice of Bernini vaporized as if by enchantment, swallowed up by a yawning maw cracking open the earth; blown sky-high with an over-indulgence in high explosives, showering the countryside for miles around with dirty marble dust and incinerated corpse debris.

Some ran, chased like panicky little beasts tripping over each other; one uncle tracked down like prey in the guise of a poor goat herder into the foothills of the Pyrenees. Locally they called it a mystery, a "holocaust of the disappeared"; without a vestige; no corpses were recovered except for, "mercifully, by a miracle of God", bits of the pious priest, which were parceled-out like sliced lunch meat to local churches; now on proud exhibition in his own parish in the diabolical monstrance. Some said the family was assumed directly into heaven to sit with their god in conclave forever, planning murders; this was before the craze of alien abductions.

This little incident gave rise to a purely local expression translated loosely as: "Don't fuck with the Americans." Only the common people connected it all to the murder of the innocent foreign lady, (and they all knew it was murder), who smiled at them, contrary to stiff-necked family protocol which decreed that they stare right through them like smelly air; a reckless unforgiveable breach on her part, not knowing her proper place, her family stature and the behavior associated with it. Without enthusiastic indigenous cooperation, collaboration really, Landzman's task would have been infinitely more difficult.

Landzman was a romantic after all; his gift; everyone heard of it. He wept bitterly:

> "There was no reason in the world to kill her. That was unnecessary... gratuitous.

> "A token settlement would have packed her peacefully on her way back home to America... where she belonged. The world she lived in hadn't reached this Old World family yet and

never would. She was caught in a time disconnect."

Too slippery, too sloppy; a church annulment would have proved expensive, enticements all the way up to the unholy "see". The local bishop frowned on such things and lined his pocket most generously in compensation; he would take the bribe but remember and always resent it. This would heap dishonor down upon the family with every crooked look of the bishop.

Drop the Names of the Famous

It is remarkable that people in conversation feel it necessary to drop the names of the famous, not necessarily admirable celebrities but definite historical personages, people of whose existence we can to some extent be certain. Is this a means of substantiating their own existence by anchoring to a public figure supposed by a greater number to definitely exist.

As a young man I spent time walking great cities and small towns. I would think nothing of walking ten or twenty miles. There is something profound, existential even, haunting in the experience, a means of absorbing the lives and all that is perceived, understood, and remembered of those who have indelibly inhabited those places; it helped that I liked buildings, great and not so great architecture. The process has been demeaned irretrievably; people shop, entertain themselves, go to restaurants, sightsee, jog, dodging traffic, oblivious; but that is not the same as walking the city.

An added dimension is found in great international cities like New York; in the days before John Lennon was shot and the paparazzi metamorphosed into the piranha-like, celebrities felt free to inhabit and walk the city. Many had open encouraging faces, some would make eye contact and even smile; others wore expressions conveying the feeling of "don't dare approach me"; and most people did not; this was New York, sophisticated if nothing else. But the thing I remember most was that it was eerie; a certain surreal amazement enveloped me; that these people existed here on this planet, not images beamed in, not some media construct, a fabrication of electronic visual engineering, some mass hallucination. They were real; or so it would seem, but really only the very vulnerable flesh which projected an artificial if believable persona for mass consumption which they could never live up to or perhaps even want to.

The downside was that people were always asking for my autograph. At first I would ask them who they thought I was: "Who am I supposed to be?" But this would scare them or fluster them; this was before everyone became so nervy, misinterpreting brazenness as a positive trait. So I learned to scribble something illegible. They would stand there staring at it, most were gleeful, others puzzled which they attempted to hide. Who was it they thought I was? I have no idea; I never found out.

Does Life Imitate Art?

We are in a media saturated urbanized world where the precise demarcations between life and art, broadcast stereotypes and strictly private individualities, has lost its definiteness and in which the question of when someone is being truly themselves is problematical or meaningless at best.

Does art imitate life or does life imitate art? Fitzgerald metamorphosed everything that moved him into fiction, and the backfire transformed fiction into reality or what passed for reality. The legerdemain left him bewildered at times about whether he was in the audience or on the stage; he questioned whether Zelda might be a character of his own fabrication; that he needed a Zelda to wield the whip he craved. Zelda was his destroyer, brandishing the shears to castrate, demean and ultimately ruin. But she was his ruthless, hallucinogenic muse plying the sweet lash, setting his imagination on frenzied fire. He is a savage islander, suddenly touched with Grace, transcending in his prayers and aspirations the grotesque little fetish he clutches in which he imagines he discovers the object of his longing.

Getting back to the primary question, which question is, none the less, hackneyed and clichéd. Are the media "arts" so commanding that the movies and advertising can present a prototype or model so powerful that it becomes an archetype to imitate? We admire, we even worship these powerful images so that life and artifice become blurred, indistinguishable.

Advertising's subtle realization into a consumer responsive system of cunning persuasion in the early twentieth century was hypnotically successful in conscripting the worker-consumers (workers who worked to consume) as obsessive accomplices in their self-enslavement.

But advertising inadvertently taught the poor to brush their teeth, shower every day, groom themselves and clean their houses, if somewhat compulsively, as no government public health campaign or educational system could ever hope to accomplish.

In the near past when a man looked for guidance for the person he wished to become he had his father, his teachers, his clergyman, the great personages of history who he could read about. These models are enfeebled in comparison to the overpowering media circus which inevitably marches forth to infect the imagination of even the most careful and meticulous decrier of mindless popular culture banalities.

Nick repeats his father's stale and trivial clichés as if they were the wisdom of the ages and yet we are thereby made glaringly aware that the rootless Gatsby has no parents, at least none that he acknowledges or would quote, certainly not his birth parents, who he does not rightly recognize as his forebears, his kin. Orphaned he becomes unmoored but also liberated, set free to create himself, adopt his own fathers floating in the heavens like disembodied intelligences. Ye Gads... Judas Priest... Gadsboy.

Nick claims that he witnessed his own version of Landzman, Gatsby that is, praying one night to the stars when he thought he was utterly alone and safe:

> "I have no mother. I have no father. I take the sun and the moon to be my only father and my only mother."

It sounds like an old Cherokee chant to me; but for the life of me I couldn't find an old Cherokee who remembered it.

Orphan

Although many said that Landzman was an orphan, he wasn't, though he often said he was. He was speaking metaphorically.... He didn't feel connected with his own people, his family. He seriously believed that these relations could not possibly be his blood, his biological kin.

He was always spinning his own yarns, like cotton candy floating in the mist, the warm updrafts from the heat of the candy making machine, conceiving myths. He was intrigued by the idea of the foundling, the king's secret son, the golden boy, given over to the care of devotedly loyal common people, salt of the earth, who are entirely ignorant of his regal origins; this for the royal heir's own protection and the threads tying him to the king broken by multiple murder and betrayal; the king's secret emissaries slaughtered by marauders and thus the king's son irretrievably lost to the care of these idiots who not knowing who he was, regularly beat him for his own good, to whip him into shape, their shape.

But if Landzman felt disconnected from his own family it does not follow that he felt some other family here on earth might fit the bill. "What am I doing in Akron, Ohio?" "Utah is not my middle-name." he cryptically mumbled. Landzman was convinced that he had landed on the wrong planet. Or was he the ultimate immigrant, a superior being, the last survivor of a vastly advanced alien world, stranded without the hope of ever mastering their language, a mean patois, a step above gibberish.

As a self-proclaimed orphan he turned out to be mysterious in his roots, unlocking himself to boundless potential. As an orphan he was liberated, could do, be, or mean anything, become one of those singular beings that belongs only to himself, no inextricable alliances; the ultimate survivor, abandoned, or set free, let loose in the woods, alone, alienated, eating his way back on a subsistence of breadcrumb tracks and magic mushrooms, leaving his own bloody trail and a holocaust of crows.

The orphan is the elemental metaphor for the dispossessed, the isolated self, a self we all exemplify as involuntary participants in a disconnected existence devoid of genuine history. We are orphans all, those who think.

Although Landzman dragged his baggage behind him in his widening wake, there was no readable label or return address.

Jackie Gleason

I had an uncle, a man I had great affection for who did a dead on imitation of Jackie Gleason, an imitation which was his life. He spoke like Gleason; he was Jackie Gleason. He ate too much; he drank too much; he was a raconteur; he was immensely lovable and he was smart and funny. Now the question is: was he like that prior to his absorbed consciousness of Gleason or was Gleason himself tying in to a whole set of values and mannerisms that preexisted, out there, in the social ether and did they both tap in to common roots? There was something quintessentially Irish about Gleason. My uncle was christened Michael but called himself Mickey, a very Irish moniker. When tanked-up he titled himself an Old Russian, which was closer to the truth, technically; certainly he had the muzhik about him. He was Leonid Brezhnev, Richard Daley, Arthur Kroc; but most of all, most certainly, he was purposefully and admiringly Jackie Gleason, the one and only; he owned every single one of his records. No, there is no doubt about it; he reinvented himself modeled against a person that he never met, that very well may not have existed, did not, in fact, exist; a creation of the performer, the image he projected; Gleason himself was never so sweet in real life, and this artificial sweetness no doubt sweetened the man my uncle might otherwise have been, that he absorbed only via an insubstantial, glittering display of flickering artificial light from a cathode ray vacuum tube. Why not Clark Gable or Cary Grant? Out of his league. In Gleason, along with the immeasurable common man charm, he could indulge the other person he himself had been, a legitimization of his gross fallibility, an easy dispensation for his most conspicuous lapses: alcoholic, gluttonous and a bit of the buffoon but a genuine character as real as rain. It granted him absolution to descend when uncontrollably, miserably drunk into Ralph Kramden, a vulgar, crude, ignorant blowhard.

But who is to say the best man is not the man of the tube; that the TV persona was not the real Jackie Gleason; his best foot forward, the man most acceptable, the man he wished and hoped to be on his best day in the best possible world.

Was my uncle real? Was this an imitation of an imitation, an act based upon an act, a submergence of identity into some nebulous mass culture or were his sources rather an ever expanding birthplace and birthright, of far richer possibility of self-realization, of deeper wells magnified and multiplied, supplying a fertile cornucopia to critically and carefully choose from? There is a mass culture that enriches and enlarges us and a mass culture that degrades and demeans us. The all-pervading modern media, the great corrupter and destroyer of societal values, also facilitates a process of class simulation and emulation; and lets us impersonate giants who blow themselves up in our faces.

John Marks

There was a consummate salesman who shattered all records. John Marks, a cold, hard man to his peers, stingy with his smiles and grudging of a word, kind or otherwise. But when a "customer" walked in he came to life like a dead man rising from the anesthetizing table, resurrected; he lit up the sky like the Fourth of July. His smile could mesmerize a concert hall and bring the congregation stomping to its feet. He was loved by his customers; they were his friends, perhaps his truest friends. Who is to say that this fabulation, this construct, this paradigm was not the real John Marks; the man he would be in a kinder, gentler world of his craftily secreted dreams ... the best of all worlds; the ultimate reality of the celebrated actor stumbling off the real stage into his accustomed protective coma. A successful salesman requires a rhinoceros's hide; but there is a kind of immunity on whatever stage; bombarded with whistles and boos, catcalls and hoots, it is all a piece with the charade; remove the bloody wounds with a costume change; nothing ventured, nothing risked your core inviolable; the purported mask is armor plate of Damascene steel.

Life is on the boards or in the magician's Chinese regalia, his inscrutable make-up, or on the tight rope or the flying trapeze; the conjuror before his audience comes to life; everything else is anticipation or anticlimax. What did Wallenda say:

> "Being on a tightrope is living; everything else is waiting."

Milton Berle

I remember an older woman born in the teens of the twentieth century who loved, was in fact hopelessly fixated on Milton Berle whom she had seen only on the small screen. Why Milton Berle people would ask in disbelief, astounded in fact? Because Carey Grant was beyond even her dreams, beyond the possible, when, as she explained, she could fully imagine Milton Berle "going for her". (Although it might have had something to do with a broadcasted tale going around that Marilyn Monroe attested to with frank reliability: "Milton Berle has the biggest schlong in Hollywood.") It seems that even mythic schlongs belonging to nebulous icons infest the dreams of Americans.

Petersen

I knew a fellow who repeated a story that was genuinely touching. His name was Peterson and he spoke of his Norwegian mother with an almost holy reverence.

Peterson:

> "I remember every Saturday night Mama would sit down at the kitchen table and count out the money Papa had brought home in his pay envelope.

> "She would carefully count out various stacks.

"'First of all for the landlord' Mama would say, separating out the money.

"'Second, for the grocer.' And yet another pile.

"'For John's shoes.' That was my older brother, John.

And we would all watch in fear as the original pile got smaller and smaller.

At last Papa would ask: 'Is that all?'

And Mama would nod and finally we could breathe easy.

Mama would look up and smile at each of us in turn. 'It is good,' she'd say. 'We have enough' ".

Peterson never tired of telling this story, endless times, like a ritual incantation, a founding, sustaining myth, varying only slightly each time. Tears would well up in his eyes and I was always moved, somewhat. It always sounded unsettlingly familiar, like I had heard it before somewhere, in a dream maybe; that it was unoriginal, a borrowed suit that doesn't fit right, big in the shoulders, too long in the sleeves; it rang false. One time when Peterson was performing his ceremonial with particular animation, his drinking buddy Joe, a prototypical Irishman, is standing in the background out of view of Peterson, making mugs, extravagant faces and an exaggerated jerk-off motion, howling in pantomime. I didn't have the heart to break up Peterson's accustomed routine, which seemed to mean a lot to him. But the next time I saw Joe I asked:

"What the hell was that all about?"

Joe:

> "I'm tired a hearing that crock a shit. I heard it a thousand times. His mother wasn't Norwegian... his father was... so he says... or thinks. His mother was a drunken Irish whore who never paid a goddamn bill in her fucking life... stole every cent the poor old man brought home... snuck out and got drunk on it... that's why the father took off when Bob was a kid... went out one night when he found her drunk in her own vomit... whacked out on the floor and never came home again. And what's this Mama and Papa shit? Every other time it's 'my old man' or 'my old lady'.

Peterson was very proud of his Norwegian roots, of the father who wasn't there and never tired of telling people, who for some reason refused to believe he was Norwegian. He looked just like the Russian general who traded insults and toasted with Patton in the movie or maybe the actor who played the general. Everyone called him a Polack, friendly-like; strangers always speaking Polish to him like a compatriot, a brother. He even learned a few Polish words so he could fake it and be friendly back. But he hated the Poles and hated even more being taken for one:

> "No, I'm Norwegian... really."

> "Yeah... sure. I'm a fucking Eskimo. Who you tryin' to kid... kid?"

It is only later that I came to realize that the story he repeated so often was lifted almost verbatim from a tear-jerking movie I had watched as a kid; the heart-warming schmaltz: *I Remember Mama*. This was curious because Peterson was a tough guy who would fight anybody, no matter how big, who looked funny at him in any bar. I think if anybody told Peterson he was parroting back a movie script and quoted it back to him he would be dumbstruck, wouldn't know what to think, might unravel right there and lose his grip; this was part of the fantasy that allowed him to exist, the sustaining myth. What do you say or do when your exact double walks into the room and claims to be you?

Peterson was intelligent and very funny, missed his calling as a stage comedian, aced the Fire Captain's test, first in his precinct, an alcoholic who got falling down drunk in a bar every night of his life, but prided himself excessively for showing up every morning for work without fail. He was always running into fires, rescuing people. They gave him his own firehouse; made him Chief but took it away almost instantly when they caught him in the act, in flagrante delicto, getting a blowjob from some bimbo in his captain's car while "on duty" outside his firehouse; he was turned in by his own men who called him a "self-hating Negro" to his face, which totally stumped him. To his last day at his own House he had absolutely no idea what they were talking about.

Paul Tripp

I had a friend who seemed especially broken up about a death one day. There were tears welling in his eyes. He was a man of fifty-seven not accustomed to tears. The year was 2002.

I remember asking:

"Was he a relative?"

Friend:

"No... until today I didn't even know his name. But it's opened up a flood of memories, like an iron gate rusted shut finally breaking open off the hinges.

"I saw his obituary in the New York Times and recognized the photograph.

"His name... I discovered was Paul Tripp. He was ninety-one.

"This sounds incredibly stupid but if it weren't for this man whose name I didn't know a week ago I don't think I would be alive today. He introduced me to the human race and made me part of it... want to be part of it. He had this television show whose name I had forgotten until the death notice: Mr. I. Magination."

This friend, more forthcoming than he usually was, remarkably so in a frightening way, described an incredibly bleak childhood in which his mother and her brothers took turns terrorizing and slapping him around. His sister, who he never remembers having a conversation with, didn't even know she was alive, inured, comatose, the unthinking slave of the adults but equally their victim. The nuns and priests were vicious, sadistic. If he could have run away he would have at four or five, anything to get away, but there was nowhere to run to.

The early days of television in the late forties and early fifties were an astonishing time, he explained as if speaking about an ancient history he had lived through:

"My mother, a vicious, stupid woman who everyone regarded as kind and generous and who I would always regard as clinically insane, purchased the magic box in 1949, manufactured by Dumont, for the astronomical sum of $900, the only rational purchase she ever made in her entire life. The small apartment we lived in had a market rent of $50 a month in an apartment house which had been owned by her dead husband, my father, a man of some wealth. Before his death the family had associated with doctors, lawyers and self-made entrepreneurs but after my father's passing she slid inexorably back to a level which accepted her, which she felt more comfortable with, from which she had risen, but much, much deeper down now to a kind of human sewer sludge of assorted low life who preyed upon her, extracting from her the ever depleting remnants of her husband's hard sweated wealth. She eventually married an old decrepit piece of the sewer sludge and gave him all the first husband's money so she could pretend to everybody that the sewer sludge had his own money; trying to prove that he may have been sewer sludge but at least he was sewer sludge with money. She became a drunk, joining the sewer sludge in getting wasted every single night; she had finally found her soulmate, descended to her perfect gutter level; happy as a pig in shit; the delivery boys weren't safe with her; forever fingering her rosary, addicted to novenas which she travelled to and hooked on suspect priests.

My father's children by a previous wife, who had died first, were taken by their grandmother. My mother warned me about these numerous half siblings as if they were demon spawn who would kill me if given the chance, break my neck or even torture me. They were all idiots, she said, rattling off their low IQs, name and number, which she was privy to. I attributed this to her spiteful resentment of the dead first wife and discounted it accordingly. But when I sought them out later in life with open arms full of naïve smiling hope for extending my family, having been isolated and "protected" from them by my crazy mother during my vulnerable years, I found to my absolute astonishment that she was right and she was right about almost nothing else. And not only about them being idiots; they would have killed me, no doubt about it; her prescient paranoia saved my life; she saved my life. I would have gone out an upper story window or drowned in a lake, "a tragic accident".

If my father had lived I, most certainly, would have died, painfully. I was too smart for my own good, which one of them warned me. Who the hell did I think I was? Be careful what you wish for. Be careful about wanting to rewrite history, of wanting to alter what you think is a cruel fate. And what did these fiends tell me about him, my father, this progenitor polluting the world with his foul semen, letting loose a brood of hateful degenerate morons?   I dreamed in a fevered dream that my mother poisoned my father, to save me, her only son, from his host of evil progeny, a strange dream considering her latter perfect union with the piece of sewer sludge. I had never met people who dripped such thick venom; the hatred was palpable, intense and unambiguous; these were people who would hunt down and kill anyone they perceived as putting on airs which was anyone at all superior to themselves. I could feel it like the beast's scorching breath, sulfuric acid burning through my back.

The building we lived in was an island whose inhabitants clung precariously to a striving lower middle class, trying desperately not to become contaminated by the sub-human scum which always threatened to overwhelm us from the adjacent, encroaching buildings and intruding mean streets. I always especially despised the writers and media hounds, the flacks, the schlockmeisters of schmaltz who romanticized and fictionalized this despicable social stratum... an inept, maladroit way of attacking the decadent rich sideways but in the process disarming and emasculating those of us who fought so mightily... so desperately hard for our very lives, our existences, to rise out of this sloshing cesspool with its vicious undertow. Even the so-called realistic writers romanticize this stratum creating a more palatable world entirely of their own creation. They don't misremember, they lived in the fantasy... they survived through the fantasy. Money has absolutely nothing to do with any of it. Give this trash, this detritus, money and they become trash with money... infinitely more dangerous.

"And so the genie's in the glass bottle; the magic box opened up the world to me, revealed to me that there were humans who walked the planet earth, putting their best foot forward no doubt, kind and intelligent... that I was not alone, that there were others like me or rather like what I might come to be, not just the monsters who held me captive in their lunacy... and if not for this miracle, this medium, this perfect confluence of time and technology, would have gobbled me up, sliced thin on stale moldy bread or reduced me to a crippled automaton. Early television saved my life or brought me to life.

"'Mr. I. Magination', I just read, was directed by Yul Brynner, another maestro ... it ran weekly on CBS TV from 1949 to 1952... the benevolent Pied Piper, Paul Tripp, the engineer in striped overalls at the helm of a toy railroad train, surrounded by young children... which passed through a magic tunnel to the land of imagination... he would tell stories from history and literature: Rip Van Winkle, the life of P. T. Barnum. Later, he performed magic tricks with the leading illusionists of the day.

"This was the unexpected captivating intrusion of what passed for high culture. The very high price of the tube insured its exclusivity, the niche market of wealthy urbanized patrons ... I was lucky to live right across from Manhattan... the signal emanating straight from the Empire State Building might as well have been a supernatural beam from a bundle of sacred stardust... live telecasts of Shakespeare and music from Carnegie Hall.

"'Studio One', 'Kraft Television Theater', 'Philco Playhouse', 'Playhouse Ninety'. They grabbed the best actors from the Broadway legitimate theater.

"We have grown accustomed to actors with marbles in their mouths mumbling inaudibly in high pitched nasally whines. But I will never forget the hallucinatory voices of Ed Herlihy and Ralph Bellamy. We seem to have forgotten what a potent and persuasive, perfectly tuned instrument the human speaking voice can be."

I wondered if his grief hadn't overtaken his common sense; he had suffered catastrophic financial reverses recently, destroyed by an only son who he loved more than anything who for irrational or sub-rational reasons plotted against his father and thereby himself, destroyed a substantial fortune which only he was heir to; having once been a rich man, now ruined, at least in his own mind; or if he wasn't having some kind of a complete breakdown, a psychological collapse, having nothing at all to do with, but precipitated by, the death of a man whose name he had long ago forgotten or never knew and whom he had never once met.

I reminded him very gingerly of the "boob tube's", (my purposeful expression), "I Love Lucy", "Uncle Miltie" and "Howdy Doody". A little taken aback he simply insisted unconvincingly that he didn't like or watch those shows. He seemed to have blocked them out. They didn't fit his picture, his holy picture, the icon on the wall of his once magnificent house, boarded up and abandoned now, crumbling into clouds of choking dust. And Herlihy, while granted had a magnificent compelling instrument; he exploited it to hawk fake cheese. Alexander Scourby similarly blessed recorded the entire Bible for the blind without pay.

Read Only Good Writers

Thomas Bucknell, from his papers, undated, uncatalogued and unnumbered:

> "It is extremely important as a writer to read only good writers otherwise your writing becomes contaminated as if by a deadly germ. This is a conundrum. How can we determine if a writer is competent unless we first read him and then we find out too late that he writes garbage and our addition is soiled by the very

determination. Are we condemned to read only long dead writers whose familiarity helped form us? The ear is a delicate instrument. If a singer repeatedly hears sour notes he too will begin to sing off key. If a gifted speaker with a beautiful voice entirely loses his hearing it is only a matter of time before his speech degenerates into an indistinguishable thick-tongued gibberish. It is the same with reading; as social beings we need constant reinforcement. I warn those who would write: stay away from untested contemporary writers; perfect your ear on the proven texts whatever that may be and rest assured that ninety-nine point nine percent of what is currently being published is shit and even though you run from it you risk carrying away its residual permanent stink just by touching it."

Crucifixion

From the archives of James Jacob Landzman, dated 1999, presumably dated by Landzman, unpublished, titled as above, catalogued by his executor's staff, numbered 11,057:

> I marvel at the often bizarre but beautiful scaffoldings that men erect to bedeck themselves, to hold themselves up and intact, to give structure where there is none, to fortify and stretch out the remnants of their collapsed ruins. We are men of straw who hang ourselves, like worn old clothes on dilapidated crosses of

castoff, broken wood which cannot hope to hold even our own weight, who even the crows violate; but do not tell me this is an unworthy crucifixion. A man stuck on a cross, especially, with focused wits which crucifixion will assuredly concentrate, should not waste his time dispensing platitudes.

Newspeak Nazis

The Christian majority has no monopoly on mind control; there are newspeak nazis of every denomination. (And there are those who would give me infinite grief for using the word "Nazi" in this context.)

The following exchange was personally witnessed in the City University of New York in its graduate program in the year 1969.

A student holding forth made the catastrophic miscalculation of using the politically charged term "Old Testament", which led to a withering barrage of venom from the professor (John Hollander):

> "The use of the term 'Old Testament' is offensive to a great many students in this class... I assure you it is not their old testament. The proper name is the 'Hebrew Bible'... I insist that in the future... in this classroom... you refer to it properly. Otherwise you will be asked to leave."

The student was dumbfounded, speechless:

"Are you reinventing the language now? 'Proper name'? Whose proper name? What you're doing is... subversive. The language is loaded. Every time I open my mouth, use language, whatever language that might be, I buy into a whole system of prejudices that I don't necessarily accept. If we redefine the language every time we speak communication becomes impossible.

"'Define your terms', the most 'jesuitical' of shouted tactics to devastate your opponent by knocking the language out from under him... Now, are men with clubs and crucifixes in long black dresses going to lay in wait for me? ... (It is to be noted that he pronounced jesuitical with the s pronounced as zju, a shibboleth which revealed that he had more than passing knowledge of this reviled order. Even the dictionaries get it wrong.)

"Are you going to rewrite the dictionaries? This is 1969 not 1984... not yet, not yet. I can guarantee you that to most Christians it is most decidedly the 'Old Testament'. In case you haven't noticed they've appropriated it as their own. You might want to pretend that Christianity doesn't exist but every time you write the date 1969 you testify to its existence... to its ascendancy. I'm sure you'd like to change that too... to hell with the chaos it creates.

'My grandfather was a proud Jew and a defiant atheist and he despised the Christians but he would have detested someone like you. You have your impregnable position of power, your irrevocable tenure and you use that authority like a club to pummel all those you imagine to have offended you. You Professor, and I use that appellation advisedly, are a pompous ass."

This was his moment of triumph; or was it? What the other students couldn't see is that his eyes brimmed full. He calmly collected his things to the infinite perturbation of the professor and ceremoniously walked out never to be seen again, not in this professor's classroom or any others in this school at least. These professors formed a tight clique; you offended them at your peril. I know for a fact that he never got his tuition back and he looked like he could have used it. This event was more cataclysmic than anyone could have understood; the end of an intended career, a life path altered irrevocably; the lost wasted savings of a struggling divorced mother who had few options. Why couldn't he keep his fucking mouth shut? Couldn't he learn to just play the game, a little bit and eat shit and smile like all the rest of us.

(There was no proof that his grandfather was in fact a Jew; but under the circumstances it sounded too good to be untrue; it was a family rumor or rather a rumor he heard from others about the family; the family denied it. He chose to believe it and would nod or shrug in mock reluctance when questioned about it.)

But there was more to it; there always is. He found this teacher excruciatingly mind-numbing; the other teachers merely unendurable. Sitting still and listening to them was punishment enough. He found most of the books he was required to read worthless and not worth finishing; and finished them only as an exercise of a steeled will. As obedient students we are expected to listen mutely in our seats to fools prattle on about less than nothing. And this the other fools regard as positive; so much so that they have named the inability to tolerate fools as a disease.

All the progress of humankind has resulted from just such deficient beings, who refuse to sit; who refuse to take notes; who write instead of read; who create; instead of consume the swill served up to them in dented dirty metal prison bowls as if it were manna from the gods. Being well-read is vastly over-rated by the soi-disant literati; the canon can be used as a bludgeon to pound us with. The vast majority of books are not worth reading and they adulterate, contaminate any style a writer might strive to develop.

I have a dream that I'll see this student's smiling face, alive and well, once again, on the front page of the literary supplement to the New York Times for winning the Nobel Prize; an unfamiliar author whose books, unknown, went unread in America; famous in Europe, living in France.

From the files of Thomas Bucknell, undated, titled as:

Arthur Miller

There are people who live only to see Roth rejected year after endless year. They look forward in anticipation, like children to a holiday, to snow on

Christmas, to the unbridled jubilation, but unnerved, shaken by the constant primal fear:

> "If he wins I'm booking the next passage out... of the world; he inflicts upon us his insular depressing narrowness which no one else outside his inbred clan should care about; dragging us into his stunted, constricted, ingrown soul, his self-obsessed sub subgroup.

> "Join the greater human race for Christ's sake.

> "Thank you, thank you again; we are forever indebted for this merciful rejection, to the infinite chagrin of the dense, self-appointed, cognoscenti who fawn all over him.

> "Give me Arthur Miller; set a precedent; award him the Prize, posthumously who had the wisdom and good sense to universalize and open his own personal world to the whole world and make us part of him."

Bucknell, no idiot; his animus is inexplicable. I read Roth and I become a Jew, persecuted, suffocated, exiled while apparently embraced; or clasped; or contained; it is not a comfortable feeling and I run from it. We are all Jews in America, most of us, who know enough, with strange dreams inflicted upon us.

Casuistry

Monsignor Fey was shadowed whenever he attended one of Landzman's parties. Why he was admitted in the first place is still something of a mystery although Nick imagined that all doors swung open as if by magic because of a wave of his hand. Perhaps Fey was the intended target and Nick the useful tool. Fey was a fund of information, rumor and innuendo; he gossiped like a fishwife and dished the dirt on the entire Roman Catholic hierarchy. The secrets of the confessional were fair game without naming names thus maintaining the technical sanctity of the sacrament, at least in his own mind. But it didn't take a genius to fill in the missing pieces and the names easily fell into place helped by a staff of stenographers, researchers and private eyes. Landzman's mansion was wired, with an attendant staff in the basement, to record any useful tidbits of information that might come in handy. It's amazing the things people will say when a little drunk and off their guard. This is presumably a transcript of a recording of Fey holding forth, made in the late summer of 1922, shortly before the murders.

Monsignor Fey:

> "The Jesuits were men before their time.... with this wonderful liberating idea. Jesuit theologians, trying to buttress personal responsibility and because of their reverence for freedom of conscience, emphasized the value of the 'case by case' methodology to personal moral evaluation and developed what would come to be called casuistry (the study of cases of conscience

case by case) where at the time of choice, individual judgements were more important than any perceived absolute moral law in itself. It is in this way that we may achieve holy ends by unholy means. And thus the means become sanctified because of the ends they produce.

"The infinite, all knowing, all powerful, all merciful God couldn't care less what I do with my silly sexual appendage; and this infinite God loves me for loving these boys in the most intimate physical way. It is essential that the boys are very young and innocent so that they can be educated about God's way, before they have been corrupted by an evil world which would turn them against the perfect love that I have for them and the sacred way I consummate that love. God knows that it is for their greater good and for the glory of God Himself; that I love these boys, selflessly, with pure Christian love, agape, the same love Jesus Christ gave to humanity; I love them more than myself; I would give my life for them. I love these boys more than anyone else could possibly love them, more than anyone will ever love them, more even than their own mothers and fathers. I teach them; I nurture them, guide them, council them to succeed at their dreams. I show them the possibilities of life; open new broader horizons, introduce them to the finest people, people who share values with me and with them, who will help them make their way in the world. I could put together a small army of my boys who would go to battle for me, die for me.

"And they come to me willingly, enthusiastically; seek me out even, because they have heard of my perfect love from the other boys and the boys together are like brothers to each other; we are a tight knit family. And the other boys love each other just as I love them and they love me and I watch over them and teach them to perfect their love for each other and they are like apostles who go forth and spread the good word and bring other boys to share our love and make it perfect in the eyes of God. I have brought scores of boys to the holy priesthood of Christ by the power of my love and they each in turn have brought scores of others; we are a powerful union of perfect love.

"I warn them always that they must be ever vigilant of those that are envious of our love and would seek out of spite to destroy that perfect love that God and His Beloved Son gives us. These are the agents of Satan that are made angry by love and will sow the seeds of disunion among our family. There are those who do not understand the details of our great love so we therefore must be secretive about the physical bonds of our love. I have explained to these boys that as a result of the sacred vows of my vocation and the holy canon law I am bound to lie even under oath to protect the Holy Mother Church from scandal and that I am bound to do anything at all to protect our Holy Mother Church. Therefore they must all take a sacred vow sworn directly to God and Our Savior never to speak of the nature of our powerful love under pain of mortal sin and eternal damnation in the fires of hell; that to break such an oath to God and Jesus Christ is the one unforgivable sin and that no priest has the power to grant absolution from this most heinous sin and that God himself never forgives it because they would have broken their direct pledge to Him.

"I have explained to them that I have a vocation, which means that I have been singled out, chosen personally by God, that this is his greatest gift, to be his servant, that what I do is good and right because I am chosen, that what I do I do as a servant of God to spread his infinite love. I am but a vessel to channel God's love to them and it is through me that they can love God.

"And the parents knowing my goodness and my power to nurture love in their boys bring them to me and beg me to help and cultivate their boys. They implore me: 'Please help my Johnny, teach him your goodness.' And they bathe him and dress him and prepare him for me, like a sacrament, a virgin to be presented to a king, through me, the King of Heaven, whose appointed surrogate I am and deep down they know the secrets of my love and are honored that I have blessed and chosen their sons, that God and Our Lord Jesus Christ has chosen their sons through me. And that God has chosen them also, because of their sons and that the doors of heaven shall swing open for them and that they shall be ushered before God by a trumpeting host of angels.

"And if ever I am accused by the forces of Satan they will stand as one by my side, all the mothers, even if they have to die for me. They will barricade the way, lay down their bodies when the legions of Satan come for me; they will stand vigil through the night with lighted candles in procession loudly reciting the rosary to the Madonna, Holy Virgin Mother of God, Mary the Immaculate who also gave Her Son as they have given theirs and she will be their strength and their courage and stand beside them, Mother to mother, as they march for me."

Monsignor

Found in the files of James Jacob Landzman, what appears to be a transcript of a voice recording. The two speakers are not identified:

"To what depths the Jesuits have fallen, from torturing Protestants and burning heretics, toppling kingdoms and assassinating kings, to little boy's dicks in their mouths."

"You're naïve. They always had boy's dicks in their mouths. Only they can't butcher Protestants anymore. More than half the fun is gone and don't think they're not intimately connected."

"I love the way these depraved demons are always so quick to forgive themselves, mouthing blasphemy like: 'I've made my peace with god.' I doubt that God has made his peace with them. May they be struck down dead and burn in hell."

Monsignor Sigourney Fey

Nick's desperate unhappiness at the Papist school opened him up, made him vulnerable to the attention, encouragement and flattery of this bizarre, ridiculous priest.

Monsignor Sigourney Fey unabashedly and mawkishly flattered his fledgling disciple, continually burying him with saccharin sweet-talk, snowing him in an avalanche of blarney:

> "I have ten thousand things to say that I cannot write. There are intimacies that cannot be put upon paper. . . . Really the whole thing is most startling; I am keen beyond words to read the rest of that book. I may be frightfully prejudiced but I have never read anything more interesting than that book. . . . The more I see of it the more amazingly good I think it is."

This about writing, long before The Great Gatsby, that was no more than run of the mill pulp; the besoted padre was hootin and hollerin over trash; anything to get in his charge's pants.

> "We are many other things— we're extraordinary, we're clever, we could be said I

suppose to be brilliant. We can attract people, we can make atmosphere, we can almost always have our own way..."

Monsignor Fey sucked him in, an old technique of practiced pederasts, escorting his protégé by the hand to the mountain-top, into his purported sphere, embellishing his own associations with celebrated figures of the greater world of religion and politics, by joining Fitzgerald with himself and by stuffing his seductive missives, love notes really, with shameless adulation.

Mentorship

Nick is always foisting mentors on his imaginary Landzman; Kodi then Wolf. Landzman, himself, considered it un-American. If America was anything it was a place where a man could rise high on his own lone efforts. There was something old world, corrupt, decadent, European, effete, a whiff of indentured servitude about it. Ben Franklin gleefully escaped the prison-like obligations of his own apprenticeship, the beatings from his brother, scuttled to Philadelphia, a new world in a new world. Mentorship: there was something girly about it, weak, like being procured an alacritous child bride or pressed into coy service, a willing prison bitch for the perks.

It was Wolf, the real Wolf, who said that any man who subjects himself to mentorship should have his manhood checked; what was left would be wrung out of him by the subservience. Wolf, the quintessential

American, not Nick's pale fiction; who counseled in his best colloquial verbiage, advice dispensed to his own young sons like a throwaway line, which they knew better than to ever quote:

> "If you ever hear the words mentorship or protégé grab your dick and run like hell."

It was the obscene Monsignor who had prepped and primed Carramel for this un-American bondage. As a result Nick was always demeaning, disgracing himself to more self-possessed men who had markedly less talent; midgets in comparison; they assumed the position of ordained noblesse, condescended and thus emasculated what little was left of him, meticulously, ritualistically. It was Wilson, his purported friend, who reinforced any way he could Fitzgerald's sense of inferiority. Even when it became obvious that Wilson had no literary talent whatsoever, Fitzgerald continued to acquiesce and humble himself to Wilson's superior posturing and also assumed an obsequiousness to a host of others who held themselves high above him.

His acute sense of insufficiency was exaggerated by his "old world", very Roman Catholic guilt and an unacknowledged desire for humiliation and punishment, his secret love of the strong hand, of the priest's whip even after his supposed abandonment of Catholicism.

Hemingway exploited and manipulated his many mentors and when he had used them up and wrung them out he discarded them with a bitter even vicious resentment that he ever needed them in the first place. No more than an amanuensis and minion shamelessly currying favor to the condescending Gertrude Stein, it is Hemingway who got the last word in and his revenge by rewriting the reality, his reality, from the grave, as writers often do, posthumously. By biting off and feeding on the many hands that had fed him Hemingway kept his balls somewhat intact and paid obeisance to no man; paid not even simple gratitude.

Edmund Wilson was viciously jealous of Fitzgerald and could never acknowledge that it was Fitzgerald who was the infinitely greater talent:

> "He has been given imagination without intellectual control of it; ... a gift of expression without very many ideas to express."

> "...a rather childlike fellow extraordinarily little occupied with the general affairs of the world... he is not much given to abstract or impersonal thought".

His "imagination suffers badly from...poverty of aesthetic ideas"; and he suffers from a Midwestern "sensitivity and eagerness for life without a sound base of culture and taste"; his values are those of the nouveau riche: a "preoccupation with display, the appetite for visible magnificence and audible jamboree" As so many did, Wilson confused the art with the artist. He had read too much of Fitzgerald's trash and couldn't recognize the magnitude of the masterpiece when it presented itself rising in glory out of the stinking shit. More than anyone he would have been astounded by Fitzgerald's posthumous triumph.

But it was not only Wilson who harbored a deep hatred and resentment of Fitzgerald. He had a knack for offending a myriad with his gross behavior and his mean, childish pranks. He was at a party in Hollywood where he gathered together everyone's jewelry and watches for a trick but the so-called trick was nothing more than boiling their personal possessions, some valuable family heirlooms in a vat of canned tomato sauce. There are people who carried an enduring hatred for him like a sacred ember in their heart. He mortally wounded people and thought nothing of it like a spoiled child inured or indifferent to all consequences.

Curdled Like a Cow Patty

It was Tom Bucknell who, seeing Monsignor Fey at one of Landzman's functions, was taken aback, waxing poetic, particularly nauseated by the old pederast who, trying to step up in the world of his boy fixation, seemed to have little success in his new endeavor of propositioning the many unattached, stylishly dressed young gentleman who seemed to be on the make for something, but decidedly not on the make for Monsignor Sigourney Fey:

> "Fey had a face creamed and curdled like a cow patty in an inundated pasture, but the color of bleached, bromated biscuit dough gone moldy; the face of a dead bloated fetus squeaking gas; an overgrown obscene corpse of a Kewpie Doll. He was a stomach churning creature who wore

his Papist priesthood like a badge of honor, who strutted his blanched pate, tilted, like a spent psycho sashaying in a perpetual Saint Patrick's Day parade. I heard the Papists were going to make him into one of their own saints which would be entirely appropriate and predictable. He was always performing cheap parlor tricks which the faithful, falling down in amasement, proclaimed miracles and have no doubt documented and sent up to the Vatican."

Champions of High Culture

The old robber barons for all their gangster ways were champions of high culture. They raided Europe armed to the teeth with new money; buccaneers buying the greatest art that mankind had ever produced; they founded and funded parks and gardens, libraries, museums and orchestras. And if they brought the same hard-nosed acquisitiveness to their purchases of high culture at least there was collateral merit in their ruthless culture climbing. And if some of their acquisitions were formless and without taste and perhaps desecrated the conceivable canons of style, in most instances, this was certainly not the case. They endowed the museums of America with incomparable treasures, the best art which enriched every one of us. It was much more than just "statuary, paintings, pottery, and rugs"; more than just "jewels, fabrics, wines, and metals".

Their descendants in stark contrast used their inherited unearned treasure to debauch themselves and degrade and cheapen the surrounding civilization by their gross acquiescence, surrender even, to an emerging popular culture at war with the culture their fathers campaigned so ruthlessly for. They pissed hilariously on their patrimony and self-declared it youth culture although the phrase was not in use at the time; the eruption of perpetual adolescence, a self-propelled pustule shooting into the sky.

Rootless as Landzman

The Bucknells and their bunch were a product of the "media", of advertising, magazines and movies, of the then current social milieu. For all their talk of privilege and family they were as rootless, more rootless than Landzman who sank his own roots where he chose to stand. They are faithful to no past; they have inherited nothing but money. They might as well have stepped out of a movie screen. There are no adults in evidence anywhere; no old patriarch or matriarchs exemplifying and demanding a standard of values. The children have inherited the house, seized control in a dark night's palace coup; snuffed out the grownups, figuratively; the great die-off of the finest. Like Nick's fictitious Jillian they are unmoored, have no real family, only an old senile aunt, irrelevant, easily placated.

Bucknell's father, an old style paterfamilias, of biblical proportions, his uncle and older brother, all the adults, died in the Spanish Flu. The 1918 Pandemic killed the most robust through a "cytokine storm"; the best and fittest having their perfectly primed immune systems turned against them, to self-destruct; like something out of a fifties sci-fi movie; which left this unholy vacuity of the inept orphaned dregs; survival of the feeblest.

Upwards of 100 million, among them the strongest, the richest and the most powerful, were dead.

Both Dodge Brothers, of automotive fame; Guillaume Apollinaire, French poet, son of Poland; Felix Arndt, American pianist, his mother was the Countess Fevrier, related to Napoleon III, composer of novelty ragtime and "Nola", composed songs for the vaudeville team of Jack Norworth and Nora Bayes, and recorded over 3000 piano rolls; Sophie Halberstadt, Freud's daughter; Phoebe Hearst, mother of William Randolph Hearst; Harold Gilman, British painter who painted "Halifax Harbour" which hangs in the Tate; Henry G. Ginaca, American engineer who invented a machine that could peel and core pineapples which exponentially increased production and revolutionized the fruit canning industry and made Dole fabulously rich; Alan Arnett McLeod, described as "the finest flower of chivalry", destroyed an enemy triplane and was immediately attacked by eight more, three of which he brought down, crash landed in No Man's Land, dragged his comrade from the burning wreckage to safety, under heavy fire, for which he received the Victoria Cross; Sir Hubert Parry, British composer, radical in his politics who shunned his own moneyed class, a free thinker who refused to go to his daughters christening and was widely described as an ascetic who spent little of his vast inherited fortune on himself; William Leefe Robinson, British flying ace, first to shoot down a German Zeppelin over Britain during The Great War; Edmond Rostand, author of Cyrano de Bergerac; Egon Schiele, Austrian painter, protégé of Klimt, he and his lover, seventeen year-old Walburga Neuzil were driven out of the small Bohemian town by the enraged townspeople, alleged by some to be carrying torches, who condemned his employment of the town's teenage girls as models; Yakov Sverdlov, whose parents were Jews, his father, an engraver, was a forger and arms smuggler for the Bolsheviks; rumors persist that Sverdlov was beaten to death with axes and clubs by workers in Oryol, because he was a Jew, who sought to destroy Orthodox Christian Russia, Bolshevik party leader, murderer of Tsar Nicholas II; Colonel Sir Mark Sykes, 6th Baronet, British politician, promoter of Arab Nationalism to counter the Turks, wrote to Faisal I of Iraq, warning of the Jews: "… this race, despised and weak, is universal and all powerful and cannot be put down"; Max Weber, German political economist, whose primary preoccupation was understanding the processes that he associated with the rise of capitalism and modernity. In The Protestant Ethic and the Spirit of Capitalism, he proposed that ascetic Protestantism was one of the major "elective affinities" associated with the rise in the Western world of market-driven capitalism and the "rational-legal nation-state". He condemned the migration of Poles into "German Lands" blaming the Junker class for promoting Slavic entry to serve their selfish interests; Prince Erik Gustav Ludwig Albert Bernadotte, Prince of Sweden and Norway, Duke of Västmanland with not enough names and titles to protect him from The Plague.

The Sudden Extinction of a Clan

For the Bucknells the Plague was a personal family holocaust, the sudden extinction of a clan, the kind of mass death that Nick invents for Gatsby's People. Bucknell's father had advised him against his "entanglement" with Delsey Fey but died before he could complete the meticulous details of his son's honorable extrication.

The paterfamilias was above all a man of honor. He was accustomed to quote the Reverend William Lawrence:

> "To seek for and earn wealth is a sign of a natural, vigorous, and strong character,"

The rich man is obligated by his very wealth to perform works of charity and is the chosen instrument of God; he, the generous rich man:

> "...is Christ's as much as was St. Paul, he is consecrated as was St. Francis of Assisi. ... If ever Christ's words have been obeyed to the letter, they are obeyed today by those who are living out His precepts of the stewardship of wealth."

He would thunder forth like an Old Testament prophet:

> "The wealth is not mine; it is given to me by God for safe keeping. I am only the trustee with the obligation to distribute it among the just and worthy.

"I am but the agent for my poorer brethren, their servant, bringing to them my superior wisdom, experience, and ability to administer, doing for them better than they would or could for themselves."

"It were better for the human race that the rich were thrown into the sea rather than fail in this sacred obligation and become slothful, drunken, and dissipated. It is better to give than to spend.

"I am not interested in ending poverty but rather I want to create the conditions for worthy men of excellence to rise in America. Like Carnegie I will give to institutions that will enable the ascent of the next generation of self-made men. I will endow libraries, colleges, museums, and concert halls where men might cultivate an appreciation of the arts, just as I have learned to appreciate those arts."

By his high standards, by his own hand Nick's Tom and his ilk would have been thrown in and drowned in that very sea.

What the children begot was a carnival, or more nearly a circus, a lewd festival of derision of what once was sacrosanct, of crazy prodigality instead of the old spirit of prudence, charity and thrift. The "youth" rebelled against their elders' American Way of Life with the same spirit of the so-called "counter culture" of the 1960s.

There is a lot of empty talk about birth in Nick's book with the concept used in its traditional sense of inherited class privilege. But they have obliterated that tradition and can invoke it only with biting irony. It's like Nick's Tom lamenting the loss of family values when he is in fact its prime destroyer.

If Tom and Delsey's "entertaining" is more staid than Landzman's lewd imitation of it, it is still mindless socializing. This generation of the Twenties fancied themselves radicals and iconoclasts but were only mindless destroyers and never found anything to supplant the old virtues of work and courage and the old graces of courtesy and politeness.

And it is this affluent decadence of incessant celebration that becomes an added means of exclusion. An upper class that practices and exemplifies the old virtues... not only thrift and diligence but chastity and sobriety... will be more penetrable, less self-protected and self-perpetuating, than an upper class that tells the aspirationally ambitious that they can't climb the ladder unless they strip down and join them in the mud, join the party first; the initiation is debauchery; dissipation the ticket in.

The perpetual jamboree, the unceasing fiesta becomes a means of rejection; if you practice the old virtues or any virtue at all you are labelled a pariah, a stick in the mud, not with it. That life must be a unending party is ingrained in the corrupt culture of the country; the cocktail parties of the fifties, the ceaseless intoxicated bull sessions of the Sixties fueled by pot, all critical capacity guttered and thus to partake of a communal intellectual love-in or more properly a know nothing orgy, union of the dumbed-down; in which people carried on upon subjects about which they knew absolutely nothing into the middle of interminable nights; the infantile need to constantly hang out. In party colleges today unless you have well-off parents to fund your party life you are marginalized, left to the side-lines, which is probably a blessing.

Tom comes to dinner in his riding clothes; Nick's fabricated Tom does; carrying with him the stink of the stables. Fitzgerald got into an altercation in Hollywood with an influential actor over just such an outrageous social breach; asking him with feigned humor: "where's your horse?" What he may not have understood completely was that the actor may not have been anywhere near a horse and was just play acting in costume; polo outfits are very pretty.

Trashing of So-called High Culture

For the Bucknells and their ilk there is this infantile need to smear their shit on the walls now that mommy and daddy are not here to reprimand and send them to their room; to break the rules of simple decorum and common sense manners; to mock all etiquette as so square, to use a square word.

The trashing of so-called high culture and all its accoutrements is not without cause. It has been the culture appropriated as the defining feature by an upper class, an aristocracy, a self-appointed, abusive intelligentsia, a bunch of stuffed shirts full of themselves.

But it can be more universally defined as a storehouse of a broader enriching knowledge, an avenue to transcend and abolish the strict boundaries of any entrenched class system.

High culture has been exploited as an instrument of exclusion; a club to beat down the aspiring, clutching masses; formal dress to the opera. But opera was at one time popular entertainment considered in some of its forms decadent by the keepers of the flame, with its shamelessly hokey melodrama. Literary Romanticism revalued and seriously reconsidered the "low culture" previously disparaged in medieval romances. The trash of one era becomes the treasure of another without ever ceasing to be trash; only the perception changes, the softness of age and an enriching patina masks the smell.

Shakespeare was a journeyman playwright, the son of a glover, ever-mindful of making a buck, peddling cheap humor to the groundlings. I'm always humorously struck by the self-proclaimed literati decked protectively, demarking themselves in evening wear, hee-hawing hilariously at his lowest jokes, gags that must have stuck sharp in his throat; a source of embarrassment to a creator who balanced dexterously on the taut hanging rope between trash and the best combinations of words ever put down on paper.

There is a pathetic tendency for particular individuals of ostensible intelligence to pay homage, toadying to the multitudes, as if to gain favor when the anticipated upheaval comes, offering obeisance even, to popularly worshipped dregs of the promulgated media culture. It's like raising a baby chimpanzee, nurturing it, pretending and truly believing in your heart that it is a gifted child only to have it grow up and eat your face off and your hands and finally your testicles for dessert. Pauline Kael, who was one of those devoted flacks for trash, a pop culture oracle as someone labeled her, belatedly remarked to a friend:

> "When we championed trash culture we had no idea it would become the only culture."

People find a commonality of blood, a brotherhood, bonding of the dumbest in their basest, most vulgar and most prurient interests; low culture, a natural herding instinct, getting high sniffing each other's armpits, inhaling each other's flatulence and wallowing ecstatically in each other's shit.

I think of talk show hosts fawning over the dredged up resuscitated corpses of old Hollywood, huffing and puffing mightily to blow life into the very dead carcasses; Victorian post-mortem photography or memorial portraiture as they euphemistically advertised it with the added kick of a real live ventriloquist bobbing the desiccated head like a grotesque hand puppet .

Although there may be as much to be learned from a soap advertisement as from a pensée by Pascal it does not follow that they have the equivalent value. I can see the usefulness of analyzing societal out-growths, like a fascinating, colorful fungus growing out of the heat of decaying compost; an intriguing jungle of life in a toxic bubbling brew of pond scum. This detritus can divulge much that is critical to the survival of the greater civilization but only on the level of an archeologist deftly sifting through the dumps and latrines of a long lost people; or the CIA cutting open the drains of the Soviet premier's hotel rooms a floor beneath to collect his excrement and thus determine the state of his physical wellbeing and the continued possibility of our own.

We Love Our Myths

We are dependent on our myths. We love our myths. When our myths become corrupt we are corrupted in our souls. Successful myth fulfills, in both primitive and modern society, an indispensable function: it communicates, enriches and methodizes our most fundamental beliefs, beliefs we may not even be fully aware of. It testifies and gives foundation to the efficiency of the resultant rituals and embraces practical rules for the guidance of our everyday lives. It is the holy covenant, a charter, a compact for moral value and social harmony. It is deep magical belief. It is the vital ingredient in what we call civilization. It is not an idle tale, a story for children, a mere legend, fable or yarn, an intellectual explanation or only artistic imagery. At its functioning best it is the glue that binds us, the sacred blood that courses through our common arteries, that makes us all brothers under the skin.

Worshipful Regard for the Individual

From the archives of Thomas Bucknell, undated, uncatalogued:

> Although we are basically social creatures the reason there has been such a resurgence in an almost worshipful regard for the individual and his "liberty" is that societal structures have been hijacked by mountebanks, charlatans, scoundrels and crooks and that the only hope for the individual is for him to cast off his corrupt myths, the fantasies and delusions, this unholy caul that blinds, and for an instant, just one instant, see clearly; throw off the chains that binds his mind and overthrow the usurpers who inhabit his mud castles in the sky.

Bill Cosby and Predator Priests

From the files of Thomas Bucknell, uncatalogued, undated. It should be noted that Bucknell died in 2003 before the Cosby controversy broke open; although Cosby's antics were well known, infamous in the industry. I have no possible explanation for its contents.

> Bill Cosby got away with raping white women because he told his white audience exactly what they wanted to hear, that Black people were responsible for their own problems. Cosby was untouchable. It could only be a black comedian

who finally had had enough of Cosby's self-serving bullshit.

Mr. Cosby is like the Roman Catholic priests. They were allowed to rape as many boys as they liked as long as they recited the right magic words at the end of any confession, no matter how vile. How many monsters did they send back into the world on a weekly basis with a wiped clean conscience? These are psychopaths skipped loose; these the friendly fiends cleansed of all their sins, enabled, refreshed, empowered to go forth into the world and ruin more souls. If this is not blasphemy, presuming to forgive in the name of God Himself, what is? This was their currency, medium of exchange, which aggrandized them, the jingling, shiny silver in their empty pocket.

"Deinde, ego te absolvo a peccatis tuis in nomine Patris, et Filii, et Spiritus Sancti. Amen."

Ego te absolvo, I absolve you; I, I, I, ego, ego, ego; who the fuck are you to absolve anybody? Say the magic words; the duck comes down; the slate washed spotless no matter how heinous the crimes or how often committed; like cracking open the prison gates of hell; go forth, with a slap on the back; come back next week, same time same place and bring a little tidbit for the good father, something to share with him, so that we may pray together for your eternal soul:

"What did you do with her liver, my son?"

299

Pouring the slops back on the deck, the innocent slip into the sea and drown. A true angel of the Lord would sit in the confessional in disguise with a 45 magnum in his lap, and God's thunder clap in his pocket:

"You did what with her, my son?"

BOOM, BOOM, BOOM; blown to hell. We need Charles Bronson with wings in the confessional, undercover.

Shortly before he was hanged by Poland for war crimes, Rudolph Höess, former commandant of Auschwitz returned to the bosom of Holy Mother Church, like a wayward son to the Roman Catholic Church of his youth, having once when young perceived in himself a vocation, a special selection, touched by the hand of God to become one of His priests. On April 10, 1947, he received the sacrament of penance and was granted absolution by Władysław Lohn, S.J., provincial of the Polish Province of the Society of Jesus. On the next day this same Jesuit priest gave him the actual body and blood of Christ into his mouth, the most sacred sacrament of his church, Holy Communion. In five short days Höess would slough off his mortal coil with the help of a Polish rope and so long as he didn't have impure thoughts or masturbate in the meantime the glory of the kingdom of heaven would be his for eternity.

Cosby's proclaimed indictment of black women's slack morals and non-existent parenting skills fed right into the hidebound beliefs of the grateful whites who flocked like supplicants to form long lines to kiss his dirty ass; they loved it; ate it up, like dogs eating their own vomit; he got two prolonged standing ovations in Melbourne Florida... after the revelations; of all places, Melbourne, beloved hold-out bastion of the Ku Klux Klan, proud murder capital for the Christmas 1951 slaughter of civil rights workers Harry T. & Harriett V. Moore who organized the first Brevard County Branch of the NAACP; a bomb blew away them and their house and their fine dust settled on all Brevard, a permanent, indelible curse; a great hurricane will come and wash it all away, Please God; fittingly famous for its crooked judges, they named a "Justice Center" after them in mockery; no doubt the good old boys shared a keg and a raucous drunken laugh over that one:

> "Five, six children, same woman, eight, 10 different husbands or whatever... ... Pretty soon you're going to have to have DNA cards so you can tell who you're making love to. You don't know who this is; might be your grandmother.'"

GRAHAM GREENE

Found among the papers of Thomas Bucknell, uncatalogued, untitled and undated. Why Bucknell cared at all about the degradation of the Catholic priesthood is only somewhat puzzling but on target to the subjects at hand. His second marriage was to a Roman Catholic who insisted on his conversion to the one true faith. His faith ended with the divorce but left its impression. She had promised him a blowjob every night of their married life as inducement to conversion and strict observance, fully sanctioned by her confessor, she insisted. "We must rally in the converts for the greater glory of Jesus Christ and His Holy Mother Church." Bucknell thought it was well worth it. He considered the pack of them deranged. She eventually ran off with a numbers runner up in Harlem who was no doubt persuaded by her negotiating skills. It is uncertain whether he too was converted to the One True Faith or whether her confessor was consulted. Actually, Bucknell was relieved to be rid of her. He was choking to death on incense:

> "The degradation of the Catholic priesthood was aided by the debauched habit of ostensible public practitioners, Catholic prep-school pranksters amongst them, who abused the confessional to explore their own obscene fantasies. Graham Greene did just that, the so-called penultimate "Catholic Writer", palpably malevolent, misused the confessional, pissed on the sacrament, to share lurid, fabricated accounts of depraved sex to get his rocks off, to horrify, demoralize and even ruin the good priests obliged to listen to his sick shit.

> "It was Theroux that said there is something ambiguously homoerotic in a man's conducting

extended affairs with married woman who remain in their husband's home continuing to have sex with that husband: to put his penis where another man's penis has just been. He was besotted by countless prostitutes, 47 of them documented in his own letters, where if he played his cards rights he could mix his semen with another man's semen in a shared communal mouth or vagina. He liked to have sex in the backseat of a car with his goddaughter while her husband drove or in the back of Italian church altars.

"His most intimate male friend was a homosexual who habitually preyed on young boys, and it has been claimed that Greene regularly targeted underage boys on the island of Capri.

"He inexplicably defended and stood by his former MI6 collaborator, the Communist traitor, Kim Philby, sidestepping the fact that Philby's duplicity and treachery had caused the death of British agents.

"He liked to feast engorgingly on the hand that fed him, describing Hollywood as 'an ignoble gang of foreign, semitic (sic) gutter people'. This sounds a lot like Fitzgerald who was an angel of light compared the demonic Greene. Fitzgerald described Hollywood as: 'a Jewish holiday, a gentiles (sic) tragedy.'

"There was something about Greene that always turned my stomach. All good writers are moral writers in that they explore the complexity of the moral dilemma, but Greene was something else again, ambiguous, equivocal, shady, shifty, purposely confusing, putting evil in the garments of good, good in the garments of evil. Greene was a committed agent of the Evil Empire, of Stalin, Castro and Ortega."

Self-made Man

The new man, the self-made man was up and coming, shrewd, practical, full of compulsive energy, his eye on the ball rolling toward the future, manic in his enterprise, indomitable in his optimistic idealism, natural openness and relentless will to succeed.

Henry Clay is erroneously reputed to have coined the expression "self-made man" on February 2, 1832 while arguing on the Senate floor for a protective tariff:

> "In Kentucky, almost every manufactory known to me, is in the hands of enterprising and self-made men, who have acquired whatever wealth they possess by patient and diligent labor."

No silver spoons in these mouths, no-siree, Bob. This is Amurica, by gosh.

In a letter signed by a Prof. Newman published October 9, 1828 in the Delaware Advertiser and Farmer's Journal the self-proclaimed professor extolled the virtues of Roger Sherman (1721–1793), the Connecticut politician who rose from humble beginnings to serve on the Committee of Five that drafted the Declaration of Independence and who later served as Connecticut's Senator in the new U.S. Congress. He was the only person to sign all four great state papers of the United States: the Continental Association, the Declaration of Independence, the Articles of Confederation and the Constitution. He had no formal education and his early years were spent as a shoe-maker. With no formal legal training he passed the exam and was admitted to the Bar of Litchfield, Connecticut in 1754.

The self-made man as the embodiment of the American Dream come true became an industry in itself, part and parcel of the dream machine; a self-satisfied America inviting itself to its own party. Charles C.B. Seymour's book *Self-Made Men* (1858) related 60 such paragons; Harriet Beecher Stowe recounted 19 American idols among them her brother, Henry Ward Beecher, who preached the American virtues of self-creation from his pulpit at Brooklyn's Plymouth Church.

We Honor the Self-made Man

We have sabotaged the meaning of the term. We honor the self-made man but destructively calculate his success, as he himself is subverted into calculating his own success, by the money he has amassed. It is that idealism itself which is sabotaged and supplanted, channeled into evaluating that idealism through the quantity of material wealth accumulated. We measure the man not for who he has become but rather for the things he has, the stuff he has acquired; money becomes the corrupted gauge of the realization of the ideal, and thereby a substitute for it and a demolisher of that very paradigm.

In the late nineteenth century a man established his worth by working diligently at his chosen vocation; he lived carefully and frugally within the confines of his class and thus achieved a certain moral wellbeing.

The new dream of success is seen in terms of limitless opportunity, sudden enormous riches achieved almost instantaneously without the plodding work previously associated with the accumulation of wealth. And there seems to be no commensurate obligation by way of morals or even simple manners attached to it.

The Confidence-Man

Herman Melville's satirical very modern novel *The Confidence-Man* (1857), dealing with problems of identity, sincerity, nihilism, existentialism, and absurdity but decorated incongruously with festoons of exuberant fancy, is attempting to instruct us in philosophical truths through the vehicle of nonsensical people talking absolute nonsense at length for the fun of it. The eponymous character, the stranger in the extreme, pushes fraudulent stock deals and solicits donations to fictitious charities on a Mississippi steamboat as it descends the magic river, a protean shape-shifter, he repeatedly reappears chameleon-like, separating the passengers from their money, reinforcing the author's belief that all that happens to a man in this life is only by way of joke and the confidence man is the jokester and joked upon, Shakespearian jester, delivering serious truths hidden in a likeness antic and ludicrous or merely absurd.

Confidence is seen not just as a method of deception, but as a needed and inevitable duplicity, a mutual surrender, a social necessity, which holds the corrupt world together. The refusal to suspend disbelief is a failure of imagination, which imagination allows surrender to the mass hallucination that affords us entrée to the social group. If we see things clearly we will be shut out or more precisely we will shut ourselves out, never able because of our clear vision, to join the pack and violently excluded from it.

American social activity, perhaps all social activity, is a confidence game. Melville presents an hallucinatory mirror image of the self-made man's success story, the promise of America's free-spirited economic engine into a menace, walking evidence of a ruined Eden.

That which makes Americans open, fluid and mobile also makes us an easy mark, exposing the naïve gullibility of the Yankee Republic. We, the down to earth Americans, don't demand impeccable references or rock solid personal recommendations. We pride ourselves on judging a man by what he is or what we see or what we think he is. The confidence man exploits this; he recreates himself, is born again and again only to dupe or to test his fellow man.

The writer's narrator is yet another form of the confidence man and comes to represent fiction itself; a mask from behind which a besieged Melville reaches out from his armed camp, fugitive and cloistered, as he sallies forth to meet the enemy, his audience.

He is different from Benjamin Franklin but not so absolutely different, who absconds from his indentured apprenticeship, shamelessly hypes his success to further prime his business, reinventing himself as a printer, scientist, inventor and founding father of a new country, a new world.

Typical Horatio Alger Story

Fitzgerald's own story was a typical Horatio Alger story: an older seemingly homosexual man, Monsignor Sigourney Fey, taking a much younger male under his wing, mentoring him, paving his way, praising him extravagantly, buying him the inevitable new suit of clothes (oh, this is the only part that may be missing.)

Horatio Alger served for a very brief period as a minister in Brewster, Massachusetts but was soon accused of practicing "evil deeds" on a young boy. A parish committee turned up further evidence of offences "too revolting to relate". Confronted by the evidence Alger "neither denied nor attempted to extenuate" the evidence "but received it with the apparent calmness of an old offender". Alger's father begged the committee not to prosecute legally. The committee decided that the scandal would do even more harm and cause "a serious injury to the church... the injury is greater the wider it is known." Alger took the next train to New York where he started a new beginning with young boys less likely to complain.

Alger cultivated New York's "street Arabs", those hawking newspapers, blacking boots, living in the streets or decrepit flop houses; he haunted the docks, wherever "friendless urchins" could be picked up; he bought them cheap with candy and small sums of money. Alger's lodgings, first in St. Mark's Place and after 1875 at boarding houses, became a "salon for street boys."

These young boys had a loyalty to Horatio Alger that rivalled the devotion of any whore to her fancy man pimp, or the prey of the pederast priests, revered by their game, their sycophants, not as good men but as saints on the fast track to early canonization. Alger's suck-ups felt an astonishing bond to their "patron and benefactor". "Mr. Alger could raise a regiment of boys in New York alone, who would fight to the death for him," gushed one of the minions shamelessly, shifting in his seat, suffering a sore ass, to a reporter in 1885. It is a symbiosis bred in hell: Alger mined them for their sordid stories which he sanitized or sterilized rather, in return for new clothes and safe haven from the mean streets; like a streetwalker elevated to the comparatively cushy life of the uptown brothel and a cleaner more limited clientele.

Wear One Face to Himself

"No man, for any considerable period, can wear one face to himself, and another to the multitude, without finally getting bewildered as to which may be the true."

This quote is actually carved in stone which attests to the durability of silliness. It's naïve. The human's skill at duplicity is myriad and enormously complex and didn't begin with the American confidence man. The practiced manipulator has a deep grab-bag of masks that he is constantly remolding as circumstances dictate. Whether simple actor, politician, salesman, promoter, entrepreneur or confidence man, any adept social being dexterously modulates his persona as circumstances and the people that he meets dictate. As for true? None of them are true or all of them are, or true in this context means nothing. The perfected pretense is the means by which we create who we are.

Through the ability to act convincingly we beget ourselves, become our own fathers. The trick is to pull off the act, to be a great actor. If others believe what we project and if we come to believe it ourselves, who is to say that is not who we are. If we pretend to be courageous, repeatedly act courageously, and are willing to die to prove it, we are courageous. If the mask doesn't slip and the wearer doesn't trip and falter, the mask becomes flesh and fuses fast to the bone, drills down arteries in blood like an enchanted plant, Jack's plant sinking roots which will catapult us to the heavens.

The more intelligent and cultivated a man is, the more multifaceted his mind, the more subtly and successfully he can deceive himself and conscript others to join in an enthusiastic chorus of his own personal subterfuge. An essential part of the performance is to believe utterly and completely in the show, which necessitates dyed-in-the-wool accomplices. It has been said that man has as many social selves as there are individuals who recognize him.

But it is celebrity, the loose little fanged sister of fame, which will devour us with its third rate play. Celebrity sinks poison roots into flesh, poisoning it, grows a mask that eats into the face like slow acting lye. Celebrity will destroy the good man. If he is stupid enough to tell the truth, they, who have granted him his moment in the scorching sun, will not take it away, rather they will turn it against him; mock him with it. But if he plays along, his elaborate lies will humiliate him. If he perfects too intricate a cover he risks self-annihilation.

The American Dream

The American Dream moves in time from a dream of perfect order and harmony to an anti-dream of total disorder and chaos; the American Dream transmutes into the America nightmare even as our eyes are glued to it. It represents a titanic theme of the shrinking and sleazing of American idealism. The idealism of the colonists and the Founding Fathers has metamorphosed into a consumerist ideology. An ethic of work and striving has degenerated into an empty-headed puzzled contemplation of "what shall we do, what do people do", of the nagging problem of filling empty meaningless time with worthless, mind-numbing activity, sports: golf and polo; travel: moving aimlessly from place to place, rootlessly taking up space, driven by leisure and consumption; a degenerate society that measures itself not by what it produces or what it creates but rather by what and how much it consumes and acquires.

The predatory cannibalism of American capitalism walks hand in hand with the Dream, which it has kidnapped, compelling it into becoming the prototype for all human relationships in America; the Beast walking down the aisle with Beauty is no secret prince. This degenerate offspring, the American Success Ethos, mercilessly tramples under foot all who are incapable of or unwilling to enter the ring.

But it is popular culture most of all that has turned the America Dream on its ear, made a mockery of it. The icons of mass culture are worshipped for the very reason that they are not worthy or deserving of their success; these personages are idolized because they are indistinguishable from the people who idealize them, with one big difference: money; they are poor people with ready cash, money to blow; big children with their pockets stuffed with big bucks; they have stepped in shit, won the lottery through a freak of fate, a cosmic disconnect: the inglorious empowerment of the talentless, of stupidity and bad taste run amuck. An American comedian hit the nail on the head by describing herself and her husband:

> "We are America's worst nightmare: white trash with money."

Plunges Herself into Gatsby's Shirts

The closest we come to a personal sexual encounter between Delsey and Nick's Gatsby is Delsey's first visit to Gatsby's house with Nick tagging along, the uninvited voyeur. Delsey is overcome with powerful emotion only when she plunges herself into Gatsby's shirts, his clothing, his cloaking, encompassing the wardrobe, coming into it at the same time ruining her meticulously applied maquillage in a rainstorm of seminal tears. This is the high point of the relationship as it is revealed to us in Nick's book: Delsey's love for Gatsby, consumerism joined inextricably with fetishism, things standing in and replacing genuine relationships, the power to purchase replacing the power to engage and control events and people. Cargo worship. Commodity fetishism.

Delsey swoons when Gatsby presents himself as a big man self-aggrandizing through his largess, securing prestige through the accumulation of goods and providing lavish entertainments. The more wealth a man could distribute, the more people subject to his obligation, the greater his prominence. Those unable to reciprocate in kind are reduced to mere "rubbish men". Consumerism becomes empty totemism, making sacred the goods in themselves which, rather that representing the sacred, supplants it and destroys any possibility of the sacrosanct. If you want to make a sworn enemy, relegate him to a rubbish man, entertain him beyond his capacity to entertain you in return. Even Samuel Johnson knew this.

Economy Is the Parent of Integrity

The following was for a time framed and hung on a corner of a wall in Landzman's office:

> "Economy is the parent of integrity, of liberty, and of ease; and the beauteous sister of temperance, of cheerfulness, and health; and profuseness is a cruel and crafty demon that gradually involves her followers in dependence and debts; that is, fetters them with 'irons that enter into their souls.' " Samuel Johnson

And directly beneath it was another quote, also framed, but more elegantly, which seems to cast a pall upon the words of the honorary Doctor Johnson and upon Lincoln also, perhaps making the point that we love to turn inferior men, with very particular talents, into our gods, mud gods which, by their worship, transmute us into mud creatures.

> "Samuel Johnson, a man of astounding intellectual arrogance, was a pompous windbag who decked out the most commonplace clichés with the gaudiest of worm-eaten feathers. He could be considered the bastard grandfather of the quotable quote, that clever sometimes witty piece of smooth but excessive glib verbiage which at first appears wise but upon examination is no more than flippant surface shine and upon deep study reveals itself often as absolute nonsense. I suggest that if ever you are subjected to a wiseacre teacher who spouts this joker with the self-satisfied smile which such fools are prone to, that you run, don't walk to

the nearest exit even if you have to trample over the more passive hearers lapping it up like neutered dogs and too dense to make way quickly enough. Johnson is proof that one can attempt to catalogue every word in a language without ever understanding the magic of a single word, that one can be regarded as a respected scholar while remaining a self-important fool.

"Let me add that he was clever at turning a cute phrase and was a fine comedian, no mean accomplishment, funnier than Mark Twain or Lincoln's favorite author Artemis Ward who wasn't funny in the least unless you're an ignorant shit-kicker starving for any amusement at all after the thrill of watching the cows being milked.

"Lincoln, of course, was famous for his interminable cracker-barrel stories which were so dull and naïve they drove intelligent men to want to strangle him. Before presenting 'The Emancipation Proclamation', Lincoln read to his Cabinet, with much uproarious enthusiasm on his part, the latest episode of Ward's, "Outrage in Utiky". Was this to annoy his cabinet; stick it to them, like the strike-it-rich host of a fancy dinner party picking his nose and grinning at the horrified guests who are required by good manners to suffer through it? But this host had chained his diners to the table and was squatting on the table defecating on their plates with his ass stuck in their face.

"Everyone should be required to read *Outrage in Utiky* to get a proper appreciation for the true quality of Lincoln's mind. Lincoln was an unabashed entertainer who played shamelessly to the low crowd who ate it up. A devoted purveyor of third rate 'literature' he recited a poem by William Knox, *Mortality*, so often that people thought he had written it himself and unfortunately he wished he had:

> 'I would give all I am worth, and go in debt, to be able to write so fine a piece as I think that is.' "

Lincoln was always willing to represent great powerful corporations, railroads particularly and had no reservations about recommending the eviction of squatters who farmed railroad land.

There is nothing wrong with admiring the worthy traits of dead powerful men but there is something juvenile and imbecilic about the need to turn them into gods; idols blown out of perfectly good rock mountainsides. It diminishes all of us.

The Most Important Day of Your Life

Found among Bucknell's papers, unnumbered, uncatalogued and undated:

> The most important day of your life is the day you figured out why you were born and the second most important day is the day you were born, which day has absolutely no importance

316

whatsoever if you don't eventually establish the most important day.

Racket and Racketeering

Discovered in Landzman's archives, catalogued by his executors, document number 2947, untitled and undated:

> Penetrating, getting underneath to some imagined significance beyond all the racket and racketeering:

> "Shh, be quiet... you talk too much. Blah... blah... blah... blah... blah... blah... blah...."

> ...overwrought lowlifes pontificating, enunciating, mercifully out-of-print longeurs resuscitated from the dead; fevered undergraduates on soapboxes in some interminable graduate seminar in the pit of hell lorded over by a pompous ass with tenure who doesn't know enough to tell them all to shut the fuck up and to shut up himself, forever.

> He blessed the bells as the bell tower tolled the time; he blessed the bells for their solidity, the solidity of their sound; they tolled and reassured him.

Flawless Memory

Thomas Bucknell, from his uncatalogued archives, untitled, undated:

> He prided himself on his flawless memory; but was it failing him? Or was he failing it? Was it working the way he wanted it to? Had he so disciplined himself in the rigorous repression of unacceptable facts that he had irreparably injured his sense of what was real, what had actually happened? Was he rewriting history or simply living in the rewrite?
>
> Had he fine-tuned his senses to a musical chord vibrating, pulsing only in his own locked head?

The Bombing of Bucharest

There is in the Bureau's, the FBI's files, a transcript which recounts in vivid very personal detail the entry of Romania into the War in August 1916 and the bombing of Bucharest by German Zeppelins, like something out of a dark fairytale, on August 28th, September 4th and 25th. The Zeppelin LZ 86 was mortally damaged by return fire from the ground during its second attack on September 26th. The speaker joined with Romanian troops and together they were able to halt the Central Powers' advance into Moldavia.

The speaker characterized this period in his life as marked by unrepeatable epiphanies. He remembers especially his entrance into a great room and that a "spectral glittering light" had turned it into:

> "an enchanted mansion... I practiced for years the formulaic regimen of resurrecting that instant of precipitous, intuitive perception, the insight into the reality, the essential meaning of everything, and in reliving it would discover again the unchanged equanimity, the complete composure, the transcendent feeling of oneness with the universe. I would slip into it as into a sliver of time, which was yet timeless, devoid of duration, lacking beginning, middle, or end. When I grappled with attacks of debilitating depression, I would find refuge in returning to the golden green light of those magical afternoons. Though the state of ultimate bliss, the beatitude, was identical, it was now unbearable to suffer; it intensified my sadness that much more, because I knew the world to which that great room belonged was a world gone forever."

I remember witnessing a conversation of a man telling his wife that the war years, the Second World War that is, something he had no doubt told her before, that they were the happiest years of his life, which she felt reflected on his relationship with her. She was dumbstruck:

> "The first half of the war you were in bloody mortal combat, the second half you spent in a prisoner of war camp. How the hell could they have been the happiest years of your life?"

"I know it sounds strange, but they were... the happiest that is. Maybe it was the comradeship, all in it together, maybe the simplicity, the moral simplicity. Things were so clear. They've never been as clear since. Everything is so muddied, confused. There is no loyalty anymore."

The transcript about Bucharest is unclear about who exactly is speaking. Obviously if it is Nick speaking it is an act of imagination; he wasn't over there long enough to witness, much less fight. But then Nick was a writer of fiction, a skilled, practiced liar. I read this passage to my grandfather who said that he liked the passage, that it was very poetic but that he had never personally witnessed the bombing of Bucharest by the Zeppelins, something he would certainly carry with him forever.

Romanian forces joined by the Russians held off the Austrians, Germans, Bulgarians and the Ottoman Turks without any of the promised troops from the French, the English or any of the other Allies; he considered this a betrayal. However, he was careful in his wording as he usually was, but more so; he did not say specifically that he did not fight there. He had among his medals a very beautiful blue cross which he called *The Star of Romania* and I'd heard from one of his surviving men that he'd fought as an officer of Romania, loaned for a limited time by the allies. But his men were always guilty of purposely spreading wild and woolly stories of absurd escapades the Colonel, not being everywhere at once, could not possibly have experienced.

My grandfather reminded me unnecessarily that over 290,000 Romanian soldiers had died fighting, over 8% of their population and he added with explosive, stinging emphasis that Montenegro, little Montenegro down on the Adriatic sea, with less than half a million people, lost 15,000 of its men, that its "warm little heart" had been irremediably rent and soaked the soil with real blood as no man who ran away could possibly understand.

The passage about the enchanted mansion is more than nostalgia. It is a view that deems linear history and time itself as an unnatural construct imposed artificially on a resisting mind, a mind that can find meaning only in going back, beginning again and again, the interminable return, the magic moment eternally relived sacramentally. This gives what is disparaged as nostalgia a philosophical foundation and thereby a self-serving rationalization which justifies or rather glorifies and sanctifies living in the past, the past reborn. This of course could be regarded as a prison house, a special circular hell never to escape from; for those who so fervently want to believe in progress. Can a man's entire philosophy, his entire life, be no more than an attempt to rationalize what is really an unhealthy fixation on the past; an intricate and convoluted validation for what is really only a gussied up form of nostalgia?

> "The past which men create for themselves is a place where thought is unnecessary and happiness inevitable." Lippmann.

"Some memories are realities, and are better than anything that can ever happen to one again." Cather

Perhaps, as I have supposed before, the Director's spooks just wanted to fill in the time and picked their favorite pieces from books and magazines or from their own skewed memories. The passage: "I would slip into it as into a slice of time devoid of duration, without beginning, middle, or end" was underlined and initialed with the note "explore further." But I have been unable to determine who the initials belong to; they're a kind of a logo or brand, stylized, indecipherable in any ordinary alphabet, which means nothing.

The Melted Snows of Yesteryear

Someone said that Fitzgerald and his heroes do not yearn for the melted snows of yesteryear, they mourn for their lost capacity to respond to those snows.

Fitzgerald himself lamented the loss of those illusions that give such color to the world that you don't care whether things are true or false as long as they partake of the magical lost glory?

At the end of "Winter Dreams" Green, the main character is told that the beauty of his dream girl has faded:

> "For the first time in years the tears were streaming down his face. But they were for himself now. He did not care about mouth and

eyes and moving hands. He wanted to care but could not. For he had gone away and he could never come back any more. The gates were closed, the sun was gone down, and there was no beauty but the gay beauty of steel that withstands all time. Even the grief he could have borne was left behind in the country of illusion, of youth of the richness of life, when his winter dreams had flourished....

"Long ago... long ago there was something in me, but now that thing is gone. Now that thing is gone, that thing is gone. I cannot cry. I cannot care. That thing will come back no more."

A portrayal not just of first love, but how a writer exploited the uncorrupted memories of the idealistic naiveté of his imagined youth and its bittersweet emotion to shamelessly feed not only his profession, as a writer, but his very existence.

The Green Light Always Shines

The door is always the same story. The green light always shines brighter in the mind. In reality it was impossible to see the green light from that distance; it was visible only in the fevered brain. I will not bore you with my story; it is always the same. I am not going to bore you to tears with a love story, of a young man. It is always the same. Does not the story always transport us back in time? Does that do us any good except as a narcotic, a drug induced sleep; to dream of past happy moments? Somewhere up the road we are looking to find sanity or clarity or oblivion.

Lean Hungry Men

The words of Thomas Bucknell, a copy secreted out of his archives by an employee of his executor, undated; allegedly removed by the executors from the archives to a separate vault and now unavailable for examination:

> The world owes all its progress to the dispossessed, the disenchanted, the lean hungry men with thick wallets or no wallets at all, who look around and see nothing but shit. You want happy? Go to the islands, the Bahamas, a desert island fed with imported water; go there, you stupid fucks, all you high muckety-mucks, go party and get sloshed, served by ostensibly obsequious Blacks who secretly reign over the place and hate your white guts and bide their time waiting for you to build their land up with your hard earned bucks; then they will serve you up on your own plates, sitting in your house, your very chair until the whole thing comes crashing down around their stupid ears for lack of maintenance, which, however, will take years.

In a Forty-Second Street Cellar

In the middle of the summer of 1922 Landzman drove in with his persistent trespasser Carramel, to the City, booming traffic and the deafening blare of horns. In a Forty-Second Street cellar full of smoke, heat and din pushed uselessly around by wobbly ceiling fans seeming to work their way loose by stirring the thick air, creating the illusion of ventilation, they met for lunch. Batting away the haze of the suffocating cigarette smoke burning his eyes, squinting away the brilliance of noon outside, yielding to blindness in the comparatively black interior his eyes sensed shadows shifting in the distance and the figure of what might have been a man began to enlarge and clarify itself, rising out of the smoke, assuming a familiar countenance.

Landzman:

'Mr. Carramel, this is my friend Mr. Wolf.'

Carramel had been pestering Landzman for a "head to head" with Mr. Wolf, hoping to gain a "connection", a stock deal to "line his pockets". Landzman excused himself after a hurried lunch leaving the table for an "urgent telephone call". Landzman didn't want to hear any of this. He wanted deniability. He wanted to be able to deny that he had ever had this meeting with Mr. Carramel.

Landzman:

"Enjoy your coffee... I'll be right back... gentlemen."

Lazarus Wolf was a large, powerful man with the deep bass voice, the trained, picked voice of a radio man announcing the morning news or a stage actor who had toured the provinces in the high heat of summer. He played King Lear when he was young. He looked like Lee J. Cobb when Cobb played in the movie "Anna and the King", but leaner and hungrier and without the make-up. If you did a movie Cobb might do him justice combined with a Chaim Topol or a Walter Mathau, but fit enough to run the hundred yard dash or go the distance, ten rounds in the ring. Wolf fought professionally in his youth. Sam Jaffe as he portrayed Erwin "Doc" Riedenschneider in *The Asphalt Jungle* would be a good third choice. Jerry Orbach would be very good; number one.

Wolf would indulge himself in a very slight Yiddish-German lilt and Yiddish locutions, self-consciously, to amuse himself, like he was play acting. This was a highly educated man, graduated from City College and NYU law school. He spoke in a strange mix of rich ironic street slang interspersed with a seeding from his prodigious vocabulary which he was unafraid to broadcast liberally. He had no tolerance for ignorance. This was back in the day when they gave elocution lessons in the public schools and students labored, hunched over long vocabulary lists in the public library; when even the city school teachers, proper spinsters, spoke in unembarrassed Mid-Atlantic accents and cracked your knuckles with an oak ruler if you didn't imitate them correctly.

Wolf's Flunky:

"Mr. Wolf, I'm sorry... half the time I don't know what you're talking about. I don't know these big words."

Wolf gave him a book. From that day on all his flunkies studied vocabulary like dutiful schoolboys.

Wolf sometimes spoke quickly with a machine gun rapidity, rattling non-stop, which some took for browbeating, which it definitely was, not giving them time to breathe much less to think; that it was purposely hard to follow, to trip them up; their guilty conscience filling in the missed words and as a result saying the wrong thing; what Wolf wanted to hear.

Wolf did not relish this meeting with Nick, feeling put upon, looking for trouble. I don't think he fully understood the implied quid pro quo, payment for services to be rendered but rendered more to Landzman than to Wolf. They were unequal partners and Wolf didn't like the risk, hanging himself out like this, to dry, for an unknown quantity, for a foreign loose cannon rolling around the deck of his own personal ship.

Wolf extended his broad, flat hand like a weapon, for examination, with not very well-concealed contempt.

Wolf:

"I understand you're a college man."

Nick:

"Yes, New Haven."

Wolf:

"Yeh... I went to New Haven too... never liked the fucking place.

"Me and Mr. Landzman opened a play there... it bombed. We took it to New York anyway... ran 480 performances there... just goes to show you New Haven don't count for shit."

Nick:

"Yes... Jay told me you invest together in shows. But New Haven..."

Wolf, insulted, purposefully interrupting, stepping on Nick's lines, every chance he got, squashing them like quick little bugs trying to run out from under a rug:

"I never invested in a fucking 'show' in my entire life. You mean that musical shit. I would die a slow painful death first. They make me sick... in the pit of my stomach sick... so I want to throw-up... vomit all over the place. I get sick just thinking about it. I invest only in serious drama... promising young writers or the classical theater... Chekhov.... Ibsen... Shakespeare."

Abruptly, as if coming to his senses, waking from a momentary lapse of consciousness, realizing what was said:

"Who is this 'Jay' character you're talking about?"

Nick, hesitating, beginning to realize he has said something wrong:

"Jay Landzman."

Wolf:

"You mean Mr. Landzman... James to his very... very close friends.

"This nickname shit always rubbed me the wrong way... got under my skin.

"This Bubba, Chuck... Curley... Billy Joe, BooBoo, Doolittle, Billy Bob, Billy Rae, JohnBoy, Cooter, Clyde, Clitus, Woody, Mooney. It's for retarded hillbillies... or is that a redundancy... retarded hillbillies.

"Jay...? You call him this? You have his permission?

"He told you to call him this?

Nick:

"No... but Delsey sometimes called him...."

Wolf:

"'Delsey'! What the... that's a fucking cow's name for chrissake.

"These crazy rich sons-a-bitches are as bad as the inbred slack-jawed cracker yokels, their Anglo Saxon brethren, with their asinine monikers already. Cookie, Cece, Paige, Piper, Peachy, Pippa, Polly, Posie, Buffy, Bunny, Bitsy, Booboo, Bambi, Heide, Happy, Sneezy, Kiki, Dede, Mimi, Missy, Muffy, Mindy, Maisie, Daisy, Sissy, Tibby, Topsy, Turvey. What an abomination... enough to make me want to toss my lunch. These people deserve to be separated from their money... cavorting like buffoons... they lack dignity, all sense of propriety. They give money a bad name."

Nick:

"Well... you see... her grandfather had a farm... a kind of gentleman's farm... where she spent the summer... as a child... over a thousand of the most beautiful acres and she had this favorite cow... the prettiest cow you ever did see... like out of an advertisement for milk at the A&P... and she loved this cow more than anything on earth...

Wolf, raising his voice:

"Stop... enough... enough already about the cow. I don't want to hear anything about any cows... goats or pigs either for that matter.

"Are we talking about this same twat he fucked down in Louisville... who's setting up the...?

Nick:

"Yes... but... but. (long, frightened pause) Don't you mean Charleston?"

Wolf:

"What the fuck... again you're at it. Does it really matter Mr. Carramel? Think about it. Who fucking cares where she comes from? This Annabel... or whatever.

"Are you a girl Mr. Carramel?

Nick:

"What...?

Wolf:

"I said... are you a girl?

Nick:

"What...?

Wolf:

"You say 'what' one more fucking time and I will blow your fucking brains out... I guaruntee. (the run and tee accentuated like a Cajun.)

"Are you a girl, Mr. Carramel?

Nick:

"No... but... but..."

Wolf:

"First the 'whats' now the 'buts'. You are trying my patience, mightily. Maybe we should have you examined... by a doctor, maybe, a proctologist psychiatrist... to get your head out from up your ass.

"There are three men in this restaurant watching us very closely... three more belong to Mr. Landzman but they're busy watching him. I want you to look around at them. They are not as inconspicuous as they would like to believe...

actually they stick out like a sore thumb... it's really comical when you think about it... they've got big heaters bulging out of their pockets... they might as well stick a sign around their neck... but that's okay... it's the deterrence factor. Like big dogs they scare people... just to look at them. What particular persons that don't last never figure out is that there is always a fourth man... that even the three others don't know about... he's tougher, quicker and smarter than the other three put together... you'd never be able to pick him out... and it is this fourth man that always saves the day. The three men, in fact, very often serve only as a distraction... like a decoy. Don't ever tell them I said that... it would hurt their feelings.

But you see... right now they all see that I am getting agitated and as a result they are getting very agitated... they don't like when I get agitated. It is their job to see that I don't get agitated.

"If you continue in this vein... I will give them a sign... two of them... it will only take two... will drag you out of here so I can personally shoot you in the nearest alley. I will shoot you in the head twice until your brains come out... so there is no mistake. If you resist they will shoot you down right on the spot... right here... in front of all these people. Then they will leave town... for the West Coast... I have interests on the West Coast. They will be gone for years until the whole thing blows over... it will blow over... it always does. But they will most likely decide to stay on the West Coast... it's nice out there... the weather... the ocean... palm trees... that's if you like palm trees... I, myself can take them or leave them... these men will sink roots... it's inevitable. I will miss them a great deal... good men are hard to find... but I will manage.

"Now... once again... one more time... so there's no question... are you a girl Mr. Carramel and is Mr. Landzman fucking you?"

Nick:

"No... no... absolutely not."

Wolf:

"So... if you're not a girl and not being fucked by Mr. Landzman then please do not call him Jay... not ever... not in my presence, or anywhere I might hear about it from someone else. People are always carrying tales to me... like they're doing me some sort of big favor, like I want nothing better than to hear.

"If a little twat wants to call him Jay that's a personal matter between the twat and Mr. Landzman... twats do and say very silly things... it can't be helped. Mr. Landzman understands this... one could say he's an expert on twats. There are certain dispensations that accrue to the station... being a recognized twat, that is. Do we understand each other, Mr. Carramel?"

Nick, shaking visibly, not knowing what to say:

"Yes.

Wolf:

"Say it one more time so there's no misunderstanding. Say: 'Yes I understand' ".

Nick:

"Yes, I understand."

Changing the subject clumsily in something of a panic, never knowing when to shut up, digging himself deeper:

"Mr. Landzman tells me you're a man of culture, that you're a patron of the arts... sit on the board of the Metr..."

Wolf, interupting:

"What? Man of culture? What does the hell does that mean? 'Man of culture.' Everybody wants to pigeon-hole everybody else, put 'em in a box... so they can make simple sense of something that's not so simple.

For instance... here, in this country, the detective mystery book is looked down on as not literature. But a writer who writes of loftier subjects, of 'social significance' even if he's a stinking writer is taken seriously. This is the 'parvenu's insecurity', if I can borrow that fancy phrase.

"But the man who can take the humble murder mystery and turn it into art... this is a

334

magician... this is the man I respect, that I can sit down and talk to. Who was it that called the fictional private detective: the new mythic hero, investigating a cultural response to universal unconscious fantasy and plunging into it without understanding society's narcissistic fixations? Boy... what a crock-a-shit. Do these bums even listen to themselves? But he's on to something... No? These writers also got murder out of the vicar's stupid rose garden and gave it back to people who are really good at it... murderers.

But it may take a real wizard to write shit one day and literature the next and not to carry the stink of the shit into the area where he lives. What serious writer dares to stray to write popular fiction in the optimistic hope of coming back by underground tunnels and devious ways into the light again, dripping with darkness? Mostly they dig down, accidently break into sewers and drown from the darkness or are asphyxiated by sewer gas.

As far as what is literature...? I know it when I see it. As for what it is, this I leave to the fat fucks... like Edmund Wilson who has the distinction in his own self-described 'serious literature' of making fornication as dull as a railway timetable... so dull that you would want no part of it... this is not an easy trick... take my word for it.

"I got side-tracked... I was off on a tangent... the tangents always get me. Getting back to the subject at hand... what the fuck do you know about culture?

Nick:

"No... I just...

Wolf, interrupting, more calmly now, getting control of himself:

"'No... I just...' You know you're a very annoying person... very annoying... What are we going to do with you? You don't learn. You don't listen.

"Whenever I hear the term culture... careful, so nobody notices, I chamber a round in my old Luger... from the war... a souvenir... pried from the cold, stiff fingers of a dead Heinie... his handsome face and blond hair pressed down in the mud... like he was nothing... and I finger it like a talisman... and laugh loud to myself.

"People who prattle on about culture are hard to stomach and don't know their ass from their elbow. These are the crumb bums that ruin it, walking around with their noses high in the air like the ground stinks... the ground does stink, sometimes... especially with people pissing on it... but not always. They have the attitude that I'm better than you because I appreciate real art. Fuck 'em... that's what I say.

"You see these cuff buttons...? Take a good close look... Do you know what they are?"

336

Nick, leaning hesitantly in to look, but not too close, afraid it was a trap, afraid he would have his head bitten off:

"Molars?"

Wolf:

"Molars? Molars... yes... very good... (like Nick had just passed an important quiz and won a contest) human molars... molars pulled from a screaming man without any anesthesia. I used to practice dentistry. I like to keep my hand in... my finger in the pie, so to speak... to keep in practice... so I don't lose the touch.

"I dream that overnight people won't want to buy pearls anymore (Nick at this point knew nothing of Wolf's pearl business)... that they'll come to their senses... that they'll regard them as silly or they'll only buy them in little cheap cloth bags for pennies like glass marbles. I worry about such things. I have a nest egg of course... what man in my position does not... but a man must keep gainfully employed... for his peace of mind and to keep himself sharp... to keep his edge. You never know... if everything goes to shit I have something to fall back on... a cushion... to catch me if I fall... my dentistry... my safety net... my first profession.

"I worked hard to be a good dentist... my parents scrimped and saved to send me to school. I wanted to be a writer but my father told me this is not a career for a real man... this is a hobby...

something to do on the side. When you make a living as a dentist... when you're comfortable... independent... then you can write all you like. But until then... you can write on Sundays... evenings... on vacation... during lunchtime... early in the morning instead of reading the newspaper. This way you can write literature... by your own standards without having to please anyone but yourself. Chekhov was a medical doctor first... the greatest writer there ever was besides Shakespeare. It is Anton Chekhov, not Dostoevsky or Tolstoy who is the greatest of the Russian writers... the grandson of a freed serf, son of a ruined owner of a humble general store... Chekhov supported his family from the age of sixteen and put himself through medical school... started writing junk... pulp... made good money at it... but once he graduated to literature he never turned to writing garbage again. And the garbage didn't suck his soul out. He could probably jump from one to the other without compromising his integrity; like it was a game... and he was on top of it. He was independent... his own man. He liked to live well... yes... I grant you... but not a slave to the dollar or the ruble... never having to demean and disgrace himself... to grovel in front of rich men... always able to hold his head high. I know there was that rich publisher, Savorin or whatever... the money bags. But he seems to have held his own.

"It is possible to write trash without selling your soul especially if it pays well... but it ain't easy...

it ain't easy... Maybe it beats teaching writing in Podunk U. But you have to keep your wits about you... leave plenty of time to write the good stuff... be able to change gears and you need a big nest egg so you never feel forced to write the shit. It's too easy to drown in it.

"My uncle... my father's brother... who I never liked very much... told me I should be a college teacher... a professor of literature and language... as training to be a writer... if that's really what I wanted to be. I told him this was no good... that they were not 'analogous' fields as he said but instead were mutually exclusive ... had nothing whatever to do with each other. The college world of literature is a totally different industry like meat packing or car tires... only they don't make anything... not anything that you can use. The papers they churn out on fiction have nothing to do at all with writing fiction... they're not only useless they're probably harmful to a writer. It's a recycling business, a boondoggle to keep otherwise intelligent people uselessly employed and taking money for it... trying to capture precious chemicals from smoke. I can say categorically that if you want to be a great writer or even a decent one stay the hell out of the universities... they wouldn't know great literature if it came up and bit them in the ass.

"Good writing is the highest form of human endeavor with the exception of the love for another human being. I have promised myself

to write one good book before I die. And if I fail...
so be it... at least I will have given it my best
shot. What more can you ask of a man? Good
writing is magic... you stare into a sheet, blank
white, slice open an artery, figuratively, and
bleed into the bottomless inkwell until there is
nothing left to give and you become rapturous...
probably from loss of blood.

"Life is funny that way... it pays to think
ahead... to be prepared for any eventuality. I was
especially good at difficult extractions... they
would call me in for special, tricky cases...
impacted wisdom teeth. I was a master at
extracting impacted, infected wisdom teeth. It's
not as easy as it looks. It's a matter of
technique.

"This screaming man called me by a nickname...
he owed me money too... very sad... a
debauched gambler... a disgusting, immoral
person... robbed food out of his children's
mouths to play the ponies... to bet on the
future... stole from the present to give everything
to wager on a future that is problematic at best.

I think deep down all of these gambling
degenerates want to lose or don't care one way
or another. They ache for the fix... the high...
that adrenalin jolt... like electrocution... they
hunger for that brush with death... no... they
want to dance the tango with a homicidal insane
lady who wants only to eat them up or teach
them crazy dance steps... hang on to her like a

bucking bronco while she's working to sink her teeth into their flesh... lie in the mud with the hooves coming down on their head... wallow in their ruin. I got carried away. I don't know what comes over me.

"You live in the past... you live in the future... the here and now is what counts... the only real world... the present instant... the past is no good when we want to dwell in it... it robs us... we squander our time reliving all of our mistakes or fantasize about some magic moment that never was... we give up our lives for a dream of what we think happened... the future full of anxiety and anticipation... both rob us of the now... strangle us... stifle us... smother us in its soft down bed.

"Grab tight hold... the here and now and live... live for God's sake...

"The past can never be recovered but truly it can never be escaped. We carry it with us forever like a sack on our back; it makes us who we are. Without memory we have no identity.... We carry it with us forever; it makes us who we are.

"I don't know. No... No... this only sounds good but I don't know if it's true. We are not the prisoners of our history... mostly but not absolutely.

"Besides, memory is just another fiction which we create.

"I got lost on a side track. Sometimes I think too loud to myself.

"Another thing... another thing is you have to pay attention... pay close attention! Most people sleep fitfully through life like drowsing through a movie... a picture they never heard of... to be startled awake by people stepping on their toes getting out of the aisle. It's too late, when they finally realize it's over. They discover how little a light the sputtering, trembling glimmer of consciousness is and have no real clue as to what exactly the movie was about. They try to divine meaning from the closing credits while people are pushing and poking against them telling them the movie is over and they're holding up the line. You can't hide and stay for another showing... the ushers are uniformed alike... they look like doormen... or those stupid looking toy soldiers on display at Kensington Palace with those high furry hats and they keep close watch wielding old-fashioned batons... not those with the rubber cushions on both ends. Don't mistake it for the fancy stick either, that's passed from runner to runner in a relay race... make no mistake it's a cudgel or truncheon and it's deadly. You only get one ticket... that's it. They don't let you stay for another showing. Thems the rules. It's a real shame though... the second time around you'd maybe learn to stay awake and might actually discover what the movie was about. Life is like money... both act like spilt quicksilver in a nest of cracks. Try to chase after that.

"Who was it that said?

> 'It is death that makes a mockery of life. We struggle to a level of consciousness, claw our way up, as if for no other purpose than to inflict upon ourselves the excruciating pain of the awareness of its fleetingness.'

"This was a wise man who said this. This is a man who knew.

"This stock 'deal' I am told you are looking for is not what you think it is, not some pump and dump... not a swindle of any kind like you imagine... not counterfeit certificates or anything like that. With such things I would never get involved and certainly Mr. Landzman, who is a very upright man, would never go near such a thing... not so much as touch such illegality. This is simply about information... nothing more nothing less... knowing what other people don't know. This is Mr. Landzman's specialty, his genius... if you want to know the truth. Where he gets his information I couldn't tell you even if I knew. This knowledge is invaluable... it's like money and must be kept scarce.... Otherwise the stock moves suspiciously and the jig is up. The more people who know... the less valuable the information. Giving you this information is like handing you money but more than that it is giving you the power to make that very money less valuable so that others who come after you suffer. We supply the information in a very particular order to a very select few. If you are near the top of the list you have the power to ruin it for those further down on the list... if you speak out of class... shoot off your mouth. It's like giving you the keys to the bank and you set the money on fire instead of only taking a reasonable amount for yourself. If you are chosen you will be given this information in a way that can never be traced to Mr. Landzman or myself. You must never speak directly to me or Mr. Landzman about these matters in any way whatsoever... ever again. You may receive a telephone call from someone you don't know or have some strange person strike up a conversation with you totally from out of the blue. He'll say something very out of the ordinary with very exact words like: 'I understand you have an interest in Oklahoma oil stocks'... those words must not be different in any way... not so much as one word out of place. And you must answer 'Texas' so he knows you understand and you're the right man. But never answer with your special word unless the words you are given are exactly right.

"By your look you seem to hesitate. He who hesitates is lost.

"Jesus! I have the unquiet feeling this is the first time you've ever done anything like this? What a fine lollipop you are! What are you going to do next... get down on your knees and pray for heavenly guidance? Never trust a man who gets down on his knees for any reason. George

Washington never got on his knees, especially not in church. God doesn't want you to grovel... it's unbecoming. Maybe you should talk it over with your grandmother or your old nanny. You did have a nanny didn't you Mr. Filtchcroft? Of course you had a nanny; all you fellows had nannys.

"Nothing... but nothing... is without risk... nothing is one thousand percent. Rarely, but sometimes... just sometimes... the information is bogus. People lie, even in secret conversations, even to themselves... especially to themselves.

"I don't know Mr. Filtchcroft. Can you be trusted to keep a secret? Or do you like to play the big man... proving to people how smart you are... what a skillful picker of stocks you are... how you're in the know, privy to the inside scoop. I'm afraid, Mr. Filtchcroft, that you're going to throw a wild and unpredictable monkey wrench into the works. But what you don't understand, is that when the busted machinery comes flying apart it will take your head off first. It won't be a pretty sight... you standing there without your head. And these things that you contemplate: are they in fact wild or just downright stupid? No matter how orderly you think your existence is, no matter how well planned, death waits for you... lurking just around the corner... for you to cross the street... and you will cross the street.

"What are you going to do with all this money you're going to come into?

"You want to gamble on some stock deal...? put money in thy purse?

"If you're intent on going to hell... at least get there in a more pleasurable way.

"Chasing after money for its own sake is a kind of homicide ... more like self-slaughter, very often gory. Money must come to you by indirection without ever hunting it down... like a wild animal which you coax and which finally comes to you entirely on its own when you're not looking... and there it is, out of the blue... all of a sudden, this huge creature, scary to look at, licking your hand like a friendly dog. And if the big beast stays in the woods... sticking out its big nose for you to see between the leaves... coming teasingly close... but never close enough... That's alright too. You have a roof over your head... food on the table... clothes on your back... some good books you buy cheap from the secondhand store... maybe even a rare public library you discovered by accident... like a jewel in the forest... that's hidden away so the bums don't ferret it out... to piss on the chair cushions, blow their nose in the books and generously share with everyone some rare highly communicable disease which drops liberally from the scabs they're covered with.

What more do you really need? This is America... no one starves to death. Do your best and do what you love and the rest will follow or maybe not. I'm this way with my pearls.

To think always of money is to think the way America wants you to think... This is what the dream has become... what the country has become... This is the trap they lay... This is the way it grinds your face into the dirt... the mud... with the boot pressing on the back of your head... then you will never be your own master.

"Save your money and save your life.

"But remember what the great Roman, Seneca said: 'a great fortune is a great slavery.' Well... it doesn't have to be... not if you play your cards right. You have to learn to delegate... to find people you can trust.

"Never forget this. Money can make you free... so you never have to humble yourself to the boss man whether that boss man is an unreasonably demanding client or an overseer with a whip. Money gives you the freedom to be yourself... to create yourself... to recreate the world... With money you buy yourself out of slavery... ransom your soul, from the heavy oppression of the clock, lift it with your own hands, from off your back. With money you buy maybe a really nice house, in a good neighborhood, a strong, solid house made of brick or stone, with a full basement... the mortgage paid off, money in a protected account and you can say FUCK YOU to any man. You do a good job and they don't like it... you say FUCK YOU. You tell them honestly and reasonably what you think and they give you trouble... you say FUCK YOU. You open your heart and arms to them and they turn their back on you... you say FUCK YOU. FUCK YOU. FUCK YOU. This is the only way for a man to stay on his feet, to stay alive and breathe clean air. FUCK YOU. FUCK YOU. These two words are the free man's prayer. It is better to save your money, to live like a monk if necessary, to pile up the greenbacks in tall stacks like armor for your soul in order to be able to say one thing and one thing only: FUCK YOU.

"I pity these poor ambitious young fellows who think they are so smart and that believe that the world is going to recognize just how smart they are and reward them... give them their due. This is bullshit. This is what the swindlers in power want you to believe. Make no mistake: it is the scum that rises to the top.

"In the classroom the most intelligent are beaten down and methodically broken by the idiot teachers who rein like despots; who deep down regard intelligence as a threat to their small brains and puny little egos. It's the ass-kissers with brown, shit-stinking noses, the shameless suck-ups who become the teacher's pet. By deciding to educate everyone we really educate no one. Where are the Shakespeares? Every single year, maybe twice a year, a Shakespeare is systematically squashed like a bug on the classroom floor. You can turn in the most keenly honed and magisterial prose and the drudge up front with terminal dandruff and the yellow teeth isn't going to give it an A... he's going to give it an F... he's going to flunk you out if he can because of the fact that you exist... can exist... and that existence threatens all that he stands for... his secure, mediocre, stupid, meaningless existence.

It's these morons on top who want to get rid of intelligence tests. They claim that the test is not predictive of either academic or worldly success. This is absolutely true. But this is an argument against the classroom and the world. I have never met a man who tested with a high IQ who wasn't extremely intelligent and worthy of better than he got. This world is not kind to intelligent men. Many were ruined, shattered men... many criminals, some in jail. What intelligent man could live in this ridiculous world without striking out, without rebelling in some visceral, violent way?

"I have been asked why I have chosen this life for myself... but I'm not sure that I have chosen it... Perhaps it chose me. I am not sure that I am much different from the artist or the warrior... the hunter... the fanatic or the martyr for that matter... At all cost I wanted to avoid an everyday life.

I want uncertainty and doubt... I want turmoil and fight... I don't want to live in peace... How can any man make peace with this world the way it is...? And if the world makes war on me God help the world.

"But this is neither here nor there... I don't know why I carry on like this... it's entirely beside the point..."

Landzman returned from his call, interrupting the never ending narrative of Wolf, his particular one man show, the well-worn, well-honed wise Mensch routine that he loved to indulge so much.

There's a story of Wolf holding a gun on a man he was trying to decide whether or not to kill and speaking at very great length, not really to his target but more to himself, trying to plead the case one way then the other; the man had finally had enough and couldn't take it anymore, blurting out:

"Are ya gonna talk me to death or ya gonna shoot me?"

Without so much as another word Wolf shot him then and there, three times in the chest. If the man had only shut up and listened he might have lived to an old age; it would have been worth the suffering. He was a wise guy; he liked the style of what he was saying, the quick, flippant backtalk... how it sounded in his head and he paid for his smartass quip with everything he had... his life.

Landzman:

"I'm sorry I took so long. I hope you men have enjoyed your conversation."

Wolf:

"Immensely... we have to do this again... soon. It's so nice to make new and interesting friends... it's always a pleasure to meet cultured... high-toned people... people who understand what intelligent conversation is. But I must be leaving. I've stayed too long as it is. I don't wish to outstay my welcome. I have much business to attend to."

Wolf rose from the table with great ceremony, putting his hand on Landzman's shoulder as if it were a sacramental ritual, a laying on, a benediction, leaning in close to his ear so only Landzman could hear but looking at Carramel the whole time with a steely squint in his eye and a forced, crooked smile:

"Where did you dig up this putz?"

When Wolf had left, Nick, visibly shaken, opined with a quaver in his voice:

"I think the stock deal is off.

"I don't think he likes me very much."

Landzman:

"No... not at all... what makes you say that?

"You didn't call him Lazarus did you?

Nick:

"No... no... of course not."

Landzman:

351

"Good... good.

"He's very European, Continental... old school... old world... proper manners are very important to him. He's out of ... not of this time. He's a real gentleman... a man of honor... very upright... lives by a strict code. You must never offend him. He's very sensitive... sentimental even... maybe a little high strung."

Nick:

"How can you call him a man of honor? He threatened to kill me... over nothing... nothing."

Landzman:

"It couldn't have been nothing to him. You must have said something that gave him offence... some sort of insult. He wouldn't kill you without a good reason. He never kills anybody without good reason. People sometimes say things without thinking. They have to learn to think before they speak. What exactly did you say?"

Nick:

"It was a misunderstanding... he took something the wrong way."

Landzman:

"The wrong way? A couple of hundred years ago something said the wrong way, an insult, would have been answered on a field of honor... by a duel. How is this different? The point is he didn't kill you... you're still alive? What are you complaining about?"

Nick:

"But I'm not even armed."

Landzman:

"Well... as the man once said: If you're going to shoot off your mouth you better arm yourself."

Nick:

"I think if you looked at him funny he might shoot you dead, then and there."

Landzman:

"I don't understand. I don't understand at all. Why would someone in their right mind look at Lazarus Wolf funny? Maybe we all need to learn better manners. He's the kind of man who kills people for good reasons."

Nick:

"You say he's honest but I heard he fixed the World Series?"

Landzman:

"Wow! No kidding? Is that what you heard? Boy... that's something... The World Series... shit.

You don't understand at all, do you...? Not at all...

That was a labor of love... a holy mission, a sacred quest even... his noblest act, for him a moment of moral grandeur. He considered it his duty to save America from itself...to win back the dream... to reestablish its purity... the purity of the dream... to rescue it from the racists, the jailbirds, the drunks and the goons, the barflies who infested it.

"Baseball to him represented everything that was wrong, what the Dream had degenerated into, a game for impoverished children played by big morons elevated to mythic status... this is what happened when the destitute had too much time on their hands and too much money... though still obstinately destitute.

But money had nothing to do with it... he wanted to show them the truth whether they wanted to see it or not, that the players were cheap, dirty racketeers always with their hand out. He risked everything by revealing that the World Series was rigged... he could have kept it hidden... it would have been better for him... He thought that the American people would come to their senses... that they'd wake up and see the light... But it was all a waste of time. Wolf wasted his time... the jury wouldn't even send the bums to jail."

Nick, as if tattling on an errant schoolboy to the headmaster:

"He asked me if I was a girl."

Landzman, laughing:

> "Oh... he's a real card... a great kibitzer. He likes to get a rise out of people. He was just playing with you. He has a great sense of humor... very dry.

> "It means he likes you... when he kids you like that."

Nick:

> "He told me his cufflinks were trophies, molars pulled from a screaming   victim who called him Lazarus and owed him money."

Landzman, laughing, forced, uneasily:

> "Ha... ha... ha... now I know he was pulling your leg... they're cultured pearls... pearls for god sakes. Those cufflinks were his first failed efforts... that's why he keeps them... souvenirs... to remind him of what progress he's made... how far he's come... how humble his beginnings were. He's a scientist... a great genius... a marine biologist... a groundbreaker... he keeps his methods top secret. No one can tell his cultured pearls from the real thing.

> "He goes to the South Pacific once a year and comes back with his treasure... so he wants everyone to believe. He comes through customs with nothing to declare but himself. He does this purposely to fuck with them. He's got them flummoxed. The customs people think he's a smuggler... they spent a whole week searching

his ship, impounding his luggage... cutting open his clothes only to find marbles... marbles everywhere.

"He runs a small operation of native divers and diggers, mostly as a front... but they're always shoving the best of the pearls up their asses and won't subject themselves to a body search... they claim it's rape and dishonors their fathers and their mothers and all their ancestors right to the beginning of time. He forced them at gun point and found a treasure trove up their anuses, but all-out war broke loose. I guess shoving pearls up their ass is alright with their ancestors. He had to jump from island to island... one step ahead. It was called the "Pearls up the Ass War" by the islanders which only sounds particularly absurd when translated into English. They took it very serious.

"Finally he was forced to smuggle pearls down to the South Seas and then declare them coming back in... just a very few to keep everybody happy.

"He's very secretive but he grows his pearls in the Bronx... in a factory... oysters in tanks tended by Chinese women who speak no English... in fact they don't speak at all. He made a deal with The Sisters of Divine Mercy for the Deaf And Dumb... a religious order in Shanghai... supervised by Chinese nuns who made the trip with them... they take a vow of silence... all one big quiet family... he pays the nuns directly and sends money to the institution. They lead a cloistered existence... work and prayer... work and prayer... never leave the property... he's got it decked out like nunnery... chapel and all... he's got it down to a science... a racket. He's got an arrangement with a defrocked Chinese priest friend who speaks Chinese... a little... an ex-con who comes in to hear confessions and say mass.

"He says it shouldn't be illegal... to sell cultured pearls as real... who's to say what's real... which is more real. Isn't it better to farm... to cultivate wheat rather than trying to harvest the wild wheat grass? His pearls are better than what's dredged up from the bottom of the sea.

"If you tell anybody they wouldn't believe you and if he finds out you're blabbing he'll be very unhappy and act accordingly."

He knew this story went on too long and sounded ridiculous but felt it served its purpose. Wolf, meanwhile, couldn't seem to drag himself away, instead roaming from table to table reminiscing with old friends... interrupting everybody's lunch as if he were at a party... in his honor. He was like this at funerals too... he lived for funerals... the life of the party.

Landzman, catching his eye, cut him off just as he was quickening his step, to slink out the door like a guilty little boy caught in the act of torturing the family cat.

Landzman:

"What the hell are you doing? You scared the bejesus out of him. Are you proud of yourself? Why must you fuck with people like that? The man has done you no harm... no harm whatsoever. There's something sadistic... I leave you alone for 60 minutes...

"You know he's important to the operation... he's Delsey's cousin and Bucknell knew him at Yale. I got Outwater to get him to rent that cottage I was going to tear down. I thought we could throw him a bone. He doesn't have much money."

Wolf:

"I'm sorry... I couldn't help myself. Someone like that... it does something to me. I don't know what comes over me. Why did you bring such a lame to meet me? Is this what you think of me? He wants a connection? I'll fucking connect him... I'll connect him good. I'll have him connected up the ass. Where do you find such people?

What you don't understand... what he didn't understand at all... is that I was trying to teach the boy something. He carries away nothing.

"Bucknell I can understand, at least... he's got a set... and if I somehow offended him and he got the drop on me he would shoot me dead without blinking an eye... without so much as a hesitation... no ifs, ands or buts. I respect a man like that... I could sit down... do business... break bread even, with a man like that."

Obviously Nick didn't measure up on a more down to earth, visceral level. I doubt that Wolf gave a hoot about family background or breeding... Patricians or Brahmans...or pondered much about Anglo-Saxons, Goths, Huns, Mongols or Magyars, except as a self-taught historian.

Put a bunch of twelve year olds who have never met into a room by themselves and a "natural" pecking order will assert itself. It takes all the king's men, all the power of society and the state to reassert a more orderly alignment.

Going off to college from a city public school isn't a rite of passage it is an ascent into a faraway galaxy. Who among the newly ascendant on return visit to the home planet hasn't been stunned to run into the homecoming king caked in layers of black grease pumping off-brand gas, the homecoming queen in a new contest to pack on weight, reeking the perfume of rancid cooking oil from bootleg, leaking, dented tins through her pores, waiting worn Formica tables at the local pizza joint for cheap tips and all she could eat and as part of her job being periodically goosed by the morbidly obese proprietor who gleefully applauds her alarming increase in girth and the reduced mobility it implies, who slyly winks at his hanger-on cronies draped on the greasy counter like the mildewed table rags: "Her pussy ain't fat." Although there was significant doubt as to whether he had touched or so much as peeked at the object of his perfervid desire.

Landzman:

> "I told him the pearl story... to calm him down...
> to distract... to confuse him. You're officially the
> Albert Einstein of pearls.
>
> You didn't tell him about the fourth man?

Wolf:

> "Tell him whatever you want. Right now he's
> scared shitless. He won't so much as squeak. So
> I told him about the fourth man... so what. Let
> me have my fun. He'll have dreams tonight and
> he will have learned absolutely nothing... taken
> away nothing."

Landzman went back to his table, paid the bill and
said little further to Nick; extending his apologies.
Once again he left Nick alone at table; he left as
quickly as he arrived, stopping to talk to only one table
and then seeming to disappear by way of a trap door
in the restaurant floor, just managing to sidestep
Thomas Bucknell with a mission, barreling inexorably
his way.

Tom, jarred by the sudden, unexpected,
disappearance, thrown off balance, practically
stumbled into Nick's table.

Tom:

> "Where'd he go? Wh... What happened?
>
> "I thought I saw you with Pearl and Diamond. I
> didn't know you hung out with such rarified
> company... you best watch your step.... You're

way out of your league... they'll eat you for breakfast and serve the leavings to the dogs. What's going on here... anyway...? I know about people... I have a sixth sense about things that tells me exactly what to do. Maybe you don't believe that, but...

Nick:

"You mean Landzman and Wolf...?"

Tom:

"Excuse me? Were you sitting with someone else?

Nick:

"No... I mean...

Tom:

"No... I mean? What the... Yeh... Landzman and Wolf.

"Wolf brokers the most beautiful pearls anyone has ever seen. I think they come from another planet. They slaughter the competition.

"I bought a string for Delsey... a buy... she fell in love with them... I've never seen her happier.

"He won't deal with just anybody. I needed an introduction... Landzman was able to help me there... very select clientele... he deals with only the 500 richest families in America... he has a strict list... and in Europe and Asia only with shahs, sheiks, sultans, emperors, emirs, princes, tsars, pashas, rajas, maharajahs, Moghuls, Mikados, khans, Kaisers, caliphs, kings, and other assorted magnates, potentates, oligarchs and particularly powerful Counts, Dukes, generals, governors and samurai... otherwise you're out of luck."

Tom was always performing these verbal acrobatics, or tripping all over himself, thinking it clever or cute or maybe just entertaining. Some found it ridiculous, inept or just plain lame, goofy and he suffered in other people's esteem as a result of it. But people will groan at even the most ingenious of word play. Why is the "unsuccessful" exercise of wit resented to such a degree? The man who tries to make a joke without it being at anyone's expense, attempts in his own personal way to lighten the world, if that's what he really wants to do? I have a grudging admiration for anyone who will put themselves out in this way, on the line for judgment, when so many people's spiteful response is a stone face or an exaggerated rolling of the eyes, when a simple smile would be so gracious and welcomed. Because this is a highly social act; the response is critical; it is elicited and when it is not forthcoming, when there is a frown instead it is like a gift that's refused or worse still, snatched from your extended hand and stomped into the ground. In a way it made Bucknell more accessible, more vulnerable, more likeable in an inane way. Because here was a man who needed to please or amuse absolutely no one, who could, if he wished, sit down and break bread with the illustrious Lazarus Wolf.

Nick, puzzled, a not uncommon reaction for Nick, not knowing what to say:

"What?... wh... what about Mr. Diam... Landzman?

Tom:

"Landzman... Landzman within a few short years had become the biggest diamond wholesaler in New York... bypassing the entire De Beers syndicate. First De Beers tried to get rid of him permanently... but they failed... they lost a small army chasing him. Then they spread the rumor that he was producing perfect diamonds 'artificially'... industrially... through some sort of process he developed. He studied physics in Berlin, after The War, after Oxford.

"Nobody could find his source... or his factory... he never revealed it... so the rumor gained traction. They say he amassed over a hundred million dollars before the De Beers campaign started crippling his sales. Then he threatened to flood the market... making diamonds worthless. Once Landzman's diamonds were out there... in circulation... no one could tell the difference... well they could tell the difference... Landzman's were better. So provenance reared its ugly head as a root of value. Buyers wanted guaranteed genealogy before they would buy... to know exactly what hole they were dug out of. De Beers tried to make certificates of origin mandatory... a birth certificate for rocks and a complete trail of records of purchase and sale...

a certificate of title... like a passport. They tried to get laws passed. But some buyers just didn't care... they were perfect diamonds... what else mattered. If excellence or perfection is to be the ultimate criterion then Landzman's were real and the De Beers were fake.

So De Beers called for a truce and the story goes that they showed Landzman hundreds of tons of diamonds that De Beers was withholding from the market... to prop it up... that diamonds were so plentiful they were virtually worthless if released into a free market... that it was De Beers... the magicians... that created value out of nothing... out of air... that it was all marketing, propaganda and illusion... smoke and mirrors, mass hallucination. Landzman was ruining it for everyone... cutting his own throat. And Landzman strangely enough respected this... as a magician himself... the sheer wizardry and audacity of what De Beers was doing... had been able to do... and the story was out... it was no secret... and still people bought diamonds... at totally fabricated prices. They gave proof to the old saw that you don't hold up people with a gun you hold them up with a smile and a handshake and thereby avoid jail. So they made him an offer... stop manufacturing ... close down his operation... supposing this was his source... they never knew for sure... and come join them... come once a year and take your pick, first pickings, up to twenty million dollars of value each and every year... endlessly into the future. Why ruin it for everyone. He decided...

reluctantly... to join them... I think he was demoralized that he had spent so much time and energy producing something that was so abundant and was so useless though beautiful... except as an industrial abrasive... the vision of those vaults overflowing with diamonds... it would take a bucket loader and a long line of dump trucks just to move the stuff. He stood fast... wrested agreement out of De Beers... keeping his operation going... but solely, exclusively for industrial abrasives... in fact, this has become his cash cow, industrial abrasives... he's the pioneer... and the last man standing... the lowest cost producer... he owns it... nobody can touch him. But it always breaks his heart a little to take those perfect gems... those perfect diamonds, bigger than ostrich eggs... far superior to anything in the De Beers's vault, picked out of the dirt... it's the only kind he knows how to make... and crush them for high grade abrasives. But I suspect that every year he takes the very best of the best and stashes them in his own private vault. Or at least so the rumor goes.

Nick:

"I don't know. It sounds like some story. I'm hearing a lot of stories today. If he's so rich why would he hang out at that big pile he erected out on Long Island? He should rule his own country. How do you know so much?"

Tom:

"A friend… a business acquaintance really… was in the diamond business and he never knew what hit him. He sent a crew of private dicks chasing after him who morphed into Keystone Cops… chasing their tail… they couldn't nail him… couldn't get rid of him either. He seems to live a charmed life.

"They couldn't dig up anything on his family… he might have sprung full grown from the bayous of Louisiana. There's his military record… there's certainty there. His academic record… Oxford… all documented… his travels throughout Europe and Asia… some on his own passport… extensively in Germany… Russia… long stays in Monaco… the south of France…

"I'd be very careful if I were you. He's dangerous… very… The private dicks who took the contract never came back. Maybe they were bought off. There's no doubt… he has connections… high up… government…? Police? I just don't know. He gets information… lots of information. The stuff he knows… it's like he hears everything. The walls have ears."

Slocum

It's a miracle Carramel wasn't shot. He insisted on repeatedly crashing the Landzman Estate, imagining that he had some special bond with the man, some vague dispensation that exempted him from the strict protocol, as if they were old army buddies, down in the trenches together. Landzman's men regarded him with a certain pity, as a benign idiot, or the walking wounded, though fully aware of his combat record or lack thereof. They imagined that Landzman had something in mind, some scheme in which Carramel would play his minuscule but critical part, which remained a secret to all but a chosen few, especially including Carramel who remained clueless.

Carramel, on his accustomed morning constitutional, shuffling through the neighborhood, had seen the horses, a party of three, granted entry through Landzman's main gate and slid in on foot with the riders under the careful acquiescing eyes of Landzman's retainers. Landsman's servant followed with a bucket and scoop meticulously cleaning up the horse manure from the previously pristine crushed white marble drive which was carefully, mechanically raked every morning like a Japanese garden.

Bucknell was with them but didn't know exactly what was going on. A pretty woman in a brown riding-habit who had been to Landzman's before had insisted that they stop to visit. Though he knew that he lived in the vicinity, Slocum, the third rider, had no suspicion this was Landzman's home. The gates were locked shut behind them as soon as they entered and guards reassumed their post; as if a trap had been sprung. It is Tom that recounted that he felt as if some bizarre plot were unfolding, that Slocum had been lured and he himself was just window dressing, part of the cover. He knew Slocum vaguely, introduced to him by Outwater, a stock broker from the city, the pretty woman he knew hardly at all; her name long since forgotten if ever remembered that long hot summer ago which otherwise burned forever in his memory.

Landzman stood on his porch, as if a welcoming host, carefully surveying the three, gleeful as a fat cat playing with a trapped mouse.

> "I'm delighted to see you. I'm delighted that you dropped in. Come right in. Sit right down. Have a cigarette or a cigar."

Dropped by? Shanghaied .

Slocum, his face drained of blood, grew increasingly petrified; would take nothing. A lemonade? No, thanks. A little champagne? Nothing at all, thanks. A breach of good manners? He was afraid of being poisoned; with good reason. In the course of the visit, through body language and furtive looks exchanged, it became increasingly obvious to the observant that the pretty woman had some intimate connection with Landzman.

As if to assert that he had not in fact died, the color began to involuntarily flow back into Slocum's frozen face, turning him instead to an alarming beet red. He began to sweat profusely, drenching his brand new prissy polo attire. He didn't enter into the conversation, but slumped back seated in a pool of his sweat, as if to disappear, in fear, shivering, too afraid to squeak.

Landzman moved in close and said something to Slocum that the others couldn't make out. A sewer smell filled the room and Slocum ran out through the front door; to his astonishment no one stopped him. Landzman yelled out after him with mock good cheer:

"I'll follow you by motor car. I'll catch up. Don't worry... I'll find you."

There was a large brown splotch on the back of Slocum's clean white jodhpurs quite obvious but which Nick, oblivious, seems to have missed; he had soiled himself. Landzman's men opened the gates and Slocum trotted off, disconcerting his horse, squishing in his saddle, oozing shit, with Tom holding back, following him at a more leisurely pace, in his wake. Carramel, on foot, followed the other two men but couldn't catch up, a little boy chasing after a sold-out ice cream truck with a broken bell that wouldn't quit; the supernumerary appendage, tag along, vacant company, a foil to bounce empty words off, tolerated, never completely welcomed, out of breath, chasing unsuccessfully after shit. What a perfect picture summing up his existence.

The pretty woman in the brown riding-habit whose name has been forgotten stayed behind with Landzman, as if overlooked in Slocum's panic, or just as if it had all been planned that way from the very beginning.

Alexander Hamilton

This was found among the uncatalogued papers of James Landzman who is most probably its author:

Alexander Hamilton embodies the relentless ambition of the outsider seeking ascendancy in a new alien land. He is the quintessential self-made man, embodiment of the American Dream come true. He was born, on the island of Nevis, part of the inner arc of the Leeward Islands of the West Indies, out of wedlock to a Scottish-French Huguenot descended mother, married but not to young Hamilton's father, who eventually deserted them, one James A. Hamilton, of Scots descent. Hamilton was orphaned at the age of 11. His mother died in the bed next to him. In probate court, his mother Rachel's legal husband, long estranged, rematerialized to seize her estate leaving Hamilton with nothing but the family's library of 40 or so books which was rescued at auction for him by a friend. He was adopted by a cousin who committed suicide.

Unremittingly resourceful in his exploitation of time and a virtuoso in the use of words, he made his name and he made himself. Hamilton was deeply in love with, courted and won the hand of Elizabeth Schuyler, with the blessing of her father Philip Schuyler, an American Revolutionary War General and wealthy landowner from one of the foremost families in New York State. By 25, Hamilton was a war hero having also been the chief of staff to General George Washington. By 35, he had written the Federalist Papers and had been a successful lawyer. By 40, he had retired as Treasury Secretary of the United States. At 47 Alexander Hamilton died, in a manner which would be regarded as criminal today and was then, for both killed and killer, victim and victor, defending his name on a field of honor, a ruined remnant of a previous more chivalric if murderous age. He met his untimely death at the hands of the notorious timekeeper Aaron Burr; almost as illustrious, who as a result of the murder would become a hunted man.

Hamilton was not without his detractors. John Adams, no admirer of Benjamin Franklin either, described Hamilton as the most "restless, impatient, artful, indefatigable, and unprincipled intriguer in the United States, if not in the world". Alexander Hamilton was neither an egalitarian nor a populist, far from it; he believed in aristocracy, a self-selecting aristocracy based not on birth but on virtue, work and excellence. His is a paradoxical and mysterious personality; his life seems to imitate art; the stuff of melodrama, of a Stendhal or Dickens; his early years so incredible as to rival the novels of Robert Louis Stevenson and Daniel Defoe. Because of his own genius, the timely support of generous benefactors and benevolent twists of fate he overcomes seemingly insurmountable odds to triumph extravagantly.

Jefferson, Adams and their minions described Hamilton as "our Bonaparte" and not as a tribute. He was called an interloper, a bounder, an opportunist (all terms traditionally used to describe a man trespassing above the class into which he is born), a military buckaroo, and most damning of all, he was described as one entirely inimical to the principles of their particular, exclusive American Revolution.

He has been described more recently as a Machiavelli, but not the Machiavelli the naïve and credulous conjure up but rather the true Renaissance scholar who penned "The Prince" as a biting critical treatise, tongue planted firmly in bloody bleeding cheek.

More than Franklin, whose bust stood prominently on Landzman's desk, it was Hamilton that was the true progenitor of James Jacob Landzman. Landzman was planning a book.

America, America

Oh... America, America, the tyranny of low popular culture has reached a deadening consummation here. No foreign totalitarian police state even at the very pinnacle of its most oppressive, murderous power had ever even come close to producing such a cohesive collective identity, such an homogenized low brow culture, oppressive prolefeed, glued together by nothing more powerful than moist shit as a binding agent.

Nick's story isn't the central fable of America it is its fundamental horror story. Its spirit torn asunder; transcendental idealism turned into the ostentatious idolization of money.

To see it merely as the fable of the fox and the grapes is to oversimplify to the point of idiocy; it is far more poignant and even profound. It is a matter of being seduced by the decadency while at the same time condemning it for the very reason it is decadent and knowing in your bones it is decadent; of knowing and understanding your most grievous sins and being at the same time powerless to stop yourself; of going to confession every single week and coming back again and again with the same old tired sins and being wracked by them. Iniquity, as with the rich, can have a mesmerizing glamour, a debauched sumptuousness, a blinding glitter to its swinishness. What child is not tempted to wallow hilariously in the mud while dressed in his best clothes; the only ones he owns?

Act in an Absurd Fashion

"It is human nature to think wisely and act in an absurd fashion." Anatole France said this; he should have said: "Human nature occasionally thinks wisely but even when it does it inevitably acts in an absurd fashion."

Should an author's intentions matter? That's exactly the wrong question. Good writing is not about intentions. Only a dopey schoolteacher would ask us how well the writer fulfilled his intentions. Nothing is so deadly to enjoyment and so poisonous to art as the writer or "artist" who has intentions to fulfill. It is not what the writer aims at but what he hits; but what he hits is not entirely a matter of accident.

Fitzgerald instinctively grasped far more than he consciously demonstrated in the irresponsible life he lived. He continually presents himself as a stupid, ignorant man and if you paid close attention to his biography you would never read his work except as a morbid tabloid type curiosity.

It has been posited that the reader's own life 'outside' the story changes the story. But the story should change the reader's own life. The narcissistic exploitation of literature as a Rorschach test to plumb the problematic depths of the reader's own shaky psyche only muddies the pool; the best writers possess a wisdom that they are not only often incapable of perceiving lucidly and logically but upon which they are often incapable of acting.

A writer shouldn't even talk about his work; by talking about it he demeans himself and his work. What good is the work if he needs to talk about it or wants to? Maybe he shouldn't even think too carefully about it once it's written. Dos Passos said that the forced contemplation of a writers' own work is that writer's hell. Well, maybe not hell but certainly artistic self-destruction which is damn close to hell. Da Vinci may disagree, saying that an artist never completes a work he only abandons it. Obsessive I'd say. Maybe he runs away from it like some ill-conceived creation, fiascos in dirty bandanas with feet chasing after him down the street. When Styron was asked to do the screenplay for *Sophie's Choice* he demurred that it would be like a dog eating its own vomit. But then, Styron talked obsessively about his own work to anyone who would listen.

In any case, if a writer sells his work to the movies he should understand that he is a whore, bought and paid for in hard cash, that his johns come from a distant degenerate planet and have bizarre and disgusting genitalia that they are excessively proud of and obsessed with and take out for everyone to admire; that is never fully extracted and continues to exude a peculiar overpowering odor long after; they leave a piece in him to lay a permanent claim to him; like some obscene insect and it festers. He must accept that he will never walk the same; running is out of the question. Collaborating with your purchasers make it worse, makes you complicit; a more active participant in the sordid details of your own prostitution. You sell your book, you go to the bank, you shut up. And you smile if you know what's good for you and want more of the big bucks in your pocket and that much sought after precious statuette of a perfect reproduction of their revered genitalia gilded in a thin tissue of gold for you to kiss and worship at.

And why in hell would any writer who knows what he's doing want to talk to other writers about his own work or theirs. This isn't arrogance; this is survival, self-preservation as a writer; the yapping fools who talk about writing misunderstand entirely what it is to write, even if, especially if, they do it well.

Bring Back Ezra Pound Alive

I'll make only one exception and bring back Ezra Pound alive and let him wield the proverbial blue pencil to his heart's content. Pound, when editing was right about half the time, which is a remarkable record as even Hemingway would be forced to admit. But please, let's limit the analysis to a simple line in thick blue magic marker that remains transparent and erasable. Although a rigorous excisor (or excisioner if you prefer) of other writer's work, humbly submitted, he seems to have been incapable of exercising even minimal discipline over his own unrestrainable output. (His mastery of Chinese was execrable; a complete sham. Pound was a man of shams.)

After repeatedly hearing that Ezra Pound did no more than echo the words of America's Founding Fathers I went back to the transcripts and listened to the recordings of his Italian wartime radio broadcasts and determined that Arthur Miller was right on target when he said that Pound was worse than Hitler, at least as far as words are concerned and as we know words were important to Pound:

> "In his wildest moments of human vilification Hitler never approached our Ezra ... he knew all America's weaknesses and he played them as expertly as Goebbels ever did."

It is only because of the benefit of clergy that Pound was not hanged for treason. Writers and other artists get away with murder. (As did Ben Jonson, the over-celebrated thug, who, however, will justly forever live in infamy for underpraising Shakespeare. There is no justice, at least not in the great writer's life time. Jonson is buried in Westminster Cathedral, while Shakespeare sits in his local church in a paid spot.)

We are incapable of separating the artist from his artistry.

Heidegger, a committed Nazi, fleshed out his great work on the philosophy of language within earshot of a death camp. 'Heidegger's pen did not stop, nor his mind go mute' because of the deafening screams of those being systematically murdered.

I feel no need to apologize for or justify Richard Wagner the man because I appreciate the unequaled excellence of his music (Mark Twain's expertly practiced kissing the ass of the masses notwithstanding); nor does the music, the words, or the painting exonerate the man though it may afford him a cozier room in jail. Let us praise and play the music while escorting whatever creator to the gallows he may richly deserve or better still, appropriately chaperoned by his supporters to the prison house splendidly endowed with writing implements, reams of paper and the best musical instruments. Let us keep the criminal caged and maintained like the goose of golden egg fame.

High Self-regard

From the papers of Thomas Bucknell:

> Someone who has a positive, coherent self-image, high self-regard and possesses self-confidence is put forth as a paragon, an example to follow; but someone who has an analogous high opinion of the entire human race is

universally looked upon as a fool and is hounded out of the room. There is an inherent contradiction here. Can the individual be laudable and the aggregate condemnable?

If our goal is to instill self-confidence in those we teach and lead we will fall victim to the curse of unintended consequences; we will have created a line of monsters who will first devour us and then, only half-sated, turn on each other and finish the job. With nothing but confidence and ill-founded self-esteem going for them they will be inevitably disappointed and murderously embittered, feeling cheated by a cruel world too stupid to recognize their obvious genius; they will feel fully vindicated only in realizing a sufficiently gory retribution.

Poetry of His Story

Presumably the words of Thomas Bucknell, found in his desk, not included with his papers:

It is words themselves that can become the embodiment of dreams, authentically exemplifying the ecstasy of emotion through metaphor and thus to strike at the heart of truth. Nick like Landzman is a dream maker; the one through the magic recreation of self, the other through the transforming enchantment of words which gives the ultimate expression of Landzman's self through the poetry of his story.

They Neither Plow Like the Farmer

The French have a marvelous tradition of anti-clericalism, anti-Catholicism really. God bless the French.

Going back even to Rabelais (born circa 1483) who said of the clergy:

> "They neither plow like the farmer nor heal the sick like the doctor; all they do is harass the neighborhood clanging their fucking bells which have no religious meaning; it's as if they, in this way tell us, I'll do whatever I damned please. I'll wake you up in the middle of the night every night like clockwork. I'll fuck your sons and I'll fuck you too if I want and there's not a damned thing you can do about it."

Rabelais's carnivalistic view was the opposite of the Mardi Gras version; he was screaming out hilariously that the "emperor" was not only naked, but a grotesque, deformed, stumbling, crippled obscenity.

Or in the immortal words of Denis Diderot:

> "Man will never be free until the last king is strangled with the guts of the last priest."

Diderot feared Christians who he believed had a thousand year legacy of destroying libraries, burning books, demolishing paintings, trashing sculptures, and torturing, with almost scientific precision, anyone who didn't agree with them. It is because of the Church's rampant history of knowledge devastation that he produced his great Encyclopedia; a compendium to safeguard all that was known, from these destroyers. His admirers and contributors included Benjamin Franklin and Thomas Jefferson. Jefferson wrote:

> "History, I believe, furnishes no example of a priest-ridden people maintaining a free civil government... In every country and in every age, the priest has been hostile to liberty. He is always in alliance with the despot, abetting his abuses in return for protection to his own."

Jefferson naively failed to realize the unholy depths of priestly power. You can exercise all the outward flourishes of a Republic, all of its so-called showcase freedoms, while remaining a slave in your own mind; a man trapped by bogus ideas is bound by chains that are uncutable, cannot be set free by glorious proclamations or Constitutional amendments.

Those who believe absurdities can easily commit atrocities.

Jon Breedlove Panders

My devout Roman Catholic sister actually married one of these priest's "queer boys". (I apologize, not my term but a quote from the whispers). She played out in real life the lead in *Light in the Piazza* without Mimieux's beauty, pathetically ingratiating herself into a family that was so stupid and talked such drivel that they didn't notice her handicap. She fit right in; possessed of a simple minded devotion to the Madonna, the

Virgin Mary Immaculate Mother of God, which insinuated her, if not at their table, at least into a secure place in a near corner.

There is an accepted subculture of homosexuality among Catholic schoolboys and their beloved priests. The pretended shock of the faithful to unveiled priest boy-rape is a perfected, practiced act, honed over centuries, a masquerade to shield their enabling complicity from the greater uninitiated non-Catholic public who weren't in on it. This was an ingrained culture, like a secret society of cannibals, close knit, tradition bound, formal dinner every evening. They had been doing it for so long they took it entirely for granted and didn't think twice about it. Shame? Does a native cannibal feel shame? This is his cultural heritage that must be protected at all costs. Remorse? They adored the taste of human flesh, its incomparable lusciousness and the good hunt for it; they gloried in it and simply pitied or dismissed those who didn't. It was a prime reason for their being.

Jon Breedlove Panders, that was his actual name; you can't make crap like this up; falling down drunk, waxing ecstatic about his wonderful, idyllic schoolboy days and his cherished Father Rogers, he of the beret and purple opera cape, pied piper trailed by dutiful goslings, entourage of gunsels, dedicated, more than willing catamites. Rogers, compassionate, magnanimous man of Christ, never laughed at Pander's teensy little child's dickie like the girls did; they had their limits; Rogers could close his eyes and imagine a six year old; he was in heaven. This priest was his savior, confessor, dispenser of easy absolution exchanged for a quick blowjob for the priest; no doubt sorely missing being fucked in the ass by the little holy man; tears in his eyes; proclaimed this godly man a saint; which priest would join in unholy league with the notorious Cuntsler, tireless, unflagging champion of terrorists, saboteurs and wreckers, in 1973, that diabolic year, to hound the university for "full recognition" of the University Gay Club, of which the priest was the proud and active faculty chairman, which back in those heady days vigorously lobbied for the ineffable glories of pederasty; having been granted "the right to open discussion and a place to meet on University grounds" which wasn't near enough for the pint-sized priest, who none-the-less couldn't help crowing in defeat how they "achieved their immediate objectives" and further bellowed: "If you allow any minority group to be discriminated against, you're in for trouble"; who propagated his contagion, diseased and loitering to the ripe and rotting age of 95, in 2007, tended by his brethren at inordinate expense and deposited with Jesuit esteems, requiems and halleluiahs, in hallowed ground, (laid in the dirt by Farenga Bros. Inc., Directors, who, if they knew, would have saved a buck and heaved his stinking cadaver, on the sly, into an open cesspit) with a paid obituary in *The New York Times*.

These priests didn't have the decency to commit their crimes quietly or in private. There seems to have been this nauseating need in them to advertise, to shove it in your face and laugh or giggle. Rogers, outrageous, would parade around with his young trophy boys like they were showgirls hanging on his arm or hard won child brides, prizes secured through protracted, hard negotiation with the fathers late into the night over cheap blended Scotch whiskey proffered by the priest over tap water ice provided by the father, the nominal host and a bottomless bowl of bar nuts, little broken peanuts, purchased in bulk in big used brown paper bags stapled shut, the daily leavings from the local gin joint down the street; which always saved a backroom for the priests, right next to the stinking can.

Writers Are a Lot like Actors

Writers are a lot like actors or media personalities; they come to life when the camera turns on with the lights, when they write:

"Lights! Camera! Existence".

It is not only their best self that becomes actuated, it may be an entirely different self or their only self; wise when they write, fools in life, or "daily life", an interesting locution for humdrum reality.

In daily life, Bellow said, I don't ask myself what is honorable and what is dishonorable but I do when I'm writing. Daily life which good writers work to avoid at the risk of their lives, that Aleksandr Isayevich Solzhenitsyn understood so well: that soul sucking deadening automatic amoral routine that serves as a stand-in, a cheap substitute for the real thing; no one should ever entirely mourn for that dumb proxy when he goes marching in lock-step back into the dirt.

At its best, to write is to commune with the gods or as a god; to speak down the long narrow echoing hall of history, to the ones who don't yet exist, who a great writer helps midwife into being, the secret father, the paterfamilias of mankind.

Do Not Get Down Off Your Horse

Roth describes Bellow through a fictionalized stand-in as emotionally surrounded by a moat so oceanic that you could not even see the great turreted and buttressed thing it had been dug to protect. Good for Bellow and his engineering skills but especially for his herculean general contracting knack; he got good help. There is something to be said for mystery and self-protection, licensed carry. This is why Bellow earned the Prize.

Where in hell is it written that we're required to bare our souls; that we must present ourselves psychically naked to enable intimacy? This requirement is modern psycho-babble, equating self-revelation with the ability to love. Sharing secrets is something little girl friends do, so they can undress, play, and cry together. How decadently bizarre that even men now are required to make public declarations of their intimate secrets. Next comes public ritual castration with everyone smiling and stomping their feet rhythmically in syncopation.

"I want to get to know the real you". Fuck the real me. Fuck the idea of the real me. Fuck the idea that the question of the real me makes any sense; that there can even be a "real" me.

Do you want a vulnerable basket case or a fully functioning ego, a knight on a huge war horse with gigantic hooves, with both man and animal in full armor decorated by a master engraver?

What's all this gibberish about being ourselves, authenticity? To hell with being ourselves; most of us are no damn good. We should be better than ourselves; recreate ourselves in a more perfect image. Hitler was sincere; said what he meant and acted upon it. God save us from sincere people. Give me a humble hypocrite or phony any day.

And as far as knowing each other, revealing the real me; this is a game we play, a futile game, a child's game to waste our time, and while our life away. No human being can truly understand another human being. Someone said that's why we invented God: a Being capable of understanding us. This turns the catechism upside-down. Why did we make God?

> "To know us, to understand us, to love us in this world and quite possibly in the next, if it exists, or if He exists."

Do not get down off your horse. I repeat: do not get down off your horse. What? To play in the mud with the other children, smear mud on each other. Do not take off your armor even when you sit down to eat; eat standing; better still, eat while in the saddle. They didn't build moats for nothing. It is an apt image. Make my walls of granite, high and thick with impenetrable battlements. I'll call Bellow for an architect with the right gifts.

More about My Grandfather

I wish I knew more about my grandfather. He grew more like his old adversaries the Anglo Saxons the older he got until he was indistinguishable from them; that is the old Anglo Saxons, the ones he admired. Even when ensconced on the North Shore in the summer of '22 he retired to his own rather small modest apartment, like a monk's retreat; the resident keeper of a great cathedral to the greater glory of his achievement. The richer he grew the more ascetic, frugal, reserved and laconic he became; he hated ostentatious displays of wealth. He rewarded his children, grandchildren and great-grandchildren according to the lives they lead as he measured them and he was not above making harsh judgments. He was a tough taskmaster; but the task, its choice and fulfillment he left up to the individual, within limits.

He gave no money to organized charity which he considered inefficient or an outright fraud. He chose deserving cases on an individual basis, those who seemed to have become the victim of a particularly cruel fate, from events entirely beyond their control. He had his own gum shoes scrutinize all cases that came to his attention. His help was given anonymously and a follow-up was always made.

He helped the victims of a crooked judicial system which task was Sisyphean; he couldn't fix the system;

that was beyond even his power and wealth. He was especially supportive of victims of crimes and those who justly attempted to defend themselves. If you died fighting back he came to the aid of your family and continued to support them as long as necessary often sending the children to college or trade school and finding them jobs, often within his own companies where he could look out for them. Very often they would win the lottery which Landzman fixed. He called the lottery a perfect tax, a tax on stupidity and lazy desperation. He thought better of this remark and took it back as inappropriately cruel.

One reporter did a detailed study of over a thousand lottery winners, every one of whom was not only in need but particularly deserving. Not one of them blew the money the way the typical old lottery winner did. No titty bars, no vacations to the islands. Only a few of them quit their job; some started businesses; miraculously they all moved up in the world. They saved their money, bought a house or paid one off; a solid house made of brick or stone with a full basement; no flood plain or hurricane or tornado zone.

It was as if they had made a pact, a covenant, some secret deal; had met with John Beresford Tipton, who himself came personally to their door with documents to sign. The reporter, a devout atheist, concluded that this was irrefutable proof of some benevolent force in the universe, divine providence, the hand of God. However, he stubbornly remained true to his convictions. He believed in a myth, of a man whose name was unsayable, whose identity he never did discover, who held a few of the levers and helped level the field just a very little.

Although the support was secret, one unscrupulous politician, a United States Senator, on the Senate floor, accused him, although he wasn't sure who <u>he</u> was, of encouraging vigilantism, claiming without any proof that individuals died fighting when they should have acquiesced, given in and saved their own skins, that they became too enthusiastic martyrs, knowing their families would be taken care of by the covert but famous, seeing but unseen, seemingly all powerful Donor. Landzman was railed against:

> "...driving men to heroism for the cash reward... battles were being won recklessly on the battlefield and in the streets".

Some crap about "impure motives". The Senator tried to have the FBI search for the secret donor's identity. But the assistant Director of the Bureau, born into a family without means, had been a recipient of more than one of Landzman's scholarships and had been guided by an unknown helping hand all of his life. He did not know for sure it was Landzman; no letters or phone calls were ever exchanged. There was no communication whatsoever. The required court orders never came or weren't requested. Landzman knew that any man or woman he had chosen, that's the word he used, "chosen", would do the right thing without any prodding or so he hoped. This was naïve.

There was a case in New York in which a man came upon a young woman being gang raped by five men; when he screamed for them to stop they opened fire on him; a crack shot, he returned fire and killed the five of them. Wounded and bleeding he was handcuffed and subsequently charged with possession of an unlicensed handgun and murder. He lapsed into a coma and was shackled to his hospital bed. At 1:00 AM one morning, two weeks after the shootings, a team of Federal agents, FBI and US Marshals showed up with three doctors, two nurses and their attendant staff to affect a transfer to a "more secure facility, with a more specialized staff", the location of which they were "not at liberty to reveal." Phone calls were made to verify the transfer and the prisoner was loaded into what appeared to be an armored military ambulance. That was the last he was ever seen.

The prisoner's family had disappeared simultaneously leaving no trace behind. The press had a field day, claiming it was an inside job, without a shred of proof; heads rolled but no one was charged; those fired all seemed to find much better jobs and very strangely two of them won the lottery.

The rumor was that he was put into some super secure witness protection program; but who would he have testified against; the dead men were all cheap violent felons with arm-long records but no connections, at least none worth the trouble. There was another rumor, unsubstantiated, that the so-called Donor, as he was called in the tabloid press, (or is that an outdated term; the press is all tabloid these days) had arranged the whole thing; relocated them to the south of France with new passports, not forged but real and new genuine identities complete with histories which they had to study and learn; to a comfortable little house and a small "cultural liaison" team to ease their transition. The children learned French quickly and loved the adventure though they missed their old friends.

Having once headed the American Legion Landzman ran with his own idea of what a Veteran's Organization should be. Any man who died for his county had his family looked after by Landzman. Anyone heroic in battle was rewarded when he came home; there were business loans, home mortgages at preferred interest rates that would never be foreclosed and jobs; his own predecessor and then adjunct to the GI Bill. There was always a welcoming committee at the train station, at the boat, girls with flowers (he had a fixation about girls bearing flowers) and a brass band no matter what time of the day or night. (One pencil pusher with an eye to counting beans found the brass band, although only a four piece affair, a "ridiculous extravagance". He was helped to move on, to find employment more agreeable to his practical preoccupations and pencil pushing ways.)

One Good Soldier to Another

Landzman never forgot the indignity of arriving back as if naked and unappreciated on the shores of America, so weighted down with medals that he could hardly stand up straight, but with empty pockets. He had stayed too long at Oxford, then Berlin. There were no brass bands, no cheering crowds, no pretty girls bearing flowers, not so much as a welcoming committee of one.

However, one old soldier from the United Confederate Veterans looked him up and bought him a hot dog at Nedicks in a storefront of the Bartholdi Hotel, at 23rd Street and Broadway. He never forgot the day. Of all the lavish meals he'd eaten in the great houses, and in the finest restaurants throughout the world, this is the one he remembered. The old timer told him to meet him at the "Orange Room of the Hotel Nedicks"; he thought that was a riot; he was on a "tight budget", expressing his regrets.

He showed up in his Confederate officer's uniform; a sight to behold, an apparition, in a double-breasted captain's frockcoat of darker Richmond grey and sky blue trim. He saluted the Colonel, long and slow, as if he were Robert E. Lee returned. The uniform was still a perfect fit, custom tailored with a brand new look; his best and only suit, saved for God knows what, for this very occasion, and had the effect of rolling back the years, a hand against the tide, like he stepped straight out of a time machine, come back especially by design so that at least one person, just one, would be there for the Colonel. The crowds gawked at him as if he just materialized from Mars and laughed like he was a buffoon; one fool asked if he was dressed for a movie part or was he going to a masquerade. He apologized to the Colonel; he hadn't meant to create a spectacle; he wore the uniform as a sign of respect, one good soldier to another good soldier. The Colonel reassured him that no apology was needed; that he was indeed deeply honored.

His grandson had served under the command of the Colonel in The War, as it was then called; and had since died; run down by a car full of drunks on a warm summer Sunday evening while he was walking home exhausted from a long day at work.

He wanted to thank the Colonel; the Colonel couldn't understand for what. He said he was sick to death of living in Yankee territory, suffocating on Yankee sanctimony; that he wanted to return home to the South, which he knew was no more, if it ever was, where everything was civilized and rotted and polite. "Never ask the names of the villages, just remember them." He was afraid to break the spell. Perhaps he lived in an unusable past, sentimentalizing a way of life that had buckled under its own weight, folded like a geriatric circus absconded in the night. He lived on dreams of the Old South rising, unscathed, out of adversity, penury and abject defeat.

He spoke at length about his grandson who had graduated from West Point; he was exceedingly proud of him but didn't seem to entirely comprehend or want to comprehend the inherent contradiction or wicked irony in all of it. His wife, the boy's grandmother, knowing better, wept when she saw him in his dress blue uniform and embraced him tightly to stop from shaking uncontrollably, burying her eyes in the blue so she didn't have to see.

The old warrior called the Colonel a good Yankee, much as one would call a German a good German twenty-five years later, as an exception, an anomaly, against nature but on good authority reputed to exist. The Colonel found the epithet jarring but held his peace. He was no Yankee; he was not taking on their sins; these were not his people, not by a long shot.

Kleinsinger

I don't remember the subterfuge that Nick employed to lure Landzman to his rented cottage; whether it had something to do with the connection that Nick was yearning after or whether it fit into Landzman's larger scheme, I never found out. Landzman, being an old school gentleman never spoke of any of it. In any event he was trapped by his good manners; there was no easy way out. When, after years, he saw Delsey his heart dropped; his usually infectious convivial high spirits guttered. He was haunted by vivid memories of her crazy family, of her father the judge chasing her around the dinner table brandishing a knife. Landzman was confident that this had not been some mock display, some empty posturing. He was convinced that if the judge had caught her he would have killed her, slashed her to her bloody death. Delsey depended on the fact that her father was slow of foot and a bit sloshed and therefore felt free to taunt him mercilessly to her heart's content. And Landzman knew that if he had continued with this woman she would have similarly taunted him, but he being quick of foot and stone cold sober would have caught her to no good end for either of them.

When exiting Nick's little cottage Delsey couldn't help but be overwhelmed by Landzman's huge abode overshadowing them, seeming to grow as Delsey stared at it transfixed in immodest wonderment:

"It's all yours... that huge thing there...? It's so... so big... my god"

she cried pointing.

Landzman:

"I'm glad you like it."

Delsey:

"I love it, I just love it. It's so big. Can I see it? Will you show it to me?"

When Landzman somewhat reluctantly gave Delsey the grand tour of the establishment after having reluctantly fucked her in Nick's thatched cottage, with Nick in unwelcomed tow, they startled Kleinsinger who hadn't been given his usual heads up; he was caught off guard, in the act, practicing the piano.

Kleinsinger was the resident property manager, responsible for keeping the house and grounds in tiptop shape but really much more than that. He coordinated the real work while the imported English butler was mostly for the entertainment and the show. Don't get me wrong; the butler was kept hopping and more than earned his keep as a performer; perfected a stiff-upper-lip obsequiousness and was re-christened Jeeves for the run of the show.

He was like the show captain on those latter day behemoth cruise ships, which, dangerously top-heavy, look like they're ready to sink or tip over; where the over-fed hoi-polloi waddle to the trough, pretend they are just like the old money rich folk and are actually, positively having fun swilling contaminated food served up by help with unclean hands and third world hygiene. The real captain steering the ship sight unseen wouldn't be caught dead in the show captain's Hollywood costume and finds his employment cloying and embarrassing; finding it necessary to lie to his family telling them that he captains a swine boat on a slow run to China. Meanwhile the show captain has infinite time to socialize with guests who pay extra. He maintains a captain's table in three separate dining rooms which he ferries between in shifts, pushing his food around the plate, smart enough not to eat it; which prompted one cheeky young lad "honored" to sit at one of his tables with him to enquire:

"Shouldn't you be steering the ship or something?"

which led to nervous laughs all around the table.

Kleinsinger occupied an incongruously luxurious apartment over the garages and an office off the big house's main kitchen but had the run of the place with Landzman's blessing. If guests were expected he was given fair warning in advance.

He was a gifted concert pianist and practiced on the Steinway grand when time and opportunity permitted; managing the estate was a 24 hour seven days a week commitment. But he was much more than manager; he was Landzman's CFO, he had become overseer of all his earthly financial affairs.

They became partners in the drugstore business with over a hundred branches in New York alone and the manufacture and distribution of alternative medicinals. He also ran the casinos.

He had played Rachmaninoff at Carnegie Hall and practiced religiously for a return.

It was with a certain, almost familial pride that Lantzman persuaded a very reluctant Kleinsinger to play his Rachmaninoff, who sensed intuitively that this wasn't the right crowd.

Half-way through the performance Delsey had had enough:

"No... No... No... something cheerful and fun.

"How about *Ain't We Got Fun?*"

Delsey broke into an impromptu Charleston, tripped precipitously and landed dangerously on her ass with knees spread wide revealing just momentarily for all to admire, her naked, wet, dripping vagina (vulva, more precisely or pussy if you prefer); she quickly composed herself duly blushing and embarrassed like the modest school girl she incongruously pretended to be. It was only later that Nick observed that Delsey was just "showing off". This from a man who was accustomed to expose himself but more in order to humiliate, degrade and self-flagellate. After reestablishing what passed for self-possession, as if nothing at all had happened or she could care less, Delsey resumed her ingenuous demeanor, giddily urging Kleinsinger to play *The Love Nest*; Kleinsinger, turning around and searching unhappily for Landzman in the gloom with the look of:

"How could you do this to me"?

Landzman was mortified, dumbstruck, though he had been a fool not to expect it.

Kleinsinger protested courteously to each request:

"I've heard it but never played it before."

He plunked out the ridiculous ditties for the delectation of the mindless interlopers.

It sounds awful and even sexist but the last thing Landzman had wanted was to have sex again with Delsey. She chased him down when he set up shop in Great Neck; she was obsessed; of all the places to open a gin joint. She kept showing up at his parties, the uninvited guest, usually mixed in with invited groups and he didn't have the heart to throw her out or bar her at the door. He tried to keep his distance, which was difficult. He was the host after all and needed to work the room.

What passes for charm in an eighteen year old can turn sickly sweet, nauseating even, in a woman in her twenties. She grew older without maturing, already beginning her slow, relentless descent into rot without any prospect of ripening. What passed as youthful rebelliousness revealed itself with age as the vicious, vacuous selfishness of the unregenerate vandal. One can see her, as in a bad dream, rising out of the mists, swinging a hammer against Roman marble. She dripped genuine blood.

He did it as an act of kindness, to keep from wounding her. It was his good deed, his mitzveh. I wonder how the priests and ministers, the self-appointed, pompous ethicists would feel about that; having sex, adultery technically, as an act of genuine kindness, and as such a highly moral act.

Landzman had met Kleinsinger in an unusual way. One day he simply showed up at Landzman's door without warning or introduction. For obvious reasons Landzman was summoned immediately by an agitated staff. He took one look at him and said simply:

"You look like blood....

"That doesn't sound right does it? What I meant to say is you have a familial look. We look related."

That was an understatement. Kleinsinger stood there speechless for a moment:

"I saw your picture in the newspaper and was struck by it."

He wasn't like a poor country cousin showing up unannounced with baggage at his feet. He was accomplished, better educated than Landzman in many ways. He had money, substantial money, but seemed to be unaffected by it, not to care about it, certainly not about spending it, which is all very convenient for those who have plenty of it.

He was just profoundly curious. Early one warm summer Sunday morning when feeling restless, with the newspaper firmly in hand, as if to serve as proof, of whatever, he simply decided to impose upon his driver and travel to the wilds of Long Island to discover, God knows what, on its sandy shores. He had no idea if

Landzman was even in or really existed. Photographs prove nothing. It was a shot in the dark.

Searching for common roots he told Landzman the story of his family. Kleinsinger's father and grandfather had been medicine men. His grandfather traveled with an entourage of wagons that looked more like a traveling fair or circus than a purveyor of healing potions. He called himself Doctor Good and had a cure for every ailment. He mixed his magic potions in New York City in his own factory which worked a double shift even when he was travelling. He traversed the rural areas of the Northeast by wagon and the cities by his own riverboat which was ocean worthy, materializing from the fog like an apparition with its calliope drowning out the fog horns; what a sound. It travelled up all the navigable rivers of the East coast, the Gulf and then the Mississippi. He had a crew of advance men who would travel ahead of him on land, booking the best accommodations, plastering the towns with posters and taking full page advertisements in the newspapers. He would line up local endorsers, prominent, respected citizens who would give enthusiastic testimonials either written or as introductory speeches, all in return for complementary product. He tried to win the support of the local physicians, usually unsuccessfully; they saw him as the competition; who they slandered as a snake oil salesman.

He may have sold snake oil but mostly he kept the ingredients of his potions a deep dark secret. Actually he sold black currant seed oil, grapeseed oil, extra virgin olive oil, coconut oil and the oil from octopus and tiny little shrimp called krill. He sold fermented milk whose recipe and culture came from Russia called Kefir and special aged cheeses and whey and his own special sauerkraut. He sold dried blueberries, sour cherries, strawberries and blackberries; and nuts: almonds, walnuts, cashews, hazel nuts, pistachios, brazil nuts, macadamias and pine nuts and peanuts which aren't nuts at all; apple cider vinegar and wild raw honey. He sold miso from Japan and natto and his own green tea and black tea from Ceylon and strong Arabica coffee from the Columbian hills and unsweetened chocolate. He sold seaweed from off the coast of Korea and blue green algae from pure inland fresh water lakes. He grew his own mushrooms: Maitake, Chaga, Reishi, Cordyceps, Royal Sun Blaze, Enokitake, Mesima, Turkey Tail, Zhu Ling, Lion's Mane, Maitake, Artist's Conk, Agarikon, Amadou, Shiitake and another parasitic growth from the dessert called Cistanche known in China as Rou Congrong. He sold a host of different spices and herbs in a myriad of secret concoctions: Curcumin, Kava, Cat's Claw, Horney Goat Weed, Maca from South America, Kalmegh, Siberian Ginseng, Chinese Ginseng, Ashwagandha, Fenugreek, Echinacea, Rhodiola, Schisandra, Milk Thistle, Tribulus Terrestris, Muira Puama, Bacopa, Cinnamon, Holy Basil, Boswellian, an extract from white willow bark and French maritime pine bark; a sleep potion made with Valerian Root, Chamomile Flower, Passionflower, Lemon Balm, Hops and just a faint touch of opium tincture; and dozens of varieties of garlic. He sold fresh onions, cabbage and broccoli. For colds he had a mix of Guaifenesin, Ephedra and Codeine. The list went on and on and on, all learned by heart and sealed securely in memory. Kleinsinger shared these secrets with Landzman as the basis for their evolving partnership in the patent medicine business; locked fast in a safe now; hundreds of ingredients based on folk remedies, Ayurveda, Chinese traditional medicine and Native America potions. Kleinsinger recalled nostalgically how his own father recited the lists to him to learn by heart like an incantation, a fairytale which lulled him to sleep at night.

The grandfather hired his own gunman as protection, who far outmatched the local thugs sent by the physicians to burn him out. He would enter a river port or town like a conquering hero with crowds cheering and bands playing (his own bands), acrobats walking on their hands and cartwheeling down the street.

He raked in so much money that he had armored wagons travelling in his wake guarded by mounted Pinkertons; when he wasn't traveling by boat. There was such an avalanche, he accepted only gold or silver coin, that he sometimes curtailed his tour to return to Chicago laden with his treasure; he owned his own bank; but its furthest branch reached only to Chicago.

Kleinsinger's father and grandfather both lived to an old age but never seemed to age. You would think that a man who was over a hundred but looked fifty would garner a great deal of attention and would receive insistent inquiries and accolades from government officials and heads of state. They were leery of him. One politician complained how "disruptive" it would be if the average person never aged. What about the doctors they complained. Do you want to put them out of business? Close down the medical schools?

> "Sickness is always with us. It is essential to the human condition. Disease allows us to cull the weak. It is god's threshing board"

one of them philosophized ridiculously.

People are grudging of even the appearance of a personal tribute. The fact that most of the health gurus today are overweight and look like shit doesn't seem to faze their devoted adherents who follow them like blinded sheep guiding their own herded way over the cliff to the tune of deafening bleats.

Kleinsinger's grandfather was killed by a runaway beer wagon pulled by huge draft horses with hair draped hooves who had been spooked or so the story was let out. But the truth is that he too was probably murdered; the murderer, protected, had connections.

His own father was shot in the back through the heart without warning by a deranged small town doctor, a religious fanatic, who he showed up by curing the doctor's wife of an "incurable" disease. The doctor had painstakingly persuaded her, prepared her to peacefully accept her fate as god's holy will, to look forward to her wonderful journey into heaven and place her faith in "the Lord, our Savior Jesus Christ". He not only embarrassed the doctor he up-staged the Lord, at least in the doctor's eyes, who was thoroughly indoctrinated with this stupid priest drivel. He seemed to be looking forward to her death so she could go up to heaven, get her reward and watch over and pray for him, his own private intercessor, a lock on the inside track.

It reminded me of my half-sister's father-in-law, a man almost entirely devoid of admirable attributes: fat, lazy, mean when drunk and often drunk; inexplicably arrogant for an entirely ignorant man, wedded obscenely to his Roman Catholic Church. He missed his calling. He was loved completely by a charming woman who worshipped the ground he walked on even until her early death. She was unduly impressed by his degree from one of those parochial colleges of indoctrination which inexplicably allowed him to teach in a public high school, proving how sick this society is with its profligate accreditation standards, failing to separate Church from State.

I remember travelling through three hours of rush hour traffic, arriving depleted, to be at her wake, to share my grief; what right had I to grieve so much? And choosing my words, crafting them ever so carefully in my mind as I sat bumper to bumper, to try to console him, which I thought would be useless in any event. I found him instead beaming ecstatically like an idiot who had found the master's whiskey. I don't think I ever wanted to beat a man so much in my life, to his senses. Here he was all puffed up and full of himself, the life of the party, strutting like a peacock, a man who was loved by a woman. He didn't even have the decency to properly mourn for her: to grieve, to rend his garments, to tear out his hair, to run howling through the street. He was intoxicated by priest rot, empty stupid words uttered by barren desiccated spiritual eunuchs who never loved or were loved by a woman, incapable of loving anything but themselves.

"She's up in heaven now... watching over us... praying for us."

So sayeth the Idiot with euphoric grin and eyes rolled heavenward.

Rage, rage against the dying of the light. Do not go gently. Do not go gently. This is no good night.

Edward Winslow

How Edward Winslow got through the heavily protected perimeter of the Landzman Estate is still unexplained. His pickups and deliveries, the extensive walking trips, his reconnaissance through the neighborhood gave him the lay of the land, imprinted the topography of the loaded on his sick brain. His repeated transport of Nick's patched up body work familiarized him with what amounted to a back door, the soft vulnerable underbelly, concealed by thick bushes, which was Nick's backyard; the barrier weakened, compromised by the habitual prying of the less than harmless gatecrasher. The guard dogs had grown accustomed to the strange, panicky smell of Carramel, and Winslow exuded that identical dull enervating fear. The ever vigilant gatekeepers, those grim heavies with their bulging roscoes, should have followed their instincts, escorted Nick to his appointed rendezvous, that boat ride on the Sound that very first night, for a moonlight swim in concrete galoshes.

Miranda inserted the long nozzle into the receptacle and with spur of the moment enthusiasm rushed out into the dusk, waving her hands joyously, shouting a friendly hello to Landzman's car. She loved Landzman and was accustomed to gush like a girl at the sight of him; she had been pumping gas but the gas could wait.

Delsey had swerved in to fill up, but seeing Miranda, hit the gas hard and... then... barreled back into the highway. Delsey, forgetting what car she was in, thought Miranda was mocking her, jeering at her in such high spirits, wearing an ecstatic grin. Delsey knew exactly who she was: Tom's woman. She had no idea she was a prostitute, the woman he would rather be with. But I think it was her extraordinary beauty and overt sexuality that enraged Delsey to this level of madness.

Winslow was inconsolable and cradled the dead Miranda in his arms and sobbed like a child.

Winslow knew what Landzman looked like; his coming and goings were no secret in this neck of the woods. He knew his extravaganza of a car; everyone knew it. At the first scene of slaughter, Tom insisted, unnecessarily protesting suspiciously:

> "... that big cream car I was driving this afternoon wasn't mine... it didn't belong to me... Listen to what I say. I was bringing you that coupé I promised you, that you've been wanting to buy."

A day late and a universe away, harrumphed Winslow in a murderous pent-up fury. He could easily kill this man now and loose nothing; but that might slow him down. As much as he would have liked to have brought them all down in one fell swoop, he would bide his time for the primary kill.

He slinked through like an animal on the prowl; an ashen fantastic figure floating surrealistically through the diaphanous trees, through the undergarments of obscene goddesses hanging from wash lines in the leaden sky. The sun was in his eyes; he was over a hundred feet away when Landzman's heavies started unloading on him. For the first time in years he stopped sweating. He instantly dropped to crouch on one knee, back in mortal combat, took careful aim, holding the gun with both hands and let loose his one shot, one shot just as a cloud brought back his sun blinded sight, long enough to know he had killed the wrong man. All the shots rang out in less than three seconds. Blood began to fill the pool, dyeing it a deep ruby red, which soon enough turned brown. Who would have thought the man would have had so much blood in him.

If Kleinsinger had been alone by the pool, as was usual, Winslow would have passed him by. It was Landzman's praetorians that fooled him, made him think that it was Landzman in the water. The armed guards protecting him were a dead give-away to a lie. They had received a warning call from neighbors that a crazy man was running loose in the neighborhood; run down by a burly grounds man up the road, narrowly slipping his captor's grip. The grounds man didn't know how lucky he was to let slip death as if by propitious accident. They stood picket as a prudent precaution. They hadn't counted on a dead-eye marksman; or the dogs inured; or the weakened worn spot through an habitual gatecrashers yard; or that Kleinsinger would be a sitting duck in the pool, powerless to extricate, to make a swift escape; the water a molasses trap in the split second he rose like a primordial god snapping chains, sticking to the earth like glue, clutched by its tentacles, the surface tension of the artificial sea, a rich man's marble pool, only to meet his death with one clean well-aimed shot from one of life's left outs. About to break free he fell back into his blood and drowned in it.

But the right man would have been the wrong man too. Sad dumb Winslow got it all wrong, as he did everything.

It turns out that Kleinsinger was ten years older than Landzman though everyone assumed he was the baby brother. His three sons, mostly grown, showed up at the abbreviated services and played their part, grudgingly, resenting the ruse, pretending to be other than who they were. There could be no crowds. They inherited the house, Landzman's house, as a negotiated settlement, the least Landzman could do, empty solace and they and their heirs own it to this day, the hub of subdivided estates and a small real estate empire and of course there is the drug company, the supplement company, the drug stores and a small interest in industrial abrasives and a chain of jewelry stores, all closely held corporations first with Landzman, then his heirs. They keep the big house mostly for nostalgia's sake which considering its history seems to make no sense. The house is open to daily tours during the Spring, Summer and early Fall. During July, August and September into Labor Day it is open to all night catered affairs; the ghostly revelry rings out into the night, all night and in the private rooms, which some say don't exist, Rot-Gut Ferrel rolls the dice and finally wins. And a man who looks just like Landzman did in 1922 and never seems to age, greets all comers at the door with a winning smile which disarms even the most cynical with its inviting charm. And in the background we hear Rachmaninoff which no one interrupts.

Simple Headstone 1896- 2000

It has been duly noted that Landzman's epitaph, which he penned himself, was a joke; that his immediate heirs found it on the great man's big mahogany desk and being stricken with grief inexplicably lost their sense of humor and took it seriously enough to have it carved in stone; which in its own way is bizarrely appropriate, that his earthly remains should be marked by a final flippancy, an over-the-top witticism from the master's own pen. There has been talk of replacing it with a more fitting memorial but level heads have prevailed; the concluding joke remains on top of his empty grave.

His simple headstone, more a marker, no cross, no star, no hammer, no sickle, no crescent, no swastika, a tall white granite obelisk polished to a high mirror sheen, simply says, anachronistically:

"Here lies James Jacob Landzman, sometime known in life as 'The Great Gatsby', a great magician, aerialist, tight rope walker, unmatched master of the flying trapeze, who spent the better part of his life in the circus and on the stage; a renowned Shakespearean actor, celebrated for his Hamlet; a skilled sea captain of sailing ships who had circumnavigated this small globe many times, who went down bravely with his sinking ship while trying to evacuate every last passenger to the lifeboats in an ice-packed sea."

Author's Disclaimers

This is a work of humor, parody if you wish. If you don't find it funny I'm very sorry for that but I can't help it. I don't in any way try to be funny; it just comes out that way. I couldn't in any way make it funny for those who don't find it funny even if I tried. I think there's just a cosmic disconnect; the word cosmic is not used carelessly. There's nothing fundamentally funny about the best humor; it's a very serious matter.

However, if you don't find this book funny, drop it immediately like a hot potato, or a red hot rivet that won't fit into the hole that was made for it; or you'll burn your hands or worse; and whatever you do, don't pick it up; step away from it; push it away gently with your foot as if it might explode. It is nothing but trouble (leave it for someone else to pick up who might find it funny); you'd be wasting your time and mine; (you might run into me and ask a silly question which misses the entire point. I don't need that, neither do you. It would be embarrassing for the both of us).

This is a work of fiction which means I made it up. Don't believe a word of it. Some people don't understand that. Pat Conroy was on a book tour for *The Great Santini*, his novel, a work of fiction; his mother picketed outside with signs proclaiming:

IT'S ALL A LIE, DON'T BELIEVE A WORD OF IT

or words to that effect. I think it was probably good publicity.

This book may seem to refer to other works of fiction; it doesn't; this is a fiction of a fiction; no actual works of fiction or what passes for fact are alluded to or quoted from. If you think I've quoted someone and the quote is wrong, rest assured that it is right; it is what I say it is; that sounds arrogant but it's not; solipsistic perhaps; it's fiction, remember.

Some of the names I have used are the same as those of historical personages, writers or writer's fictional characters. If you look in the phone book or what passes for the phone book these days you will find many people with those same names. I do not refer to any of those people either and certainly not to the historical or fictional personages; any resemblance to any of those people is purely coincidental and if you compare them closely you will find that they don't even vaguely resemble each other. The places referred to or named do not exist, not on this earth and are a product of my mind, such as it is.

The thing about fiction is the writer doesn't have to look anything up; whatever the memory re-conjures is good enough or better; an imaginative act of recreation. What we remember is usually fiction anyway, the purest fiction because we manage to convince ourselves it's true. In this sense we are all fiction writers or conjurors of reality. The question inevitably comes up: why is it misremembered? By what alchemy has the brain reconceived it in the way it has; rewritten history. But written history is a constant rewrite; a self-serving concoction whipped up by the victors, survivors or the last man standing to justify their existences after the fact.

The world of our memory is its own world made of bits and pieces vaguely suggested by true facts, riddled with empty pot holes, pitfalls and bear traps that we plaster over with twigs and shattered branches of supposition and fill in with the detritus of our past history of beliefs and prejudices or obscure with mob-sourced rumors which are often vicious and plainly fallacious.

Intricate Jigsaw Puzzle

A novel is a long piece of prose or poetry disguised as prose founded upon a creation of made-up persons and events; there is enormous freedom in the form which defies simple definition. A novelist should struggle to grasp his subject from every angle, to attempt to uncover some unifying whole or explore it in such a way as to reveal its inherent and inescapable contradictions; that a cohesive whole is not possible.

If you think this novel is disorganized or fragmentary you are blind; there is not a piece that does not carefully fit like the bits of an intricate jigsaw puzzle of a thousand seemingly incongruous sizes and shapes. You may not like it, fine; hate it if you wish; but don't tell me it lacks unity or structure. I'll send you a schematic in fifty different colored inks.

It is a novel, an amalgam: ironic or perfectly serious essays, old fashioned story-telling, slices of pure drama, some characters that play act, are phony and insincere, who themselves don't know who the hell they are, bits and pieces, letters sent and unsent, pompous speeches and speeches from the heart by pompous people and not so pompous people, what passes for historic fact or factoid, realistic excursions into unreality.

The synthesizing power of the novel is like the distinct voices of polyphonic music, the convergence of two or more simultaneous lines of independent melody. It's like a choir with every one singing a different song, in a different language but in communication, in ordered counterpoint. What's important is that the singers keep on singing no matter what; and can carry a tune in the middle of heavy traffic at the risk of getting run over.

It's a symphony orchestra crashed by Gypsy Tango guitarists, violinists and pianists playing "Por Una Cabeza" with El Mago; pickers and pluckers, fiddlers from the Ozarks and from off the roof, Jazz trumpeters, trombonists and saxophonists, a guy off in the corner playing a trap set to music in his own head in rhythm with the kettle drum and a Jamaican steel drum played by a Rastafarian, and a sorry bunch of squeeze box players from every corner of the known world including Zydeco and a quartet crying out the haunting street call of the Jewish ragman's song; a New Orleans funeral band with wailing Mexican trumpets drowning out the mourner's tears in its own tears. I love the squeeze box.

Plot, if it flows naturally, is useful but unnecessary. The questioning of ideas can hold it all together; call it theme if you like; but the themes can only spring naturally from the characters and their unfolding and their perhaps non-sequential progression of events (plot is too structured and constricting a term). To use characters as a mouthpiece is absolutely anathema; so is allegory. The author should stay the hell out of it and never show his hand; he shouldn't even sit at the table, but be the money man behind the curtain or a one-way mirror. The world he creates has to come alive on its own and continue to run on after he is long gone.

The manipulator steps aside and is often the one who winds up manipulated. If you want to preach or teach find a pulpit or university easy chair.

Plot is too often ill-used: an artificial scaffolding to hang common romances and pulp detective stories on. It can be a cheap trick to keep the small mind otherwise occupied or distracted; a dancing shill, a third rate audience grabber. If any plot develops it should grow organically, naturally like magic mushrooms in a lush black mulch with a rich unseen, underground matrix, insinuating mycelium, white vessels, capillaries like Queen Anne's lace by which it mysteriously propagates.

Shakespeare borrowed almost all of his plots. If you read the originals they show little promise. The plots, themselves, sound like hokey melodrama. Yet he took these well-worn almost hackneyed stories and turned their lead into pure gold. The same can be said of Nick's story; read a plot summary and you have nothing but a cheap pulp murder-detective mystery.

If you're looking for answers you've come to the wrong place. People who have the answers are exceedingly dull and murderously dangerous; they lack humor and the human touch. You can see it in their serious benumbed eyes; hear the dull thud of the Gestapo on the stairs in the night, the Storm Troopers singing in perfect harmony marching down the boulevards, flags waving, with church choir voices; the inevitable police state of the certain mind coming to methodically hunt you down like a dog in the street.

The skill is to pose the right questions and to word them precisely in beautiful language. It is the trick of any good riddle which has no answer; to provoke thinking and to arouse an appreciation of the splendor and intricacy of the riddle itself which somehow is enough; must be enough.

We find the answers as we may, only when the intellect has withdrawn its watchers from the gates.

When you ask the right questions, the only questions that count, you take the stairs all the way down, descend into primeval chaos and pull up a chair and feel right at home there with your feet to the fire.

The Talking Cure Was All the Rage

A friend of mine went to a psychiatrist, back when the talking cure was all the rage; the doctor was very big on dreams. My friend didn't remember his dreams mostly because he wasn't at all interested in them or found them too dull to be worth repeating or too embarrassed by their dullness, or so he said, perhaps too insistently. Also he didn't want to hurt the doctor's feelings; but mostly he didn't want to confront this grand authority figure by refusing to comply with his wishes; so he made them up. Other aspects of the treatment seemed to be working so he continued making up his dreams to keep the doctor happy. Finally after many years of this and eventually displeased with where the treatment was taking him he decided to stick it to the doctor, to tell him how he was duping him all along and how gullible the doctor had been:

> "You're so smart you didn't even know I was making it all up."

But the doctor, unfazed, replied by telling him he knew they were 'lies' all along.

Patient:

> "Then why did you lead me on?"

Doctor:

> "I didn't lead you on... your so-called dreams, these 'lies', as you call them, were your most telling revelations.
>
> "They told me more about you than anything else you exposed to me."

Of course there's always the possibility that the doctor was a shark raking in the bucks from the poor slob and couldn't care less one way or the other.

Was it Freud that said that literary fiction is controlled psychosis? Or not so controlled; which control varies with the writer; a ring master locked in his own ring with the lions circling around him; it is only the ceremonial master that provokes them to dance in seeming unison.

I, Myself, Do Not Speak One Word

I, myself, do not speak one word in this book and have tried to stay out of it as much as possible and tried not to take sides. We have a narrator whose dependability you must determine for yourself. We have no independent corroboration that he is who he says he is, but that is a problem with most narrators. I can vouch for him to some extent, but only outside the novel, which doesn't count.

If you have a problem with what some of the personages say, as I expect you would, I suggest you take it up with them. I would if I could but most are long dead. And though a good writer can raise them from the dead, he does so at his peril. I don't expect them back anytime soon. In any event I'm not sure I would want to see any one of them again. It would be like meeting the summoned son from *The Monkey's Paw* knock, knocking at the door and like a fool opening that door and letting him in. Be careful what you wish for or who you summon from the past, including your own creations. The past is not what you think it is and never was.

That Fucking Lion

And then there was that lion without whom none of this would have been possible. I'm not one to sit for any length of time. I'm writing because I had no other choice, laid up as I am with crippling pain in my best leg, all because of that fucking lion. There must be poison in a lion's teeth or in its mouth; like a Komodo Dragon infecting its ill-fated quarry with the bits of filth, previous prey, rotting in its stinking maw. How else to explain this refusal to heal, the wound breaking open, inexplicably on the anniversary of the mauling and the healing forced to begin all over again.

The poison was in the wound, you see; and the wound wouldn't heal; at least not permanently. I'm searching for the tincture made from the juice of fire-flowers which I understand are extinct and always have been. Doctor Good knew the formula but refused to sing the song of it. We weep for it on the banks of the rivers of Babylon, but as hard as we try we fail to remember it. The formula is useless without the flower.

The lion is not the mighty hunter it is cracked up to be; it is just as often the scavenger gorging the fetid flesh snatched from the wily hyena or the jackal with sense enough to cut and run.

Believe it or not, I was once a crack shot; the irony or ineptitude. I'm sick to death of lions. Are there any "white hunters" left, in any country, anywhere? Or is that politically incorrect? But enough of that; this story's not about me.

For some reason I've been consumed by this ordeal. I feel like an exhausted traveler who's journeyed to an incredible land that the others insist doesn't exist; from which he has lost the power to return; or if he, by some incredible trick, by some miracle, manages to make it back, it is without the ability to speak or write in any recognizable language. I don't like lions anymore.

Fictional Construct

This so-called "author" is a fictional construct, a literary invention, once removed from the narrator. The actual author, that is the author of the "author", has nothing further to say except to say he has absolutely nothing further to say. The book is the book; period; end of story. There will be no question and answer session, ever. The fictional "author", who seems quite chatty, might have entertained questions but alas, he has left the theater; he is no more; there will be no encore.

I refuse to meet with villagers bearing torches in the night; torches I take as a bad sign, even if they profess friendly intentions and carry my books; for autographs they say; in bundles I say, smelling of accelerant.

And if I lose my mind and give a speech, or even worse an interview, ignore it. Undue influence has been exerted. I am under extreme duress and being held captive at gunpoint; my family held hostage in a remote, secret location. Whatever I say is no more than self-serving unadulterated horseshit or entirely in the interest of my captors. I am being forced to read from a cue card script held off camera by men with Uzis, itchy fingers and dark sunglasses, in black suits, disguised as limousine drivers, hired pall bearers and camera crew. Or regard it as a coerced deference to show business, a bow to Hollywood and Oprah, mindless entertainment for entertainment's sake, irrelevant and misleading, designed to humiliate both the entertainer and the entertainees.

Just remember, many fine writers when they open their mouths sound like idiots. They have no idea what they're doing, or how they are doing it, especially if they're doing it right, and have a tendency to run off at the mouth. Some of them actually think they can teach people how to write and they clog up the schoolrooms indulging their futile, ineffectual subterfuge; a nonsensical sinecure, an easy ride while stealing time for the real work.

Never... never give interviews; and stay away from other so-called writers. There is, of course, as evidence the recent pathetic calumny by David Lipskin, a second rate scribbler who out of envy attempts to bring down a comparative giant to his own measly size for the sole purpose of aggrandizing himself. He scrawls a schmaltzy, mawkish smear of a screed that parades as accolade; painfully, pathetically aching after the very celebrity that David Foster Wallace dismisses while at the same time falling victim to it and professing to loathe it. A world teeming over with piranha fish who masquerade as your most devoted fans, who Wallace seemed powerless to distinguish or exterminate on sight, cut a straight line to the doom of 2008. The leeches who feed on vulnerable greatness, the likes of the slimy, sycophantic media hound, intent on unarmoring Wallace's justifiable protective cover like a burrowing, grubbing, parasite dredging up his victims guts with a grappling hook, to lay bare and parch in the withering sun for the little vultures and scurrying rats to gorge on, covered with flies and rotting blood, scrapping viciously with each other for the choicest tidbits to choke and heave on.

This is a haunting replay of the defamation perpetrated by another second rate scribbler parading shamelessly in the stolen clothes of a literary writer. Bud Schulberg set himself against a red wood giant with his puny little ax. But like any proficient little witch he knew the secret poison and how to employ it. He fed whiskey (Champagne, actually) to a known alcoholic to unhinge and finalize the dethronement of a relative colossus and insinuate his own little writer friend ready and waiting to pounce from the wings. Don't be fooled by the phony acclaim. The worst defamation is couched in extravagant tribute. *The Disenchanted* is a diatribe, plain and simple. There is no envy like the envy of the second rate writer for the great writer. We are talking lightning next to the lightning bug and the burned bug knows it, holding tight to its venom like an old man holding on to his piss. They ache to the bottom of their black insect soul which though they have tried they cannot sell. They hawk it on the street corners like cheap goods, but there are no takers. No matter how hard they work and sweat, no matter who they are willing to kill or what crime commit, they cannot hope to even touch the hem of the garment of the literary giant; they can only soil themselves, busting a gut, attempting to topple over his tower but get caught in the falling shadow.

In a hundred years both Lipskin and Schulberg will be known only for their slander, a footnote at the back of the book in barely readable print that burns the eyes with straining, possessed of the derivative fame of the unsuccessful assassin.

Publisher's Note:

The author of the author is a literary invention. On the advice of the publisher the actual author, that is the author of the author of the author, has absolutely nothing to say. If anyone comes forward to speak about this work claiming to be that author rest assured he is an impostor and up to no good. Call the police.

If anyone signs this book claiming to be the author, that signature should be regarded as a forgery or a fraud. The author has assured me that under no circumstances will he sign a copy of his book.

Publisher on the Author

I have known the author for over twenty years; however to this day he is a mystery to me. He has asked me not to relate the details of his life which he regards as totally irrelevant to his work. He has specifically requested that I not mention the schools and universities he has gone to since he regards them as having been barriers to his intellectual development, such as it is. Anything he has achieved is in spite of them. To give them any credit would be like Solzhenitsyn crediting the Gulag for his Nobel Prize. If our time in hell inspires in us a motivation to write, it does not follow that we should praise hell; quite the contrary; let us learn to damn hell eloquently and repeatedly.

The author's whereabouts are unknown; somewhere in Europe I presume. Geneva was the last I heard. I don't expect any book tours anytime soon.

The photograph on the back cover came with cryptic instructions which I didn't understand. I couldn't reach the author for clarification. It could be the author; it looks like him, at fifty; but then again it could be Landzman; or Kleinsinger, if he had lived. Photographs are funny that way. Take it for what it is.